Deep Fried
Reservations

KATHLEEN IRENE PATERKA

Deep Fried Reservations
Copyright 2017 © Northern Ventures Literary Group
First Print Edition: 2017

ISBN-10: 0-9892838-4-4
ISBN-13: 978-0-9892838-4-7

ALSO BY KATHLEEN IRENE PATERKA

The James Bay Novels
Fatty Patty (Book #1) (2012)
Home Fires (Book #2) (2012)
Lotto Lucy (Book #3) (2012)
For I Have Sinned (Book #4) (2013)
Deep Fried Reservations (Book #5) (2017)

Women's Fiction
Royal Secrets (2013)
The Other Wife (2015)

Nonfiction
For the Love of a Castle (2012)

DEDICATION

For my mother, Rita Geraldine Gay,
who taught me how to read,
how to write,
and what love is all about.

ACKNOWLEDGMENTS

WRITING A NOVEL IS LIKE being locked away in your own little world. You sit down at the computer, and begin telling yourself a story. Soon you're floating away in what appears to be the most pleasant dream (or, worst case scenario, the stuff of which nightmares are made). When the story is finally finished, you emerge from the room, take a giant leap of faith, and place your darling into the hands of readers. So many of you continue to contact me, letting me know how much you've enjoyed my books. I'm very grateful. Thanks for keeping in touch, for supporting my work, and for leaving reviews. And to my loyal readers who hung on and demanded another James Bay story: I hope you'll feel that this book was worth the wait.

To my team of beta readers: Virginia Conlon, Marsha Braun, Claudia Guerra, and Nan Kirvan, for their thoughtful commentary and insight through the initial writing and subsequent drafts. Authors Catherine Chant and Jackie Bouchard, for their unflagging support, sharp eye for detail, and continuing friendship. Dear friends and fellow authors Jenna Mindel and Christine Johnson, travelers along the way. Long live the Queen of Hearts Club! Editors extraordinaire

Samantha Stroh Bailey and Francine LaSala, whose invaluable feedback encouraged me to push and polish, even when I felt like quitting. Any mistakes are mine alone.

Research can be tedious and time-consuming. It can also be fun, provided you're working with the right people. Many thanks to Terry Left, Jodi Shepard, Lori Silva, and Linda Cuca, for the inside scoop when it comes to running a restaurant and bar. Lonnie Allen, for sharing feedback about life in the Marine Corps. Lorraine Sakamoto, for her stories of Hawaii, its people, and its different cultures; Diane Ford, for her perspective of life on the island. Donna Swanson, for insight into homeless shelters and pulling volunteer duty.

And finally, a big shout-out for my husband Steve. Not only is he the best brainstormer in the business, but Steve also provided me with the quiet and space I needed as I struggled to find my way through this book. He was also quick to assuage my fears, reminding me every time I wanted to give up and said I couldn't do it: *"Yes, you CAN."*

Mahalo to you all!

Never turn your back on the ocean.

~ Hawaiian Proverb ~

CHAPTER ONE

~ Who Ordered the Appetizer? ~

FUNNY THING ABOUT RUNNING A restaurant? You never know who's going to walk in the door. Chuck's Tavern & Grill always draws a crowd, and that means all types of customers. *No matter what they say or do, the customer is king*, Pop reminds our staff when he catches them complaining.

But Pop isn't on the floor right now, and I'm the one in charge of keeping the bickering in check. All of us are feeling hot and frazzled on this crazy busy day in mid-July, including me, Katy Malinski, alone behind the bar. I pour shots, blend sweet frothy concoctions, and serve beers, while keeping one eye peeled on the growing line of customers crowding through the front door. The summer high season, with its glorious weather, is nothing short of organized chaos for places like Chuck's. After a day spent packing our Northern Michigan beaches, strolling the sidewalks, and jamming the exclusive downtown resort shops, tourists wandering into Chuck's only want three things: air-conditioned comfort, a cool drink, and a good meal. And just as soon as I finish pouring this next shot, I promise myself, I'm calling Pop up from his basement office, so he can play host. That line isn't getting any smaller.

Then the front door opens, and she walks in. She stands alone, a mere slip of a thing; a small, sleek presence near the front of the line. The hair on the back of my neck prickles as I catch sight of her, and I'm suddenly spooked. I know I've never seen her before. If someone showed up with a Bible right now, I'd be able to swear I don't know her. I rarely forget a face. And she's the kind of woman you don't forget. Beautiful. Exotic. Intense.

Dangerous, something deep down inside warns.

If I thought my day was bad before, I'm suddenly convinced it's about to get a whole lot worse.

Nettie, one of the long-time fixtures at Chuck's, is busy scribbling down reservation numbers for next-in-line. Narrowing her eyes, she points a crooked finger at the woman. "How many?"

"Just me. But I don't—"

"Estimated wait time ten minutes," Nettie says. "Name?"

"Never mind," she says, slipping from the line. "I'll sit at the bar."

And suddenly she's directly in front of me. Our eyes meet as she takes a seat, and I throw her a nod, acknowledging her as I finish up with the round I'm pouring. I peg her as slightly older than me, maybe in her early thirties. Long jet black hair frames her face, and dark expressive eyes the color of toasted almonds search the room. A sleeveless red dress hugs the curves of her body in all the right places. I give a fast yank to my t-shirt and khaki shorts, the standard uniform at Chuck's, and swipe one arm across my forehead, pushing back blond curls frizzing around my face, brushing away a light sheen of sweat. While I probably resemble a spent dandelion threatening to burst, she looks like she's accustomed to wearing satins and silks, with a delicate bloom tucked behind one ear.

I doubt the woman even knows the meaning of the words *to sweat*.

She settles on the bar stool next to Kevin, our town's You-Don't-Have-To-Sleep-With-That-Drip-Tonight plumber. His eyes light up. "Hello there."

Tucking her purse in her lap, she promptly ignores him.

"Hey, Katy, let's have another beer over here." He points at his glass.

"Sure thing," I say, and grab it.

He leans in close to her. "How about you, honey? Can I buy you a drink?"

I pour his beer, wait for the deep freeze sure to follow. Kevin's about to get shut down with one of those frosty you've-got-to-be-kidding glances any woman would immediately recognize for exactly what it is, but which men seem to have a problem differentiating. Why his wife puts up with the guy and doesn't divorce him is beyond me. But Kevin's a Happy-Hour regular, and pays his tab on time. I'm not into dissing customers.

"Anything you want," he urges.

She stares at him a moment. And just when I'm sure she's about to zap him with a pithy one-liner, she smiles.

"Yes, thanks. A drink would be lovely."

"What can I get you?" I ask, and wait for her to order. It'll probably be something like a Mango Daiquiri, or a smooth pineapple foo-foo drink filled with brandy and rum, garnished with fruit.

3

She glances over my shoulder, searching the variety of liquor bottles, premium and middle grade, lining our shelves. "Do you have Grey Goose?"

"We do."

"Perfect." She fingers a thin silver chain hanging around her neck. "Make it neat, please."

I turn and reach for the bottle. Tending bar, you quickly learn it's none of your business what your customers drink… until they hit that limit of one drink too many. Then you quickly make it your business.

"Twist of lime?" My fingers hover above the citrus peels heaped on a nearby steel tray.

"No, thanks," she says, and I place the glass in front of her.

He leans in. "The name's Kevin."

"And my name is Mai." She samples her drink. "Mmm, perfect."

She rewards him with the hint of that enigmatic smile that ramps my curiosity up another notch. Where do I know this woman from?

"Vodka, huh?" Hands cupped around his beer, Kevin peers at her drink. "Me, I never touch the hard stuff."

"Maybe you should experiment a little." Mai takes another sip. "You might be surprised."

He shifts on his stool. "Really? You think I'd like it?"

"No doubt in my mind," she says coyly, slightly lifting one eyebrow.

I blink. Is she flirting with him? Working behind the bar, you hear it all: blatant flirting and flat-out rejections. And while I've heard plenty of pick-up lines, they usually come courtesy of the guy who's hitting on the girl. Does Kevin know what he's doing? He's a six-pack beer kind of guy, while Mai is a top-shelf woman.

He tosses back his beer in one quick gulp, and slaps his hand on the counter.

"Katy, bring us another round," he prompts. "But this time, gimme one of what she's having."

"You got it," I say, nodding.

Kevin hauls himself off his stool, pauses long enough to lightly touch Mai's shoulder. "'Scuse me, I'll be right back. Got to use the men's room."

"I'm not going anywhere," she promises.

With a sloppy grin, he points himself in the right direction, and heads down the room past the other end of the bar where our restrooms are located.

I grab Kevin's empty beer glass, submerge it in the soapy wash sink directly below the bar, then pluck a clean glass from the rack and reach for the bottle of Grey Goose.

Mai places her hand atop her own glass. "No thanks, I'm good."

"You sure?" I say, a little surprised by her change of heart.

"Quite sure," she confirms. "I don't want to encourage him."

"Wise decision." I decide right then and there to save all of us—including Kevin's wife—some time and grief. "Word of advice? He's married."

"Word of advice? You're crazy if you think I intend to let him get anywhere," Mai says, serving me up a chilly smile as cold as the ice cubes we add to our drinks. She settles back in her chair, eyeing me with a skeptical look. "Seriously? Can you see me with a guy like that?"

"I suppose not," I admit, starting to feel sorry for Kevin. Granted, the guy can be an overbearing loudmouth know-it-all, but that's no reason to talk like he's dirt. Meanwhile, she only took him for one drink. He's lucky he got off cheap.

"And did you see his shirt? It's covered in grease stains." She wrinkles her nose. "And he smells."

I shrug, trying not to listen as I busy myself filling other drink orders.

"Men like him think they're God's gift to women. Why do they assume they can pick up a woman because she's alone in a bar? I hate that. It's insulting and rude."

But not as rude as she is. Plus, not all men are like that. Especially not Pop, I silently fume, reflecting on the story of how he and my mom met in a bar. I push ice cubes into a glass, add a shot of rum, follow it up with a splash of cola, and purposely keep my mouth shut. I have no interest in trading witty comments, or discussing my family history. The longer Mai sits in front of me, the more I wish she'd leave.

"Order up!" I flag the attention of our newest waitress.

Ellen hurries over and I push the mixed drink and a couple foamy beers toward her.

"Thanks, Katy." She loads the drinks on her tray and throws me a quick smile.

"No problem." I grab my bar rag and attack the spotless counter with a burst of ferocious energy. What I'd really like to do is scrub that coy look clean off Mai's face. But Pop prides himself on running a family-friendly establishment, and insulting customers isn't something he tolerates. He's drilled me in the necessity of being polite since I was a kid. No matter what type of customer sits in front of you.

No matter what type of customer.

I force a deep breath, wishing Kevin would hurry up and get back.

"Is the owner around?" she suddenly asks.

I blink. What does she want with Pop?

"He's not here right now."

"Do you know when he'll be back?" Mai presses.

I hope she doesn't intend on waiting. "Why do you ask?"

"I don't see that's any of your business," she replies.

"Excuse me?" My I-can't-believe-you-just-said-that meter is now on high alert.

"*The owner*," she drawls, as if I'm an imbecile. "I'm here to see him. His name is Charles Malinski."

Hearing her casually drop Pop's name startles me more than the nastiness she spewed about Kevin. What does she want with Pop? Not to mention, no one calls him by his formal name. Around town, my father is simply known as Chuck. Even our restaurant—Chuck's Tavern & Grill—trades on his nickname.

"Do you have an appointment?" I ask, though I already know she doesn't or Pop would have mentioned it. But he disappeared downstairs after lunch without a word. A creature of habit, his routine rarely varies, and today is no exception. He hung around until the lunch crowd departed, then headed down the narrow staircase behind the kitchen for the cramped basement office the two of us share.

He's probably down there right now, either hunched over the desk crunching numbers from this week's suppliers, or catching the latest baseball score on the office's tiny television. I glance at the muted big screen TV behind the bar. Sure enough, the baseball game is on, with Pop's beloved Tigers playing. It's bottom of the eighth, Minnesota vs.

Detroit, with the Tigers down by 1. A die-hard Michigan fan no matter the sport, Pop's undoubtedly muttering obscenities as he watches Minnesota's batter take the plate.

"Do you have an appointment?" I repeat.

Mai pauses long enough for me to catch a shadow of uncertainty slide across her face. Just like I thought, I nod to myself. No appointment.

"I've come a long way to speak with him." She tucks a strand of jet black hair behind her ear.

"If it's about the restaurant," I say, suddenly determined she won't be getting anywhere near Pop, "you can talk to me. I'm the general manager."

Pop brought me into the business last winter after suffering a mild heart attack. His cardiac episode scared the hell out of both of us, and—for him, at least—sped up the process of my taking over. Pop's been grooming me on the ins and outs of running the restaurant since the day we opened when I was a teenager. My education has proven hit and miss, especially given my underwhelming lack of ability in anything but basic math. Then there's that other niggling fact I've yet to discuss with Pop: I'm not sure if I really want to take over the family business. The announcement that he was making me general manager and a limited partner came as a big surprise to me. I suppose he thought it made sense, seeing how I'm managing more and more of the daily operations. But am I ready to devote the rest of my life to spending it in a restaurant? It's something we need to talk about, but for now I'm putting the discussion on the back burner. Pop's the only family I have since Mom died, and I want him around for a long time to come. And if that means my picking up the slack, I'm glad to do it. After what I did, I owe him that much, and plenty more. I'm more than capable of handling things.

Including whatever business Mai thinks is so important.

"Like I said," I add, "if it's about the restaurant, you can talk to me. Though I have to be honest. If you're here about a job, we're not hiring." And it's not exactly a lie, I reassure myself. We've adequate staff at present, but we're always on the lookout for good help. And since I'm the one who does the hiring and firing, I could take Mai on. Throw her some hours, see if she works out.

If I want to.

Which I don't.

Who knows what might happen if she worked here?

Jake, our regular bartender, chooses that moment to return from his dinner break. He glides behind the bar to join me. His eyes widen, and he hisses a low whistle through his teeth. "Man, Katy, why didn't you call me?" He nods toward the front door. "Look at that line."

Cursing myself for not paying attention, I peer over Mai's shoulder at the line now snaking out the front door. If the pre-dinner rush is any indication, today could very well end up breaking sales records.

"Sorry, guess I lost track of time."

"No worries, I've got things covered." Doffing two fingers to his forehead in mock salute, he heads to greet a noisy group of customers as they step up to the bar.

I have a fleeting thought that maybe I should call him back, ask him to deal with Mai. Jake's excellent at handling women. He wouldn't have a problem finding out who she is, why she's here, and what she wants with Pop. I ponder on it for another few seconds, then decide to let it go. Jake has better things to do. Such as, run the bar. I don't need him running interference for me.

Like it or not, Mai is my problem.

"If you want to fill out an application, I'll make sure—"

Any pretense of a smile drops from her face.

"What is your problem?" She stares down her nose at me. "I think I've made myself perfectly clear: my business is with the owner, Charles Malinski... not with you. I suggest you quit stalling and tell me when he'll be back. Or maybe he's been here all along, and you're not telling me?"

I open my mouth to respond, but her remark has me so flabbergasted, I only glub air instead of words.

She stares at me a long moment, then gives a dramatic eye-roll and huffs a sigh. "Never mind. I'll wait."

We glare at each other over the bar counter, and I begin to realize that she's not going to leave before she talks to Pop. I glance toward Jake, who's busy pouring shots, then cast a quick eye on the growing line twisting out the front door. I should be over there playing hostess like I normally do until Pop relieves me. Can I afford to waste precious time arguing with her? She's here at our bar, and she's not going anywhere.

"What's your name?" I struggle at getting the words out. Conceding is never easy.

"Mai Kaido," she says smoothly. "But he doesn't know me. Tell him I'm here on behalf of Yumiko."

"Yumiko?" I frown. "And who's that?"

A flash of displeasure flits across her face. "Just tell him. He'll know."

Mai Kaido might think so, but I have my doubts. Yumiko isn't the kind of name one expects to come up in ordinary conversation around our little resort town of James Bay. Is it a man or a woman? Does Yumiko even exist? I wouldn't be surprised to hear Mai's conjured the whole thing up, just so she could gain access to Pop. Then again, why does she want to talk to him? She freely admitted he doesn't know her.

But I've run out of time, with every minute bringing us closer to the dinner rush. I throw down my bar rag and head for the back stairs. Whoever this mysterious Yumiko turns out to be, and why Mai was sent on his or her behalf, had better be important. Pop hates being interrupted during ball games. And I don't appreciate being dismissed like I'm some pimply-faced teenage messenger sent off to do Mai's bidding.

This restaurant is my business, too. And Pop never holds anything back. He'll fill me in with a full report once she leaves.

If Mai Kaido—she, with the exotic features and sultry eyes hinting of shadowy secrets—thinks she can hide something from me, she should think again.

***

The dinner rush is as crazy-busy as I guessed it would be. The mingled aromas of French fries, deep-fried perch, and barbecued ribs slathered in sauce wafts through the air, greeting hungry guests who jam the tables and booths. Someone, however, proved to be a no-show tonight. Finally, I find a minute to myself, and fish out my phone. The restaurant is too noisy and crowded for a decent conversation, so I end up resorting to texting.

"*Record crowds tonite,*" I tap out the message and hit send.

I'm not surprised when the screen stays dark. Not only

does Pop loathe *all-this-technology-crap*, as he likes to put it, he also thinks my generation is way too obsessed with our phones. But with Mai long gone, my curiosity (and concern) has ramped into overdrive. I'm curious to hear all about the mysterious Yumiko, and exactly what Mai wanted with Pop. I expected him upstairs as soon as she left, but he never showed. As far as I know, he's still holed up in our office. It isn't like him to skip playing host. He likes to glad-hand the regulars, welcome the tourists, and make his presence generally known. With his towering 6'5" frame, booming voice, and penchant for cracking bad jokes, Pop's a hometown boy who made it good. Everyone loves him. He's as much of a legend at Chuck's Tavern & Grill as our Friday night all-you-can-eat fish fries.

"*Everyone missed u,*" I text.

Still no response.

"*They asked where u were.*" I try again, waiting to see if he'll respond. I give him a good ten seconds, though with my impatience and frustration, it seems more like thirty, before my annoyance flips to concern. What if he's not simply ignoring me? What if something's wrong? The man suffered a heart attack last year. With a flick of my finger, I pull up the camera feed, displaying it on my phone courtesy of the numerous surveillance cameras located throughout Chuck's. Most are strategically mounted to catch video from the high-traffic areas and kitchen, but two are downstairs. One is in the hallway, and the other, inside the office, is high in a corner and aimed directly at the oversized safe. It's the second feed that provides me with a partial view of Pop.

I sigh, relieved to see him sitting upright in his chair,

fiddling with something in his hands. At least he's not passed out, slumped over the desk. I spy his phone, close beside him.

"*U okay?*"

I watch him tap his phone, check my message, then promptly ignore it.

If he's trying to drive me crazy, he's doing a great job.

"*Big brother is watching,*" I text-taunt. "*U can't hide.*"

Scanning my message, he glances up at the surveillance camera, then sticks out his tongue.

I chuckle to myself. Pop hates the surveillance cameras as much as he does smart phones. "*Smile, u r on camera.*"

Muttering under his breath, he grabs his phone and punches in a number.

I answer on the first buzz.

"Nice of you to finally get back to me," I say. "Good to know you're still alive." Not exactly funny, when your lone surviving parent has already been close to death, but he knows I worry about him.

"I was busy."

"We were busy too. Or maybe you forgot we have a restaurant upstairs? Oh, and by the way, that restaurant has your name on it."

"Look, I don't need the grief, okay? You're always saying I should let you handle things. Guess I picked the wrong night to take you at your word."

The quick tease I meant to fling back at him catches in my throat. Pop can be gruff, but he's never mean. And he isn't one to say things lightly. But he's right. For months, I've been nagging at him to slow down and let me pick up the slack. The restaurant business is fast-paced and demanding for everyone involved: wait staff, cooks, dishwashers, and busboys alike. But owning a restaurant is a whole different ballgame. You're the one responsible for managing every aspect of the business. Hiring and firing, managing inventory, marketing and quality control; it's a 24/7 job, with your financial livelihood at stake.

"Sorry, kiddo," he says quietly. "You didn't deserve that."

"I'm sorry too. I didn't mean to be so snarky." I rake a hand through my hair, remind myself to go easy. Pop doesn't need the grief.

"Were you really busy?" he asks, curiosity emerging from him like an itch between his shoulder blades that he can't quite reach.

"Yes, but no worries, things are fine. Everyone pulled together and we managed. And Pop, honestly, I didn't mean to make it sound like we couldn't..." I break off. There's no point in reminding him again that he never showed up. It's over and done with.

"No, you're right. I should have been there, and I wasn't. That's my fault, and I'm sorry. I meant to come upstairs, but... well, I guess I needed time to think."

The knot in my stomach tightens. Pop isn't the type to sit around and think. He's an action type of guy.

"Katy, I think you better come down here. We need to talk."

The quiet firmness in his voice ratchets up my anxiety to full alert. Not only is Pop not the kind of guy to do anything quietly, he's also not the type who likes to *have a talk*. For that matter, neither do I.

"We still have quite a few customers up here." It's a flimsy excuse. True, the tables and booths are full, but the dinner crowd has thinned out, and there are plenty of waitresses to cover the floor. One of them could easily take over my hostess duties.

"Obviously, if you're busy, stay and help."

"Things should clear out in another ten minutes or so," I say, knowing I won't be able to put him off indefinitely.

"That's fine. Come down as soon as you can."

"You didn't eat dinner. Want me to fix you a plate?"

"I'm not hungry."

I blink. It's not like Pop to turn down a meal. He can still put it away just as fast as guys half his age. Though how he stays fit is a mystery to me, especially since he loathes any type of exercise. I'm assuming his hearty appetite and trim figure are courtesy of the self-discipline drilled into him during his long-ago stint with the US Marines.

"I'll be down as soon as I can," I promise, though having a chat with him is something I'm suddenly reluctant to do.

"Good," he says, then hesitates. "Katy?"

I pick up on the sad, sorry sound in his voice. The way he says my name makes the hair on the back of my neck prickle. Why do I have the feeling that the world as I know it is about to change?

"Yes?"

"Make it as soon as you can." He clears his throat with a gruff *harrumph*. "It's important."

It takes another good twenty minutes or so before I pull myself off the restaurant floor and head for the basement office. Pop slouches deep in his dinged-up chair. He throws me a tired smile as I cross the threshold and sink into one of the battered leather chairs facing his desk. He rubs a hand through his trademark crew cut. His eyes are smudged with a dark and sunken look, and worry lines carve deep grooves in his forehead. I take a closer look and see tiny beads of sweat pop on his face. My heart pounds like I just swam forty laps. When was the last time he saw his cardiologist?

"What's going on? Are you sick?" I ask point-blank. Better to get it over with then pussy-foot around the subject.

"Not exactly," he says.

I peer at him. "Something's wrong."

He tilts his head, as though contemplating how much he should tell me.

"Whatever it is, you know I'll find out eventually. Besides," I remind him, "you're the one who asked me to come down here. And now, here I am." I sit back expectantly. "Let's have it."

He scratches his ear.

"Come on, Pop, tell me the truth."

"The truth." Blowing out a long sigh, he tips back his head and stares at the ceiling. "Funny thing about the truth. What one person considers to be the truth can turn out to be a different truth entirely for somebody else. You go along, living your life, thinking things are fine. And then one day, when you least expect it, something happens, and pow! Turns out, things aren't as hunky-dory as you thought.

"And there's the kicker, Katy." He turns his gaze back toward me, and his eyes lock on mine. "You just never know."

What the hell is going on? The sort of existential tangent Pop's currently spouting isn't like him at all. Our staff is accustomed to his spur-of-the-moment discourses on all sorts of topics, but this doesn't sound like one of his usual rants or raves. And I don't like how ashen his face looks. Maybe his biorhythms are all screwed up. Has he quit taking his high blood pressure medication again?

"Did you take your pills this morning?"

He frowns. "What's my medicine got to do with this?"

"Because you look horrible, and you're not making sense." Bouncing to my feet, I lean over the desk and place one hand on his forehead. It's clammy and cool to the touch.

"Are you having chest pains?" I ask. "Where are your nitro tablets?" The cardiologist warned us that Pop should always keep his pills handy. "The hospital's only five minutes away. How about if I get my car and—"

"Whoa, time out. I'm not having a heart attack, okay? And as for my pills, I got 'em right here." He pats his shirt pocket, forcing a quick smile that doesn't fool me in the slightest. "When will you quit worrying about me, Katy-Did?"

Katy-Did. I was notorious for chasing grasshoppers when I was a kid. Hearing Pop casually toss out my childhood nickname has the nerve endings in my body suddenly humming like electrical lines on a hot summer day. He seldom uses my nickname anymore; mostly when he's feeling nostalgic, or the rare times he screws up.

Has Pop screwed up?

Seizing his shirt collar, I yank it in a threatening tug. "Worrying is part of the deal when you love someone," I remind him. "And I love you, Pop. I love you very, very much."

Does he seriously believe I could ever quit worrying about him? I was only thirteen when my mom died. Thinking about her isn't something I like to do. Even after all these years, the hurt is too big, and the loss too much to bear. Maybe even more so because of what happened, and what I did. But since she died, it's been just Pop and me. Pop moved us north to James Bay shortly after her accident, and within a year, started up the restaurant. Since then, he's been the one steady, guiding presence in my life. And no matter what, he's always been there. He was the one holding my hand during every one of those dreaded appointments as the orthodontist clamped and tightened those painful braces. *Someday your teeth will be beautiful, Katy-Did*, he'd assure me, *and this will all be worth it*. It was Pop assuring me that not everyone understands math, that *no, you are NOT dumb* and *yes, you will survive, you will not flunk out*; then hiring a tutor to make sure I didn't. And Pop was the one who was crushed when I made the decision not to attend college. *Your mother was a teacher*, he reminded me more than once. *Having a degree will make things easier. Don't be like me; I had to learn the hard way when it came to the business side of owning a restaurant.*

But is that what I really want to do with the rest of my life? Pop would like nothing more than to see me settled down, running the restaurant, getting married, and having a few kids of my own. Kids who would call him Grandpa. But you don't marry someone just to please your dad. And while I really like Don, my on-again-off-again boyfriend, I'm not sure I'm in love with him. What does being in love really mean? Pop never remarried after my mom died. I asked him about it once, and he told me that, for some people, love like that comes around once in a lifetime. He said there could never be anyone else for him, and he was thankful for the time they had together.

Growing up, I hung on to those words, and took them to heart. That's the kind of love I want, which makes this whole thing even harder. How do you know when it's the real deal? How did my mom know Pop was the one? How will I know if Don is the one? Life with Don would be so easy, if it weren't for the fact that we're both so stubborn. Hence, our frequent break-ups—though I must admit the making up part is nice. And while Don and I might end up together someday, I don't want to force either of us into doing something we'll later regret.

But no matter what, I can count on Pop to take my side. Life without him would be unimaginable.

"You're sure you're okay?" I press.

"I'm fine. At least, as much as I can be." He gestures toward the chair behind me. "Now sit down and let's get this over with."

I ease myself back into my seat.

Wordlessly he opens the top drawer of the desk and pulls out a silver necklace which looks vaguely familiar. Pinching it between two fingers, he carefully places it on the desk before us. Two metal tags, battered and worn, hang from the chain. Made of stainless steel, each has its own markings. Reaching out, I finger one of the tags, pulling it close enough that I can read the words *Charles Roy Malinski* etched at the top. Pop's social security number, O blood type, and religious preference of Catholic are listed beneath his name.

He taps his finger against the stainless steel. "These are my dog tags."

"You mean, from when you were a Marine?" When it comes to detailed family history, my memories are sketchy at best. I know that Pop was a civilian, honorably discharged from the military, way before he'd met my mom.

"They issue you a set of dog tags when you enlist. You're required to wear them at all times." He shakes his head. "I still can't believe it. They went missing more than thirty years ago."

I stare at the tags and silver chain, and swallow over the lump rising in the back of my throat as I realize it's the same necklace I saw earlier. The one hanging around Mai's neck. I jerk my finger away, as if the metal might suddenly begin to sizzle and burn. But it's too late. The damage is done. On some deep gut-wrenching level, I'm aware I'm caught up in a scorched-earth policy.

Take no prisoners. Is that Mai's motto?

"I don't understand," I say slowly. "You said they were missing. So why did she have them? Because I saw—"

Pop blows out a long sigh.

"I've got something to tell you." His face is grave, and his eyes contain the same haunted look as the day he told me about the car accident, and that my mother was dead. "It's about something that happened a long time ago. Something that will be hard for you to hear. But before I tell you, I need you to promise me something."

He pauses, watching me with wary eyes.

"All right," I agree uneasily.

"Promise me that you'll remember that all of this came as a surprise to me, too. Because I didn't know, Katy. Swear to God, I didn't know."

And in this moment, I realize that things are worse—much worse—than I originally feared. Because things aren't fine. Things will never be fine again.

Pop starts talking. Watching him hunched in his chair, staring at the floor, hands clasped together, it's like he's praying for strength to get him through. His voice falters at first, but he keeps going, and I keep listening, though his story grows more implausible with each passing moment. Cold and numb, I sit there. It feels as if I'm caught up in a tsunami that I'm helpless to stop. Pop can't save me, and I can't save myself. Wave after wave of what he assures me is the truth churns up everything in its path.

Ten minutes later, he's finished. Pop bows his head lower, still unable to meet my eyes.

"I'm sorry, Katy."

I sit in stunned silence. I'm sorry, too. Sorry for myself, and sorry for Pop. But most of all, I'm sorry for our little family, because it no longer exists. The tsunami shook up an alternative reality that never, in my wildest dreams, would I have believed. A reality which, according to Pop, is the truth. And while I'm not sure I can—or should—believe him, one thing is certain. The life I woke up to this morning is gone forever. It's been washed away in a flood of emotions and judgments courtesy of a long-lost relative from Hawaii.

My older half-sister, Mai.

CHAPTER TWO

~ Table for Three ~

I KNEW KATY WOULD TAKE IT hard. What kid wouldn't, hearing that kind of news? And she doesn't deserve it. Life's already been plenty tough on her. No kid, especially a girl, should have to grow up without her mom. Katy was devastated when Katherine died. I tried to step up to the plate, be both Dad and Mom, make sure she had what she needed. It wasn't easy, and it still isn't easy. Ask anyone who's been in my situation, and they'll tell you the same thing: being a single parent can be damn tough at times. And while I always tried to do my best, I didn't always do a great job. What do I know about teenage girls? I'm a man.

One thing kept me—and keeps me—going: I love Katy with all my heart. My love for her is absolute, and I'd do anything in my power to protect her. Still, I couldn't protect her from what happened this afternoon. Because everything changed the minute Mai walked through my door.

The resemblance was amazing. I haven't seen Yumiko in over thirty years, but I'd recognize her and her daughter in a heartbeat...

Mai stands before me, small and fragile, her eyes

feasting on me like she's a waif from a third-world country who suddenly finds herself treated to an all-you-can-eat buffet. Meanwhile, my head is buzzing, my thoughts zipping around in all sorts of scattered directions. Yumiko's daughter must be in her early thirties. Yumiko's daughter. The timing works; her age fits. Yumiko's daughter. That would have been around the time I was stationed in Hawaii. Yumiko's daughter, here in my office. I shake my head, trying to gather my sloppy thoughts and arrange them in some type of semi-coherent fashion.

Yumiko's daughter.

My daughter.

What do you say to a daughter you've just met? *Hello, glad to meet you. Hello, you surprised the hell out of me.*

Mai slips into the chair facing me and removes the thin chain from her neck. She lays it on the desk before me. "I brought you a gift."

The chain snakes across the wooden surface, with military dog tags on full display. *My* dog tags, issued to me when I joined the Marines. The tags look exactly like I remember them. I reach out and finger the worn metal inscribed with my name and other information the military deemed necessary.

"I haven't seen these for... well, for a very long time." I glance up at Mai. "Where did you get them?"

"From my grandfather, my Ojii," she says. "He gave them to me a few weeks ago. My mother left them behind in a drawer at his house, and he kept them all these years. He said they'd belonged to my father." She folds her hands in her lap and sits quietly with an expectant look, eyes trained upon me.

I study her silently and contemplate my next words. They

23

will be crucial, but talking might prove difficult. The looming lump in my throat is greater than any hill we stormed during practice maneuvers while stationed in Hawaii. And though the buzzing in my head has stopped, I'm still trying to absorb what's happened. Things like this don't happen in real life, except maybe on one of those idiotic reality TV shows. Yet when I look at Mai—really look at her—I can't ignore what I see reflected in her face, nor the memory of my final day in Hawaii, and Yumiko's surprise news that she was pregnant.

"But what will become of me?" Yumiko wept when I confessed I had my orders and would be shipping out the next day. "How can you leave me? How can you leave your child?"

And now that child sits in front of me. A grown woman, with Yumiko's delicate features, plus my Aunt Sis's smile. The sweat pops across my forehead, and there's a sudden insistent pounding in my chest that I haven't felt in months. I grip the arms of my chair, aware my heart is racing way too fast. I take a deep breath, then force myself to blow it out in a slow, steady huff like I learned from the therapists in cardiac rehab.

"I'm sorry. I don't know what to say. You caught me by surprise."

I should have known. Yumiko told me, but I didn't believe her. Why didn't I believe her?

I reach for the dog tags and pick them up, rub them between my thumb and forefinger, like doing so will help me absorb the reality of what Mai's laid on the table. "The last time I saw these, your mother was with me. It was the night before I shipped out."

"I knew you'd been in the service, and were stationed in

Hawaii. But she rarely talked about you." Mai breaks off, hesitation and mistrust hanging in her voice, uncertainty clouding her eyes. "She said you left because you didn't want us."

"But that's not true," I protest, clutching the arms of the chair. My palms are sweaty and it's hard to get a good grip. "I didn't know. I never knew about you."

And I didn't, I assure myself. Not really. *Yes, you did*, a silent nagging voice reminds me. *You just didn't listen. You chose not to listen.*

"I always wanted to meet you," she replies quietly. "To know the man who is my father."

How the hell do I tell her the rest of the story?

I was a kid straight out of high school; a wild-ass know-it-all looking for a fight when I joined the Marines. Those four years I spent as a cook in the Corps are a hazy blur of serving up chow in the mess hall, and blasting my way through all the booze, drugs, and women I could get my hands on. Yumiko was one of those women. I met her in a bar one night on a street near the base a few weeks after we put in to port. She was hanging around inside, hoping someone would buy her a drink and maybe shell out a bit of money for something more besides. I took her up on the offer; after a couple of nights together, I made sure everyone knew she was off the market.

For the rest of the time I was stationed in Hawaii, Yumiko was my girl. She was young, she was beautiful, and she didn't whine. I liked having her around. She did my laundry, cooked, and cleaned—she did whatever I wanted to keep me happy. Yumiko had plenty of experience in keeping a man happy.

Knowing I had Yumiko waiting for me every night got me

through the daily drudgery of frying up eggs for breakfast, burgers at lunch, and mixing up batch after batch of creamed beef for dinner. But come night, I was living every guy's dream. I had a gorgeous Asian beauty in my bed who kept me satisfied and never said no to whatever I wanted. Back then, you could get away with having your girl on base if your bunkmate didn't care. Fortunately, mine didn't, which meant Yumiko and I were together a lot. Did we use protection? I never gave it a thought. That was something women took care of, as far as I was concerned.

We were together for six months, right up until the day before we shipped out. We'd gotten our orders weeks before, but I put off telling her until I started packing. I had little fear of squaring off against an unknown enemy armed with bayonets and long-range cruise missiles, but I didn't have the guts to face up to Yumiko's tears. When I finally broke the news, I expected her tears… but not her stunning announcement that she was pregnant. A baby? We'd made a baby together? Part of me, a big part of me, believed every word she was saying. But there was no time to think. No matter what, I still had to ship out; I couldn't risk going AWOL. But that didn't mean I was going to abandon her. I wouldn't leave her alone and pregnant. A man steps up and gets the job done. We could work something out, I feverishly promised myself. I'd put a ring on her finger and make an honest woman of her. Then, maybe in a few months, she could join me on the mainland. And maybe, once my tour of duty ended, she could return with me to Michigan. Or we could live in Hawaii. We would settle down, buy a house, raise a family.

That's when my bunkmate walked in. Five minutes later, he hauled me out of there. *An intervention*, he told me, *before you do something stupid. You gotta get a grip, man.* Within an hour, he and some other guys were pouring beers into me, talking sense into me. *"There's no baby,"* they warned. *"She's just telling you that to make you stay. Don't you know you can't trust women? Especially women like her."*

And when I eventually got back to my bunk, Yumiko was in my bed, her back turned to me, face to the wall. Obviously, she'd cried herself to sleep. I slipped off my clothes and crawled in beside her. When I woke up hours later, she was gone. Yumiko had slipped away sometime during the middle of the night, taking my gold chain and my dog tags with her.

We shipped out the next morning. I sweated through the next months, waiting to see if she'd contact me, but I never saw or heard from Yumiko again. And as time passed, and the years went by, it got easier to believe my buddies had been right. Yumiko wasn't pregnant. It had been a ruse to get me to marry her. There was no baby.

Boy, was I wrong.

Tilting her head, Mai eyes me in an eerie imitation of Yumiko. "I don't remember a time in my life when I gave up wondering about you. Who you were, where you lived, what you were like. When I was little, I used to ask so many questions. But no one would give me any answers. Eventually, I quit asking." She bites her bottom lip. "You aren't even listed on my birth certificate. I didn't know your name until a few weeks ago."

"Yumiko didn't tell you?"

"She wasn't around. My grandparents raised me," Mai says slowly. "My mother... well, she has her problems. I was taken into my grandparents' home when I was a baby. My mother said it was better for me to be with them than to live with her. It was only as I grew older that I understood the reasons why. She meant well, but there was—there is—a sickness in her soul that she could never lose."

"Drugs?"

She dips her head, unable, or perhaps unwilling, to meet my eyes. "Yes."

I'm not surprised by Mai's answer. Back then, life was different, and I was different. And while I'd done my fair share of dabbling in some of the hard stuff, I'd also been perfectly content chilling out with dope and a six-pack. But not Yumiko. Once she had a taste of something, her cravings intensified, and she wanted more. And more and more and more.

"Is she still alive?"

Mai nods. "The last time I saw her was a few months ago. We bumped into each other in downtown Honolulu. She didn't say much." Her face draws quiet. "She didn't look good."

What if I had stayed? Would it have made a difference? Would Yumiko have given up the drugs?

And what if I *had* stayed? I never would have met Katherine. Abruptly I push away the disturbing thought and the equally inconceivable consequences: if I hadn't met Katherine, there'd be no Katy.

"Eventually, Obaa and Ojii banned her from their house," Mai says. "She couldn't kick the drugs and alcohol, and she only showed up when she wanted money. I think she used to steal things. It wasn't a happy home during her visits. They were always fighting."

"I met them once."

Mai's eyebrows lift high. "My grandparents?"

I nod. "Your grandmother wasn't exactly thrilled when your mother introduced us—"

"Obaa will never change," she quickly cuts in. "She believes in the Japanese way of life, and insists our family adhere to the traditions of our ancestors. According to her, there should be no intermingling between the races."

"Yep, that's pretty much how I remember her," I say darkly. My visit to her grandparents' home in Kaneohe Bay hadn't been a long one. While Yumiko's father had been unfailingly polite, his wife's dislike for me had been on full display. As far as she was concerned, I was a no-good white trash Marine from the mainland who had no business being anywhere near their daughter. "When it came to me, she definitely didn't hang out the welcome mat."

"I'm not surprised," Mai says. "Obaa listens to no one. She's always been impatient and judgmental. When she learned that my mother was pregnant by a white man, she…"

My face heats up faster and hotter than it does when I'm standing behind the grill helping fill orders for barbecued ribs. There's no need for Mai to continue. We both know her grandmother, and we both have no problem filling in the blanks. I wish to hell we weren't having this conversation, but I can't ignore the facts, or the consequences.

Tiny as she is, the biggest consequence of them all—Mai herself—now sits directly across from me.

"What about your grandfather? I only met him the one time. Granted, I don't remember him saying much, but he seemed like a nice enough guy." Stiff, formal, the classic epitome of a Japanese gentleman. Still, he hadn't been the one who threw me out. His wife had done that.

"Ojii was the sweetest man." Mai's eyes soften. "He was

open to dealing with people of all cultures. But Obaa insisted upon following tradition, and Ojii never argued with her. He got sick last winter. The doctors said there was nothing they could do. By late spring, he couldn't leave his bed. A few weeks ago, he called me to his bedside, and that's when he gave me your dog tags. He told me he wanted me to have them. He made me promise that after he was gone, I would look for you." Tears well in her eyes, but she blinks them away before they can fall. "That's why I'm here. I'm keeping my promise to Ojii. All my life, I wanted to meet my father. And, according to Ojii, you are my father."

Is Mai telling me the truth? I scan her face, see the captured glint of Yumiko's eyes resting upon me, the faint trace of the same smile as Aunt Sis playing round her lips. Is Mai playing me for a fool, or do I believe her?

How can I not believe her?

Fantastic and disturbing as her story sounds, it has the ring of truth. Then there's also that undeniable evidence on her face, in her eyes, her smile. Mai is my daughter. And suddenly it seems vital that she understand my part in what happened, and why I've never been involved in her life. This is my responsibility, and I need to suck it up. I need to admit what happened in the past, and accept what's in the present... and future.

Rising to my feet, I stride around the desk. I grab her shoulders with both hands, like I do with Katy when I want her full attention. Mai flinches at my touch and I ease my grip slightly. Still, I don't let go.

"You don't deserve the way your life turned out," I say. "It was tough, and it wasn't fair. Every kid should have a father around. I'm sorry I wasn't involved. I'm damn sorry about that, Mai. And I'm sorry I can't change the past. But I can change the rest of it. Starting right now."

Mai blinks rapidly and I know she's listening, which helps rally my courage. I allow myself to breathe. "We're going to make a new start. Together. All of us. Starting today. What do you think? Would you like that?"

And what about me? Will I like it? Only time will tell.

"Yes," she says. "Yes, I'd like that. I'd like that very much."

Opening my arms, I gather her in and rest my chin atop her head, the way I used to do with Yumiko. Mai's such a tiny thing; the top of her head barely reaches my shoulder. I've forgotten what it's like to hold a small woman in my arms. Katherine was tall, and Katy inherited her mother's height. I inhale the floral fragrance lingering about Mai, feel her beginning to relax against me. And then I hear a faint sound, then another. It takes a minute before I realize she's crying. Tears for a father she never knew? If so, I can relate. For the past thirty years, I've had a daughter I didn't know. And much to my surprise, I find that my own eyes are wet. Mai trembles and I can feel her heartbeat, fluttering against her chest like a wild butterfly. Yumiko and I gave her that heart. Who could have guessed that Yumiko and I could have created this beautiful creature?

My daughter. My daughter Mai.

And then, without warning, another thought creeps up. *What about Katy?*

Katy. How am I going to break this news to her? How will she react, learning she has an older sister? I doubt she'll turn cartwheels at hearing the news. She was none too pleased earlier this afternoon when she showed Mai into the office. Though she'd been polite, she kept her distance as she retreated and left the two of us alone. But no way could Katy have known the truth. I'm sure she was still in the dark.

But she isn't anymore. Not after the conversation we just finished having.

"I'm sorry, Katy-Did." I reach for her hand. "You have no idea how sorry I am about all this."

And I didn't even tell her the worst part: how I turned my back on Yumiko, and took a wild gamble that the pregnancy story was simply some story she dreamed up. How I listened to my buddies, fled the island on a military transport, and never once looked back. What kind of a man does that? What kind of father?

"I'm sorry, too." Her voice is glum, and she turns her head away, pulls her hand from mine.

"Katy, please don't be…"

"Stop it," she says, still not looking at me, her face growing whiter with each passing second. "Just… stop. Don't you understand, Pop? I can't, not right now."

"Tell me what I can say to make this right." I'm not above begging.

"Nothing. There's nothing you can say. I need time. This is all too much."

I quiet, wishing to hell things were different, that there was something I could do or say that would wipe away the hurt and betrayal I see on her face and in her eyes. I'm the one who put them there. It's my fault we're in this mess.

But what's done is done, and I can't change it.

Katy leaps to her feet and heads for the door.

"Where are you going?"

"Home," she says in a voice I don't recognize.

"Katy, wait."

But she's too fast for me. She tears out of the office before I can stop her. I know she's upset, and I don't blame her. When Mai walked in the door today, life as we knew it got blown to hell. Things will never be the same.

There's a bad feeling churning in my gut, but I know it's not heartburn.

It's heartache. And fear.

Two daughters, one father, and a potential battle brewing.

What the hell do I do now?

CHAPTER THREE

~ Family Brunch ~

POP RARELY DEMANDS ANYTHING FROM me, so his early morning phone call asking me to join him for breakfast is a request I don't ignore. In fact, by the time I rap on his door and show myself into his second-floor apartment above the restaurant, I've convinced myself that his invite is a good sign. Pop's not an early riser, and he's never been one to preach the benefits of eating a good breakfast. What happened yesterday must still be weighing heavily on his mind. Maybe, like me, he lay awake most of the night, thinking things through. Such as: is Mai really who she says she is? Why did she suddenly decide to show up in James Bay? Does she have some ulterior motive? And what about the horrible way Pop and I left things between us?

I still don't understand everything. His story has so many holes, and me bolting from his office left so many questions unanswered, so many things unsaid between us. And I still feel betrayed. How could any of this be true? But no matter what, I never should have run out of his office. I should have stayed and talked.

And I need to apologize. Now, before things get even worse.

But the heartfelt *I'm sorry, Pop* ready to bubble forth from my lips dies an immediate death as I round the hallway into his kitchen/dining/living room and take in the cozy scene playing out before me. Pop and Mai, chatting at the breakfast table. They've drained the coffee pot, and she's made herself comfortable in what's normally my chair.

This isn't going to be the quiet breakfast I expected, with the two of us talking in private and working things out. He summoned me here so I'd be forced to talk with her.

I take a few steps backward, hoping I can slip away before either of them notices.

"Katy!" Pop's eyes light up as he catches sight of me, and he waves me over with an enthusiastic curl of his arm. "Hey, kiddo, glad you made it. Come join us."

I hesitate in the doorway. Pop and I aren't accustomed to being at odds with each other. Just like I'm not accustomed to the intense dislike surging through me when I glance at Mai. I don't want to be in the same room with her. I don't like her, and I don't trust her. But leaving now will only make things worse.

I move toward the table and take the seat across from Mai, squint against the glaring sunlight streaming through the windows. Everything looks different from this angle. I moved out years ago, but I'm still up in Pop's apartment one or two nights every week after the restaurant closes, chatting about business and other things. Don joins us sometimes, but mostly it's just Pop and me, taking in the killer views of evening sunsets through the floor-to-ceiling windows overlooking James Bay. I took it all for granted, blithely assuming things would always stay the same. How could I have been such a fool? The world goes on. Things change. People change.

"How about some coffee?" Pop grabs the pot, eyes the bit of brown sludge barely covering the bottom. "Sorry. Guess we drank it all. Want me to make more?"

"Don't bother. I'm good." I shield my eyes against the sun as I take in the veritable feast of breakfast goodies spread across the table. Warm bagels, sliced cheeses, fresh fruit, orange juice. The fact that he's managed to scrounge up any type of food isn't lost on me. Pop's never been one for keeping his refrigerator stocked. He must have raided the restaurant cooler. Though I'm not sure where he managed to find the bagels. Chuck's doesn't open until 11 am, and breakfast items aren't included on our menu.

"How about some juice?" He lifts an empty glass, tilts it sideways in a pouring motion.

"No thanks." The thought of putting anything acidic in my already-jumpy stomach only serves to ratchet up my uneasiness. I grab a bagel from the heaping stack centered on a plate, then proceed to rip it into two pieces, then four.

"It's nice to see you again, Katy," Mai says in a guarded voice. "I'm sorry we didn't have much of a chance to talk yesterday."

"Yeah, that was unfortunate," I say, recalling the brief chat we had before I took her down to Pop's office. She'd been rude to me, and the way she talked about Kevin the plumber had been downright mean. If she doesn't curb that snippy tongue of hers, today's little gathering could turn into a brawl.

But Pop's watching, so I keep my head down, mouth shut, and focus my attention on shredding my bagel. Why in the world does he believe she's part of our family? I want some proof. How about DNA testing? That would be way more conclusive than a set of military dog tags and Pop's stubborn insistence that Mai's telling the truth.

Mai and I sisters? I don't think so. Put us side by side, and even the most impartial witness would have to admit that the two of us look nothing alike. She's short and I'm tall. Her dark brown-black eyes are deep and expressive, while my own green eyes are mirror images of Pop's. Her hair is a glossy jet black, while mine's more a faded strawberry blond. Her skin tone is a beautiful shade of pale brown, while my skin burns a scorching lobster red even when I slather it with SPF 100. Fashionably dressed, immaculately coifed, perfectly made-up, Mai's even more impressive than I remember from yesterday's encounter at the bar. As for me, I'm all too aware of how I look in my t-shirt and shorts, hair pulled back in a quick ponytail and eyes smudged with dark circles. I'm not a pretty picture, and I doubt things will improve anytime soon.

Exactly how long does she plan on staying?

"Katy, you gonna eat that bagel, or play with it all morning?" Pop points at my plate, and I take in the pile of mangled bread crumbs before me.

"Sorry." I pop a piece in my mouth.

He grabs a bagel for himself, neatly halves it, then proceeds to slather both sides with cream cheese. The real stuff, the kind that's loaded with saturated fat which Pop isn't supposed to eat. Has he forgotten everything his cardiologist and the dietician cautioned against?

"A little heavy on the cream cheese, don't you think?" I say.

"Aw, what's the point in living if you don't indulge yourself occasionally? Besides, we're celebrating."

"We are?"

He beams. "Sure, we are! Our little family just got a little bigger."

Our little family. It's been just Pop and me for nearly half the years I've been alive, yet now I'm supposed to accept Mai as my sister (granted, half-sister) merely on his say-so? Sorry, but I'm not buying. I swallow over the jumble of raw emotions, the accusations burning inside me which I feel like spitting on the table. Doesn't Pop understand how I feel? Any kid would feel this way, blindsided and betrayed.

But I'm not a kid anymore.

Pop crams a large bite of bagel into his mouth. Swallowing, he produces a wide grin and smacks his lips. "Delicious," he says with a nod for Mai. "Thanks for bringing them."

I should have figured she's the one responsible for the bagels and cream cheese. I rip more pieces between my fingers, scattering a trail of messy crumbs across my plate. "I never thought bagels were part of a typical Hawaiian breakfast."

"They're not." Her smile for me is both indulgent and condescending. "They're served in the restaurants and big hotels on Waikiki Beach, but not in the house where I grew up. We ate eggs, fresh fruit... and rice, naturally."

"I'm not much of a fan of rice," I say.

"It's a staple for most of the cultures living on the islands. Many Japanese and Hawaiian dishes are made with rice, including at breakfast."

"Thanks, I'll stick with bagels," I say, wrinkling my nose.

"Obaa wouldn't allow them in her house."

"Obaa?"

"My grandmother. I lived with my mother's parents, Obaa and Ojii."

"You didn't live with your mother?"

Her face colors slightly and I catch Pop's frown. The plot thickens and so does my interest level. What happened to Yumiko? Why was Mai raised by her grandparents?

"Her mother was sick," Pop interjects. "Mai grew up in Kaneohe, a city on the island of Oahu. Kaneohe isn't that far from Honolulu. Maybe ten, eleven miles."

Mai nods. "It's an easy drive, across the mountains."

Visions of tropical beaches, lush green mountains, pineapple fields, and huge waves crashing on the sand flood to mind. Mai is like a fragile sea star that washed up on a Northern Michigan beach... except she's on the wrong beach. She belongs to the ocean, and a different way of life. A life that isn't ours.

I shrug off her explanations. I know it's borderline rude, but I can't help it. I'm mad at Pop, for putting us in this situation, and with Mai, for showing up in James Bay. But most of all, I'm angry and frustrated with myself. I'm supposed to be an adult, and that means keeping my emotions in check. Instead, they're bouncing all over the place. It feels like there's a giant tug of war going on inside me. My stomach is in knots, twisting and turning over this unexpected anger and resentment, plus guilt and shame over the foolish way I'm acting.

But dammit! Haven't I got a right to feel this way? This whole story sounds way too suspicious. Too much is wrong here. Way too wrong. If Mai's really Pop's daughter, why didn't she come searching for him years ago? And why is he so willing to believe what she says? What's the matter with him? In the world I used to live in, Pop would have been pouncing all over a story like this, poking holes in it. But instead he seems willing to believe whatever she says. Me, I want proof. I sit back, glance back and forth between them. How hard would it be to convince them to take a DNA test?

"Have I done something wrong?" The soft lilt of Mai's voice breaks the silence.

"What do you mean?" Pop asks.

"Oh, I think Katy understands," she says.

I lift my head and stare at her. What exactly is she up to?

"It's confusing, isn't it, Katy? I mean, obviously you're upset. And I suppose, if I were you, I'd be feeling the same way, too. It's so confusing." Mai's eyes begin to water, as if on cue. "When I decided to come here, I was afraid. I didn't know what people would say, or if I'd be welcome. But I couldn't help it. I had to come." She bows her head, long black hair framing her face. "I'm sorry if my being here is a problem. I never meant to cause trouble."

Then turning slightly, her back sheltered against Pop's vision, she peeks at me with the oddest smile. It's as if she's taunting me, daring me to say anything contrary.

And at that very moment, an absolute certainty floods through me that I should never, ever, dare underestimate her. To do so would be at my peril. Mai is not the sweet delicate flower she wants Pop to believe. She's a force to be reckoned with; a fierce adversary who knows precisely what she's doing, and who will not allow anyone to stand in her way. For whatever reason, she's here to claim a place at the table with Pop.

She's already sitting in my chair.

Oh, Pop. Can't you see we're in trouble?

"Let's get something straight." Pop clears his throat. "I know this is an odd situation, but we'll get through it."

He shifts his gaze back and forth between us. "And we're going to make the best of it. The three of us together. Is that understood?"

"Yes, of course," Mai says agreeably.

"Katy?" His frown is suddenly directed at me. Despite the fact I'm all grown up, he still has the power to make me squirm. "Katy?" he demands.

"I get it." I'm no fool. There's a battle looming, but this isn't a hill I'm prepared to die on.

"Good." He shifts his attention back to Mai. "So, no more apologies, okay? You haven't done anything wrong. I want you to quit thinking that any of this is your fault. Like I told you yesterday, we can't change the past, but we *can* change the future. Starting right now. And that's exactly what we're going to do."

His face relaxes slightly. "You did the right thing, coming to find me. And I'm glad you're here."

Mai studies him for a moment, then suddenly dips her head and offers him a quiet smile. "Thank you."

Pop gives a quick nod, the way he does when his mind's made up and he's moving on. "Okay, now we've got that settled, how about the three of us take the day off and celebrate?"

A day off? In the middle of what's already proving to be our busiest summer season in years?

"What did you have in mind?" I ask, careful to keep my gaze centered solely on him.

"Just what I said," he replies in a hearty voice. "It's shaping up to be a beautiful day. We can take Mai around, show her the sights. Let's give her a nice introduction to James Bay and Northern Michigan."

"But what about the restaurant?" A quick check of my watch shows it's already mid-morning. "We'll be opening soon."

Pop shrugs. "No big deal. Nettie can be in charge for the day."

"Are you serious?" Nettie's one of Pop's original hires, but she has plenty of years on him. It's hard enough for her to work a full load of tables, let alone take over managing the restaurant. "Do you think she can handle it?"

"Why are we arguing about this? I don't care who you get." Storm clouds begin brewing on his face again. "Ask Nettie or Jake. Hell, go ahead and let Pete do it, for all I care. He knows what's going on, and he can cover things from the kitchen. Besides, it's only for one day. There's no reason someone else can't handle it. Today's all about celebrating remember?"

Not all of us feel the way he does.

"I appreciate the invite, but I think I'm going to pass." Throwing down my napkin, I jump to my feet and start for the hall. "You show Mai around and I'll take care of the restaurant."

"Katy, wait." Pop rises and reaches out to grab me, but I'm too fast and too far away. "You should come with us."

Mai nods quietly and smooths her hair with a long stroke of her hand. "If you can't, don't worry. It's all right. We understand. We'll miss you."

"See, Pop?" I throw him a brilliant smile. "Mai doesn't mind."

I'm positive she doesn't. In fact, she's probably gloating over the fact that I'll be *persona in absentia* all day, and she won't have to deal with me.

"You two go play," I urge him, "and let me handle the restaurant. No worries."

"I wish you were going with us," he says, trailing me to the door.

"I'll catch up with you later tonight once the restaurant closes," I promise, even though I have no intention of doing so. I don't like lying to Pop, but there's no way in hell I'm subjecting myself to another face-to-face meeting with Miss Hawaii. The less I see of her, the better.

"But I thought a day together would be nice," he says. "Just the three of us. You girls need to get to know each other better."

"Oh, that won't be a problem," I assure him. "Mai and I are already beginning to know each other quite well. Besides, I don't think she's going anywhere... at least, not anytime soon. Isn't that right, Mai?" I challenge her with a sideways look outside Pop's line of vision.

She meets my gaze without flinching. "You're absolutely right. I'm so happy to finally be here. And now that I am, I think I'll stay awhile."

"Great news, honey." Pop beams. "Isn't that great, Katy?"

"Absolutely," I say, though for all I care, Mai can go jump off the end of the pier. She comes from water; drowning seems like an appropriate fate. As for me, I've sunk pretty low myself. If I'm not careful, I'll hit bottom. I already told two lies this morning, but I'd do it again if it meant I could rescue Pop from this strange hold Mai seems to have over him. But he doesn't look like he wants to be saved.

So, my first priority will have to be to save myself. Which means I have no intention of stopping by his apartment after the restaurant closes. Once I lock that door, I intend to head home to bed, where I'll throw the blankets over my head, and pray like crazy that, when I wake up tomorrow, I'll discover the past two days have been nothing more than a bad dream.

Except for one indisputable fact: I'm wide awake, and this is really happening.

And that's the scariest thing of all.

"Bye, Pop. You two have a great day." I plant a hasty kiss on his cheek.

"Katy—"

I hear the plea in his voice. It's rare for Pop to beg, but I can't let it stop me. I whirl away and open the door.

Mai hangs back behind him. "Bye, Katy," she calls. "See you soon."

"Looking forward to it!" I slam the door behind me. Our little-Hawaiian-hula-girl can bet her sweet patootie we'll meet again. And when we do, she'd better watch out.

Game on, sister.

CHAPTER FOUR

~ À La Carte ~

"I T'S SUCH A PRETTY TOWN," Mai says, close at my side as we stroll down the sidewalk. "I can understand why you like living here."

We're nearing the end of our tour of the downtown area, and Mai looks suitably impressed by the things I've shown her. I normally get a kick out of playing host, whether it's in my restaurant or my hometown, but showing Mai around has been somewhat of a game-changer. It's not every day I get to introduce James Bay to someone who also happens to be my new-found daughter.

"I was born and raised right here in James Bay. There's no place like home, right?"

"Is the house still here?"

"House?" I throw her a sideway glance.

"Where you grew up," she explains.

"We lived above the restaurant," I say. "My Aunt Sis owned the place. She's the one who raised me." Katy can relate our family history backward and forward, but Mai has no clue about the details of our life. "My mom died when I was born, so my dad sent me to live with his sister. He was career military, and he was stationed all over the world. But he always came back to us in James Bay. After he was killed in the war, Aunt Sis took over raising me. She never married, she never had any kids. Well, except for me, I guess." I swallow hard. "She was a great lady."

"It sounds as if you loved her very much," Mai says softly.

"Yep." I don't trust my voice to say anything more. Aunt Sis has been gone for years, and I know she's in a better place. But sometimes, when I catch myself suddenly thinking about her, the hurt is so strong, it sucks the breath right out of me. I suppose it's the same thing people go through after losing their mom. I never knew my own mom, but Aunt Sis was like a mother to me, and I miss her. I guess I hadn't realized how much, until yesterday when Mai showed up. She's brought Aunt Sis back to life. Each time Mai smiles, I catch a glimpse of the woman who loved me.

"Look, you can see the restaurant from here," Mai says, craning her head and pointing down the street in the direction we're headed. "Such a perfect location, right in the center of town."

"Gotta give Aunt Sis credit for that one. She's the one who bought the property and started her business."

"And you renamed the restaurant after she died."

"Not exactly," I say, chuckling to myself. While a few older people around town still remember Aunt Sis, most of the locals have long forgotten there once was a dress shop where Chuck's Tavern and Grill now stands. "She owned a ladies' dress shop," I say, remembering how the place looked when I was a kid. The windows were filled with mannequins, decked out in frilly dresses and frothy hats. "I inherited the property after she died and turned it into a restaurant."

I slow a bit. The day is shaping up to be another hot one, with the sun beating down on our heads, and the air thick with humidity. I gesture across the street at the green space nestled against the marina and waterfront.

"Over there, that's our city park. And right there you've got Lake Michigan." I point out the whitecaps crashing against the break wall which guards the harbor entrance not far from where we stand. "They call Michigan the Great Lakes State. It's surrounded by water, and divided into two peninsulas, which are connected by the Mackinaw Bridge. It's pretty damned impressive, you know, especially seeing that it's the longest suspension bridge in the world." I hesitate, suddenly wondering if I've got my facts straight. "Well, if it's not the longest, then it ranks right up there. Over five miles long, and pretty spectacular."

"Really?" Mai's face shines, and I can tell the stats have impressed her. "We don't have any bridges like that in Hawaii."

"It's only forty miles north of here. We'll have to take a drive up there sometime, so you can see it."

"I'd like that," she says, and throws me one of her Aunt Sis smiles.

"And there are plenty of other places around here worthy of a visit. Northern Michigan is great." I give an abrupt laugh. "I probably sound like a travelogue, right? Well, I suppose I can't help it. This place has always been home, and it always will be. I love it."

"It's understandable why you'd feel that way," she says as we turn away from the marina and start back toward the restaurant. "There's something special about being on the water." She gestures toward the small waves lapping against the adjacent shoreline, a shimmering oasis of blue. "All this water reminds me of home."

"Home's important," I agree. The winters can be harsh, but the gorgeous weather during the other three seasons balance things out; especially the ten weeks of summer when tourists flood our little town, intent on taking advantage of the lakes, the natural wonders, and everything else the area offers. Like beer and barbecued ribs at Chuck's. I've got us on a five-year plan, and the restaurant's doing better than expected. Reviews are favorable. Profits are up. Katy and I make a great team. Life is good.

And even though having Mai here will mean some changes in our lives, that doesn't necessarily mean they'll be changes for the bad. I'm determined that won't happen.

We fall silent, walk a few feet with our separate thoughts to keep us company. The restaurant isn't far, only two blocks ahead as we cross the street.

"Nice," she murmurs as we stroll past exclusive summer boutiques. "Wonderful shopping."

"But nothing like what you're used to, right?" I guess.

Mai bows her head, but her long hair can only partially hide her smile, which I know she's trying not to let me see. And her preference is completely understandable. After all, she grew up in paradise. The islands have a unique laid-back way of life, and its peoples, cultures, and weather are like nothing else on earth.

"It's okay," I assure her with a quick laugh. "You're not going to hurt my feelings. We both know there's no way James Bay can compete with Honolulu."

Comparing the two is like trying to match up apples to pineapples. I haven't been in Hawaii since I left in '84, but I remember plenty, thanks to Yumiko. She loved living on base, and the cheap prices of things for sale at the PX. But she loved glitter, too, and she wasn't above dragging me downtown to window-shop at all the fancy places she couldn't afford. "Island life is so expensive," she constantly complained... the same way she groused about the influx of visitors—national and international.

We pass another few stores. Mai slows, lingering, window-shopping just like her mother.

"What kind of work are you in?"

"Sales. Retail sales."

"Clothes?" I take in the outfit she's dressed in today, a sleeveless cream-colored linen dress with plain simple lines that might look dowdy on other women but somehow suits her. She has a knack for wearing things well.

"I've worked at a jewelry store on Kalakaua Avenue for the past several years."

"Kalakaua Avenue. I remember that street." How could I forget? Yumiko loved strolling down the avenue, like a glittering bird of paradise perched on my arm. "It's like the Fifth Avenue of Honolulu."

"Tiffany's, Gucci, Coach, Yves Saint Laurent, Chanel. They're all there," she says. "You can buy anything on Kalakaua Avenue... if you have enough money. I bought this last winter." She moves her right hand, allowing the sun to catch myriad sparkles from the array of diamonds circling a stunning black oval stone on her ring finger.

"Very pretty," I admire.

"Black coral," she explains. "It's Hawaii's state gemstone.

It's very rare, very protected. It took months of saving before I could buy it. Even then, I couldn't have bought it without my employee discount."

I'm guessing that ring on Mai's finger is worth thousands, even with a hefty discount. You'd never catch Katy wearing something like that. Katherine loved jewelry, and while sometimes, on special occasions, Katy dons her mother's signature pearl necklace, I've never seen her wearing the emerald engagement ring which she inherited when Katherine died. Maybe it's because her hands get so beat up from working in the restaurant. And Katy's never been one to bother with manicures. "A waste of time and money," she's groused more than once. I sneak a second glance at Mai's ring, note her polished nails. How can two girls be so different?

"Obaa was angry with me when I bought the ring. She called me frivolous and vain, and said I shouldn't have spent my money like that."

I keep my mouth shut, even though I agree with Obaa. This generation—X, Y, Millennials, whatever you want to call them—most of them seem to think the future will magically take care of itself. There's no thinking ahead. They don't realize how hard money is to come by. As far as I'm concerned, blowing a substantial wad of cash just to put a fancy piece of jewelry on your finger seems like a waste. That's money that could be spent on education. Saving up for a down payment on a house, like Katy did before she bought her little place a few years back. Nothing big, nothing fancy, but at least she owns it. There's a case to be made for building equity in your future.

Mai halts on the sidewalk, turning to face me. "You think

I was wrong, don't you?" she guesses. "You think I shouldn't have spent the money."

"Did I say that?" I ask, quick to defend myself.

"You didn't have to," she says quietly.

I look away, suddenly ashamed of myself. Where do I get off, judging her? Mai's an adult, and it's her money. She earned it. If she wants to blow it on jewelry, she has every right to do so.

"Do you want to know why I bought this ring?" Her voice is not defiant; her face betrays no anger; her tone holds no offense. But her look is determined, and I realize we're not budging until she has her say.

"Sure," I say, sweat beginning to pool under my arms and around my neck. "Let's hear it."

"Because Obaa can't touch it."

"It won't fit her finger?" I ask, even though the image that leaps to mind doesn't make sense. Mai's grandmother strikes me as the plain and simple type who prefers wearing a scowl over a piece of jewelry.

"No, you misunderstood. Obaa was born in Japan. She and Ojii moved to Hawaii shortly after they were married. But she hasn't forgotten the old ways. To Obaa, traditions are sacred."

I nod. Sounds like an accurate description of the mean old woman I remember tucked away in my long-ago memories.

"My mother broke one of our ancestor's sacred traditions."

"Wearing jewelry?"

Mai's face is solemn. "No, it happened when she met you. When she was with you."

"But that doesn't make sense. What do you mean, *when she was with me*? Why would…"

I break off, my face reddening as I catch the subtle phrasing behind her words, and the drift of what she's trying to tell me. Yumiko was full-blooded Japanese, while—as far as Obaa was concerned—I was nothing but no-good white trash. A man who would always be second-rate. A lowlife, a man born of another race, an *inferior* race, who got her daughter pregnant.

"I don't blame my mother. She is who she is. And if she couldn't help herself, how could she help me?" Mai's voice is patient beyond her years. "But I do blame Obaa. There was no reason for her to say and do the kind of things she did."

"What do you mean, '*the things she did*'? What happened?" I cock my head, feel a frown spreading across my face, carving deep grooves in my forehead. "What did she do?"

"It happened long ago. It's over and finished."

"The hell it is," I blurt out. "Tell me what that crazy old woman said. And what she did," I demand. "Did she hurt you?"

"No, nothing like that," she assures me. "Not physical abuse. She never beat me, though she often threatened me with her broom. But she used to call me out, call me names, tell me I was stupid. Nowadays, I suppose what she did and said would be called emotional abuse. But that doesn't mean it's any easier to live with."

She breaks off, and gazes at the ring on her finger, touching it as if it's something sacred. And suddenly, I get it. I'm a long time removed from my days in the Marines, but some things you don't forget. I was a kid. A scared, lonely kid, mad at the world. Those years I spent in the service were rough, but they knocked some sense into me, and helped me become the man I am today. Back then, when I was mad or scared, or lonely and homesick, all I had to do was reach for my dog tags. Rubbing the burnished metal back and forth between my thumb and forefinger kept me grounded, like a touchstone. They carried my name and credentials, reminding me of who I was, where I came from, and everything I could be. Those tags helped me remember that no matter what had happened in my past, that I could make a life for myself. The future was up to me.

Is that how Mai feels about her ring? Everyone needs a little something to get themselves through rough times, and Mai's had her share of those. Yumiko deserted her; no dad around; the abuse she suffered at Obaa's hand. What a nasty old woman; God only knows what she did and said to Mai. But if this piece of black coral helps Mai claim a piece of dignity for herself, then I'm glad she treated herself. She deserves it.

"Your grandmother was wrong." I squeeze her hand, rub my thumb against the smooth black stone of the ring. "Forget about her, and everything she said. None of it matters. It's over and done with. The world's a different place now."

"Not for everyone," Mai says solemnly. "Many people, especially the older people, think the same way Obaa does. They wouldn't agree with you."

"Then that's their problem," I reply. "And they're definitely people I don't want to know. Meanwhile, you can't let it stop you from doing the right thing."

She tilts her head. A curious expression crosses her face, one I can't decipher. Then suddenly she smiles. "Now I understand."

"Understand what?"

"Why my mother fell in love with you," she says. "You're a good man, Otosan."

"*Otosan*..." I've heard the word before but don't recall the meaning.

Mai nods. "It's Japanese. It means *father*."

I suck in a deep breath. I know she's meant it as a term of endearment, but instead it reminds me of all the things I could have done, would have done, and should have done, for Mai.

"You don't mind, do you? I won't call you *Otosan* if you don't want me to."

Hell no, I don't like it, I want to say. I deserted Mai and her mother. I'm the last guy who deserves an honorary title. Hearing *Otosan* from her lips will only remind me of the lousy things I did, and the decent things I didn't do, and kick-start my shame into overdrive.

"Honey, if it makes you happy, then you go right ahead." I drop her hand and clap her on the shoulder, though what I really want to do is take her in my arms and catch her in a tight hug. Right here on the sidewalk, in front of all James Bay. But that would bring me close to tears. I'm normally not a crying man, but this whole situation has me thrown me for a loop. And if I start crying now, I might never stop.

"We should get going," I mumble, run a finger under my collar and feel the dampness cling around my neck. "Today's going to be a warm one."

We walk in silence, weaving our way through crowds of tourists thronging the streets. It's a busy day in James Bay. I'm guessing the hotels are booked to capacity and the beaches are packed. Tourists mean sales. People here for vacation come to stay, play, sleep... and eat. Good news for area businesses, and good news for Chuck's, which is coming up directly in front of us. We're nearly there when Mai suddenly halts in front of the adjacent empty store front. She glances at the sign hanging above the entrance, and peers inside.

"Used to be a furniture store," I say. "It closed down the end of last month."

Joining her at the window, I scan the empty interior. I had my eye on the place way before Eva decided to sell, and I still have hopes we can cut a deal. Eva and I have always been on friendly terms, and I know she's anxious to move to North Carolina, so she can be closer to her family. Plus, Don's the listing agent. With him acting as broker, there's no doubt in my mind the three of us can make this sale happen fast.

"Eva, the woman who owns the place, decided to retire." I step out from under the awning and back into the sunshine. "Her husband died last winter. Now that he's gone, she wants to sell the business."

Bad news for Eva. Good news for me. For us. *If*—and that's a big if—I can talk Katy into agreeing to the sale. I've mentioned it once already, but she shut me down fast. She's not keen on expanding. "I have to think about it," was all she said a few days ago. "Don't think too long," I warned, trying to tamp down my frustration. I want to move ahead, but I also want Katy on board even though I don't need her signature on the paperwork. She's only a limited partner, but I want to keep her involved in the deal. After all, she'll be taking over Chuck's someday.

"You'd never see a furniture store in downtown Honolulu," Mai says. "The real estate's much too valuable."

"The place will sell fast," I predict.

"And then?" She lingers in front of the window. "What will come in?"

"Not another furniture store, that's for sure."

"Maybe a restaurant," she suggests.

"Maybe." I hesitate for a minute, wondering if I should share my plans with her. It's not like they're any big secret. After all, Katy already knows.

"As a matter of fact, I'm seriously thinking about buying the place," I blurt out.

"Really?" Mai says in surprise. She glances at me, then back through the storefront window. "Are you going to do it?"

"Haven't quite made up my mind yet," I confide. "But it would make a great addition for Chuck's."

"It would," she agrees.

"You think so?" I hadn't expected her to echo my sentiments.

She nods. "How could you go wrong? It's right next door to your restaurant. If you're really interested in expanding, this place seems perfect."

"I've wanted to do something like this for years. We could bust out a wall and make a second dining room," I say, warming to the project. "It would double our current floor space. Plus, we'd gain an additional ten parking spaces. Parking in this town is at a premium, and Eva's ten spaces are right behind her building. Even if we didn't move on the expansion right away, those extra parking spaces would come in handy."

Even more reason to nail down the details, and get moving on this deal. We already lost out once before when the property directly behind the restaurant came available several years ago. Since Katy wasn't a partner back then, I was flying solo and calling all the shots. But the project had major problems right from the get-go. The second-floor loft area, with its existing staircase, was the first stumbling block. I had a go-round with the new zoning inspector, some young guy who'd only been in town a couple months. He was a real hot-dog, somebody with something to prove. *Regulations are regulations*, he insisted, refusing to meet me halfway. First thing I'd be required to do, he insisted, was install an elevator for handicap accessibility. It was either that, or rip out the staircase and block off the upstairs. Then there was the issue of the one lone bathroom, with its single sink and stall. It needed a total gut job, he informed me, again refusing to budge. His arrogance and insistent demands ticked me off to no end. While I understood the need for the bathroom renovation, upgrading it would have decreased the existing floor space, and caused a severe drain on financial aspects of the project. As the days and weeks passed, the inspector's list continued to grow. Eventually I gave up. Zoning regulations doomed the sale.

But that wouldn't be the case with Eva's property. It would be a simple renovation.

"I've already talked to the bank," I confide. "The financing's in place and I'm ready to sign."

"And you haven't," she says.

"Not yet," I admit.

She throws me a curious look. "What's stopping you?"

I pull up short. "Well, I guess in this case, you might say, it's not so much a matter of *what*, but *who*."

"Oh. I see." Mai's eyebrows raise slightly. "You're talk-ing about Katy, right?"

"Maybe," I agree, though we both know that's exactly who I meant.

"And she's against you expanding?"

"She has her reasons," I concede, thinking maybe I should give Don a call, ask him to try and talk some sense into Katy. He's savvy about business, he knows the market, and he knows that opportunities like this are rare. When they come along, you need to act fast. That's something Katy doesn't seem to understand.

"Could you go ahead without her?" Mai asks.

"I could."

"After all, it's your restaurant, not hers," she points out.

"That's true," I say, suddenly uneasy about carrying things any further. Though I'm not certain where this conversation is headed, I'm pretty sure I don't want to go there. Meanwhile, Mai's given me something to think about.

"So why let her stop you?"

"You're right." I give a brief nod as we reach the canopied entrance of Chuck's. A group of tourists are gathered studying the posted menu, conferring between themselves before joining the line. An icy puff of air-conditioning blasts through the front door. I glance inside, spy Katy working her way through the crowd as she scratches down names of parties waiting for tables. The restaurant is already standing-room-only, and it's not even noon. Katy was right. Looks like today is turning out to be another one for the record books. I tamp down my guilt as I stand there in the growing heat.

I belong in that restaurant. I should be inside, alongside Katy, doing my job. I told the girls over breakfast I wanted today to be a celebration, but I'm starting to have second thoughts. Playing host is a job that's normally mine.

So why am I out here?

"Aren't we going in?"

I hesitate. Mai's been in town for less than twenty-four

hours, and we're still getting to know each other. I think about that black coral ring on her finger. I think about her calling me Otosan. If we go in, and I go to work, what will she think? And what's she supposed to do? I doubt she wants to sit around for hours on end, watching me play host. And I can't very well put her to work bussing tables. But the hot summer sun already promises another scorcher, and that will mean plenty of foot traffic for the restaurant. A busy lunch hour, and a dinner rush that will probably last for hours. Long lines for tables, demanding customers. A typical summer day in downtown James Bay; a normal part of doing business. And with my name prominently displayed outside in glowing neon letters, I'm the one ultimately responsible for making sure things run smoothly.

Or am I?

For months now, Katy's been bugging me to slow down and smell the roses. "You're not getting any younger, Pop," she's admonished countless times. "I know what I'm doing. Why don't you relax and let me handle things?"

Maybe it's time I took Katy up on her own advice.

"They can get along without me," I assure Mai.

"Are you sure?" she asks. "They look busy."

"They sure do," I say, my gaze trained on Katy, watching as she darts from customer to customer. I trained that girl right. She knows what she's doing. I chew over her words until they've lost their flavor. And suddenly, the feeling passes, and I no longer have any taste for working today.

"How about the two of us take a little drive?" I suggest. "I can take you to see the Mackinaw Bridge. A friend of mine owns a great restaurant up there, right on the Straits. We'll have lunch on the deck and watch the freighters go by."

"I'd love it." Mai's face lights up and she slips her arm through mine, exactly the way Yumiko used to do. But there's a big difference between mother and daughter. Yumiko wasn't above using people to get what she wanted. Mai isn't like that. She didn't press me to take her anywhere. She waited for me to make up my mind.

Maybe I should make a practice of doing that more often. Making up my own mind, instead of waiting on others. What am I trying to prove? I don't have to be everything to everyone. It's high time I start trying to make myself happy, and making others happy, too. Mai deserves some happiness in her life, especially after all she's been through. Today is supposed to be a celebration. It's supposed to be fun.

No restaurant. No worries.

A rare drive north on a beautiful summer day. I'll have a chance to get to know my daughter better. My daughter.

My *other* daughter.

"My car keys are upstairs," I remember. Crap. Just my luck. Now I'll have to go inside. I grab Mai's arm as she starts for the entrance. "We'll go through the kitchen door and use the back steps. No use trying to push our way through the crowds."

I steer her away from the clumps of people waiting in line and briefly think I'm safe. But the feeling only lasts a moment.

And the fleeting glimpse I catch of Katy's face as she turns and spies me in the crowd—first surprise, then relief, then a look of growing hurt—haunts me as I turn my back on her.

CHAPTER FIVE

~ In a Pickle ~

"Y OUR DAD SAYS YOU HAVE some big news."

"Are you purposely trying to make me mad, or are you just being a jerk?" I ask, my temper suddenly flaring. Spouting off at Don is a stupid thing to do, especially since I'm glad to see him. But ever since Mai showed up, my emotions have been running the gamut, to the point where I no longer even trust myself to say or do the right thing.

"Now why would I do something like that?" He throws me a wink. "I thought you knew me better than that."

I'm not about to give him the satisfaction of a reply. Good old Don. This love/hate relationship of ours drives me crazy enough as it is, without having him twist the knife. If he's talked with Pop, Don knows all about Mai. Then again, she's already been in town three days. At this point, everyone in James Bay probably knows about Mai.

Grabbing a menu, I whirl around and head toward the back of the restaurant. It's long past lunch and the crowds have disappeared. I halt in front of the small single booth we stopped using last week after one of its springs broke. I slap the menu on the table. "Enjoy your lunch."

"Aw, come on, Katy," he coaxes, grabbing my arm. "Don't be like this."

"Like what?" I slip from his grasp with one quick, smooth move, even though what I'd really like to do is plop down beside him and sob out my heart in the safety of his arms. "I have no idea what you're talking about."

"Au contraire, sweetheart. You know exactly what I mean." Sliding into the seat, he bounces on the busted spring, then grimaces. "Hey, did you know this seat's broken?"

"Really?" I lift my eyebrows. "I had no idea."

"Ha!" he says, with a chortle loud enough that two customers near the front turn and stare. Don gives them a quick wave, turns back to me. "The hell you didn't," he murmurs.

"Look at it this way." I lean in close enough that I catch the faint scent of his favorite cologne, an expensive designer fragrance I gave him for Valentine's Day. "You know those little kids who beg their parents to take them out for hamburgers and fries at the restaurants with the big bouncy playrooms? Well, now you have your own personal bouncy booth. It'll give you something to do during lunch," I add, darting backward a few feet before he has another chance to grab me.

Sighing, he settles back in the booth, wincing as the springs attack once again. "You're really ticked off, aren't you?"

"About what?"

"You know what I mean. According to your dad, her name is—"

"Look, I know her name, okay? It's Mai. Mai Kaido."
I spit it out like a piece of spoiled fruit. "And if it's all the
same with you, I'd really rather not talk about her."

"Okay, fine, we'll talk about something else." He jerks
his chin at the vinyl-covered bench across from him. "Have
a seat. You look like you could use a break."

"I can't. I'm busy."

He glances around the nearly empty restaurant. "You
don't look busy."

"Well, I am." I fold my arms across my chest. "Right
now, I'm playing hostess."

"Doesn't your dad normally handle the lunch crowd?"

"It appears we're no longer living in normal times." For
the second day in a row, Pop and Mai are incommunicado.
Yesterday they disappeared for hours, and today they left
shortly after breakfast. Where did they go? Color me clueless.
Not only did Pop not bother to fill me in on the details, he
also didn't invite me again to tag along (not that I wanted to,
but that's beside the point).

"I think I'm starting to understand." Don's eyebrows
arch together in a temple of understanding. He gives another
nod at the seat across from him. "Sure you don't want to talk
about it? Talking it out might help make you feel better."

"Since when did you become a psychiatrist?" I lean
against the booth and rub the spot on my forehead where a
dull headache has taken up semi-permanent residence since
the day Mai arrived. I scrounge through my apron pocket
for another Tylenol, hoping to bang back the headache to a
manageable level. Too bad it isn't possible to pop a pill and
make Mai disappear. And there's nothing I'd like better than
to see her gone. In the space of merely three days, she's done

a splendid job of cozying up to Pop and establishing a place for herself in his life. I still don't get it. This random stranger shows up out of nowhere and somehow manages to convince him to accept everything she says is the God's-honest truth. And Pop's fallen for it—every word of the sob story she fed him. It's not like he's stupid or gullible. So, how did she do it? Did she shame him into it?

Whatever's behind it, *Mai-Mai-Mai* is all Pop has on his mind... and—according to what he told me last night—also in his apartment.

His news caught me completely by surprise.

"What do you mean *she's moving in*? Pop, are you crazy?" I hiss, straining to keep my voice at a whisper. The two of us are huddled together in the kitchen which takes up a small corner of the spacious living room. Supposedly Mai was in the bathroom, but I wouldn't have put it past her to be lurking around the corner, eavesdropping on what's meant to be a private conversation. "You barely know her. She shows up and suddenly you're inviting her to move in?"

"Probably sounds like I'm moving too fast, right?" he says sheepishly.

"*Probably*? You can say that again," I sputter. "Why are you doing this?"

He sighs, pinches the bridge of his nose with two fingers, shakes his head. "Katy, I sure wish you'd try and understand. Don't you see I really don't have much choice?"

"Yes, you do," I say. How can he not understand that? How could he have lost touch with reality in such a short span of time? "Letting her stay with you is a huge mistake. How can you not understand that?"

"Because it's not true." His face reddens. "It's not a mistake."

"It is," I insist. Knowing that I'm not getting through to him is beginning to scare me. Pop and I have had more than our fair share of heated discussions in the past, but nothing has ever come close to this. *Nothing.*

"Katy, listen to me." He squares himself in front of me and places his hands directly atop each of my shoulders, the way he does when he wants my full attention. His eyes are cloudy and troubled. "I know what you're thinking, but—"

"No, you don't. You have absolutely no clue. But if you really want to know, then I'll tell you: I think you've lost your mind." My normal, rational don't-give-me-any-crap father has disappeared, courtesy of a woman who barely clears five feet. How can someone so tiny do so much damage?

"How can you trust her?" I ask. "We don't know anything about her, except what she's told us. We have no proof that anything she's said is true. She could be feeding us a bunch of lies. For all we know, Mai could be anyone. She—"

"But she's not," he insists. He pulls me further into a corner, lowers his voice so we can't be overheard. "Look, I know it sounds crazy. And I know I'm asking a lot from you. But you've got to trust me on this, Katy. Everything Mai's said about her past, her mother, and me being in Hawaii before I shipped out? It all happened the way she described it. And don't forget, she had my dog tags. She brought them back to me."

Those dog tags you think are so important? They don't prove a thing, I want to hurl back. Instead, I press my lips together and keep my mouth shut, despite the fact I want nothing more than to refute everything he's said. But I can't.

I don't have any clear answers. The only thing I'm sure about is how I feel: confused, hurt and betrayed.

"I know the two of us don't keep secrets," he says quietly. "And believe me, this wasn't something I was trying to keep from you. But I'm telling you now: I believe what she's saying. I know it's hard for you to accept. But won't you at least try? Please, Katy-Did? Can you do it for me?"

I glance at the floor, unable to meet his eyes. Pop's right about one thing: we don't keep secrets from each other. Well, except for the horrible thing I did that I've kept from him all these years. He still doesn't know, and as far as I'm concerned, he never will. And right now, I can't afford to give him the chance to spot the regret and unhappiness, the guilt and grief hanging in my heart. I'm vulnerable, and I know it. I can't chance him finding out.

"I need a promise from you, Katy." He draws me even closer, drilling his gaze into mine with a piercing stare with the intensity, passion, and resoluteness of a U.S. Marine. "I need you to do something for me."

"What?" I mumble. I dread hearing what he's about to ask, especially because I already know I'll do it. I won't be able to help myself. Love makes you do all sorts of things and I'll do anything for Pop. But I already blew my first mission today. I came upstairs hoping to save him from Mai.

How am I supposed to save him from himself?

"Give her a chance," he says. "That's all I ask. Spend some time with her. Get to know Mai. I know you don't want to, and—"

Damn right I don't want to. I open my mouth to object, but he stops me, gently putting two fingers over my lips before I can speak.

"Consider this, then: Mai wasn't as lucky as you. Growing up, her family life wasn't the most stable environment. She needs to know we trust her. And if we can do that, then everything's going to work out the way it's supposed to. So, at least for now, the best thing we can do is to give her the benefit of the doubt. Mai deserves that much."

Pop's jaw has that square set to it, the one he gets when he's already determined which way to plant his feet. No matter what I say, I know I won't be able to change his mind. Not right now.

"I'll do it if you answer one question," I say. "Just one question."

"You got it."

"It's about Mai moving in. Did you invite her to stay with you, or was she the one who asked? That's all I want to know."

A funny look slips across his face, as if he expected something else from me. Then, just as quickly, the look is gone, replaced by a quietness that sinks my heart. I have my answer.

"Why should she spend her money on some fancy hotel when I can put her up for free?" His voice is laced with disappointment. "Besides, it's not like I don't have the room."

I swallow over the growing lump crowding the back of my throat. The only reason Pop has the extra room is because I moved out years ago. My bedroom, small and cramped, with its one tiny window overlooking the back alley, still has the posters I tacked up as a teenager during my New Kids on the Block phase decorating its walls. Garish beaded necklaces, left over from an old Mardi Gras celebration, are still draped across the dresser; snapshots of Pop and me peek out from between the edges of the mirror where I tucked them long ago. Or at least they were there the last time I looked. Did Mai take things down? If I still lived with Pop, I could have rescued everything. Mai wouldn't have moved into my old room. She wouldn't be sleeping in my old bed.

"Aw, Katy. Why are you so scared of her?"

"Scared? What makes you think I'm scared?"

He tilts his head, shakes it softly, then catches me in a tight hug. I choke back the tears as he presses his face against mine, his cheeks rough with day-old whisker stubble. The faint trace of tobacco lingers on his shirt collar. Pop's sneaking cigarettes again. Having Mai around is adding to his stress.

"Everything will be okay," he whispers in my ear. "I promise it's going to be okay."

I want to believe him. More than anything, I want to believe him. Pop's never let me down.

"Earth to Katy," Don says. "Come in, Katy."

I look up in a kind of daze, surprised to find myself in the restaurant, still on my feet, one hip propped against the booth. Don looks at me like I've just beamed down from the Starship Enterprise.

"I hate to tell you this," he says, "but you look like hell."

My legs suddenly feel wobbly, and I'm hot and cold all over.

"I... I don't know what—"

Don's on his feet, his arm wrapped around me. "Sit," he commands. "Sit down now. Before you end up on the floor."

Shouldering me into a corner of the booth, he slides in beside me. Snapping his fingers, he snags Ellen's attention. "We need some water over here, pronto."

I lean against him, grateful for the support.

"Here, drink this," he prompts, forcing the glass into my hand.

"What happened?" Ellen hovers in the aisle, a worried frown on her forehead. "Katy, are you okay?"

Nodding, I force myself to sip the water. I need to get a grip on myself. The two of them are staring at me like they're contemplating putting in a quick call to 9-1-1.

"I'm fine," I assure them, waving away their concerns. Hopefully they believe me. "I guess the heat got to me."

"I'll bring more water," Ellen says.

"Make it a pitcher," Don calls as she hurries away.

I lean into him, allowing his body heat to chase the chill away. He still has one arm around my shoulder, and with his other hand, he strokes my hair in a slow, steady way that I find comforting. It reminds me of something my mom might have done when I was upset. Out of nowhere, the grief wells up from deep inside, surging through me like a dark wave. Behind my eyes, hot tears spring to life at the thought of my mom. She was strong and smart, and she always knew how to handle things. She'd know how to handle this situation with Mai.

I draw in a sharp breath. Did my mother know about Pop's secret past? Did he confess to her? Did she know about Yumiko?

Don scrutinizes me closely. "Are those tears I see? What's going on, Katy? You never cry."

I lean into the softness his shoulder provides. Maybe I should reconsider talking things over with him. Don's a smart guy, and he's sure to have a cooler head than me. After all, he's not the one involved in a family crisis. Maybe he could help me figure things out. I glance up and find him still staring at me. His face, highlighted by the glint of early afternoon sunlight reflecting through the windows, is filled with concern.

"Remind me again why we broke up?" I ask.

"You said you needed space, remember?" he chides in a soft tease.

"And you listened to me?" Sitting up straighter, I punch him lightly on the arm. "Why?"

He laughs softly. "You weren't exactly in a reasonable mood."

"I'm sorry. Why you put up with me, God only knows." I've been a fool, stringing him along. Don's one of the good guys, and I know that. But I'm the one who'll end up the ultimate fool if I allow myself to believe he'll be willing to stick around forever. Because he won't, no matter what he says. Eventually he'll get tired and change his mind. Someone will come along; a woman who doesn't throw arguments in his face on a regular basis; someone who appreciates him for exactly who he is.

Ellen reappears and refills my glass. I sip slowly, trying to rid myself of the crazy memories from last night's conversation with Pop, and the seismic shift which cracked our lives apart when Mai appeared in town.

"Don't get me wrong, I'm not trying to pressure you," Don says, "but sometimes it helps if you talk things over."

"Mm." I drain my water glass. What's the use in trying to deny it? He knows. We both know.

"Honestly, Don, I don't know where to begin. Mai Kaido is like no one you've ever met. And no one you'd want to meet, either," I add darkly. "The sooner she's back in Hawaii, the better off we'll all be."

I slouch back in the booth. The smooth glossy center surface of the table is marred by an unsightly nick. Probably courtesy of some kid goofing around with a fork when his parents weren't paying attention. It's something we constantly see at Chuck's. Swear to God, if I ever have kids of my own, I'll make sure to teach them manners. I scratch the slight groove carved in the wood. It's not too deep; it can probably be salvaged. For some serious damage, a knife would have worked better. Not a bad idea, come to think about it. I have plenty of knives and forks at my disposal. Maybe I should grab one, find Mai, and let her know exactly what I'm capable of.

Don leans forward, elbows propped on the table. "She can't be that bad. Some of the things they're saying—"

"You mean, people are talking about her? About Pop and me?" Holy crap. Mai and her nasty little paternity claim isn't exactly the type of dirty laundry I want flapping in the breeze. When it comes to the public forum of James Bay, there's no such thing as politically correct. Everyone has opinions, and they're not afraid to voice them, either. I grab his arm. "Tell me what you've heard. What are people saying?"

"Ow!" He yanks it away. "Hey, take it easy. Remember, I'm not the enemy."

"Sorry." The needle on my guilt meter ratchets five degrees higher. He's right. None of this is his fault.

"It's okay," he relents, still rubbing his arm. "You're stressed. I get it."

"Forget about how I feel... so?" I press.

"So, what?"

"*So-o-o-o*...tell me what you've heard."

He pauses a moment. "Like I said, your dad told me."

The hedging in his voice is obvious. "Come on, Don, please tell me the truth. You've been hearing stuff about Mai all over town, haven't you?"

He waits a full ten seconds before finally conceding. His face is grim. "I guess I did hear some things at the coffee shop this morning."

"I knew it," I mumble. "People in this town live for fresh gossip."

"It's not gossip if it's the truth."

"But that's my point." I leap on the semantics. "How do we know it's the truth? Think about it, Don. Mai shows up out of the clear blue sky, claiming to be Pop's daughter. What the hell? Why now, after all these years? And, here's the most unbelievable part: Pop thinks every word out of her mouth is true. Pop, the most practical, sensible man I know. You know how he is. He thinks for himself and he doesn't take any guff from anyone. When he started this business, people predicted he'd fail. They said there was no room for another restaurant in James Bay. But that didn't stop him. He put Chuck's Tavern & Grill on the map, and he's managed to make a nice living for us. And he didn't do it by being stupid.

"But he's being stupid now. He's not thinking straight. Mai could be anyone. She shows up one day, spouting some ridiculous story and what happens? He falls for it." My hand trembles as I pour myself another glass of water. "It's sickening to watch how easy she's managed it. Mai's manipulating him by claiming to be his daughter. It's all one big fat lie."

"How do you know she's lying?"

I glare at him. "I thought you were on my side."

"And I am." He grabs my hand. "Look, Katy, I get it. What you're feeling is normal. It's only human nature to be jealous of—"

"Seriously, that's what you think? That I'm jealous of Mai?" I snatch my hand away. My heart is galloping in crazy circles round and round inside my chest.

"But this isn't about me," I say. "It's about Pop. He's not himself. He's—"

"He's what, Katy?"

"Nothing." I can't bear to say anymore. To Don, or anyone else, Pop probably still looks the same: craggy eyebrows, military crew cut, stern square chin. But the rest of him, the Pop I know and love, is gone, having abandoned all sense of propriety and balance. And the man in his place isn't anyone I recognize. He's excited, elated, and eager to please. Most of all, he's hopeful. One look at his face, and anyone would know exactly what he wants.

He wants to believe her. More than anything else, he wants Mai's story to turn out to be true.

Getting my emotions under control won't be easy. Last night Pop asked me to extend an olive branch. Can I do it? Mai's already proved herself an expert at pushing my buttons. But who knows? Maybe if I try hard enough, I can pull it off. Maybe she isn't as smart as she thinks. Maybe if I play nice, I can lull her into a false sense of security, and learn something that could prove useful later. And who knows what I might find? It's worth a shot.

Right now, it looks like it's the only strategy I've got.

CHAPTER SIX

~ Man Does Not Live by Bread Alone ~

WHOEVER FIRST SAID *WOMEN ARE the weaker sex* had no clue what he was talking about. Fast forward a couple thousand years, and plenty of men are still clueless. Meanwhile, I've got no illusions. Men might think they're in charge, but it's the women who run the show. Case in point, my own life.

Aunt Sis was one tough strong woman. I was only eight years old when my dad died, and she took me in, raising me as her own. He was a gruff old guy, a gunnery sergeant who loved his country as much as he loved me. Dad lived for the Marine Corps; he died for them, too. Aunt Sis did what she could to uncover the details, but back in that time, the early 70s, the government was a tight box of secrecy. The only thing she managed to learn was that the helicopter transporting my dad and his unit was brought down in 1970 by enemy fire somewhere in North Vietnam. They returned Dad's body home to us, and he was buried in James Bay with full military honors. Through it all, I had Aunt Sis.

She stood right beside me, never wavering, never crying, never letting go of my hand as the priest presided over Dad's funeral mass at our parish church, St. Mary's of the Lakes. Her arm tight around my shoulder, we stood together, heads bowed, before the open grave, listening as the priest recited the final prayers commending Dad's soul to God. And she was there, too, in all the days, weeks, months, and years that followed. Aunt Sis never gave up on me, though she must have been sorely tempted at times. I put the poor woman through hell. She knew I was headed down the wrong track, though I didn't know it. I only knew I wanted to fight. And fight I did. I got myself into plenty of trouble, picking fights with other kids, ready to prove I was as good as anyone else. I'm sure she got tired of being called to the principal's office to plead my case yet one more time. If it hadn't been for Aunt Sis, it's anyone's guess how or where I might have ended up. I might even be dead.

But she wouldn't give up. One day, after a particularly messy skirmish in high school that landed me with a broken nose and my opponent with two black eyes, she hauled me home, sat me down, and gave it to me straight. "No more messing around," she warned. No more excuses; no more exceptions. I'd go back to school, I'd toe the line, and after graduation I'd join the military. "It was good enough for your dad, and it's good enough for you," she declared. Joining the Marines, I'd have a chance to see the world, and experience things I'd never have a chance to know if I stayed in James Bay. "It will make a man out of you."

Aunt Sis was right.

God, I miss her.

I miss Katherine, too. We met at a bar, believe it or not, one cold winter night in downtown Detroit when she and a group of her girlfriends stopped for drinks after a concert at

Cobo Hall. I was sitting at the bar when the door opened, blowing in a bitter swirl of wind, snow, and one of the most beautiful women I'd ever seen. I couldn't take my eyes off her as she and her friends shook the snow from their coats and stomped the ice from their boots. Laughing and chattering, the other women filled up a booth, but Katherine, with her thick chestnut hair, glowing complexion, and deep merry laugh, filled up my heart. I tossed back a shot of whiskey to fortify my courage, then tossed back one more *just in case* before I worked up enough nerve to step away from the bar. My legs wobbled in a good imitation of Popeye, and I swore under my breath, hoping I wouldn't come across like a drunken sailor. I reached the table, sober enough to deliver what I hoped was a semi-coherent greeting for each of them, playing round-robin with the flattery until my gaze finally came to rest on her.

God, she was gorgeous. I went down hook, line, and sinker. Her emerald green eyes sparkled as I delivered a rapid-fire round of what I hoped was brilliant rhetoric but feared was utter drivel. But I didn't stop talking. I didn't dare. Her friends giggled and whispered among themselves, but I kept going. I only had eyes for the woman in the stylish black coat at the end of the booth who, for some unearthly reason—thank God—was keenly intent on listening to me. I talked as fast as I could, hoping to impress her.

When Katherine flashed me a brilliant smile and crooked her finger at me, I couldn't believe my luck. Score! I crouched down beside her. Hell, I'd kneel before her, prostrate myself, if that's what it took. I breathed in the crisp tang of frost lingering on her coat mingled with a trace of light floral perfume. Our heads nearly touched. She was close enough to kiss. I searched her face, took in the luminescent glow of her skin, and realized she was even more beautiful close-up. And suddenly, I pulled myself up short. Where did I get off, thinking someone like her would be interested in someone like me? She was so far above me, in every way I could think of; I had no business anywhere near her. And to think she'd allowed me to go on and on. Right then and there, I thought about cutting my losses. *Get out before you get shut down.*

So, I did the only sensible thing I could think of: I started talking even faster. After another few seconds, she raised her palm, stopping me mid-sentence.

"I have a question." Her voice was pure music, each word like notes of the sweetest melody I'd ever heard.

"Yes, ma'am," I said.

She gave me a curious smile. "Do you ever shut up?"

Mortified, I took my lumps and slunk back to the bar, listening as her friends all had a good laugh at my expense. I hunkered down on a stool and ordered another whiskey to soothe my sorrows. But when the drink arrived, it wasn't whiskey but a cola.

"What the hell?" I scowled at the bartender as he placed the drink in front of me.

"Compliments of the lady." He jerked his chin over my shoulder.

I turned on the bar stool. There she stood, directly behind me, calmly buttoning her coat. Her friends waited at the door.

"Next time," she said, bending close enough and speaking softly so only I could hear, "it would be nice if you gave a lady a chance to speak."

"You mean, there'll be a next time?" I managed to croak.

"That depends," she replied with the same merry laugh

that I swear sounded exactly like tinkling bells. "Are you going to ask me?"

"You bet I am." I stood up so fast, I nearly upended the barstool. "Will you go out with me?"

She fastened her scarf around her neck, tucked the ends inside her coat, then once again trained those bewitching green eyes upon me. "I don't even know your name."

"Charles Roy Malinski." I sucked in a deep breath, inhaled the faint fragrance of her perfume over the smoky stench of the bar. "But everyone calls me Chuck."

"Well, Chuck, I'm Katherine. Katherine Mallory."

"Nice to meet you." I offered my hand, and to my surprise, she accepted it. The physical connection between us as we shook hands was brief, but electric, and it took every ounce of effort within me not to draw her into my arms and never let her go. "So, Katherine... Miss Mallory... will you please go out with me?"

"My friends think I shouldn't." Turning, she eyeballed the door where the other women waited, and gave them a brief wave. They all laughed, and a few rolled their eyes. Katherine herself was laughing as she turned back to face me. "They think you're a fool." She leveled me with a shrewd glance. "What do you think?"

I decided to throw the dice. "I think they're probably right," I said. "Though some people think I'm a dangerous fellow."

"Goodness, you don't look dangerous." Her eyes widened in mock horror. "Should I be afraid?"

The back of my throat clamped shut and I knew right then I couldn't make a comeback. Not to her. Not to Katherine. If anyone should be afraid, it was me. No woman had ever reduced me to silence. No woman had ever made me feel weak in the knees, sucker-punched in the gut, with my heart turned inside out.

"So, Chuck, you caught me in a good mood tonight. And just between us, I don't think you're a fool. Far from it. Not after hearing the way you talk. Besides…" She leaned in closer, her mouth close to my ear. "I think you're cute."

I caught my breath, then burst out in a big grin. Lots of women from my past had called me lots of things (liar, cheat, scumbag, and loudmouth all came to mind), but the word *cute* had only been used by one other woman: Aunt Sis.

"I'll go out with you on two conditions," she continued.

"Name 'em," I said, making a silent vow right then and there to do whatever she asked.

"You drink too much. You should think about cutting back."

"Done," I replied fervently, hardly daring to believe my luck. A beautiful girl like Katherine deeming to go out with the likes of me, a good-for-nothing ex-Marine? Sure, I'd recently landed a decent job working the line in one of Motor City's auto factories, and I had some money in my pocket. But money didn't buy everything. And it sure as hell didn't buy you class.

And Katherine sure as hell had class.

"I'll meet you somewhere. Let's make it dinner. Take me someplace nice." Her eyes narrowed. "But remember, it's only dinner. Nothing more than that. If it works out, there'll be a second date. Maybe, maybe not."

"There'll be a second date," I promised.

"You think so, do you?" She raised her eyebrows. "But that depends."

"On?"

"On my second condition," she reminded me.

"And that is…?" I prompted, though I was suddenly scared to hear what it might be.

"I expect you to mind your manners."

"I'll be the perfect gentleman," I vowed. Right then and there, I swore my allegiance to Katherine. And I never looked back. Within the year, she was wearing an engagement ring, we'd set the wedding date, and I was off the booze for good. An occasional beer now and then, but I was done with the hard stuff. I was done with the hard life.

I had Katherine and she was my world. Soft as silk, tough as nails.

She and Aunt Sis got along great.

We married, and a year later, Katy made us a family of three.

"Just because I had a baby doesn't mean I quit being my own person," Katherine informed me in bed one night a few months after giving birth. "I'm Katy's mother, but I'm also a teacher, and I belong in the classroom."

"But why bother? It's not like you need to work." I was working the line, racking up all the overtime I could handle, trying to make a decent living for my two girls. They deserved everything the world had to offer, and more. "I can take care of you and Katy."

"It's not a matter of if I have to, but that I *want* to."

I wasn't happy about it, but I knew there was no use arguing with her. Katherine was a force of nature. Once she made up her mind, there was no stopping her. "I don't want you wearing yourself out."

"You don't think I can do it all?" she teased, and suddenly raised herself to lay on top of me. Her body was warm and supple, her breasts full and inviting. She traced a finger down the line of my jaw and across my lips. I caught the smile on her mouth captured in the moonlight.

"My money's on you, kid. I know you can do anything," I whispered.

"You bet I can. I'm one of those modern woman, remember? *I can bring home the bacon, cook it up in a pan, and keep you happy you're my man*," she joked, like the perfume commercial that had run ad nauseam a few years back.

"I have no doubt," I said, but she shushed me from further talk by catching my face between her hands and sealing her vow with a deep, throaty kiss, which led to the sweetest lovemaking between us since we'd found out she was pregnant.

And I never doubted that she would succeed. Somehow, Katherine made it work. She was a product of the 60s and 70s, and her parents were ardent activists who worked to promote the causes of feminism and social issues. Katherine grew up with loving parents who believed in standing up for what they thought was right, and who taught their daughter to do the same. And Katherine passed that same passionate spirit, that quiet determination, that unwillingness to take *no* for an answer, on to our daughter Katy.

Katy. What am I supposed to do with her now?

I know she's upset about this situation with Mai. She wouldn't be her mother's daughter if she wasn't upset. Katy had the benefit of Katherine's wisdom and strength for the first thirteen years of her life, and I know she remembers her mother, though we rarely talk about her. What would Katherine do if she was here? What would she say to Katy? Even more important, what would she say to me? She knew

I'd been stationed in Hawaii, but I'd never told her about Yumiko. It's not the kind of thing a man confesses to the girl he marries. The last thing I wanted to do was diminish myself in Katherine's eyes. I wasn't proud of the man I was back then. That man attacked life armed with a chip on his shoulder, a know-it-all attitude, and two fists constantly primed for a fight. Meeting Yumiko marked a turning point in my life, and not a good one.

"Buy me a drink, GI?" she'd asked when I walked into the bar near base that night. Buying her that drink was my first mistake. The second was allowing her to lead me outside and down the street to the seedy apartment she shared with two other women. I'll admit I was an all-too-willing participant when it came to her seducing me with sex. And I was hooked from the start. It was like freebasing a darker side of life I'd never been exposed to before. Once I met Yumiko, my time in Hawaii dissolved into a hazy world of booze, kinky sex, and mind-altering drugs. How I managed to keep myself sane and relatively sober, along with showing up for duty and serving up chow to the enlisted men, is still a mystery to me. I'm surprised I never got thrown in the brig.

The thing that eventually saved me was our transfer orders. We were shipping out, stateside. I was finally going home. The orders came just in time. I knew Yumiko was traveling down a road that would take me places I wasn't sure I wanted to follow. Aunt Sis hadn't spent all that time trying to raise me right, only for it to end swallowed up in darkness. But Aunt Sis was in Michigan, and I was on my own, a man with a messed-up mind fumbling his way through a messed-up world. Yumiko and the drugs, the booze, and the sex, had a firm grasp on me, and each day only made it worse. So, when my orders came through, I kept my mouth shut; even on that last day, when Yumiko told me she was pregnant. I took the easy way out, listening to my buddies. The Marines threw me a life preserver and I grabbed it. With thousands of miles between us, I'd never see Yumiko again.

Or so I thought.

Yumiko walked back into my life the day Mai walked into the restaurant.

This girl, my daughter, is a stranger to me. Katy's like a firecracker with a lit fuse, while Mai's quiet and reserved. She doesn't say much, but that doesn't mean she isn't paying attention. She's asked lots of questions these past few days, as I've taken her around and introduced her to the places that mean something special to me: the school I attended as a kid; the restaurants I worked at; the cemetery where my dad and Aunt Sis are buried. Katy's familiar with everything, but Mai isn't. Katy's had me her whole life; Mai hasn't.

I've already had one heart attack. It's time I put my affairs in order, and make things right. And while I have no problem doing it for Mai, how do I convince Katy it's the right thing to do? She's been handling things in the restaurant all by her lonesome since Mai showed up. Not that she's been complaining about it, but I know she's not a happy camper. But Katy's going to have to figure out a way to deal with it a bit longer. I know she won't like it. Most likely, neither will I. Because my gut's already warning me that things might turn out bad. All those years ago, when our ship left port and the shoreline of Oahu faded in the distance, the feeling I remember most was overwhelming relief that I'd made it out of the darkness. And though I knew it wouldn't be an easy journey, at least I was headed for the other side. But now

Mai's here, some of the sunshine has disappeared. When she walked into the restaurant, Yumiko's darkness followed. And there's nothing I can do about it.

But I can't turn my back on her. I turned my back on her mother, and I'll always regret it. And the thing that scares me the most?

Getting lost in the darkness again.

CHAPTER SEVEN

~ The Customer is King ~

"HI FOLKS, HOW CAN I help?"

I offer a smile to the party of four—two couples, probably in their mid-forties—seated in one of our front window booths. When they breezed in an hour ago, I had a hunch they might cause problems, and my fears have been realized. First, they demanded one of the best seats in the house, then voiced loud complaints at being forced to endure a ten-minute wait. Once I finally got them seated, I did my best to keep an eye on them, but when the dinner rush exploded, all my good intentions evaporated like a blast of hot steam from the kitchen's deep fryer. Today is one of our busiest days yet, and with Pop *in absentia* once again, I'm pulling double-duty, and never made it back to check on the demanding foursome. Now, thanks to their rudeness and my neglect, Ellen's reduced to tears after they ran roughshod over her.

After advising Ellen to stay in the kitchen and take a few minutes to calm herself, I head for their booth, silently urging myself to heed my own advice. Deep breath. Stay calm. As manager, it's my job to make sure things flow smoothly, and to solve people's problems: customers and staff included. A happy staff equals less headache for me. Happy customers mean satisfied customers and (hopefully) repeat business.

"How can I help?" I repeat.

"For starters, you can take this charge off our bill." The stockier of the two men shoves the slip toward me. "Those ribs were overcooked. Talk about terrible food."

"I'm sorry to hear that." A complaint about our ribs? Chuck's is famous for serving up delicious barbecued ribs. The only menu item more popular is our Friday night all-you-can-eat fish fry.

"And greasy," says the woman next to him. "Much too greasy," she adds with a sniff, wiping her fingers clean with one of the numerous paper napkins tossed around the table.

I pick up the bill, study it quickly. Four full slabs of barbecued ribs, and sides of coleslaw and fries, multiplied by four. Add in the booze, of which they've consumed plenty, and we're talking a nice piece of change. Any restaurant owner in James Bay would hate to see that kind of profit walk out the door. If Pop was around, he'd be through the roof.

But Pop isn't here. I have no clue where he is, or what he's doing. But rest assured, wherever he is, it's with Mai.

"All of you had the ribs?" I ask, though the question is redundant, given the four dirty plates stacked high with the remains of rib bones picked clean, still littering the table.

"We told that waitress they weren't any good, but she didn't listen." The second man's voice is equally scornful. "Why should people have to pay for lousy food? They shouldn't!"

I nod sympathetically. He's right. The first rule of

business for any retail business—restaurant or otherwise—is never to dismiss a customer complaint. And when it comes to customer complaints, our staff is drilled daily that any criticisms—concerning food, drink, or anything else—are to be brought directly to either me or Pop. Granted, Ellen's new on staff, but she didn't alert me about a potential problem. And as far as I know, there haven't been any other complaints about the ribs tonight.

"We only came here because of a friend," the first woman says. "She ate here last summer and raved about what a wonderful place it was, with such delicious food."

"That's a bunch of bullshit and you know it," the man next to her scoffs. "Julia's drunk half the time and she never knows what the hell she's talking about." He glares at me. "So, crappy food, crappy service. I want to know how you're going to make this right."

I eye his empty glass, study his flushed face, then consult the bill once more. According to the tab, one of them has consumed three Jack on the rocks, and I'm guessing he's the culprit. I sneak a glance at the fourth guest in their party. Up until now, the other woman has remained silent. But she doesn't look composed. Her bottom lip is white, as if she's been biting back words.

"And you, ma'am, you also had the ribs?" I ask. You need to draw the line somewhere. The customer is always right... except when they're not.

"What's the matter with you?" The first man slams his fist on the table and silverware goes flying. "You're as dense as that stupid waitress who served us. Didn't you hear me? We all had the ribs."

"Yes, I can see that. And I also see that you ate them,

too." I'm careful to keep my tone neutral, mindful that other customers are watching and that our heated discussion is being served up as the latest newsworthy topic in the restaurant tonight. "Here's what I'm happy to do for you: free dessert for everyone, on the house. Our cherry pie is very popular."

Our cheesecake is the dessert menu's best seller, but I'm not about to offer them that. These people want something for nothing, and I refuse to let them take advantage of our good graces. They're already getting more than they deserve.

"Pie?" the first man sputters. "If you think some damn piece of pie will—"

"Bill, honest to God, would you please shut up?" The second woman suddenly throws her napkin on the table and glares at him. "Because I swear, if you don't, and I mean right now," she threatens, "I will walk out of this restaurant and never speak to you again." She glowers at the man seated next to her, and the other woman. "And that goes for both of you, too. I've never been so embarrassed in my life."

I do my best to keep a straight face as Bill sputters and spits while the other two remain silent.

"Fine." The woman turns to me without a smile. "Thank you," she says in a civil tone. "We'll all have the pie."

"Coming right up," I promise, and head for the kitchen. The sooner they polish off their dessert, the sooner they'll leave. You can't please all the people all the time. The best I can do is settle for trying to please most of the people all the time.

"I'm so sorry." Ellen, positioned just beyond the swinging door, gnaws at a ragged cuticle as I enter the kitchen. "Are you mad at me?"

"Silly, of course not," I reply, heading toward the dessert counter.

"Honestly, Katy, those people were horrible. They complained about everything."

"The food?" I ask.

"No, not that. But they sure were vocal about everything else. The booth wasn't comfortable. The table was missing a fork. The service was slow. Nothing I did made them happy." Ellen lifts a hand, swipes a faint sheen of sweat from her face. The narrow kitchen is hot and steamy, unlike the dining room, which features an air conditioner working overtime to keep customers cool and content. "And some of the things that one man said to me?" She blushes to the tip of her blond roots. "I can't believe someone could be so mean."

"Believe it," I say with a grim smile, doing my best to forget the foul language he used. "The guy is a creep. And unfortunately, while he might be the first you run across, he won't be the last. So, don't worry about it." I grab a full cherry pie, and place it on the counter.

"But I do." Ellen's forehead wrinkles in a worried frown. "You took a chance on me by giving me this job, and I don't want to mess up. Swear to God, Katy, they never said a word about the ribs being bad, not until I took out the check. If they'd complained, I would have come to you right away."

"Somebody says my ribs are bad?" Pete yells across the room. "Who says so? No way." Pete is the balding middle-aged line cook who's been with us since Chuck's opened. He stands before an open flame grill slathering generous portions of barbecue sauce over racks of juicy pork, all while keeping a careful eye on the full and half slabs. "These ribs here are some of the best we've had all month."

"Forget it, Pete," I advise.

"If somebody got a complaint about my ribs, just send 'em back here. I'll show 'em what's what."

"No doubt," I say.

"You think I'm kidding?" Squinting, he points an over-sized sauce spoon at me.

"Absolutely not," I vow, despite the fact I'm pressed for time. I grew up around Pete, and I'm not going to say or do anything that would jeopardize our friendship. Our line cook might talk a rough and tough game, but underneath that crusty exterior of his, he's a true sweetheart. "Everyone knows you're a man of your word."

"Damn straight." Nodding vigorously, he turns his attention back to his grill.

I grab the stainless-steel pie cutter and center it over the pie while Ellen continues to hover at my elbow.

"Best advice I can give you?" I say. "Just do the best you can. Waiting tables is a tough job, one of the toughest you'll ever have. You're going to run into all kinds of people. Some of them will be great and some will be jerks. But you can't let the jerks get to you. Do your job, do your best, then move on and let it go." With one swift thrust of my palm, I jam the cutter through the pie, slicing it into eight neat pieces.

"You make that look so simple," Ellen says.

"Years of practice," I reply. "Grab some plates, will you?"

"Sure." She heads off, and I let out the deep whoosh I've been holding in since she cornered me. Hopefully tonight's incident won't rattle her too much, and she'll stick it out. The last thing I need is Ellen losing her nerve and walking off the job. With nearly half our current staff soon headed to college, Chuck's needs her. I need her.

Plus, I like her. Ellen's friendly and funny. I hired her a few weeks ago, despite her lack of experience. Despite the fact Pop didn't want me to do it.

"Are you crazy?" he sputtered when I told him about our newest waitress. "The woman is a convicted felon. You can't let someone like that work here. Before you know what's happening, she'll have her hand in the cash register and rob us blind."

"That's not going to happen," I said, trying not to roll my eyes. Pop can be so dramatic at times. "And it's my decision," I reminded him. "I'm in charge of staff."

"I hope to hell you know what you're doing," he muttered, shaking his head.

"I do," I promised.

"Maybe she'll quit before she cleans us out," he said darkly before stomping off.

But I trust Ellen, and I have faith she won't let me down. We met about six weeks ago, when Ellen moved into The Bungalow, James Bay's local halfway house for women. I volunteer there once a week, and Ellen and I struck up an immediate friendship. Yes, I knew she'd been convicted of a felony for shoplifting, and yes, I knew about her having spent thirty days in the county jail. But I hired her anyway. If anyone deserves a break, it's Ellen.

Raised in a family drowning in alcohol and drug problems, Ellen ran away from home at fourteen, after being molested by her father. A few years later, following a brief nightmare of a marriage to a man who turned out to be a deadbeat husband and drug dealer, Ellen found herself on the streets, a single mom struggling to raise two little boys. When she was caught stealing food, the grocery store refused to drop the shoplifting charges. Granted, she did a foolish thing, but most people would understand the motivation of a mother trying to feed her children. But not the national corporation which owned the grocery store. Their *no exceptions* policy resulted in Ellen serving a jail term, and losing her boys to foster care. Now she's living at The Bungalow while serving out her probation period; her five-year old twins visit once a week. The three of them won't be eligible to be together as a family again until she graduates from the halfway house system, and establishes herself as a contributing member of society. That means Ellen needs a steady job that can pay the bills. After hearing her story, I hired her on the spot, though I told her up front that the fact we were friends didn't mean I intended to cut her any slack. She had no experience as a waitress, and I was willing to give her a chance. But she needed to learn how to handle herself in a fast-paced environment, and cope with the stress that comes in dealing with the public. Ellen promised to do her best; up until now, I haven't been sorry about my decision to hire her.

And I'm still not sorry, even after tonight's clash with her customers. Rudeness isn't something we tolerate at Chuck's—from our staff or our customers. That table Ellen served isn't the type of trade I want to encourage. People like them can find someplace else to eat. James Bay has plenty of other restaurants in town.

I glance around the kitchen, take a swift survey. Everything seems under control, including the noisy commercial-grade dishwasher. It was on the fritz nearly two hours this morning, but it seems to be working now. I turn to Ellen. "Do you want me to serve the pie, or can you handle it?"

"No, I'll do it. They're my table." She stacks the four

plates of cherry pie on an empty tray. "It's like you said. The world is full of people like them. The faster I get used to dealing with them, the better I'll be able to handle it."

"There you go," I say, silently cheering her on and wishing Pop was here so he could witness how she's stepping up. *Way to go, Ellen!*

She moves to pick up the tray, then suddenly halts. "Katy?"

"Something wrong?"

"No, nothing," she quickly assures me. "I only wanted to say thanks. Thanks again for the vote of confidence. I appreciate it."

"You're welcome," I say, proud as any parent watching their little one who, the day before had been in tears, confidently wave goodbye and hop into line the second day of preschool. I nod toward the swinging door. "Better get going, before they start complaining how long the pie took."

Ellen plasters a determined look on her face, picks up the tray, and heads back to the main dining room.

"She's still a little rough around the edges, but she'll make it," Pete says as I near his grill. He flips racks of ribs with an expert hand. "Give her another week and she'll be handling more tables than any of those college kids you got out there."

"Think so?"

"I know so."

I smother a smile. If Ellen's already managed to get Pete on her side, chances are good that she'll work out fine.

"Uh-uh, hands off," he says as I reach for a clean spoon, intent on sampling the barbecue sauce. "I can't afford any taste testing, not the way these ribs are moving tonight."

"Not even from the boss lady?" I tease.

"Nope, not even her."

Laughing, I drop the spoon. "You're a horrible man, Pete. Anybody ever tell you that?"

"Yep, all the time." He grunts, brandishing the supersized serving spoon at me like a deadly weapon. "Go on, get out of here. You wanna bother somebody, go check on that new kid your dad hired to do the dishes. Last I saw him, he was headed out the back door with a pop and some smokes."

Great, just what I need. Dreading the encounter, I head around the corner in search of our new dishwasher. Pop seems to have a talent for hiring losers. While a few work out, most walk off the job or end up with me having to fire them. Pop's a big softie when it comes to kids in need of a job. *How can they be expected to make something of themselves if we don't show them the way out?* he's said time after time. He draws the line when it comes to drugs, but alcohol-related run-ins with the law don't seem to bother him. *Once upon a time, I was just like them*, he's said more than once, without elaborating.

Yet now, I can't help but wonder if Pop's involvement with the mysterious Yumiko was somehow tied to an alcohol-induced lifestyle? He likes his beer, but he never touches the hard stuff. Was there a time in his life when that wasn't the case?

How much do I know about his past?

Why haven't I ever asked him?

Rounding the corner, I find Pop's new hire back at his station in front of the dishwasher, scraping and racking dishes at a furious clip. Thank God. Maybe he'll turn out to be one of Pop's success stories. And thank God, the commercial sized stainless-steel dishwasher is fully operational again.

I'm already dreading the plumber's bill that I know will eventually show up in the mail, but I had no choice but to call him. Clean, dry, sanitized dishes are a necessity. If we don't comply with health safety standards, the Health Department will shut us down in a heartbeat.

People who routinely go out for dinner assume they know everything there is to know about running a restaurant. Chalk it up, I suppose, to the rising popularity of celebrity chef and other reality TV shows on the Food Network and such. But running a successful restaurant is much more involved and intense than the TV audience and dining public will ever see.

First and foremost is hiring—and keeping—a competent staff. Having the right team in place is crucial to success. And, except for alcohol, the profit margin is slim. A prep cook who tosses out a soft tomato or a bit of slightly wilted lettuce; a line cook who regularly messes up or burns orders; a surly teenager manning the dishwasher who decides to cart a case of frozen food out the backdoor and stash it in his car; a waitress with a bad temper and a mouth to match; all can easily ruin a day's or week's profit. Staff who can handle the pace, cook a decent meal, keep up with the orders, and serve them with a smile, are worth every cent we pay them, and more.

Up until a few months ago, Pop handled Chuck's day-to-day operations, but since his heart attack, I've taken over more of the responsibilities. He still manages the alcohol, beer and wine inventory, but I'm now in charge of the daily and weekly food orders, tracking supplies, overseeing deliveries. And just like the other restaurants in James Bay, Chuck's has a fully stocked basement. It's easy to get lost down there in the maze of metal shelving. Canned goods, the six-or-seven-pound commercial grade variety, are neatly lined up on shelf after shelf. Dinnerware of all sizes—bowls, salad, dinner, and dessert plates—gleaming silverware, sparkling glasses, and glistening stemware take up an additional two metal shelving units. Another contains overstock items: salt and pepper shakers, condiments of all sorts, an ample supply of paper products. Industrial-sized freezers stand next to the shelving, fully stocked with frozen shrimp, chickens, and other meats. A large walk-in cooler holds fresh produce, with deliveries coming in five days a week.

Customers would get an eye full if we gave them a tour, but people who show up for lunch or dinner are only interested in three things: comfortable surroundings (note to self: fix the booth with the broken spring), good food, and a friendly atmosphere where they can relax and enjoy themselves. They never see the cleaning lady who shows up religiously every day at five am, putting in her four hours with bucket, broom and mop, then quietly disappearing before the lunch crowd arrives. People aren't interested in our struggle to contain costs, to keep inventory and utility bills from soaring, and the ever-complicated bookkeeping business end of things. Customers could care less how tough it is to juggle employee work hours to maintain a happy staff who show up when they're scheduled. The dining public doesn't care if we have the appropriate HR posters displayed in a prominent spot. They don't want to know how many metal napkin holders are stocked on our basement shelves; the only thing that matters to them is having plenty of napkins available at their table. And customers shouldn't have to care about these things. That's my job. When I told Pop about my plans not to attend college, to work alongside him at the restaurant, he advised me to make sure I knew what I was doing. *Owning and operating a restaurant isn't easy*, he warned. *Figure out what you love to do, and it won't be work.* I've paid attention, listened to everything he said. I've done my best to follow his lead, because I know I'll never find a better teacher.

Pop's always loved Chuck's Tavern and Grill. It's his restaurant. It's his home. It's who he is.

Or so I thought.

I don't think I'm wrong about Mai.

But have I been wrong all along about Pop?

And have I been wrong about me?

CHAPTER EIGHT

~ Chef's Special ~

"Now's your chance," Don says. "Eva wants to sell, and you said you've been wanting to expand for years. And a property located right next to Chuck's? You'll never find a better opportunity."

"I know, I know." I blow out a deep sigh, slouch lower in the cushy leather chair across from Don's desk. His spacious glass cubicle, though smack dab in the middle of the busy real estate office, affords us some privacy.

Don leans forward, phone in hand, and gives me one of those looks. A look that says, you'd-be-crazy-not-to-act-on-this-deal. A look that says, we-need-to-get-this-done-and-we-need-to-get-it-done-now. "What do you say? Do we make the call?"

"Give me a minute, okay?" I hate feeling pressured, especially when I know it's my own damn fault. I'm the one who started the ball rolling. I'm the one who told him I was interested. And if not for Katy's objections, it would already be a done deal.

I shift in my seat, allow myself a breather. I know Don's

got my best interests in mind. My interests—and his own. He's smart, I'll give him that. He's only been in town a few years, but it didn't take long for him to make a name for himself. Now he's the lead local listing agent in the firm he works for, and his name and face are prominently displayed on real estate signs all over town. His office is a busy place, with phones ringing steady, and a constant flow of people in and out. But to me, it feels like heaven. No one knows I'm here. No one to bug me. No customers. No staff.

No daughters.

"Eva's ready to sign," Don reminds me. "We can get this deal done today."

"I dunno." I hunch forward, scratch my head like it might help my thoughts line up straight.

He leans back in his chair and folds his hands over his stomach. "Okay, what gives? Either you want the place, or you don't."

"I do." Still, I hesitate. "I'd like to get my hands on the property. It's just... well, I'm having a little problem with Katy."

This purchase is a major deal. I talked with the bank a few weeks back, and the loan is already pre-approved. But it's a lot of money. I wish Katy would understand how expanding into Eva's location makes perfect sense. Adding a second dining room to our existing building gives us more floor space, which means more tables. And more tables will mean more people eating at Chuck's. We improve our visibility, grow our customer base, raise our market exposure; ultimately, it all adds up to increased profits. Why can't she understand that? It's good for business.

A quizzical look covers his face. "Katy doesn't think expanding Chuck's is a good idea?"

"She doesn't think right now is a good time for us to take on any debt."

"But I thought you didn't have any other debt."

"That's right. We don't."

"It's not like Eva's asking for the moon," he reminds me. "It's a fair price."

"I'm not arguing that."

Katy is the one who's been doing the arguing. And that was *before* Mai showed up. I hate to think what my younger daughter will say if, and when, I broach the subject of the property purchase again. Katy's barely talking to me now. Meanwhile, Mai thinks the deal is great, and wonders why I'm dragging my feet. And she's right. What's holding me back?

"What's wrong with women, anyway?" I blurt, throwing up my hands. "Why are they always hellbent on making such a big deal out of stuff?"

Don eyes me carefully. "I assume you're talking about Katy and Mai?"

"Who else?" I stretch out my legs, consider my scuffed brown shoes. "Frankly, I don't get it. Why can't they get along?" I run a hand across my buzz cut. "Men don't have these kinds of problems. Something comes along, we accept it, and we move on. Why can't women do the same?"

"Because they're women. They're wired differently."

"Boy oh boy, that's the truth." I shake my head. "Look, I'll admit that when Mai showed up, it threw me for a loop. But it is what it is, and she's part of our lives now. I accept it, just like I accept her. But Katy? Well, she's a whole different story."

This growing rift between us makes me sick to my stomach.

"Has she said anything about it to you?" I ask.

His face tightens. "About...?"

"You know what I mean. Has she said anything about Mai?"

We sit there for a good minute, eyeballing each other.

"Maybe she did," he finally admits. "But is that really important?"

"It could be," I say.

"Want to know what I think?"

"I do," I say firmly.

"Okay. I think you're talking to the wrong person. Yes, Katy and I have talked about things, and how she feels about Mai. But I'll bet it's nothing you don't already know. So, even if I told you what she said, I doubt it would help. Because I'm not the one you need to talk to. Am I right?"

I grip the arms of my chair so hard, my knuckles turn white. "I guess so."

His face softens. "Look, Chuck, I get it. You're upset. And hey, that's understandable. You love Katy. There's a special bond between you. Anybody who knows the two of you can see that. And what you're feeling is probably the same thing any father who loves his daughter as much as you love Katy would feel. But think for a minute about how she feels. All these years, it's been just the two of you. Then Mai shows up, and suddenly... everything changes."

"You think I don't know that?" For some reason, his comments irritate the hell out of me. They sound like something that could be coming directly out of Katy's mouth. But like it or not, it's also the truth. Haven't I been thinking the same thing for days now?

"Katy loves you. She's just confused."

"She's not the only one," I say. "Why do things have to change?"

"Change is hard," he agrees.

"Crap, I hate this stuff. Life can be damn unfair."

I hunch forward, turn my head, take in the view out the window. Everything looks the same as it did when I walked in his office. There are tourists gallivanting all over downtown James Bay. They stroll through the shops, wander along the marina, admire the beautiful view of the bay. But I don't need a reminder of what this place is like. This is my hometown. It's where I grew up. Even with my eyes closed, I can picture it all in my head. The town, the people; they're seared in my memory, like the odor that lingers in Chuck's kitchen when Pete occasionally burns the ribs.

And yet... though everything looks the same, there's a subtle shift in view.

Pete hasn't burned anything, but it stinks to high heaven. Something is different.

I'm different. I'm the one who messed up. I'm the one who burned things. I'm the one to blame.

"You ever make any mistakes in your life?" I blurt out.

Don blinks, then chortles. "Sure," he admits. "Who hasn't? It's part of being human."

"But what about the big ones?" I press.

He frowns. "I'm not sure I follow."

"The big ones. Things you wish you'd done different," I say bluntly. "How do you live with them?"

He grows quiet, rubs the back of his neck. "I guess everybody has stuff they keep deep inside," he finally says. "Stuff they wish hadn't happened, things they regret."

"Yep, that's what I'm talking about."

"Maybe the trick is learning to let go of the regrets," he muses. "If you don't, they'll eat you up inside."

Damn right. I wish I had some antacids. My stomach is on fire. Aunt Sis raised me to be a man. That means owning up to your mistakes, accepting the consequences for your actions, even if they're not what you want for your life. I fish a handkerchief out of my pocket and mop the perspiration from my forehead. I can hear an air conditioner humming in the background, but Don's office feels as humid as an afternoon in Honolulu. I feel the sticky wetness spreading under my armpits. I grab my shirt collar, fan the fabric away from my body, try to get some air circulating.

"You okay?" he asks.

"Thinking about the past... and the stupid mistakes I made."

"Everyone makes mistakes."

"Well, I made more than my fair share," I reply, "and some of those things I'm not proud of."

I swallow hard, remembering how I took the coward's way out. The pressure tightens in my chest. Guilt isn't an easy weight; some days it's worse than others. Today is the worst by far.

"Chuck, hey, take it easy. You didn't know. Don't be so hard on yourself. It's not your fault."

"Yes, it is," I insist, with another swipe at my sweaty forehead. "Mai deserved to have a father around."

I mop the sweat from my neck and throat. Dammit, it's hot in here. Why don't they crank up the air conditioning?

"I should have done right by her mother, and stayed in Hawaii."

"If you'd stayed, look how different your life would be now. Plus, there would be no Katy."

I close my eyes, try to imagine a life without Katy. I hadn't thought the pain in my chest could get any worse, but I'm wrong.

"That would break my heart," I say quietly.

"Maybe you need to tell her that," he suggests.

"Maybe," I agree, drawing a ragged breath. Am I ready to do it? A total confession would mean admitting to Katy exactly what happened with Yumiko. The good *and* the bad. And Katy and I don't talk about things like that. She doesn't need to hear about all the mistakes her old man made. She's my daughter.

But so is Mai.

Enough. I fumble through my pocket for the little brown bottle my doctor advised me to always keep on hand.

Don eyes the bottle. "What's that?"

"Don't worry about it." Unscrewing the cap, I fish out the tiny white pill no bigger than a mustard seed. I slip it under my tongue, then lean back and wait for modern medicine to work its magic.

"Did you just pop a nitro tablet?"

"It's nothing."

"The hell it's nothing," Don mutters. "Your face is gray." He grabs his phone and punches in some numbers.

"What are you doing?" I sputter.

He shoots me a harsh look. "What do you think I'm doing? I'm calling 9-1-1. You need medical help."

"No, don't," I insist. My voice sounds tiny and echoes in my ears as the narrow tunnel closes in on me. "Give me a minute or two. I'll be fine."

"Too late," he says. "They're already on their way."

"You shouldn't have done that." I struggle for breath. Damn pill. Why isn't it working? It usually does. "Katy will be worried sick."

That's the last thing I remember before blacking out.

CHAPTER NINE

~ Heartburn ~

"IT'S CALLED AN ANGIOPLASTY," I explain. "He had a partially blocked artery, and they put in a stent. They kept him in the hospital overnight, and now he's back home."

"And he'll recover?" says Ellen, who's nestled at the other end of the couch in The Bungalow's living room. "He'll be okay?"

"According to his doctor, yes," I say, nodding. "But he also said that Pop was lucky this time, and that he needs to take better care of himself."

Which he is going to do, whether he likes it or not. Because if he doesn't, he'll have me to deal with. I tuck my feet under my legs, curl up deeper in my corner of the couch, and give the throw pillow a good smack. Doing it feels so good, I punch it a few more times.

Ellen eyes me over the sewing in her lap. "Are you trying to kill that pillow?"

"Better the pillow than my dad," I reply, giving it another whack. I'm thankful Pop's alive, but that doesn't mean I'm not still furious about the situation. He was popping nitro for more than two weeks and never told me? Talk about stupid.

"He's already had one heart attack. He knows the symptoms. He knows better. But when he started having chest pains a couple weeks ago, do you think he admitted what was going on? Nope, not my father," I fume. "He popped a nitro and hoped the pain would simply disappear, like magic. Damn it, Ellen, he could have died. Doesn't he know that? What's the matter with him?"

"He's a man. Most of them don't like to admit they're mere mortals, like the rest of us."

"That sounds about right." It's still impossible to shrug off the feeling of dread that crept over me when I heard Don's voice on the phone letting me know what had happened. It was a different scenario when Pop had his first heart attack. The telephone call from the EMS crew caught me in my car on my way home from work. Pop had been fine a half hour before, and I'd just finished closing the restaurant. I broke every speed limit and raced through two red lights on my way to Bay Memorial Hospital, beating the ambulance with Pop and the EMS crew by mere minutes. I still remember how scared I felt watching them make their noisy entrance into the Emergency Room with Pop strapped to a gurney, an oxygen mask covering his face. I was terrified he wouldn't survive, that I would lose him, that I'd be all alone in the world.

"It's lucky he had someone there with him."

I nod. "Thank God Don had enough sense to call 9-1-1."

And while I'm grateful to Don for taking charge, I'm still plenty mad at him, too. Don knows Pop's health history, and he has no business goading Pop on. The two of them shouldn't have been talking business like that. I'll grudgingly admit that owning Eva's property would be mostly a good thing for the restaurant, but I'm still not convinced we're up to it; more specifically, if Pop himself is up to it. The last thing he needs is more stress in his life. Like his cardiologist told us, it isn't a matter of *if* Pop will ever have another heart attack, but rather, *when* the next one occurs.

Pop was lucky this time. He dodged a bullet. Who knows what's going to happen in the future?

Especially with Mai still here. Having her around only adds to his stress. She's been in town for more than two weeks, but she still hasn't given us the slightest indication that she's interested in leaving. Someone should set her straight. Hasn't she heard that old adage: the one about guests who overstay their welcome? After three days, they stink like fish. And Mai's from Hawaii, where the ocean swarms with fish. But she seems to be an expert at covering her stench. Probably that expensive designer fragrance she wears.

If you can't say something to someone's face, then better not to say anything at all, Pop taught me when I was growing up. And I shouldn't be talking about Mai. It's wrong. It's mean. But if I don't tell someone how I feel, I'm afraid I'll explode.

"You should have seen her fussing over Pop at the hospital." I punch the pillow again, grinding my fist into its satin softness as the memories resurface. Mai, showing up at the hospital. Mai, lingering at his bedside. Mai, listening intently to every word the doctor uttered. If I'd had my say, I would have banned her from the room. But that's not what Pop wanted. And it galls me to no end that he allowed her to stay.

"Who are you talking about?" Ellen asks.

"Mai. Who else?"

"I'm sure she must have been worried."

And I'm still worried, even now, with Pop back home and supposedly on the mend. His meds have been switched out, his cardiac rehab appointments scheduled, and I've laid down the law about him working at Chuck's. I'll handle things at the restaurant until he feels stronger. Better that he takes some time off, eases back into things gradually. The less stress on him, the better.

And that includes Mai. My dear, sweet, older half-sister Mai, who, at this very minute, is probably pretending to be thoroughly engrossed in yet another of his stories. She hovers over him, a constant presence at his side whenever I run upstairs for a quick visit. It's impossible for Pop and me to have a private conversation. I love him. I miss him. Why doesn't she leave us alone?

Every time I see her, it gets more difficult to keep my mouth shut.

"This all would be so much simpler if she'd go home. Everything would go back to the way it used to be."

"No, it wouldn't." Ellen glances up from the pair of boy's pants she's mending. "Think about it, Katy. Things will never be the same. Even if she leaves, she'll always be your sister."

"That remains to be seen."

"You think she's lying?"

"Personally, I find it odd that everyone is willing to believe her story."

I've been leery of Mai since the day we met. It's hard to put a finger on why. There's something about the way she carries herself, especially when she's not aware of others watching. She's good at concealing it, but it's always there, lingering beneath the surface. There's an attitude, an edginess about her—a quiet assumption that she's entitled to something. What that might be, I'm not sure... and maybe it doesn't matter. Because, the bottom line is, I don't trust her.

And Pop isn't helping matters. When she drove away from the hospital the night he was admitted, I kept thinking about where she was headed... back to his apartment, where she spent the night alone. She could have snooped through all sorts of things she has no business poking around in—Pop's private papers, his office files, our family things. Who knows what she did? While the restaurant has plenty of surveillance trained on various locations, Pop's apartment isn't wired with security cameras. He lives alone. What would be the point?

But Pop doesn't live alone anymore.

"I still don't understand why she makes you so upset," Ellen says. "Mai seems nice enough."

"I don't trust her," I say bluntly.

"Has she done something? What exactly is it about her that makes you not trust her?"

I don't have a ready answer. Mai might think she's pulled off a perfect job of playing the role of a quiet, loving daughter, but she can't fool me. This passive act of hers is merely a ruse—or a noose. Give her enough time, and I bet she hangs herself. And I hope I'm around for the lynching.

"I can't explain it. When she's around..." I break off, searching for the right words. I don't want to come across as cynical and spiteful, though that's pretty much how I feel inside. "She makes me feel—"

"Inadequate? Like you're not good enough?"

"Maybe," I reply. It's simpler to let Ellen think what she wants, and it's safer than admitting my true feelings. I'd be embarrassed if anyone knew. I scrunch deeper into the couch, watching as she labors to hem the worn clothing.

The Bungalow is a regular drop-off point for community donations and Ellen's an expert at scrounging through the boxes for children's clothing. One recent donation contained numerous pairs of boys' trousers requiring only minor repairs, which she's working on right now. When her twin sons show up for their next visit, they'll find new (for them) outfits waiting. Ellen was so proud when she showed me the hand-me-downs. But she and her boys deserve so much better. Why do some people seem dogged by rotten luck? The only difference between Ellen and me is an accident of birth. Why did I get off so easy? So lucky? One could say I live a charmed life.

Except for my mother's death.

Except for Mai.

"What I notice about her, mainly, is the air of confidence Mai has." Ellen works her needle through the fabric. "Then again, beautiful women tend to be like that."

"True." Mai could intimidate even a crowded room of former Miss-Americas. Any woman would find herself coming up short next to Mai. Especially me. I wasn't like all the other girls at school, fussing with their make-up, hair, and clothes. Those kinds of things never mattered. I dress up when necessary, but given a preference, I'll choose jeans and a sweatshirt, or t-shirt, shorts, and flip-flops every time. Maybe it's because I was raised by Pop. He never complained about the way I looked, or gave me any reason to believe that clothes, make-up, and jewelry are what define a woman.

But maybe I'm wrong. Maybe I haven't been paying attention. Maybe those things *do* matter to Pop.

"Have you ever thought about talking to someone?" Ellen says.

"I thought I was talking to you," I say.

"I mean, talking with someone who could actually help."

"You think I need a therapist?" The thought disturbs me more than I care to admit. Granted, my life these days is a little crazier than usual. But that doesn't mean I need professional help. Or does it?

"You might be surprised. Seeing a therapist has helped me. I always felt different. Like I wasn't good enough."

"But you're good enough," I assure her. "Don't you know that? You're better than good. You're great. You're amazing."

"You're sweet," she says. "But honestly, Katy, talking things over with someone really helped open my eyes. I learn more and more about myself at every session. Things I had no clue about."

"Such as?"

She pauses, the sewing forgotten on her lap. "Things about my family," she replies after a moment. "Things from school. I can't tell you how much I hated school. It was torture. I was short, and the teacher always put me in the front row. I'd hear the other kids behind me, laughing, and I always thought they were laughing at me. And when it was time for recess, I would sit alone on a swing. I would watch all the cute little girls, the ones with their pretty clothes and all their nice things. They always seemed to be together, you know? Their hair was neatly braided, and their clothes were so clean. I knew I could never be like them. Just looking at them made me nervous. Ugly and ashamed."

"You have nothing to be ashamed about," I say. "And don't let anyone tell you that you're not pretty. Because you are." Ellen has a way about her, an elegant simplicity, a calm, quiet presence that gives her a natural beauty, and makes a person glad to call her a friend.

"Thanks, Katy."

"It's the truth," I insist.

"Thanks." Then a sudden half-smile lights her face. "*Thank you*. Do you realize how long it took for me to be able to say that? Without putting myself down, or giving an explanation? And each day, things are a little better. I'm getting better."

I lean my head against the back of the couch, blow out a long sigh. "I guess what really concerns me most about this situation is how it's changing Pop. He's normally so level-headed and rational. But Mai's got him completely turned around. He doesn't know if he's coming or going. He believes every word she says."

"And you don't?" Ellen reaches for her scissors to trim the remaining thread.

"No." I straighten on the couch. "I don't."

Her eyes widen slightly. "You don't think she's your sister?"

"I'm not sure," I say. I'll admit there's a family resemblance, but that could merely be coincidence. "But I don't think so."

"Why?"

"Mai's older than I am. That means she's had more than thirty years to find him. Let's think through this logically. If you were Mai, and Pop was your dad, don't you think you would have come looking for him long before this? Why did she wait so long?"

"Maybe she didn't know. Maybe she just found out."

"I find that hard to believe," I mutter. It would be good

to have more information on her, but Pop hasn't exactly been forthcoming with details about Mai's life.

"There must be a way you could figure it out." Ellen scans the hem of the pants she's working on. "It's hard to know what's going on in someone's mind, or why they do the things they do."

Ellen's right. Who knows why people act the way they do? There's always an underlying motivation. Ellen's a perfect example. The only reason she's a convicted felon is because she got trapped in a no-win situation trying to feed her children. And what about the other nine women living in this halfway house? Each has their own sad story to tell. Some, the lucky ones like Ellen, will probably make it. But how many other women have passed through this house only to end up inside a jail cell again? I have a lot of respect for Ellen. Already she's different from the woman she was a few weeks ago, her first day on the job. She seems happier, more confident, and proud of what she's accomplishing. Watching her find her way in the world, land on her feet, find a decent place to live, and eventually be reunited with her two little guys will be the perfect happily-ever-after.

"Has Mai said how long she plans on staying?"

"Good question," I say with an eye-roll. "I wish I knew the answer. Meanwhile, she seems to have taken up permanent residence in Pop's apartment, and she doesn't seem interested in leaving." Grabbing the lumpy pillow, I punch it a few more times, then stuff it behind my back.

"What do you know about her family history?"

"Not much," I admit. "She mentioned something about a grandmother and grandfather in Hawaii; other than that, I don't know." Trying to figure it all out is like trying to connect the dots in a puzzle while blindfolded. I'm sure Pop knows more than he's saying, but the way things are between us right now, I can't ask him. He'd assume I'm criticizing, and he'd take offense. The last thing I want is to trigger a shouting match between us.

"Have you tried the Internet?"

"Not really." With Pop virtually leaving me to run the restaurant by myself, there hasn't been much time left to engage in any cyber-snooping.

"It could be worth a shot."

"I guess it's worth a try." Maybe two or three quick searches will produce some answers to my questions.

Ellen stifles a yawn. "Sorry to punk out on you, but I think it's time I called it a night. I'm working the lunch shift tomorrow... well, actually, make that today, seeing how it's already after midnight." She folds her mending in a neat little pile.

"Sleep well."

"You're not going to bed yet?"

"I have some things to do first."

"'Nite," she says, and starts up the stairs. Then suddenly she pauses, one hand on the banister, and looks down upon me. "Katy?"

"Yes?"

"Don't worry too much about this thing with Mai. It'll all work out for the best."

"I know."

She hesitates, and seems on the verge of saying something more. But then, with a quick nod, she turns instead and heads up the stairs.

I sit alone in the living room, think about the soft little bed in the next room reserved exclusively for volunteers.

It's been a long day, and the thought of stretching out and falling into a long, dreamless sleep is tempting. But despite my scratchy eyes, there's no time to sleep. Not with my brain hot-wired the way it is right now. I'm foregoing sleep for my hot date with Google.

Who knows what interesting things I might discover about Mai Kaido of Kaneohe Bay, Hawaii?

CHAPTER TEN

~ I'll be Your Server Tonight ~

KATY GLARES AT ME. "EXACTLY what do you think you're doing?"

"What does it look like?"

"Like you're not following doctor's orders," she replies. "Seriously, Pop? I take a few minutes to run to the bank, and when I get back, I find you downstairs in the restaurant. You know what the doctor said. You're supposed to be resting."

"How in the hell am I supposed to rest with the kind of crap going on around here?" I grumble. The minute I saw her breeze through the door, I figured she'd start in on me. Sure enough, she made a beeline for the small table near the kitchen that we keep reserved for management and staff.

"People quitting whenever they feel like it," I add, throwing in a snort for good measure. "Goodbye and good riddance, that's what I say. Who needs 'em?"

"What are you talking about?" Katy gives me one of her this-better-be-good looks she's honed to perfection and slides into the chair next to mine. "I wasn't gone more than twenty minutes. Who quit?"

"Tiffany and Barb." I spit the words out like they're pieces of deep fried fish cooked in oil gone bad. "They worked the lunch shift, then walked out the door."

"You're kidding." Her eyes pop wide open. "Barb quit?"

"She did."

"Just like that?"

"Just like that," I confirm, with a snap of my fingers.

"Great. Two more staff members gone. Exactly what we don't need."

I nod. We always expect a slight decrease in staff when the college kids head back to school. But timing is everything. And we need every living breathing body on board doing their job until Labor Day Weekend is over.

"Losing Barb is really going to hurt. She was a great waitress." Katy's forehead scrunches together in a bundle of little worry lines. "The locals love her."

"She's good with people, I'll grant you that." Personally, though, I'm not that upset to see Barb go. While she knew how to treat a customer right, she wasn't so great when it came to handling her private life. I never told Katy about the night a couple years ago when Barb surprised me by showing up uninvited at my apartment door, six-pack in hand, ample cleavage on display in a sheer blouse. It was right after Katy moved out and Barb's boldness caught me off guard. I learned long ago not to mix women and booze, and I wasn't about to mess things up for a one-night stand with a waitress whose weekly paycheck includes my name and signature. She took it as a personal offense when I refused to invite her in, instead telling her (very kindly, I might add) that while I liked her as a person, I had no desire to get involved. Barb didn't like it, and things between us have never been the same. Frankly, I'm surprised she stuck around for as long as she did.

"I still can't believe she quit," Katy says.

"Supposedly Sid Meyer hired 'em for that new seafood restaurant of his. They open this weekend."

"That's crazy. Everybody in town knows his place won't last. Granted, it's on Loon Lake, and has a killer view. But who wants to drive seven miles outside of town just to eat fried shrimp?"

I shift in my chair and settle in to listen as Katy takes off on one of her rants. Better to have her complain about Sid and his staff then having her nag me about my health. When she gets going about something, she tends to gnaw it to the bone, like an old dog. And while I appreciate that she's worried about me, this whole you-could-have-had-a-massive-heart-attack thing is wearing on my nerves. I've got Mai upstairs watching my every move, and Katy downstairs playing doctor-dictator. I'm sick and tired of the two of them treating me like I'm an old man ready for the nursing home. I'm only sixty years old, and I've got a lot more living to do.

"I bet Barb will be back and begging for her old job sooner than you think," Katy predicts.

"Don't be too sure about that," I say. "Sid promised her a dollar more an hour than we're paying."

Katy's eyes blaze. "A dollar more an hour? How can he afford to pay his staff that kind of money? Talk about ridiculous."

My thoughts exactly. When it comes to slicing the difference between profit and loss, a good restauranteur needs to know exactly how to wield a sharp carving knife, and exactly where and when to make the cuts. And Sid didn't build his reputation on being stupid. He's a successful business man with two area restaurants, each offering different ethnic menus and catering to clientele who prefer to indulge in gourmet dining experiences. He's been touting his newest venture as Up North Casual Cuisine. Granted, the prices are substantially higher than we charge at Chuck's; but pricey or not, opening a seafood restaurant means Sid is garnering for the same market share. James Bay is already saturated with restaurants. The only one not in direct competition with us is Penny's, the local diner which opens daily at 6 am and caters exclusively to the breakfast crowd.

"He'll never make a go of it," Katy predicts.

"That doesn't matter. We've got bigger problems right now."

"What's wrong?" That concerned-doctor look returns to her face. "Are you feeling okay?"

"Forget about me, will you?" I jerk my head at the clock high above the door. "We're about to get hit with the dinner shift."

"And with Barb and Tiffany gone, we're two waitresses short." Katy's voice falls flat.

"Three," I correct. "Marty called in just after you left."

She tilts her head back, looks at the ceiling, blows out a deep sigh. "Please tell me you're kidding."

"I wish to hell I was."

"Did you tell her how much we need her tonight?"

"I did."

"Did you tell her about Tiffany and Barb?"

"No, but—"

"I'll call her." Katy, suddenly all action, grabs her phone and scrolls through her contacts. "Maybe once Marty hears how short-staffed we are, she'll agree to come in for a few hours."

"I don't think so. She said she was at the ER. Her kid had another allergy attack."

"Ugh. Well, scratch that idea." She props her elbows on the table and rests her chin in her hands. "Okay, looks like I don't have any choice. I'll pick up her shift."

"Sure you want to do that?"

Katy shrugs. "Who else is going to do it?"

I wish to hell there was some other way than putting the extra work on her. The only time she fills in as a waitress is when we're in crunch-mode. Our dinner shift normally operates with five servers on the floor; being down three means we'll be running with a skeleton crew. I scan the restaurant. Nettie's already out on the floor, but she can't handle things by herself. And with Ellen still in training, Katy has no choice. Now she'll be hustling dinner orders, dealing with cranky customers, overseeing the other waitresses, plus handling closing on her own once the front door is locked.

"Okay, here's the deal," I offer. "You pick up the shift, and I'll cover as host. I'll even take care of reconciling the receipts and processing tomorrow's orders."

She shakes her head. "Nice try, Pop, but no go."

"There's no reason I can't—"

"I don't want to hear another word about it. Not one word, understand?" she says, her eyes flashing golden sparks of anger. Katy looks so much like her mother right now, I could swear Katherine herself was sitting beside me. "You aren't going to be host tonight, and you're not going to do any paperwork. What you *are* going to do is go back upstairs and rest, like the doctor ordered. I'll take care of things down here, and I'll finish up once the restaurant closes."

And maybe, if she's lucky, she might make it home before midnight. I take a good look at the dark shadows under her eyes, remembering how Katy spent last night volunteering at

The Bungalow. There must have been trouble at that place, since she looks like she didn't get much sleep.

"You look like hell," I comment.

"Geez, thanks a lot," she says with a dramatic eye-roll. "When you find out I joined a twelve-step group for low self-esteem issues, don't bother asking me why."

"Aw, come on, you know what I mean." I grab her hand, give it a little squeeze. Katy's been having a rough go of it lately, with all this stuff about Mai. And instead of talking about it, we're letting it sit on the table between us like some appetizer neither of us ordered off the menu. But once the dish is served, you can't send it back to the kitchen. That wouldn't be fair, especially to Mai; she's already been served enough hard knocks to last her a lifetime. And while I can't change the past, I can change the future. Mai came looking for her father, and now that she's found me, I intend to do right by her. I owe it to her.

Meanwhile, don't I owe Katy something, too? Somehow my poor girl has got lost in the shuffle. She looks tired, and what little tan she had earlier this summer is nearly disappeared. Hard to get a tan when you're cooped up inside a restaurant day and night. She's been working way too hard. Me being sick isn't helping. A girl her age should be out having fun.

"I miss you, kiddo," I suddenly say.

Her eyes widen in surprise, then she gives me one of those smiles that melt a father's heart.

"I miss you, too, Pop."

"It's been awhile since we talked like this, hasn't it?"

"Yes." She gives my fingers a little squeeze, and, swear

to God, I nearly start bawling like a baby. This damn heart medicine they've got me on has me all screwed up inside.

"Well, go right ahead and blame me for that. I'm a stubborn old guy, and I need to learn to do things better."

"Like, listen to your doctor?"

"Like, listen to my daughter... and be a better dad."

She laughs like she was ten years old again, without a care in the world.

"I love you, Katy-Did."

Her breath catches, and she suddenly fingers away a few tears of her own. "I love you, too."

The tears confuse me. They always have; they always will. Women cry, but never Katy.

"I'm worried about you," I say, clenching her hand tighter. "You're working way too hard."

"No, it's not a problem. I'm okay."

"You sure?"

"I'm fine." A small smile trudges across her face. My little girl's always been a brave soldier, even during that horrible time when Katherine died.

"I'll take some time off once we hire another waitress and things slow down," she promises. "Meanwhile, I'd better get to work."

"Grab some coffee," I say. "That will perk you up."

She stands and throws me a sweet smile, which disappears just as I catch it. She's noticed something behind me, and the wary look that appears on her face is one I've come to recognize all too well these past several weeks. When Katy looks like that, it only means one thing. Turning, I look behind me.

Sure enough, there she is.

"You scared me." Mai slides into the chair beside me, and wags her finger under my nose. "I slip out to make one phone call, and when I come back, you're gone."

"Just checking in to see how things are going down here," I say.

"And now," Katy says, "it's time you march yourself right back upstairs."

"Yes." Mai covers my hand with her own. "Let's do that, shall we? We can sit on the balcony and watch the people go by."

And before I can stop it, I blow up.

"Did the two of you ever think that I might be sick of sitting around and *watching people go by*?" I shout.

"Pop, calm down," Katy says, her eyes wide.

"Don't tell me to calm down." Still, I purposely lower my voice, aware people are watching. "I don't need the two of you telling me what to do." I shrug off Mai's hand, my gaze darting back and forth between them. "Swear to God, you girls need to back off and give me some room. I didn't have a heart attack. The doctor called it *an event*, remember? He put in a stent, and I'm fine now. And this is my restaurant, dammit. If I want to come down here and check up on things, I sure as hell can do that."

"We'll see about that," Katy says.

"You need to rest," Mai's words collide with Katy's.

I fold my arms across my chest and settle in my chair. It's anyone's guess which will kill me first: my heart or all this fussing from these two girls.

"I'm not going anywhere," I say. "I can rest down here as good as upstairs."

"Fine, have it your way." Katy glares at me. "You want

to sit and watch? Go right ahead. But don't you dare budge from that chair."

"Who's going to be host?" I remind her.

"It's not going to kill us to do without. And I don't care if the waiting line is fifty feet out the front door. If people don't feel like waiting, they can go eat somewhere else."

Out of nowhere, an idea comes to mind. I turn to Mai. "You ever work in a restaurant?"

She blinks. "Years ago, when I was just out of high school."

"There you go." I throw up my hands, give Katy a knowing smile. "Problem solved."

"You are unbelievable," Katy says, staring at me.

"I don't understand." Mai glances at me, then to Katy, then back to me.

Laughing, I sling an arm around her shoulder and pull her close. I've been looking for a way to help Katy and Mai get to know each other better, and now I've just been handed the perfect opportunity.

"Mai, honey," I say with a big grin, "welcome to the family business."

CHAPTER ELEVEN

~ Let Them Eat Cake ~

"**A**ND IF ALL THAT WASN'T bad enough, now Pop's got her working in the restaurant." I keep my voice purposely low as I wrap up reciting my litany of woes for Lucy. *The Journal's* office is one large open room, and I don't want the rest of the newspaper staff overhearing our conversation.

"Personally, Lucy, I don't believe a word she says," I continue. "Mai shows up out of the blue one day, and claims to be Pop's daughter. Where's the evidence, that's what I want to know. Because I think her story stinks. But it's painfully clear Pop doesn't feel the same. He believes every word out of her mouth, and he refuses to listen to me, no matter what I say. I'm desperate, Lucy. I need to figure out who Mai really is, and I need to figure it out fast."

"I'm not sure exactly how I can help, Katy."

Lucy Carter-Graham, owner and publisher of the *James Bay Journal*, studies me from behind her desk. Her face and voice are like a blank page, impossible to read. But there's no doubt in my mind that Lucy will be able to uncover the truth. If anyone can help, she can. Lucy and I have been friends since eighth grade, when Pop and I moved to town. She and her husband, Max, play a big part in this town's success. He runs a popular boys' summer camp on Loon Lake, while Lucy, who hit it big a few years back with a $70 million lottery win, bought our hometown newspaper and turned it into something James Bay can be proud of. *The Journal* has a reputation for fair and accurate reporting, and Lucy and her team thoroughly vet their information. If anyone knows how to track down a lead, it's Lucy Carter-Graham.

"You started out as an investigative reporter, right?" I try to encourage her before she shoots me down. "You're bound to have better luck than me."

"Which part of her story don't you believe?"

"I don't know," I admit. Part of me wants to believe the whole thing is a hoax, while another part of me urges to proceed cautiously. Mai knows plenty about our family. Someone provided her with the information... maybe the same someone who gave her Pop's dog tags.

"Tell me why you don't believe her," Lucy presses. "Do you think she's looking for money?"

"If she is, she's out of luck." Pop isn't rich, not by a long shot. Chuck's Tavern and Grill provides a comfortable living for us, but only because the building was paid off long ago. If we still owed money, or were leasing the property like so many other business owners in town, we'd be totally dependent on a successful summer season to keep the doors open year-round. But Pop's also made some sound investments over the years, providing us with a little wiggle room in case the season doesn't cooperate. He granted me total access to his legal and financial affairs when he made me a partner in the business. But Mai isn't privy to his financial matters. She doesn't know how much money he has in the bank.

Or maybe she does, I realize, dismayed by the thought. It's anyone's guess as to what Pop might have told her.

Because, according to Pop, he has two daughters now.

"It doesn't make sense." The words rush out of me. "I don't trust her motivations. I think she wants something from him. Where's she been all these years? What's she been doing? And why did she suddenly show up like this?"

"What if she only now found out who he was?" Lucy suggests. "Is your dad listed on her birth certificate?"

"I don't know," I admit, feeling the quick flush of color rising high in my cheeks. I'm sure Pop knows, but I don't dare ask him. Mai's very existence is a sore spot between us.

"What about DNA testing? That would be a simple solution."

"You'd think so, right? And it would prove things once and for all. But honestly, I can't figure out how to facilitate it, not without their consent. Even if I managed to somehow collect samples from them both, no lab would touch it without their authorizations." The words sit there between us. "Please, Lucy? You're my last hope."

She considers me for another moment, then her face softens. "You said you already did some research on the Internet?"

"Right. But I didn't find much. At least, not anything that would be helpful." A reference to Mai in her grandfather's obituary, dated six weeks earlier. But that doesn't qualify as news. The other mention was a lengthy feature piece that ran last year in the *Honolulu Star*, which linked Mai's name to an upscale jewelry store. I quickly clicked into the article, only to find Mai identified as a sales associate who provided a quote as to what customers visiting the store might expect. Obviously, she's knowledgeable enough about the jewelry business that she qualified to be interviewed for the story. Nothing to pique interest. Mai isn't a jewel thief.

"Have you tried social media?"

"Facebook. Twitter. Pinterest." I nod. "You name it, I searched it… and unfortunately, I came up with nada. It's like Mai doesn't exist." I slouch further in my seat. "I've tried everything I can think of, and now I'm tapped out. That's why I came to you. I was hoping *The Journal* has access to other resources. Things beyond what the general public, someone like me, can find and read. Maybe police records?"

She hesitates.

"Please, Lucy?" I'm desperate, and if it means reducing myself to begging, then that's what I'll do. "I wouldn't ask if it wasn't important."

She gives me a long look, and the more seconds that tick off, the surer I am that she's going to refuse. Then suddenly she grabs a pen and yellow legal pad.

Thank God, I breathe, flinging a silent prayer up to heaven. My mom must be watching over Pop and me.

"Okay, first I need the details you remember," Lucy says. "Tell me everything you know about her, and exactly what you're looking for."

I fill her in with the few facts I've committed to memory about Mai's history, plus everything I can remember about Pop and his time in the service.

"I'll start working on it this afternoon."

"Thanks, Lucy." I give her a quick hug. "You're the best."

"Don't thank me yet," she warns. "We don't know what I'll find."

***

It hasn't been an easy week, but thankfully Ellen has proven to be a great multi-tasker. She's now fully trained, and can handle a full load of tables better than Nettie (not to mention, without Nettie's constant griping). I do my best to fill in where needed, covering both lunch and dinner, while trying to eke out time to interview people applying for the positions. Meanwhile, Mai seems to be loving every minute of her new job. I hate to admit it, but she's doing better than I thought she would. She also knows how to handle a crowd. She has a way of swishing her hips, flourishing menus, and offering up coy smiles and amusing remarks that soothes even the most irritated customers. The management at Duke's trained her well.

I followed-up on Mai's casual reference to her former job from years ago, when she supposedly waitressed at Duke's Restaurant on Waikiki Beach. When I put in the call, Duke's not only confirmed her employment, but also gave her a glowing reference.

Whether I like it or not, Mai knows her way around a restaurant.

And exactly how to provoke me, I thought to myself earlier, watching as she untied her apron and fluffed her hair.

"Are you going somewhere?" I ask.

"I'll be back in half an hour."

"It's not time for your break yet," I remind her. The lunch crowd is thinning out, but I don't want to be caught short-staffed. "If you're hungry, go grab something in the kitchen. But I'll need you back on the floor in five minutes."

"I'm leaving." She hangs her apron on the peg near the bar. "They're waiting for me. They phoned a few minutes ago, and I told them I'd be right over."

"You told who?"

"The people at the print shop." She fishes a pair of glittery designer sunglasses out of one pocket and rests them atop her head. "I'm going over to proof the new copy."

I'm totally confused, since we don't have any new orders at the print shop. I haven't talked to them in months. "New copy for what?"

"The menu inserts," Mai says, starting for the door.

I blink. What is she talking about? Pop and I discussed the issue long ago, while there was still snow on the ground, and decided against using menu inserts this summer.

"Wait a minute." I grab her arm. "I didn't order any menu inserts."

"No, you didn't... but I did." She struggles to pry herself loose.

Amazed by her audacity, I drop my hold on her. "And why did you do that?"

She lifts one shoulder with a dismissive shrug.

"Why?" I insist.

"We decided to add some new items to the menu."

"What new items? What are you talking about?"

"We thought the menu could use a little spicing up. We're adding a few Japanese dishes."

"We?" I sputter, unsure I should believe my ears, since this is the first I'm hearing about this. "And exactly who is *we*?"

"Pete and me. He's been helping me work on them. People love Japanese food."

I do not believe it. Our top-line cook has joined Team

Mai? Pete and I have been buddies since I was a kid. Why didn't he say anything to me?

"Chuck's is not a Japanese restaurant," I say through clenched teeth. It's not the idea of Japanese food I mind; I'm as much a fan as anyone. What I don't like is Mai assuming she can take control. Pop hired her to be a hostess. This is *not* her restaurant.

"Don't worry." She offers up a sweet smile, which comes off as foul. "We're not deleting, only adding. And there's no reason we can't include a few extra dishes. Sukiyaki, yakitori. Wait till you taste what Pete's done with the yakitori. He's preparing it with a barbecue sauce that gives it a special Northern Michigan twist. You'll love it," she adds confidently.

I'll hate it.

"He also came up with a wonderful recipe for curried rice. Oh! And we're adding a new dessert, too. A yummy new flavor of ice cream."

Ice cream? I feel the freeze settling in. There's no way in hell I'll allow ice cream on our menu. Never in a million years. "We don't serve ice cream at Chuck's."

"Not yet." A slow smile melts across her face. "But we will, once I pick up the menu inserts. Pineapple ice cream."

I step forward, close the distance between us in two quick steps. I'm probably invading her personal space, but I don't care. She's doing a good job of invading my space. Not to mention, undermining my authority. Mai doesn't give a damn about my feelings. Why should I care about hers?

"Who do you think you are?" I growl, taking care to keep my voice low enough so no one can overhear. "What makes you think you have the right to walk in here and do as you please?"

Mai stands there, not looking the least bit surprised by my outburst.

"I can," she coolly informs me, "and I did."

"On whose authority?"

"Who do you think?" she says with a brazen smile. "Otosan."

My heart is pounding so hard against my rib cage, I'm afraid it's going into overdrive. "You won't get away with this forever, you know," I say. "Eventually the truth is going to come out."

"The truth about what?"

"About who you are."

"I know exactly who I am. And you know it, too."

Is she calling my bluff? "Well, maybe we'll just see about that." I swallow hard. "Maybe a DNA test will prove otherwise."

"Oh, Katy, you poor little fool. I thought you were smarter than that." Her eyes glitter as she stares me down. "Here's the truth, little sister: I'll be glad to take a DNA test if Otosan asks. And why wouldn't I? I have nothing to lose, and everything to gain."

And with that, she promptly turns her back on me, and strolls out the door.

I stand there for a moment, my emotions a mess of misery, as I absorb the lessons just learned.

Lesson No. 1: Never, ever underestimate Mai. She's much smarter than I originally thought. I don't know how she did it, but somehow, she managed to manipulate Pop and bring him around to her way of thinking. And now that she has him exactly where she wants him, it's dead certain that she has no intention of cutting him loose.

Lessons No 2: If she's not afraid to take a DNA test, then she obviously isn't afraid of learning the results. And if that's the case, then it doesn't bode well for what I've assumed has been the truth up till now.

Lesson No. 3: Mai and I are engaged in a full-out war. At some point during the week, especially since she started working here, the two of us have dropped all pretense of liking each other. Today's altercation was the final turning point. I don't like Mai, and she doesn't like me. And this has nothing to do with sibling rivalry.

This is now a fight for my family. This is a fight for Pop. For me. For life as we know it.

But no matter who wins, my gut tells me things will never be the same.

CHAPTER TWELVE

~ Specialty Items ~

"**W**E GOT A PROBLEM HERE?"
Obviously, something's wrong. Katy's glowering as she hovers over the POS terminal, her face flushed and hot. But it can't be the heat. Our air conditioners are blasting continuous bursts of cold air, which roll over the restaurant like cumulous clouds dropping dollar bills from the sky. How many plates of barbecued ribs do we need to serve to afford an hour's worth of electricity? To heat the place in winter? To cover the water and sewer? Without someone keeping a close eye on things, the utility bills alone could swallow up our profits.

"What's wrong?" I press.

"I'm not sure." Tapping the touch screen, she studies the page, but her frown only deepens. "There might be a problem; then again, maybe not. This new computer program still has a few kinks."

I shuffle back and forth, jingle the change in my pocket, trying to keep my mouth shut. Katy has an eye for detail, and she's good at catching problems and figuring out solutions. Unfortunately, her solutions usually don't come cheap.

First it was the surveillance cameras, right after my heart attack. *Believe me, Pop, you won't regret it. The cameras will keep an eye on things, even when you're not around. And the best part is, you can even check them on your phone.* While I wasn't crazy about investing any of our hard-earned cash in modern technology, eventually I gave her the go-ahead. Being able to see what's happening real-time in the restaurant, no matter if I'm upstairs or two thousand miles away, definitely has its advantages.

Then came last winter, when she approached me about purchasing a new POS—Point of Sale system. "Why spend the money for something we don't need?" I asked. "Our old computer program worked fine."

"Exactly my point," she countered, referring me to the system's outdated technology.

Reluctantly I gave her the go-ahead, and the POS system and terminals, which tie into our beverage and food service, were installed early last spring. Theoretically we were supposed to be able to work out all the glitches before our summer season was in full swing. But that hasn't happened. As far as I'm concerned, our POS, supposedly the brains of our operation, barely deserves a passing grade. Maybe a D+.

I lean in close beside her, scrutinize the screen. "Any idea what's going on?"

"The till came up short."

Exactly the kind of news I don't want to hear. "How short?"

"Twenty dollars and some odd change. But don't worry." She shoots me a quick smile. "It's happened before; it's probably just a computer glitch. Or even a slip someone voided."

"Wait a minute. What do you mean, *it's happened before*?"

Forget the glitch. I already know what's going on. Theft is one of the biggest headaches a restaurant owner faces. "Why didn't you tell me?"

"Because I knew you'd get all fired up, exactly like you are now," she says, without bothering to glance up from the screen. "Quit worrying, Pop. I've got this."

If she thinks I'm going to quit worrying merely because she says so, Katy needs to think again. It isn't that I doubt her abilities. She's smart, even though she didn't go to college. But theft isn't something to be taken lightly. Especially employee theft. Two months ago, we fired a busboy plus a cook for stealing two cases of meat from the freezer. Good thing I'd logged onto my phone that night to check out the feed on the new surveillance cameras. It was nothing more than pure luck that I happened to catch the incident live. I called the police and we caught them before they had a chance to load the meat into the truck they had waiting in the back alley. But if I hadn't been watching in real-time, we never would have caught them. The meat shortage eventually would have been noticed, but probably not until it was too late, since the tapes are recycled on a weekly basis and overwritten by new footage.

"People stealing from us is nothing to mess around with."

"We don't know if that's what happened," she points out.

"How much you wanna bet?" I've got my suspicions. That friend of hers isn't to be trusted. "You need to get this figured out fast."

Katy pulls her gaze from the screen. "Exactly what do you think I'm trying to do right now?"

"Sorry," I say, holding up my hands to ward off any further outbursts. "You're right."

I need to cut her some slack. She's been testier than normal lately. Some of it I'm chalking up to me being sick, some to this thing going on with Mai, and the rest is the general the-summer-people-are-driving-me-crazy malaise we're suffering from. But everything will work out. I'll be back up to speed in no time; Katy and Mai will learn to trust each other. Come Labor Day, the crowds will die down. Meanwhile, I shouldn't be sticking my nose where it doesn't belong.

"Sorry I said anything."

"I'm sorry, too." Gripping her hands on both sides of the monitor, she bends back over the screen, then glances up a few seconds later, a triumphant smile marching across her face.

"There, see? I found it!" She points at the monitor.

"What is it?" I hunch over the screen, peer through my glasses at the tiny text. Dammit, these eyes of mine are getting worse by the day. Next thing I know, the doctor will be saying that I need cataract surgery.

"Right there, see?" She taps her finger on the screen. "A voided slip. Just like I suspected."

"Who did it?"

She pauses a beat too long, and I know exactly who's to blame. Didn't I tell her not to hire that woman? Twenty dollars here, thirty dollars there; it all adds up. The last thing Chuck's needs is a convicted felon on staff. Maybe now she'll listen to me.

"Come on," I press, "you know I'll find out eventually."

"It was Nettie," she finally admits.

"Hunh." I straighten up.

"Let me talk to her," Katy suggests. "You know how

Nettie is. She probably only needs a little more training on the system."

"I thought everybody got trained."

"Yes, but everyone has their own learning curve. You yourself said that this system is complicated."

"Yeah, well, I'm not the one overcharging our customers. And this program was installed way before the season started. Don't you think she should have learned it by now?"

"I know it's frustrating, but give her a chance. Once Nettie gets the hang of things, she'll be fine."

The reminder isn't necessary. Nettie's been with us since the day I opened Chuck's. A small, wiry woman with a feisty attitude, she keeps everybody—customers and staff alike—in line. But the clock catches up with all of us and Nettie was already straddling the line between middle-age and qualifying for a senior discount when I hired her. I glance around the restaurant and spot her on the floor, taking an order. She blends in with the rest of the staff, except for the gray hair cropped close to her head and the wrinkles carved deep in her forehead. Nettie could be Katy's grandmother. Would I want my own mother, God rest her soul, working this job? We all get tired. Lord knows the day-to-day grind can wear you down. And I know Nettie must feel it, the same way as me. She isn't afraid to voice her opinions, and sometimes I think she grumbles even louder than I do.

"Okay, fine." I shove away from the register. "You're in charge. You talk to her. But make sure she knows what to do, and how to do it."

"I will," she promises. "No worries."

Maybe she's not worried, but I am. Because no matter what Katy says about Nettie being the one who's messing up on all the voids and overrings, I don't believe it. Not for one damn minute. I know what's really going on around here, and all I need is a way to prove that I'm right. Maybe Mai could help. That's a thought worth pondering.

***

"What do you think?" Mai hangs over my shoulder as I study the glossy menu inserts. "Do you like them?"

"Nice. Real nice. And I especially like the way you included these photos and tag lines." I point out the picture of big, burly Pete behind the grill, grin on his face, hamming it up for the camera as he slathers sauce on a full rack of ribs. Being included in publicity shots has got to be a first for him. "Adds a little flair to the menu."

"I think the customers will love it. People like human interest stories. And being able to read the history behind Chuck's and learning about our staff will help them feel like they're part of it all. Plus, once they're interested in the stories, and the people who work here, they'll be more likely to come back and eat here again."

"And that's exactly what we're looking for: repeat customers," I say, sliding the insert back to Mai. "Good job."

It's good to see her smiling again. It hasn't been an easy couple of days for any of us. I'm not sure what's going on, but Katy's barely talking, and Mai's been quieter than usual. Which is one of the reasons I readily agreed to her suggestion about adding those Japanese dishes. Granted, Japanese food isn't exactly what our customers expect, but why not celebrate her presence with a nod to her heritage? Mai's part of the family now. A little rice and chop suey will spice up our menu. And if Pete says he can cook it, and people enjoy it, then life's good and everybody's happy. Meanwhile, Mai's got plenty of good ideas. Her recommendation to halt our Friday night all-you-can-eat fish fries, at least throughout the summer season, made perfect sense to me. If you limit the portion size to two pieces of fish, she pointed out, you save money. How come Katy and I never thought of that? Mai's fresh insight is exactly what we need around here.

"As soon as we slow down, go ahead and get these put inside the menus. If you need help, pull a busboy and a waitress off the floor."

Mai hesitates.

"Something wrong?"

"Maybe we should ask Katy first," she suggests.

"I already told you they look fine."

"I know, but…"

I peer at her over my glasses. "But what?"

"I don't want to cause trouble. Sometimes… sometimes I think Katy doesn't like me."

"That's nothing but crazy talk," I scoff. "Why would you think she doesn't like you?"

"Just some of the things she's said and done." Mai stares off into the distance, her fingers worrying the silver chain which used to hold my dog tags but now displays a polished Petoskey stone pendant I bought her. "Sometimes I get the impression that she thinks I've overstepped my boundaries. And I've tried not to do that. I know she's in charge, and—"

"No, I'm in charge," I remind her. "Don't forget, I'm the one who owns this place."

She nods, bestows a small smile. "Yes, Otosan, I know. But I don't want Katy mad at me."

I jerk my chin at the inserts. "Has she seen these yet?"

"No, I've been afraid to show her. Something she said to me once about Japanese food... I don't think she likes it."

"See, that just goes to show you that you're wrong. Katy's crazy for Japanese food. Why, when she was a little girl, her mother and I used to take her to this one restaurant every—"

I stop before I breach a boundary that's off limits. Mai doesn't need to hear about Katherine, and I don't need to be constantly rehashing the way things used to be.

Katherine is dead. Life goes on.

"Look, everything will work out. So, no more worrying, okay?" Reaching out, I chuck a finger under Mai's chin, tilt her head upward, force her to meet my eyes. "That's a direct order from the boss, understand?"

She hesitates, then finally nods.

"And if Katy gives you any grief, I want to know about it," I add. "You can tell her to come talk to me. I'll set her straight."

Mai bows her head once again. "Yes, Otosan."

"Good. Now, how about we get those inserts into the menus, so our customers can read all about Pete, and he can start cooking up those new dishes."

Her smile breaks forth as radiant as the sun after one of the frequent cloud bursts over Diamond Head. "Pete will love it. He'll be famous."

I chuckle. "Just so he doesn't get too famous and hit me up for a raise."

CHAPTER THIRTEEN

~ This Is Not What I Ordered ~

"SWEAR TO GOD, DON, IT'S like she's an invasive species from Hawaii that's infested the Great Lakes." I curl up on my side of the bed and punch the pillow beneath my head. For a few sweet hours in the darkness of his bedroom, Don's helped me forget about the mess in my life. But now my mind's back to running full tilt, and holding hands with my fears. "Everywhere I look, everywhere I turn... somehow Mai manages to be there. It's like she's taken over our lives. She has her hands on everything: the restaurant, the menu..."

And Pop. That's what hurts the most: seeing how easy it's been for her to manipulate Pop.

"Katy, you've been obsessing about her for the past ten minutes."

"Have I?" I reach out, draw a finger down his cheek and the rough stubble of his beard, trace the outline of his lips. "Sorry. Are you mad?"

"Nope, not mad." He strokes my hair with his fingertips, playing with a few of the springy curls spread across the pillows. "Your hair's getting long."

"I haven't had time to get it cut."

"You're the boss," he reminds me. "Book yourself an appointment and take some time off. That's what normal people do."

"These aren't normal times."

"You're going to make yourself sick if you keep this up," he predicts. "You've got to make time for yourself."

"Easier said than done." Never in my wildest dreams would I have guessed that my life could dissolve into the bizarre kind of fairy tale I'm caught up in today: a real-life fairy tale featuring an evil half-sister. "The truth is, I'm afraid to leave her alone in the restaurant. Who knows what she'll be up to while I'm gone? I could walk back in and find out I no longer have a job."

"You're doing it again," he quietly reminds me.

"What?"

"Talking about her."

"I'm sorry. It's really hard to get my mind to shut up." I lay my head on his chest. Quieting, I listen, taking measure of his heart pumping in a slow, steady rhythm. My own heart is quiet, too, but not in a good way. It's on the verge of breaking.

I've never been one of those people particularly adept at dealing with their emotions. Then again, I've never had to face something like this. This is different than the horrible hurt at saying goodbye to my childhood friends when Pop and I moved up north. And it's different than the guilt I felt at crushing Pop's hopes when I finally admitted to him I had no intention of going to college. This is different than the absolute worst time of my life: the day my mother died, and then having to live through all the days, weeks, and months that followed. Nothing can touch those memories; the ache of knowing she was gone, and that it was my fault. That hurt will never go away.

Having Mai around is like living under the imminent threat of a tsunami. I'm in a continual state of panic, waiting for the sirens to blare. Waiting for her to let loose, washing across the landscape of my life, her path of destruction sweeping away the things and people I love most. And the worst part is, I have no idea how to stop her. All my spare time and energy has been devoted to shoring up the beachhead against the deluge. I'm terrified that, despite my best efforts, we'll end up drowning in a valley of fears, tears, and heartbreak. And the thing that scares me most? If I somehow do manage to break the surface and come up for air, it will only be to find that Pop has disappeared forever.

"Don?"

"Right here," he whispers.

"I'm scared." I nestle my head in that safe sweet spot between his shoulder and neck. "I'm really, really scared. What am I going to do?"

"Give it some time. She won't be around forever." He kisses my forehead. "My guess? She'll be back in Hawaii long before the first snow."

"But it's only August. I don't think I can wait that long." The wave is building, and every day brings it crashing closer to shore. "And... what if she doesn't leave?"

"Why worry about something that might not happen?"

"But I don't think—"

"Okay, this needs to stop. *You* need to stop." He props himself up on one elbow, squaring me in his gaze. "Want to know what I think?"

145

Do I want to know? I hesitate. Maybe. Maybe not. "I guess so," I finally say.

"I think it's time we talked Truth."

"No!" I sit bolt upright in bed. "Don, I can't."

He grabs my arm, halting me before I can scramble away. "Listen, Katy, do you want my help or not?"

Truth is a game we've played before, and it's not one I'm fond of. While gut-level honesty can be cathartic, it can also be scary. And hurtful. And cruel. Not to mention, Don and I are great at pushing each other's buttons. Last time we played, a few months before Mai arrived, he accused me of being a workaholic, a perfectionist, rigid in my thinking. That was the night I tore his diamond ring off my finger and threw it in his face, followed by some terrible words like boorish, overbearing, and (cringe-worthy) a swaggering idiot. It was a bitter fight, our worst fight, and we're still recovering from the aftermath. And now he wants us to play again. Then again, it's my fault we're having this discussion. I'm the one who's been complaining. And by the rules of the game, I'm now honor bound to tell-the-truth-the-whole-truth-and-nothing-but-the-truth-so-help-me-God.

"Have you talked with your dad about how you feel?"

"No," I admit.

"Why not?" he presses.

"Lots of reasons."

"You're stalling."

"You're right," I say.

"This is Truth, remember?"

"What if I don't want to?" I challenge.

"Sometimes we don't always get what we want."

"It's so not fair," I say.

"Give me some specifics," he prompts.

"Mai," I reply. "Everything about her. Is that specific enough?"

"Did you ever stop to think that maybe this isn't about you?"

I clamp my hands over my ears even. "Would you please shut up?"

"You started this."

"Whose side are you on, anyway?" I throw him a furious glance.

"I'm not playing sides," he reminds me. "And I'm not the one with the problem. You are."

"Yes, I have a problem, and her name is Mai. And I don't want her in my life."

"You're sure about that?"

"Of course, I am," I say, then pause, eyeing him uncertainly. "Why?"

His eyebrows rise slightly. "Your life?"

"Who else would I be talking about?"

"Give it a second," he advises, "and you'll figure it out."

And then I get it.

"All right," I concede. "Maybe it's not just about me. This involves Pop, too. But Don, have you seen the way she handles him? I know it sounds cliché, but it's like she's got him wrapped around her little finger. He does anything she wants."

"Anything?"

"Pretty much," I say, feeling the storm brewing inside me, big black thunderheads looming close.

"You've always said that your dad's the best," he says.

"He is."

"That he's kind and good, and that you're so lucky that he loves you so much."

"That's right."

"And that he'd do anything for you."

"He would," I insist. "He does."

"So, if all that's true, why does it bother you so much if he wants to do the same for Mai?"

"*Because*," I say, offended by his words. Don has no business pushing me like this.

"Great answer," he scoffs.

"Because it's not fair!" I suddenly shriek. "Because I don't want to share him!"

The words fly out of me, accompanied by a wild tangent of heartache and tears.

Don clucks his tongue softly. "And finally, we reach the heart of the problem."

Maybe it's the shouting, or all those smacks I inflicted on my pillow. But whatever the reason, all my anger abruptly disappears, and I collapse against him.

"I sound like a selfish brat, don't I?" I whisper.

"Yep," he agrees, calm and quiet, without a hint of malice.

Selfishness. Greediness. I have so many character defects. I'm not a particularly nice person. Not only am I self-centered, I can also be nasty and cruel.

"What am I going to do?"

"Like I said before, I think you should talk to your dad. Think about how he feels."

It's a scary proposition. Am I willing to consider Pop's side of things? To open my eyes and ears and heart to what he must be going through? How would I feel, if it was me? The thought of discovering I'd abandoned my own child, and that it was my irresponsibility that led to that child growing up without the love of a father.

Which isn't the reality I grew up with. Pop's always been around to cheer me on. He's given me such wonderful opportunities in life, beyond my wildest dreams. I had everything, while, according to Pop, Mai supposedly had nothing.

How can I begrudge Pop for wanting to give her those things now?

How can I begrudge Mai for what she wants and needs from him?

Then I remember how she showed up at the hospital after his heart attack and pushed her way into his room. At the time, I'd thought of her like she was an intruder who didn't belong. Yet if she's really his daughter, then Mai *does* belong. I think of how she glides through the restaurant, a constant presence. But is that merely my selfish pettiness? Is it my paranoia at work, assuming that she's listening, scheming, and planning her next move? Much as I hate to admit it, I can't fault her work ethic. Mai's wonderful with the dining public. She's polite, charming, and excels at what she does. I can't even accuse her of wheedling her way into the position, since Pop himself was the one who came up with the idea of bringing her on staff. She's only doing the job he asked of her.

But that isn't really true. She's doing that, and plenty more. Things she has no business doing. Like somehow managing to talk Pop into halting our popular Friday night all-you-can-eat fish fries. Like going behind my back and colluding with Pete about those new menu inserts. Like blithely informing me that the Japanese dishes she's added to the menu were a done deal, then tripping off to the printer, leaving me to stand alone in her wake.

Do I begrudge her for who she is, and what Pop's doing on her behalf?

Yes.

Do I understand his motives?

Yes.

Would I do the same if Mai was my child?

The answer rushes over me in a tidal wave: *NO*.

I should be over this, shouldn't I? I should be handling this better. *You should*, I hear that little voice in my head, the adult Katy, admonishing me. *I should*, the reluctant child Katy agrees.

But I'm not over this. And I feel horrible. Guilty. Frustrated. Angry.

And lonely. I've never felt so lonely in my life.

I bury my face in Don's chest. "I'm afraid that if I tell him how I feel, Pop will turn against me."

"He won't," he assures me. "Your dad's a good guy. He loves you, Katy. He'll understand."

"That doesn't mean I'm not still scared."

"Think of it like a mission. *Your mission*. You've got to tell him how you feel. Remember, the last thing he wants to do is hurt you."

"I know." And deep in my heart, I know exactly that. Six months ago, I wouldn't have been afraid to approach him. Pop's never given me any reason to question his love. But things are different now. It's as if overnight someone slapped up a wall between us. Sometimes that wall appears only two inches high, easy enough for a toddler to manage; other times, it looms in front of me, with steep craggy peaks scratching the sky. Do I dare try scaling it by myself? What if I lose my balance? What if I slip and fall? I'm no longer sure Pop will be there to catch me.

I finger away a few tears welling up behind my eyes.

"Don't cry, Katy. Please don't cry." Don pulls me closer.

Lying there in the warmth of his arms, I try to clear my mind, think only of this time, this place, this moment. For now, I feel safe. But it won't always be like this. Tomorrow morning, I'll go home, back to the restaurant, back to reality.

"Things will get better. But you need to talk to him. Remember: *nothing changes if nothing changes.*"

"You're right."

"And you'll talk to him?"

I nod. There's no point in arguing about it any further. Don will never understand. And I can talk to Pop until I'm blue in the face, but it won't change a thing. The only way things are going to get better, the only way things will change, is if—and when—Mai leaves.

***

Lucy's text asking me to stop by *The Journal*'s offices at my convenience lights a fire under my feet. I don't even wait for the usual lull between the lunch and dinner break. I know I won't rest until I find out what she's discovered about Mai.

"I'll be right back," I tell Ellen, then head out the kitchen door and down the alley. The irony isn't lost on me. A few weeks ago, Mai walked in the front door, and now I'm sneaking out the back.

"That was fast," Lucy says.

"What can I say?" I settle in the chair across from her. "I'm anxious to hear what you found out."

"I wish I had better news."

I feel the dismay fall across my face. "Nothing?"

"Not much, other than the things you'd told me about. Her grandfather's obituary, and that article on jewelry stores. She also popped up on a high school graduation list."

"College?"

Lucy shakes her head.

So, neither of us has a college degree. "What about a birth certificate? Did you manage to get a copy?"

"No access. It's protected by privacy laws."

"Even for the press?"

A brief smile washes over her face. "I hate to disappoint you, Katy, but the press is not the end all, be all that everyone thinks. Contrary to public opinion, journalists don't automatically have access to confidential files. Some things, yes, but we're also limited in our search results. So, unless you're a member of law enforcement, part of the Federal Government, or can prove you're someone with authority to act on a relative's behalf, things like family records—birth and death certificates, marriage licenses, divorce decrees— are off limits. According to the Federal Government, some things are sacred."

"Sacred, my eye," I mumble. "What about genealogy searches? I thought that people could access birth certificates through those."

"It takes seventy-five years for a record to become public."

"I haven't got seventy-five years." I slouch deeper in my chair. "So basically, if I understand correctly, you're saying I'm screwed. There's no way I can prove who Mai is, and I also can't find out if Pop's listed on her birth certificate."

"I'm sorry, Katy. I wish I could be more help."

The downcast look on her face only makes me feel guiltier. Lucy's not responsible for her search coming up lacking. I surfed the web myself with similar results.

"It's not your fault. At least you tried, and that's something. I appreciate it." I feel the pressure building, the dull familiar pain climbing up the back of my skull, a result of stress. I do a few neck rolls, trying to relieve the tension. This is crazy. I can't understand why the trail is cold, especially in today's world of TMI. There must be plenty of information about Mai out there somewhere; I just haven't stumbled across it yet.

"I'll keep looking if you want," Lucy offers, "but frankly, I doubt we'll find anything else." She hesitates. "If you like, I can put together a small piece and run it in *The Journal*."

"You mean, an article about Mai?"

"Sure. I'll interview her and write something up. It wouldn't be much, probably only a few paragraphs. But since she's been around, a few people have started asking about her. They're curious who she is. It might be a nice way to showcase the restaurant, let people know a bit more about her, and welcome her to town."

"Thanks, Lucy, but I don't think so." It's obvious Mai already feels plenty welcome. Why make it seem as if we're encouraging her to stay?

"Let me know if you change your mind," Lucy says as she walks me to the door. "I'll be glad to run something."

"I'll think about it. Thanks again. Tell Max I said hi."

"Will do," she promises.

Five minutes later, I'm back at the restaurant, walking in the front door.

Mai, posted at the entrance, menus in hand, blinks as I walk past. "You left?"

I nod. "And now I'm back."

"No one told me."

"Guess I forgot." A minor fib, but I'm not about to admit that I purposely headed out the back door, just so she wouldn't spot me.

"Next time, it'd be nice if you let me know," she says, the reproach in her voice evident.

Who exactly does she think she is? She's not the boss of me. I stride past her and head for the kitchen, berating myself with every step I take. I'm not answerable to her, and there's no reason to feel guilty or let Mai get on my nerves. I can take off whenever and wherever I please. *Where I go is none of your business*, I should have said. *What gives you the right to question me?* I should have said.

I should ask her. I really should ask her.

I should do a lot of things.

But right now, there's one thing, more than anything else, that I absolutely need to do.

Don is right. *Nothing changes if nothing changes.*

Whether I like it or not, I can't see any other way around it.

I need to talk to Pop.

CHAPTER FOURTEEN

~ **What's on Today's Menu?** ~

"Y OU BUSY?"

I look up and find Katy in the doorway.

"Nope, come on in." I lean back in my chair, eyeballing her as she slips into the seat across the desk. I used to be able to read her in one glance, but that's no longer the case. The last few weeks have changed things between us. I feel like she's purposely been avoiding me, and I don't like it. The same way I don't like the fact that the two of us aren't talking much these days. I need to get a handle on that, make sure it changes.

Lots of things need to change.

"What's up?"

She sucks in a deep breath, holds it for a minute, then lets it out in one fast whoosh of air. "I guess you could say I'm here on a mission."

"Sorry?" I cock my head, not sure I heard her correctly.

"A mission," she repeats, as if that's supposed to explain everything.

"I'm still not following."

"You know, *a mission*. People go on missions all the time."

"You're going somewhere?" What's she talking about? What's all this talk about a mission? Is she joining the Peace Corps?

She throws back her head, watches the ceiling. "I knew this was a stupid idea."

"The mission?"

"Yes. I mean, no!" She shakes her head faster than Jake can shake a martini. "Sometimes, I wonder why I bother. I never should have listened to him."

"What'd Jake tell you?"

"Who said anything about Jake?" Katy asks, frowning. "What's he got to do with this?"

"I thought you said you'd been talking with Jake."

"No... but maybe I should have. He might give better advice than Don."

"Is Don going on this mission with you?"

"Look, Pop, forget the mission, will you? And forget about Don. This is about me and you." Katy leans forward, clasping her hands between her knees. Her face gleams with an earnest look she reserves for those special occasions when she wants my full attention.

And suddenly, I understand. She's talked with Don, and somehow, he managed to talk some sense into her about buying Eva's property. Eva wants out, and fast. I want to buy the place, and fast. Up until now, Katy's been the only thing holding me back.

That, and the recent scare involving my heart. But that's all resolved now. I'm taking my meds, going to cardiac rehab, and eating right. I feel better than I have in years.

Especially now I know Katy's on board with the property purchase.

"So, this mission I'm on? It's specifically to see you. I thought it's time we talked."

"You're absolutely right." The longer time goes by without signatures on the closing documents, the slimmer our chances of locking in a low interest rate.

"Look, Pop, I'll be honest with you. The first thing I need to say is, I'm sorry. I hate the way things have been between us lately. I hate that we haven't been talking. It feels like everything started when... well, no, never mind. It doesn't matter *when*, it only matters that we fix it. Anyway, I'm sorry. So much of what happened is my fault. And this—"

"Aw, kiddo, why don't you stop right there," I rush in, cutting her off before she confesses anything else. Katy's not the only guilty party involved here. A lot of what happened is my fault. In normal times, the two of us sit down daily and chat about the business, how things are going, potential problems, foreseeable solutions. But since Mai showed up, I've been derelict in my duties, and I've left Katy to handle things by herself. "It's not fair to let you take all the blame. I should have handled things better."

And from now on, I will. I'm going to get on the phone and call Don, get those papers lined up for our signatures.

A large smile blooms across her face. "You mean it?"

"I sure do," I say fervently.

"I'm so glad to hear it."

I chuckle. "You sound surprised."

"Not surprised, exactly. I guess you could say, more like, *impressed*." She relaxes in her chair. "But why didn't you say anything before now?"

I shrug. "You know how I hate talking about stuff like this." Like father, like daughter. I've never been one for talking about my feelings, and neither is Katy.

"You have no idea how happy this makes me." Her voice trembles in a shaky laugh. "Thinking about all this, I've been worried sick."

"Me, too," I say, wondering if I've got time to give Don a quick call. Maybe I can catch him in his office, and he can bring over the paperwork.

"We should have talked about this long ago," she says. "It was getting to the point where I was afraid it would drive us apart."

"Never," I vow. "Not in a million years." I reach across the desk and grab her hand, give her fingers a tight squeeze. "Not in a billion years."

She claps her other hand over my own. "I love you, Pop."

"And I love you, Katy-Did." I add to the growing tower with my other hand. It's the best feeling in the world, having things squared between us, the way it's always been. The way it should be. "How about we give him a call right now?"

She blinks. "Call who?"

"Don," I say. "Who else? Maybe, if he's available, we can get him over here right now. Sounds like you're good to go."

"*Good to go* with what?" She yanks her hands away from mine, her face suddenly bunching in a frown. "What does Don have to do with this?"

Now I'm the one who's frowning. "I thought you said the two of you talked."

"We did." Her eyes narrow in sudden understanding. "Exactly what do you think we talked about?"

"Why, buying Eva's property, naturally. What else would you talk about?"

"Don't tell me you've started up with that nonsense again?" she asks in an incredulous voice.

"What do you mean, *nonsense*?" Why is she questioning me? "The deal's nearly done."

"Deal? There's no deal," she sputters. "That damn store. It's always about that damn furniture store, isn't it? And that's the reason you think I wanted to talk to you today?"

"What else?" After all, I'm not the one who went searching her out. I know how she felt about the deal. She's thrown it in my face enough times. But she's the one who mentioned Don, not me. Why else would she bring him up, unless it was about the sale? She knows the two of us have been working together to get the deal done.

"Do you honestly think I'm crazy enough to say yes to you buying that store?"

I snort. "I think you're crazy *not* to. Everyone I've talked to says it's a great buy."

"Not everyone, obviously." Then she pauses, and her eyes suddenly narrow. "Wait a minute. Did you discuss this with Mai?"

"What if I did?" My chin tilts higher. "I guess that's my prerogative, seeing how she's part of this family, too." And Mai's all for the expansion. Why can't Katy understand how us buying the place will be a win-win all around? Why can't Katy be more like Mai?

"Just so we're clear, I'm not about to sign off on the sale." Glaring at me, she jumps to her feet. "Do you understand? I'm not giving my permission for you to go ahead with some stupid idea you've got stuck in your head about that stupid store."

"Stupid? For your information, I'm not stupid." Who does she think she is, calling me stupid? "And neither is my store."

"It's not your store," she hotly reminds me. "And it's not *our* store, either," she corrects herself. "We don't need the space, and we don't need the business. It's only going to mean more work and more stress. And stress is the last thing you need in your life."

"Don't I? Ha! Well, let me clue you in on something, kiddo. Right now, you're doing a damn good job of making me stressed."

"Fine. Maybe I should leave."

"Maybe you should," I shoot back, glaring at her.

"I'm so done with all of this." She waves her arms in large circles, encompassing the room, taking in both of us. "This... this is utter nonsense, and you're going to be sorry."

"Don't bet on it."

"Do you honestly think I'm going to stand by and watch while you kill yourself?"

"I'm not going to kill myself!" I holler.

"Keep it up and you might."

"Fine. You don't want to stick around, then don't." My voice is growing louder by the minute, and they probably can hear me all the way upstairs, but I'll be damned if I care. "Go on!" I shout. "You want to leave, go right ahead. I don't need you. I don't need you at all."

I realize my mistake the minute the words are out of my mouth. But it's too late; the damage is done. The sudden wounded look on her face is a combination of incredulity, hurt, and heartbreak.

"Seriously, Pop? I can't believe you said that." Katy's voice is barely above a whisper.

"I've never been more serious in my life," I growl, despising myself more with every word I speak. What have I done to my little girl? But some things are beyond fixing. And I can't have her challenging my authority. Katy might be all grown up, and I might not be her boss anymore. But she doesn't get to tell me what to do. I'm still her father, dammit.

"I meant every word!" I bellow.

She looks at me a long moment, then turns away and starts for the door.

"And close the damn door!" I shout after her.

She obliges, slamming it with a vengeance.

"Goodbye and good riddance," I swear under my breath, and throw myself into my chair. I stare at the wall a good long time before it finally occurs to me that I still haven't the slightest clue what kind of mission Katy was here on and why she wanted to talk to me.

CHAPTER FIFTEEN

~ Diet Plate ~

I SHOULDN'T HAVE STORMED OUT OF his office. Just because Pop chose to act like a stubborn moron doesn't mean I should have done the same. But I was so stunned and hurt by the harsh words he lobbed at me, and the spiteful way he shouted about not needing me, that I never gave it a second thought before slamming the door in his face. It was only after I calmed down and thought about things, that I realized what—or more precisely, *who*—exactly was to blame. Because none of this is Pop's fault. She's turned him, and he just can't see it yet. Meanwhile, I knew I'd have to swallow my pride and make amends. I acted out of hurt and spite; I was wrong, and I need to admit it. Not that I think I'm wrong about the way I feel on buying Eva's property. But I never should have allowed myself to get into a screaming match with Pop. And I never should have called him stupid. Pop might be lots of things, but stupid isn't one of them. We need to get things fixed between us, and fast. I'm determined to apologize to Pop before the day's over. I'm an adult. I can take the high road.

But that high road doesn't include Mai, despite the fact

I've treated her horribly at times. Some of it she deserved, some of it she didn't. But I can't allow her to distract me from my primary purpose, which is salvaging my relationship with Pop. And if that means keeping my mouth shut and playing nice with Mai when he's around, then that's what I'll do. She might be the catalyst, but she isn't included on this stretch of highway. This road of forgiveness belongs to Pop and me.

I step up to his table and stand before him. He takes his time before finally glancing up from the menu he's studying.

"Here to dish out some more?" He eyes me with a skeptical glance.

"Excuse me?" The accusation halts me in my tracks.

"You know what I'm talking about."

His eyes are brown slits, blank and dead, putting me in mind of the stuffed deer head that hung above our fireplace when I was small. Supposedly Pop was quite the hunter once upon a time. He took the deer down with one clean shot during one of his annual pilgrimages north for deer season. After he brought it home and had it mounted, nothing he said could convince me that the deer wasn't dead; rather, I was certain it was merely stuck halfway through the wall, watching me with its glassy eyes, biding its time until no one was watching so it could burst through the wall and attack me.

Then one day it disappeared.

"Deer don't belong in the house," Pop replied when my five-year-old self screwed up enough courage to ask if he knew where it had gone, and if he thought it might be coming back. "Not if you don't want it to, Katy-Did," he whispered in my ear, followed by the kind of hug that told me I had nothing more to worry about. It was only when I was older that I learned he'd banished the monstrous head to the garage once he realized how much it scared me. And when he thought I was old enough, and without making a big deal of things, he calmly took me out to the garage, letting me see for myself there was no body attached.

That was Pop. Always thinking things through; always making certain I had what I needed. He was such a great dad. Growing up, I remember feeling like I didn't have much in common with the other kids at school. Some of them complained about their mothers being mean, or their dads being too strict. In middle school, the grumbling grew louder; by high school, it had exploded. Everyone seemed to have a beef with their parents; everyone, that is, except me. I couldn't find any fault with Pop, except for the few times that he drank too much beer and yelled too loudly at the television when the Detroit Tigers came up to bat. Other than that, my life was sane and pretty much normal. I remember thinking I was lucky not to have all the troubles my friends had with their parents. Yes, my mother was dead; yes, it was my fault; yes, I missed her terribly. But through it all, I still had Pop. As long as he never found out what happened, I still had Pop.

And now I don't. I might have found the courage to tell him what happened, but even that no longer matters. I never told him, but I lost him anyway.

How have we gotten so far away from each other?

Pop jerks his head toward the door. "Look at that. See how hard she's working?"

I watch as Mai slowly ushers an elderly couple, the beginning of tonight's dinner crowd, to a table. She helps them be seated, offers to store the man's wheeled walker in an out-of-the-way area. They beam under her attention, then whisper between themselves as she leaves the table. Trading compliments about her, probably.

"She does a great job." I force a smile to my face. And I can't deny it: at work, Mai's deferential, respectful, and everything a business owner could wish for in an employee.

But not in a sister. I don't want a sister. And especially not Mai.

"You ever stop and think about how hard her life's been?" His eyes follow her as she moves about the restaurant. She looks up suddenly, catches him watching her, and throws him a little wave.

"I just don't get it, Katy. How can you begrudge her any of this?" he says.

"Did you ever hear me say that I—"

"You didn't have to. It's pretty obvious." His face is as hard and stern as one of the figures chiseled on Mt. Rushmore. "Well, let me tell you something. As far as I'm concerned, she's exactly where she belongs. And you'd better get used to it."

Is he serious? "She's not going back? She's actually told you she plans on staying?"

Pop doesn't say a word, only swings his head slowly back in my direction. And when his eyes meet mine, I swallow hard, realizing how high the wall between us is growing, faster than I thought possible.

"We're done talking about this," he says. "And by the way. What's the story with those two?"

I follow the direction in which he's pointing. Two little boys in shorts and t-shirts sit hunched over one of our back tables, oblivious to everything but their crayons and coloring books.

"They're Ellen's little boys," I explain, relieved to be

talking about something besides Mai. "Marty called in sick again, and Ellen agreed to come in for a few hours."

"What's that got to do with those kids?"

"Today is her day to have her little guys for a scheduled visit."

"That still doesn't explain why they're here."

I'm confused. It sounds as if he's objecting, but why? Other waitresses have brought their kids to work in the past if they got in a bind. Granted, it doesn't happen often, but when it does, our staff knows they can count on us. Working at Chuck's has always been like being part of a big, happy family.

Or rather, that's the way it used to be.

"They're good kids," I assure him. "They won't cause any trouble."

"That's not the point. Haven't they got a grandmother or someone around to watch them?"

"No, they don't," I shoot back. "Honestly, Pop, I don't understand why you think this is a problem. Ellen's doing us a favor, remember?"

"And you think that means I'm supposed to be impressed?" He shrugs, stands, and gives me a flat look. "You want to hire a thief, Katy, that's your decision. Meanwhile, like I've said before, I don't like having her around. And I especially don't like those kids hanging around my restaurant. I'm not running a nursery." With another quick look, he jerks his chin at their sodas. "Make sure she pays for their drinks."

I watch him as he strides away, sick to my stomach by the way he spoke to me, and embarrassed by the things he said. Hopefully no one overheard him.

"Katy?" Ellen halts next to me, a tray stacked with dirty glasses in her hands. "Is everything okay?"

Somehow, I muster up the little positive energy left inside me. "Yep. Things are cool."

She pauses, cautiously shifting the tray to one hip so the glasses don't slide. "You're sure?"

Ellen and I are friends, and friends share their problems. But some problems she doesn't need to hear... especially when one of those problems directly involves her.

"Absolutely."

Her eyebrows scrunch together. I know she doesn't believe me.

"Things are A-Okay. Hunky dory. Never better." I need to extract myself from this conversation right now, or it will drag us into places I don't want to go. And Ellen wouldn't, either. Especially if she ever found out how Pop really feels at having her on staff. I know exactly what she'd do. She won't stick around waiting for him to catch her in the slightest mistake, just so he can have the pleasure of firing her. She'll quit before that happens.

And I'll quit before I allow her to quit. Things can't go on like this, no matter what Pop thinks. I need to draw a line somewhere.

"Thanks again for coming in today," I say. "I appreciate it."

"No problem. I'd planned to take the kids to the beach, but they love being here." A smile spreads across her face as she watches her boys. "Guess what Ryan told me this morning," she confides. "He said he wants to work in a restaurant someday. And Desmond said he's going to own the restaurant."

"They're both so cute."

"They are, aren't they?" she says, with a loving look at her two little guys. "Thanks again for letting me bring them in with me."

"They're always welcome." The lie rolls off my tongue as smooth as if I swallowed a skein of silk. "You're the one who did us the favor, when you came in to cover the shift." Why can't Pop understand that? "In fact, if you want to go ahead and take off, that's fine. I'm sure we can handle the rest of the dinner shift without you. I bet the boys would like you all to themselves."

"Oh, that's okay, I can stick it out. And the boys won't care. I put in their dinner orders about ten minutes ago, and they should be up soon." She laughs. "Little boys are so easy to please. A burger, fries, and a bottle of ketchup, and they're happy."

"Let dinner be my treat." I stick my hand in my pocket, fish out enough cash to cover the bill and then some, and crush the money into her hand. "That should cover things."

Just in case Pop asks.

"That's not necessary," she protests, attempting to push the money back at me.

"No, take it."

"You're sweet, Katy, but it's too much," she insists.

"But I want to," I say. "It will cover their meal and drinks."

Ellen hesitates. "But I always thought the drinks were free?"

For you, and for me, but not for your boys. I bite back the words.

"Oh. I see." Her voice is flat and funny-weird as she looks

at the money, then back up at me. Then abruptly, she crushes the bills into a tight wad, forcing it back into my hand.

"Thanks, but no thanks. I don't need your money."

It's a defining moment in our relationship, and one I never expected. Financial information is personal and private, but both of us know that Ellen's budget is tight. It doesn't include room for frivolous expenses, like so many other families take for granted. Things like, not stopping to consider if you can afford the occasional dinner out. Or being able to order the gigantic plate of fries that would make any kid's eyes bug out. Like, I'm-going-to-order-dessert-Ryan-and-Desmond-do-you-want-dessert-too?

"I don't need your money," Ellen repeats. Chin high, she backs away, eyes blazing. "I don't need it and I don't want it."

"I'm sorry. I only wanted to help." As usual, I barged ahead without thinking, assuming I'd ride in and save the day. Katy to the rescue. Turns out, the only thing I've done is embarrass us both. Why am I constantly poking my nose into matters which don't concern me? Why can't I be more sensitive? When will I learn to quit tromping on people's feelings?

"I can take care of my boys. And if you're so worried I can't pay, let me reassure you right now that there's no need for concern." Digging deep in her apron, she pulls out a five-dollar bill and slaps it on the table between us. "That should cover their drinks. I'll catch the food order bill after they eat. Now, if you'll excuse me, I have a table waiting."

"Ellen, wait," I plead. "Please don't go."

But I'm too late. She's already turned her back on me, and I'm left alone to stand and watch as she heads back out on the floor.

CHAPTER SIXTEEN

~ You Are What You Eat ~

J AKE SNAGS MY ATTENTION WITH a two-finger alert and waves me over behind the bar.

"What's up?" I ask when we're standing shoulder to shoulder. I don't want anyone overhearing.

"The till came up short again last night," he replies quietly.

"How short?" I ask, keeping my voice as low as his. I asked him on the sly last week to keep me posted if he spotted any shortages. Katy's been responsible for the till for a long time now, and I don't want her catching me sifting through the daily receipts, and then start thinking that I'm checking up on her... even though I am. But it's not as if she left me much choice. I no longer trust her to keep me informed. And Chuck's is my restaurant. I need to know what's going on.

"How short is short?" I repeat.

"Twenty dollars last night." Turning his back on the crowd, Jake edges closer to me. "And I did some poking around. Turns out, the same thing happened the night before last—which happened to be my night off. It rang up short that night, too. Fifteen dollars."

A hot flush spread across my face faster than a grease fire in our kitchen. Fifteen bucks here; twenty bucks there. It all adds up. And Jake's news only confirms my smoldering suspicions that we have a problem. Still, suspecting it is one thing; but having it verified, and—worst of all—knowing Katy purposely didn't tell me, makes the revelation burn even deeper. One of our employees has been ripping us off, and I don't need to think too hard to figure out who.

I know exactly why Katy kept it from me: she's trying to protect her friend. From the day Katy hired her, I knew that woman would turn out to be nothing but trouble. I tried to warn her, but Katy wouldn't listen. Instead she chose to bluster ahead on some crazy do-gooder quest without taking the time to think things through. Now all of us are facing the consequences.

Well, that's about to end.

"Good job, Jake." I clamp a hand on his shoulder. "You notice anything else funny going on, I want to know about it."

"Will do," he says.

"And don't forget, this little matter stays between us."

"You got it, boss," he promises.

I push away from the bar and scan the restaurant. This time of day—between the lunch and dinner crowd, when the afternoon heat causes a drowsy lull and things quiet down— is normally my favorite time to escape downstairs. I shut myself up in my office, turn on the TV, and kick back in my chair to catch a few innings of the Detroit Tigers. But not today. I've got an appointment to keep.

And a thief to catch.

I snag Mai from her hostess duties. "I'm expecting a

visitor. Let me know when she gets here, will you? She's in her seventies, with gray hair, and kinda short."

"Is this the person who's buying your car?"

"No, I'm selling it to a guy from Wisconsin. But he can't get here till next Tuesday." I've been running an on-line ad for my classic convertible for the past couple weeks, and finally have a legitimate offer on the table. "This woman, Eva, owns the property next door."

Mai's face blossoms into a smile. "You're going through with the restaurant expansion?"

I choose not to answer, and I don't smile back. Instead, I eyeball Katy, hunched alone scribbling notes at the staff table. I should be feeling happy about this deal, but knowing she's against it puts a sour swirl in my stomach.

"One more thing," I tell Mai. "Let's not bother Katy with any of this. When Eva gets here, send her down to my office. I'm headed there right now."

"I'll keep an eye out for her," she promises. "Would you like me to fix you a plate? Today's the first day we're serving the yakitori."

"Thanks, but I ate a late breakfast." Still, I don't want to discourage her. Mai's worked so hard with Pete, and she's so proud of our new Japanese dishes. "I'll try some later," I promise, nodding at the menus in her hand. "Things going good? People like the new stuff?"

"Very much." The hint of a smile lights her face, and the flash of color in her eyes—like a rich toasted almond—has me suddenly thinking about Yumiko. Mai inherited her mother's best features, but—thankfully—not her demeanor. "Excuse me, Otosan, I must see to these guests."

She glides toward a group of four men at the door. I

watch as she greets them, then lithely turns to escort them to a table. One of them touches her arm, says something which makes her laugh.

The bell tinkles above the front door and I turn toward it, but my expected visitor hasn't arrived, only more customers. That's when I notice Katy at the employee table, staring straight ahead, glowering as she watches Mai.

My back stiffens. I clench my teeth, my resolve hardening. Katy's given me nothing but trouble for the past month. So much trouble, that if I still harbored any doubts as to what I'm about to do, she's just made it easier for me. Katy needs to get over herself and move on with life.

Just like we all have.

Just like we all will.

Turning my back on her, I head downstairs.

CHAPTER SEVENTEEN

~ Manager's Special ~

"WHAT DO YOU THINK YOU'RE doing?" I stand in The Bungalow's kitchen and stare at Ellen, arms folded across my chest. How could she betray me like this?

"I should think it's obvious." Ellen, knife in hand, doesn't even bother to glance up as she smears a glob of mayonnaise across a piece of bread. "I'm making myself a sandwich."

"That's not what I'm talking about, and you know it," I hotly reply. "Mai told me you took off your apron and simply walked out."

"She's right. That's what I did."

"But you must have had a reason, or you never would have walked out right in the middle of the dinner rush. So, what happened?"

She lifts one shoulder in a dismissive shrug, and stacks a slice of turkey atop the bread.

"Was there a problem? Because, if there was, you know you could have come to me."

"You weren't there," she says.

"Exactly my point!" I'm frustrated beyond belief. "I'm

off the floor ten minutes, only to get back and find you gone. I think the least I deserve is some kind of explanation."

Not to mention, an apology would be nice. Each time I relive Mai's recount of what happened earlier tonight—how Ellen hung up her apron, walked off the floor, then out the door—my anger kicks up another notch. The minute we closed, I drove to The Bungalow, where I found her. "Tell me."

She presses her lips together. "I may not be the smartest girl in town, but I know better than to stick around where I'm not wanted."

"Who says you're not wanted?"

She drops the knife and faces me. "See, Katy, that's one of your problems. You have no idea what's going on in your own restaurant. You can't expect people to keep doing their jobs when no one knows who's in charge."

"I'm in charge," I snap, not even bothering to hide my annoyance. Ellen's the one who walked out. She's the one who betrayed me. And if she had a smidgen of decency, she'd understand why I feel so hurt and frustrated. She walked off the job without coming to me first, without letting me try to put things right. And the thing is, I still don't understand why she did it. My employees—our employees—aren't in the habit of walking out the door.

"I'm in charge," I repeat. "I thought I made that perfectly clear when I hired you."

"Really?" One eyebrow arches slightly as she screws on the lid of the mayonnaise jar, returns it to the refrigerator. "You might want to check with your father. He seems to have a different opinion."

"Look, do me a favor and just tell me what happened."

I've had a crashing headache since Mai gave me the news that immediately turned my stomach inside out. I took a huge chance when I hired Ellen despite Pop's opposition. I trained her, and she's good. She's more than good; she's great. Then again, maybe that's why she left. *Green, good, gone.* I remind myself, recalling the common mantra of employers suddenly left in the lurch when their staff disappears. Train a new hire, get them up to speed, and suddenly they're gone, hired away by the competition. "Why did you walk out?"

"Why?" She picks up her sandwich, plucks a stray piece of lettuce from between the bread, examines it carefully, then discards it with a sniff. "That's what people usually do when they get fired."

"Excuse me?" I say, unable to stop myself from staring. "What do you mean, *fired*?"

She pokes a finger at a bit of mayonnaise oozing from the sandwich. "He fired me."

"Pop?" My heart thumps in my ears, loud sickening thuds that vibrate all the way into the pit of my stomach. "I don't believe it."

"I didn't either, until he told me to get out." She licks the mayonnaise from her finger. "He said I had five minutes to get out of his restaurant before he called the police. So, I left. And here's something else you might be interested in hearing. Thanks to your dad, I might soon be homeless. When the director of The Bungalow found out I lost my job, she told me I have exactly two weeks to find a new job, or I'll need to leave."

I sink onto one of the wooden chairs surrounding the large kitchen table. The chair is sturdy and solidly built, but it feels like I'm on one of those county fair amusement rides that promise thrills and spills as they spin and whirl you in circles till you've lost all sense of balance and focus. "Pop actually fired you?"

"Yes, ma'am." Ellen leans back against the kitchen counter and munches her sandwich, coolly surveying me from a good six-feet away. "It was pretty clear he meant it. I tried talking with him, but it was obvious from the start that he had no desire to hear my side of things."

"Did he give you a reason?"

"He accused me of stealing... of lifting money from the till. Not once, but several times, he said, *according to my sources*. Then he told me to get out."

This is insane. Ellen's not a thief. I feel it in my gut; I know it in my heart. She'd never steal from Pop. And as for Pop and his so-called sources? I don't have to think very hard to figure out who exactly his source might be. She's everywhere.

"It's not true."

"Of course, it isn't," she calmly asserts. "Why would I want to put everything in jeopardy?"

She's right. Ellen would never do something that would mess up her chances of getting her boys back. She'd never risk their prospect of being someday reunited. She loves them too much.

"Let me talk to Pop," I say. "I'm sure I can work everything out. It's probably only a simple misunderstanding. He's been having some health problems lately. He hasn't been himself." None of us has been; not since the world as we know it was shot to hell the day Mai walked through our front door. "And you know all the problems we've been having with our POS," I add. "It's hard enough for me to figure out what's going on, let alone Pop. He and the digital world aren't exactly friends." Which is one reason I hadn't bothered informing him about the minor cash discrepancies we've been experiencing lately, with the till not balancing. It's only a few dollars; I'm not in panic-mode. Why would I bother Pop?

"We can salvage this." I think hard for another moment. "Let's give him a day to cool off. Then I'll sit him down and explain why I re-hired you."

"Don't bother," she says. "I'm not interested."

"What do you mean?"

Ellen shrugs. "Why do you care?"

"I'm your friend," I say. "Of course, I care."

"Think whatever you like, Katy, but we're not friends." A glint of anger shoots across her eyes; her voice carries an edge sharper than any of the kitchen knives Pete uses in the restaurant. "I used to think we were friends... but not anymore. Friends don't let things like this happen."

"That's not fair."

"You actually want to talk about what's fair and not fair?" she scoffs. "You're not the one who got fired, remember?"

"But I didn't know," I stutter in my own defense. "Pop didn't tell me."

"I find that hard to believe," she says flatly.

"It's the truth." I lift a palm to my forehead, try to rub down the nasty headache before it spreads out of control. *Damn it, Pop.* Why did he do this? Ellen is innocent, no matter what he thinks. And he had no right to let her go. I'm in charge of restaurant staff. He agreed to let me do the hiring and firing.

"I'll fix this," I promise. "All I want is a chance to talk to him."

"Talk all you want, but it won't change a thing. I'm not coming back."

"Ellen, please don't say that."

"Why not?" Narrowing her eyes, she looks at me as if she sees right through me. "I'm telling you right now: don't waste your energy. Even if he does apologize, I'm not coming back. Your father has never liked me. And don't try and tell me different, because we both know the truth. He never wanted me on staff. If you go behind his back and re-hire me, he'll hate me more than he already does. And I won't put up with that. I refuse to put up with that. I don't need the grief." She shakes her head. "There's been enough negativity in my life. It's time for me to move on. I'll find another job."

"But where? Who do you think would..."? I cut myself off before I can give voice to the thought, but it's too late. My doubt already hangs in the air between us like wet sheets hung out to dry.

"You think no one will hire me? Every restaurant in town is looking for staff. And, I've got some experience now. I doubt I'll have a problem."

She's probably right. It won't be difficult for Ellen to find another place to work. Help Wanted signs are posted all over James Bay. With their seasonal employees now back in college, most restaurants in town have been reduced to operating on a skeleton staff, the same as Chuck's. Ellen's brush with the law might raise a few eyebrows, but people will overlook it.

"Are you sure about this?" I can understand her frustration, but I still hate to see her go. Especially under circumstances like this. "I wish there was something I could say or do to convince you to stay."

Her face tightens. "My mind's made up."

"When you find something else, give them my name and tell them to call me. I'll give you a great reference, and tell them what a great job you do... did," I correct myself.

"I appreciate that," she says stiffly.

"I guess that's it then." I stand up and shove in my chair.

"I suppose it is."

"Tell your boys I said hi."

"I will," she says, without even the hint of a smile.

There's nothing left for me to do but walk out the door. But hearing it close behind me doesn't sound like the end of things. If anything, it only furthers my resolve. It's too late to do anything tonight; but come tomorrow morning, I intend to have a serious talk with Pop. I'm determined to find out exactly what happened, and what caused him to make such a terrible mistake. Because no matter what he might believe, that's exactly what firing Ellen was: a horrible mistake.

It's up to me to make things right.

***

If the events of last night weren't enough to convince me, my breaking point comes this morning with a phone call.

"No way," I say. Don's phone call catches me fresh out of the shower, wet hair wrapped in a towel. "No way," I repeat, plopping down on the unmade bed. "I don't believe it."

"You didn't know?" His voice downshifts from confident into uneasy. "Sorry, I assumed that the two of you had already talked."

"No, we haven't." I glower at the overstuffed chair piled with clean clothes I haven't had time to put away and the walls I'm forever promising myself that I'll get around to painting someday. *Someday*. So many things I put off doing, and for what? I've thrown my time and energy into managing Chuck's, to help relieve Pop from needless stress. And what has it gotten me? He's gone and added more stress to our lives. How much more does he think he can handle?

How much more can I?

"And you're absolutely positive that it's a done deal?"

"I have the signed paperwork right here on my desk," Don confirms. "Eva called me last night and told me about their meeting. She just left my office."

Pop signed the paperwork despite everything. He knew I was against the sale, so instead of consulting me, he cut me out of the deal. He bought Eva's building and tied us up in a bank business loan for God knows how long.

Why didn't he talk to me? Did he actually think he could do this on his own?

Or maybe he had encouragement from another source. She's sleeping in my old bedroom, she's working in our restaurant, and now she's taken over managing Pop's life.

"Katy? You okay?"

"Let's say I've had better days."

Mai's turned him against me. The man who raised me, the man I used to know and love, is gone. *That* Pop never would have gone behind my back and cut this deal. Until today, I never put any faith in the expression that you can hate someone with all your heart... but now I get it. Because that's exactly how I feel about Mai. I hate everything about her. And I have no doubt she's the one behind all this. A restaurant expansion I don't want to deal with. A third person involved in our daily operations. And where exactly do I fit in? I've spent years turning myself inside out, taking care of Pop, helping him run the business.

Is she taking my place? Is he forcing me out?

I've made Chuck's my life because of Pop. This restaurant, this town, is all I know. Closing my eyes, I think about that January evening when he upped the stakes and brought me in as general manager. Pop was recovering from his first heart attack, and I'd moved back in with him on a temporary basis to make sure he was taking care of himself. Then, right after dinner, he abruptly excused himself, went into his bedroom, only to re-emerge with a neat stack of paper-clipped documents which he pushed into my hand. I quickly skimmed the paperwork, filled with legal jargon. "What's all this? I don't understand."

"A more formal version of our business arrangement," he answered. "I'm bringing you into the business, kiddo."

"Seriously?" My voice squeaked between incredulity and pure panic. I'd been working at Chuck's since Pop bought the place. Those years while most of my high school class departed for college, then began marrying, raising their families, I hung around. True, my responsibilities in the restaurant gradually increased, but he'd never talked about formally bringing me in on the business end of things. "Seriously, Pop?"

"I've never been more serious in my life," he replied. "All this heart stuff I've been going through... it makes a person stop and think about what's important. Sure, you think about the things you have, what you've done. But most of all, you think about the people in your life and how you feel about them. And I didn't have to think very hard about that one, because it's all about you, kiddo. You're the one who's always mattered, and you always will be. I love you, Katy-Did."

"I love you too, Pop," I said, big fat tears welling up in my eyes. Pop, who up until then no one would ever have defined as particularly sentimental, seemed a changed man. I'd heard heart attacks could do that to people. His heart attack had made him morph into one big mushy pile of emotions.

And me, as well. If I wasn't careful, I'd turn into a big blubbering blob.

"I didn't mean to make you cry," he said gruffly as I scrounged in my pocket for a Kleenex.

"I'm not crying," I said, dabbing at my eyes. Neither of us were experts at dealing with emotions. "It's allergies."

"Uh-huh." He pointed at the paperwork. "Rose said all we need to do is have you sign the papers, and we're all set. Nice and legal."

I knew if Rose Gallagher had drafted the document, it was a virtual guarantee that everything was in order. Rose has been our family attorney since she inherited her practice from a local judge who died years ago in an arson fire. When Rose drafts documents for clients, they know they can rest assured that all the details have been thoroughly addressed.

A Limited Partnership Agreement. So much, so fast. Part of me had been expecting something like this for a few years now, but another part of me had dreaded the thought of Pop presenting me with such a document. After all, partnerships didn't come cheap; family or not, I'd surely be expected to put up money to buy my shares. Could I afford it? I'd just bought my house. And while I was pretty sure the bank would grant me a loan, I wasn't certain if I wanted to commit. Accepting part ownership of a business would mean assuming even more responsibility. I'd told Pop years ago that I wasn't going anywhere, and planned on being at Chuck's for the long haul; but had I really meant it? And did I still mean it? Granted, it's the family business. But it's Pop's business, not mine.

Is working in a restaurant what I want to do with the rest of my life?

"I'm flattered, Pop, honest I am. And I appreciate your confidence in me."

"Why do I hear that *but*... in your voice? Just sign on the dotted line."

But things aren't always as easy as they seem. I hadn't expected the offer to come at this particular time; certainly not before my thirtieth birthday. "I'm not sure how to say this..."

"Spit it out," he suggested.

"I don't think I can afford to buy into the business right now. I bought my house and then that new car last year. I'm not sure—no, I'm trying to be honest—I *know* I can't afford to kick in any money. Maybe in a year or two. But not right now," I finished lamely.

Granted, the balance in my savings account was starting to accumulate again, but only because I'd been saving like crazy. I don't like being beholden to anyone, especially to a bank.

"Who said anything about money?" he asked. "Did you hear me asking you for money?"

"No," I admitted. "But I guess I assumed that if we're going to be partners, then I'd be required to buy into the business. Isn't that the way things are supposed to work?"

"Maybe for other people, but not for us. A business is

only as good—or bad—as the people involved. And you're the best part of this business, Katy. If you don't know that, then I'm to blame. Guess I don't tell you as often as I should.

"Anyway, I've made my decision, and I think that now is the right time to do this. And why not? You've been a part of Chuck's since you were a kid. At this point, you probably know the business better than I do. Why shouldn't I bring you in as a partner? And as for your question about money—I don't see the point of asking you to buy in when we both know the whole place will end up being all yours someday."

"Katy?" Don's voice echoes across the phone line, tugging my thoughts back into my bedroom. "You still there?"

"Where else would I be?" I'm still sitting on the bed, naked beneath my bathrobe, wet hair snugly wrapped in a towel.

"Look, why don't you come down to my office and we can talk about it."

"I don't see that we have anything to talk about." My brain races down a side track that's taking me places I never thought I'd visit. Is this paperwork even legal? Pop and I are partners. How could he buy Eva's property without my signature?

"Talking will help. It always helps."

"But will it change anything?" I ask. "Will it change the fact that Pop signed the paperwork? That he bought Eva's store?"

Don hesitates. "Well, no."

"So, what's the point?"

"I thought he would have explained it."

"Explain what?" I demand, quickly beginning to lose patience with him.

"The way all this works. When I questioned him about it, he showed me your Partnership Agreement. I assume you know that you're a limited partner," he says.

"Yes, I'm aware of that."

"That comes with some contingencies."

"Meaning?" I press.

He pauses for a minute. "For one thing, he doesn't need your signature. Your dad's the controlling partner. His signature was the only thing needed to close the deal."

Everything inside me goes numb. "You're kidding."

Don's silence is all the confirmation I need.

I take a deep breath. "All right, I guess if that's the way it is, then that's the way it is."

"But you're still coming down to the office, right? You're—"

"Nope, I'm not. What would be the point?"

"We can talk," he says.

"There's nothing to talk about."

"Katy," I hear his voice plead.

Traitor, I think, hanging up on him.

And that goes for Pop, too. Plotting behind my back all along, when I've been working my butt off since January trying to get things ready for the season. This summer has been great for business, and our foot traffic hasn't slowed down. And it won't, not for another few weeks. And now that he's bought Eva's property, things will get even busier.

How am I going to handle it?

I feel my resolve harden; suddenly, my mind's made up. I'm not the one ultimately making the decisions and switching things around. I'm not the one heaping more troubles and concerns on plates already overflowing with responsibilities.

This is no longer my problem. I'm going to give myself a little break. I'm done worrying.

Then, for a brief moment, I have a twinge of regret. What about Pop? How will he manage the day-to-day business of running the restaurant? Opening in the morning, closing out at night, seeing to the suppliers, overseeing deliveries, managing staff. How's he going to do all that, plus play host, fill in as bartender, and keep the customers happy? I've been doing those things up until now; how he's going to manage if I'm not there to help?

Then I remember how he shouted at me. Horrible things were said. *I don't need you. I don't need you at all.*

And no wonder he doesn't need me. Not now, when he has someone else right beside him. Someone I'm sure will be more than happy to fill in.

If Pop thinks he and Mai can run Chuck's together, then the two of them have my official blessing to go ahead and try. I have better things to do.

Like, appreciate the chance to take some time off. Discover what it means to live an ordinary life. Enjoy what little's left of the summer doing the things I want to do.

But what *do* I want? I've been so busy taking care of Pop and the restaurant, I haven't had time to take care of myself.

I head back into the bathroom and towel my hair dry, though by now it's one big, frizzy mess and a lost cause. But who cares? I pop it in a ponytail and ready myself for my adventure. I've already wasted too much time. I have no intention of wasting what's left of this morning.

But I can't help wondering: exactly how long will Chuck's Tavern and Grill be able to get along without me?

CHAPTER EIGHTEEN

~ Running Short-Staffed ~

"I SUPPOSE SHE SENT YOU?"

"Sorry?"

"You know what I mean. You're her intermediary. Well, I'm telling you right now that you can save your breath." I squint at Don from behind the hostess stand. The longer we stand here, the madder I get. This is all Katy's fault. She's the one who landed us in this mess. She should be the one who bails us out. "You'd think she'd be old enough to fight her own battles. Well, you can tell that daughter of mine that if she's got something to say to me, she can get her butt over here and tell me herself."

"Hey, don't get me involved in your family feud," Don says, raising his hands, palms spread wide. "Whatever's going on between you and Katy is strictly your business. I'm here for lunch, that's it. I'm a lover, not a fighter."

"I'm not interested in your love life." Shrugging, I grab a menu. "Come on, we've got an open table for two."

"It's just me."

"Yeah, whatever." A paying customer is a paying customer, regardless of whose side he's on. I shoulder my way through the crowd, Don close behind me, and halt at one of the side booths. "Have a seat."

He eyes it cautiously, then slides across the vinyl bench. "See you got the spring fixed."

I slap the menu on the table. "Beer?"

"Sure," he replies as he glances around the busy restaurant. "Looks like business is good."

"Can't complain," I say, though my feet hurt and my hips ache. I lean against the back of the booth, allowing it to take some of my weight. I haven't worked the floor since that episode with my heart laid me up last month. And while part of me feels good being back in the swing of things, by day's end, my energy is gone. I hadn't realized how much I'd come to depend on Katy until she suddenly wasn't here. Running a restaurant involves a lot of hard work; she made it look so easy, I forgot how hard it actually is. And now the whole shebang is back on my shoulders, I've got to admit that I'm running into problems. I'm not getting any younger, and I can't run this place by myself. Mai's tried her best to pick up the slack, but she doesn't have Katy's expertise or experience, and she can't keep up the pace like Katy can. It's impossible for one person to be in two places at once. And seeing how Katy called in supposedly sick again today, we're super short-staffed.

She's playing games with me and I don't like it. What's her problem? Is she mad because I bought Eva's property? Is it because I fired her friend the felon? Or does this have something to do with Mai?

I eye the floor. Jake's behind the bar, Pete and his crew are working the fryers and grill, and supposedly Mai and

189

Nettie are covering the tables. I spy Nettie at a nearby booth taking an order, but Mai's nowhere to be seen.

"Guess you lucked out," I say in an aside to Don. "You got me as your waitress today."

He grins up at me. "Where's your apron?"

"Keep it up, wise guy," I retort.

"How's the whitefish?" he asks, not bothering to open the menu.

"It was swimming in Lake Michigan yesterday."

"Sounds good. Bring me the whitefish sandwich."

I snatch the menu from his hand. "Chips or fries?"

"Make it fries," he replies. "And my beer."

"You got it," I promise.

"If you're my waiter, does this mean I have to tip you?"

"Very funny," I shoot back, and start for the kitchen to place his order.

"Excuse me." A woman snags my arm as I pass her booth. "Do you work here?"

"Yes, ma'am." I glance up from the noisy din, take in the party of six older women. Empty plates and glasses litter their table. I grab as many dirty dishes as I can safely carry, and load them in my arms. "What can I do for you ladies?"

"You can find our waitress," a second woman, with graying hair and even steelier gray eyes, demands. "She said she'd be right back with our checks, but that was at least ten minutes ago. First, we had to wait for our food, and now we're waiting for our bills. Frankly, we're tired of waiting."

"Coming right up," I say, mentally adding the table to my growing list of things-to-do. Find their waitress, place Don's food ticket, and see to the line of hungry customers crowding out the front door. Where in holy hell are all these people coming from?

"And could you bring us more water?" a third woman adds. "Please?"

"Hey, we could use some water over here, too," calls a man from a booth across the aisle.

"I'll bring a couple pitchers," I promise, kicking into high gear and hightailing it back to the kitchen.

"Hey, you." A man further up the aisle manages to corner me just before I reach the safety of the kitchen. "Who do we need to talk with to get some service around here? No one's taken our drink order yet."

"I'll send someone right over."

"Yeah, well, if they don't show up in the next couple minutes, we're out of here," he replies with a scowl. "Me and my wife are sick of waiting around."

"Yes, sir. Sorry about that." I juggle the dirty dishes in my hands, trying not to focus on the beads of sweat dampening my shirt collar, beginning a slow drip between my shoulder blades. One more thing to add to my list: check the air conditioning system pronto and make sure it's not acting up again. The dining room feels steamier than a hot grill, and that's not good. People want their food hot and their restaurant cold.

"I'll bring out your drinks myself," I say. "On the house. Meanwhile, if you're ready, I can take your order."

Two drink orders, four empty platters, and one pitcher of water later, I finally reach the kitchen, only to find it a hot mess of steaming chaos. With the barbecue grill suddenly on the fritz, Pete's in a foul mood and swearing up a storm.

"You think I can cook with shit for equipment? Somebody better fix this thing fast."

"Hey, watch your damn mouth," I growl. Pete isn't the only one who knows how to swear his way out of a problem.

"Otosan?" Mai hovers at my elbow.

"What now?" I bark, my voice gruffer than I expected.

"I... I'm sorry." She takes a few steps backward.

Crap. I take a deep breath, trying to tamp down my frustration and get myself under control. It isn't Mai's fault that we're three waitresses short, or that my irresponsible younger daughter selected one of the busiest weeks of the season to walk off the job. I blow out the numerous annoyances vexing me and force a smile. "Nothing for you to apologize for."

"You look tired," she says, searching my face. "Are you okay?"

"Nothing a good night's sleep won't cure." I stretch my mouth into a grin so wide my face hurts. "What do you need?"

"The POS is offline, and we can't place orders."

Double crap. It probably needs a reboot or whatever the hell you call it. Katy usually handles that kind of thing. But she isn't here, and I don't have a clue when she plans on coming back.

What if she doesn't come back?

"Give me a few minutes, and then I'll take care of it." I swipe a hand across my forehead, leaving a trail of grimy sweat on my palm. Great. Now I'll have to wash my hands before heading back out on the floor. "I need to get these food orders going first."

"You think I can do more than I'm doing now, you better think again," Pete punctuates each word with a sharp stab of his finger. His face, covered with sweat, blisters an angry shade of red. "I can't cook without a goddam grill."

"Didn't I tell you to watch your mouth?" I caution him, conscious of Mai right behind us. I swing my head, but she's disappeared. "I said I'll take care of it."

"Yeah, well, you better make it quick... that is, if you plan to keep serving food today."

I can't afford having Pete walk off the job. If he does, we'll have to shut down the kitchen. "Sorry, I didn't mean to lose my temper. I'll take a look at the grill right now."

He eyes me over the non-functioning grill, then slowly relents, shrugs. "Yeah, well, whatever." Turning to one of the two deep fryers, he raises a wire basket filled with deep fried shrimp bubbling away in burning oil. He deftly unloads it with a flick of his wrist onto a glistening metal tray. "Order up!" he barks.

"About time," Nettie says, sidling in beside me.

"Don't you start in," Pete says. "You got your food, didn't you?"

"Fin-ally," she says, dragging it out for emphasis.

"I told you not to mess with me."

"Yeah, well, guess what? You mess up in here, and it's me who has to deal with the customer complaints," she snaps. "And believe me, they're complaining today."

"Quit your bitching. You waitresses think everything's so hard. Ha! You don't know how easy you got it."

"You think so?" She snorts. "I'd like to see you give it a try."

"Yeah, well, I just might do that," he says, shoving messy piles of shrimp and fries onto two plates. "It sure as hell beats standing around in a hot kitchen trying to cook on a grill that don't work."

Nettie grabs the two plates. "I'd like to see you spend five minutes trying to explain to people why they've had to wait nearly half an hour for their—"

"I said, that's enough!" I roar, losing my temper for the third time in less than five minutes. "Both of you, just shut up right now!"

A hush falls over the kitchen, and Nettie and Pete stare at me like I just announced all dinners and desserts would be free today.

"You okay, Chuck?" Nettie asks. "You look a little funny."

"Yeah," Pete slowly agrees, a peculiar look on his face as he eyes me over the grill. "You don't look so good. Maybe you should sit down."

"I'm fine," I retort, trying not to panic at the irregular thump-thump-thump pounding inside my chest. The cardiologist warned me not to allow myself to get worked up about things. Too much excitement, he said, isn't good for your heart. It's a good thing my doctor isn't in the restaurant. Last thing I need is someone else hanging around, telling me what to do.

I slide Don's order across the counter at Pete. "I need a whitefish sandwich and fries, and I need it right now."

"You got it, boss," he says, his voice registering only one tenth the resonance it had only moments before.

"You want me to take that order out for you?" Nettie asks. "I can do that."

"Thanks." I lean against the counter and close my eyes. When I press my fingers against the lids, bursts of silver stars explode against a fuzzy black backdrop. Except for the fact it's happening in my head, it's almost like watching fireworks. When was the last time I took the time off to watch real fireworks? I didn't take time off this year, and catch the display. I was too busy closing the restaurant. What if I have another heart attack? What if I don't recover? What if I never live to see another Fourth of July? Fireworks. Family. Fun. Patting my shirt pocket, I come up empty. Damn! Where did I put my nitro? God, I hate getting old.

"Chuck?"

"Huh?" I ask, blinking rapidly to clear my vision.

"Whitefish sandwich and fries." Nettie holds up the plate. "Where do they go?"

"Don McLane. He's at table eight," I say slowly, as much for my own benefit as to make sure she understands my instructions. "And grab him a beer. On the house."

"You got it."

I take another minute, stand there quietly, try not to focus on the continuing commotion surrounding me. I don't dare get involved even if the deep fryer blows up. My top priority right now is to get this galloping heartbeat under control. Dammit, this isn't funny anymore. I'm doing way too much around here. I don't know what kind of game Katy thinks she's playing, but this has gone way beyond being funny. Has she forgotten we're trying to run a business? She'd better get her act together soon, and get back here... or else.

Or else... what? Do I think I can lay down the law, serve her up an ultimatum the way I used to do when she was little? Katy's all grown up. My little girl has disappeared, and there's nothing I can do about it.

I take a deep breath, concentrate on counting my heartbeats. The therapists in cardiac rehab taught me how to breathe correctly, and to focus on meditation—not that I practice it on any regular basis. But what I'm doing now seems to do the trick; the ticker in my chest slows considerably, enough for me to figure it's safe to move. And as soon as things slow down, I'm going upstairs and hunt down those nitro pills. They're probably in the bedroom, still on my night stand where I put them last night. But first, I still have things to do. Standing around won't get the work done.

"Move over, Pete." I start behind the counter, nudge him aside to gain a better position. "Two heads are better than one. Together, hopefully you and me can figure out what's wrong with this grill."

CHAPTER NINETEEN

~ Eat, Drink and be Merry ~

"**I**'M SO GLAD YOU DIDN'T have a problem finding another job," I say. Also gladdening my heart this afternoon: Ellen didn't flat-out refuse my invitation to meet for coffee. I've missed our chats. I've missed my friend. I haven't seen her since our nasty quarrel at The Bungalow. And while it feels as if there's a layer of frost distancing us as we skate around certain issues, at least we're together. We're talking.

"And wow, talk about fast," I add. "It only took you... what? Two days?"

"I was surprised when Penny called," Ellen admits. She opens a creamer, and empties it into her coffee. "She said she'd heard I was available; next thing I know, she's asking if I want to work for her. It was weird. In a good way, I mean. But Penny doesn't even know me. So, how did she know I was looking for a job? I never even filled out one of her applications."

"This is James Bay, remember," I point out. "News travels fast in this town."

And it helps when someone (such as me) places a quick

phone call to a friend (such as Penny), with a glowing recommendation for a former employee (such as Ellen), advising she'd be crazy not to snatch Ellen up while she has the opportunity. *But if Ellen's so great, why isn't she still working at Chuck's?* Penny's question got directly to the heart of the problem. A personality conflict between her and Pop, I assured her, then added my personal guarantee that Penny wouldn't regret hiring Ellen. And that's all it took: one phone call. Now Ellen has that new job she needed, Penny has a valuable employee she can count on, and my guilty conscience has eased considerably. It's a win-win for us all.

"So, how do you like the new job?"

Ellen's face thaws slightly. "It took a few days for me to get used to it. For one thing, getting up so early in the morning. Penny's opens at six, and I need to be there an hour early for the breakfast prep. But I really like it, and I'm glad I took the job."

"I'll bet Penny's glad, too."

"Did you know she's pregnant with twins?" Ellen says. "That's probably why she hired me so quick. She said she wanted to make sure she had a dependable crew in place before the babies are born."

"I'm so happy to hear things are working out." Ellen deserves it.

"It was strange at first. No more working nights, and no more serving alcohol. And the atmosphere is so different than Chuck's. Penny's is open for lunch, though she mostly caters to the breakfast crowd. Men, mainly.

"And the funny thing?" she confides, her voice warming. "It doesn't seem to matter what kind of jobs they have. The tables are filled with construction crews, store owners, doctors, lawyers, judges. Some show up in three-piece suits and others are decked out in jeans and steel-toed boots. But no one cares." She grins. "At that time of day, those guys are only serious about two things: strong coffee and fresh gossip. And Penny's serves up plenty of both."

I can't help laughing. "Remind me to call you when I need to know what's happening in town."

"The pace is fast, but the hours are great. Not that I didn't appreciate you giving me a job," she hastily adds, "but it's like I'm living a completely different life. Take today, for instance. If I was still working at Chuck's, I'd just be finishing up with the lunch crowd, and starting to prep for the dinner shift. And I'd never be having coffee with you this afternoon."

"True," I echo, glancing at the large black utility clock behind the front counter of the fast food restaurant. We're on the outskirts of town, and none of the people I know are away from their offices at two o'clock in the afternoon.

"Speaking of the time," she says, "I have to admit I was a little surprised by your phone call. Shouldn't you be at the restaurant right now?"

"I had some things to do, so I took a few days off." Ellen doesn't need to hear about my problems.

"Good, you deserve some time to yourself. And I'm..." Abruptly she clams up. "Never mind."

"What?" I press, noting the uneasy glance on her face.

"I don't know if I should say anything. I don't want you getting mad at me."

"Are you crazy? Why would I be mad?" I reply, my curiosity meter jumping off the scale. "What is it?"

And just like that, the polar express disappears, leaving no tracks of any tension between us.

"Okay, I know this sounds weird," she says, "but I'm glad I'm no longer working for you. Don't get me wrong," she quickly adds. "I'll always be grateful to you for giving me a job. And I know it caused problems between you and your dad—"

"Ellen, that's not—"

"No, please, let me finish," she prompts. "Let's be honest, Katy. Both of us know he doesn't like me. But that plays into exactly what I want to tell you. Because when I was working at Chuck's, I never felt like I could say what was on my mind. Do you know what I mean? Even though you and I were friends, there was always a wall between us. But now I'm working for Penny, things are different. Our relationship—you and me—that's different. We're no longer employer and employee; we're friends. And I love that. It gives me the freedom to say what I want. I can tell you what I really think."

"And there's something important you want to tell me, right?" I ask, unable to halt the growing smile spreading across my face. I can always count on Ellen to have an opinion, no matter what the subject.

"Absolutely there is," she confirms. "I think you're working way too hard. And you let people take advantage of you. Do you realize how many things you're responsible for? The ordering and inventory, the customers and staff. And Katy, you're so good at what you do, and you make it look so easy. If you weren't around, that restaurant would have to close its doors."

"I'm flattered, truly, but I also think you're giving me way too much credit."

"And you're too modest," she replies. "I hope your father appreciates the job you do."

"He does," I assure her.

"Does he?" she challenges. "Because frankly, sometimes I wonder. I know how much you love him. But when we love someone, it's that very act of loving that gives them an opportunity to take advantage of us. And it would be such a shame if that happened to you. I'd hate to see you get hurt."

I'm not sure what does it: her sympathetic tone and words, my attitude today, or the flat-out relief at knowing I have a friend I can trust. It's been a lonely couple of days. I miss my daily routine. I miss being around people. I miss Don, even though I'm still miffed about the major role he played in the Pop-and-Eva property fiasco. I've been ignoring the numerous voicemails and text messages he keeps sending. And I really miss Pop. I never expected to miss him so much. And suddenly, despite my best intentions and all my lofty promises to keep quiet about the personal struggles going on in my life, everything comes spilling out. I even let slip my fears about Mai trying to replace me.

"Don't worry." Ellen reaches across the table and covers my hand with her own. "Your father loves you, Katy, no matter what you think, or how things are playing out right now."

"He might still love me, but things have changed." How can I explain all this, so it makes sense? "Pop knew I was against buying Eva's property. He knew I thought it was risky, but he went ahead and made the deal anyway. And worst of all, he didn't bother to tell me. I found out from Don."

A weary heaviness tugs at my heart as I remember how hurt and betrayed I felt when Don accidently disclosed the news about the pending sale. Pop never would have gone through with it if he truly cared about my feelings, not in a million years.

And least not in the world pre-Mai.

"I used to think he valued my opinion. But in the end, I guess it didn't matter. And so," I conclude, "I decided to take a few days off to assess and re-group."

Ellen thinks for a moment, then nods. "I don't think it's necessarily a bad thing. Look at it this way, maybe if you're not around, he'll begin to see how much you do, and how much he needs you."

"I don't know. He still has Mai, remember?"

"But she isn't *you*," Ellen reminds me. "Give yourself some credit, Katy."

"Right. But that still doesn't mean—" I break off, ashamed to admit the truth. It's been hard enough to admit it to myself.

"What?" she prompts.

It takes a moment before I can finally respond. "But what if Pop doesn't come around? What if me doing this, taking a step back, only drives him further away? What do I do then?"

"You deal with it. But remember, you don't know for certain that's going to happen. None of us can predict what the future will bring. Right now, the best thing you can do is not think ahead. Try and stay in today."

"Easier said than done," I say, as numerous scenarios involving Pop and Mai tumble through my mind, the same way they've done for the past few days. Mai and Pop. Pop and Mai. I'm no longer part of the equation.

"Cheer up," she says. "Why not use this time for yourself? There's still plenty of summer left. How long has it been since you went to the beach? When's the last time you were on your bike?"

"I don't remember," I admit, thinking of my road bike, safely stashed in a corner of my tiny garage, where it's languished most of the summer. Working twelve-hour days and late shifts isn't exactly conducive to cycling.

"Give yourself some time to relax. Play a little."

"Maybe." I mull over the idea. I've been working hard for what seems like forever. And I can't blame anyone but myself. Pop cautioned me long ago not to make the same mistakes he did, and allow the restaurant to consume my life. As usual, however, I didn't listen. I was so busy playing super-hero-restaurant-manager-daughter-extraordinaire that I somehow lost track of myself.

"What about Don? Maybe the two of you could take a few days, and have a mini-vacation."

"The two of us aren't exactly speaking right now."

"I'm sorry to hear that. He's a good guy," Ellen says quietly. "I always liked him."

"Me too," I muse. Don *is* a good guy. And it's not entirely his fault that the two of us aren't speaking. I'm as much to blame. I can be impatient and demanding, and I know it. I'm hard on the people I love, and it takes time before I trust someone enough to let down my guard, let them into my life. Up until the Pop-Eva disaster, I'd been starting to think I could trust Don. And despite what's happened, deep down in my gut, I still think he has my best interests at heart. I'm lucky he's continued to hang in there. Hopefully he'll continue doing so, and he won't give up on me—on *us*— before I figure out how to work through my troubles.

And it's at that precise moment when the cause of all my troubles walks through the door.

"I don't believe it," I say, sucking in a deep breath and slouching low in my seat.

What's she up to? And who is that man with her?

Ellen frowns. "What's wrong?"

"You won't believe who just walked in. No, don't look!" I hiss, grabbing Ellen's arm and keeping her from turning toward the door. "I don't want them to see us."

"But who is it?" Ellen strains to keep her voice at a low whisper, and not to twist her neck for a good look. "Is it your dad? Is he with Mai?"

"It's Mai," I say, "and she has a guy with her." I duck my head, try to stay inconspicuous. Why here? Why now? James Bay isn't that big. There are plenty of other restaurants in town. Didn't she notice my car in the parking lot? Can't she respect my privacy? Why does she always have to snoop around where she isn't wanted?

"Do you know who he is?" Ellen presses.

I stare at her. If I thought my day was bad before, it's about to get a whole lot worse.

"No, but it looks like I'm about to find out. Brace yourself. Here they come."

CHAPTER TWENTY

~ Will This be Together or Separate Checks? ~

"YOU GONNA INTRODUCE ME TO your friend?" I lean against the bar, peer over my glasses at the character hovering close beside Mai. Who is this guy? Decked out in designer blue jeans, fancy black leather cowboy hat, and mirrored shades dangling from the neck of his shirt. He sure isn't the type we normally see hanging out in James Bay.

"Otosan, this is my friend, Dennis Kailani."

"Chuck Malinski." I stick out my hand, surprised to discover the guy has a nice, firm grip. You can tell a lot about a person by the way they shake hands. And Dennis seems sharp. On his game. Someone to deal with. "Pleasure to meet you."

"Likewise," he says with a squint and a smile. Deep brown eyes, warm brown skin kissed by the sun.

"You from the Islands?" I venture.

"Oahu," he confirms. "Born and raised."

"You're a long way from home," I say, glancing back and forth between them. Mai never mentioned having someone special in her life. So, who is this Dennis character, anyway?

He's traveled a long distance, and flights to and from Hawaii via Northern Michigan don't come cheap.

"You here on vacation or business?" I deliberately allow a thick dose of authoritative curiosity to layer my words. I'm Mai's father. It's my prerogative to play the heavy.

"Dennis and I have been friends for a long time," she says.

Friends? Lovers? Her quick smile betrays nothing.

"Mai's been gone too long. I was getting lonely." One corner of his mouth curves in a lazy smile as he clutches Mai's hand and laces his fingers through hers. "Had to come see for myself what my girl's been up to."

His girl. Now I have my answer, but for some reason, I find myself disappointed. Not with him, but with Mai. Why didn't she tell me? Take me into her confidence? Katy never would have kept him a secret.

I offer a thin smile. "It's always about a girl, isn't it?"

He tilts his head, grin widening as he casts a sideways glance at Mai. "Love makes the world go 'round. Isn't that right, baby girl?"

She looks flustered, and I step up to rescue her. "Been here for a while?"

"Caught a flight up from Detroit this morning," Dennis says. "Beautiful country you've got here."

"It's home," I say. "I suppose you feel that way about the Island."

He touches a finger to his hat. "No place like home, man. Right?"

"Right." I give the restaurant a perfunctory look-around, satisfied to see that things appear to be settling down for the night. With the dinner rush over, our staff—what little we have left—have kicked it down a notch and are taking their sweet time finishing up their daily tasks. Only a few tables are left, lingering over cold coffee and nursing tepid beers. If Katy was here, she'd be bugging me to close the doors and lock up early. But Katy isn't here. And I can't close, not yet. I'm expecting the guy who's buying my car, and until he shows up, the doors stay open. Meanwhile, it's just me by my lonesome. I'm right back where I started, handling things by myself, the same way I did before Katy took over. The bank runs, the ordering; everything's on my shoulders. And not only am I supervising our staff, I'll be closing out tonight.

"You hungry, Dennis?" I asked. "Our kitchen's still open and the grill's hot. We can rustle you up something to eat."

"No, thanks."

"How about a drink?"

He gives me a thumbs-up. "Now you're talking."

We claim seats opposite each other at the staff table. I peer up at Mai. "You're not joining us?"

"I'll get the drinks first," she says.

"Thanks, honey. I'll have a beer. Draft," I add, with a quick glance for Dennis, who shows Mai another of his lazy grins.

"You know what I like," he says.

"Ever been to Michigan before?" I ask as she heads for the bar.

"Nope. Never saw the need to travel much. Everything I wanted I had at home." He pulls off his hat, places it to one side of the table. His eyes search out Mai, chatting with Jake as she loads our drinks on a tray.

"You miss her," I note.

He nods. "The Island's not the same without her."

"The two of you grow up together?"

"Oh, man, no way." A short laugh erupts from his belly. "Her Obaa would have put a quick stop to that. She is one nasty woman."

"I'll drink to that."

His eyes widen. "You've met her?"

"Once," I say, "a long time ago. And believe me, once was enough."

"Man, I hear you loud and clear," he says. "We met last year, and I don't plan on ever going back again." He shudders in mock horror.

"Have you known Mai long?"

"A few years now. A friend of mine owns a kiosk in the mall. I was running it when Mai started working at the jewelry store next door. Once I saw her, I couldn't take my eyes off her, man. And we've been together ever since." He studies her intently as she approaches us with the tray. "I knew right away she was something special."

"Don't believe a word he says," Mai says as she serves our drinks, then joins us at the table, sitting between us. "Dennis can't be trusted."

"Is that so?" He grabs her wrist with a deep-throated laugh. "Says who, baby girl?"

"Says me, that's who," she says. "Stop it, Dennis. Enough is enough." Pulling her hand from his grasp, she massages her wrist, then turns to me and rolls her eyes. "Dennis's problem is that he doesn't know when to stop."

"You're like a drug to me, baby girl. I can never get enough," he croons. "You should know that by now."

"I know lots of things," she chides with an arched look clearly meant for him alone.

I watch Dennis take a sip of the drink Mai delivered. Jack, straight up, I wager. "Make sure she gives you the grand tour of our town. That is, if you plan on staying awhile."

"Oh, I'll be around. I'm not leaving until I get what I came for." Reaching out, he fingers Mai's hair, playing with it until she gently swats him away. Immediately one of his hands strays to the back of her neck, massaging it. "What do you say, baby girl? Wanna play tour guide and show me around?"

"This isn't all fun and games, Dennis," she replies. "I have a job."

"A job?" He hoots with laughter. "Don't tell me you need the money?"

For some reason, his flip manner and the way he's teasing her suddenly irks the hell out of me. "Mai's been working here at the restaurant," I inform him.

His eyebrows lift with mild interest. "Doing what?"

I wait for her to speak up, but Mai ignores him, so I wade in. "A bit of everything. She's doing great."

"Yeah, she's one talented little lady." He glances at Mai. "What's going on in that pretty head of yours? You thinking ahead? Maybe planning to work your way up to manager?"

Her face dissolves in an angry scowl. "Shut up, Dennis."

"She's definitely manager material," I reply, then stop right there. What the hell am I doing? Chuck's already has a manager; not that she's seen fit to grace us with her presence these past few days.

Dennis takes another sip of whiskey, sizes me up over the rim of his glass. "She looks like you, man," he says after a moment's reflection. "Like father, like daughter."

"You don't know what you're talking about," Mai says.

"I know what I see," he retorts. "Faces don't lie." He turns back to me. "Mai's been wanting to meet you for a long time."

I spare a glance for my older daughter. Her appearance in our lives brought about lots of changes; some for the good, others, not so great. But when all's said and done, and no matter what the outcome, I know I'll never regret Mai coming to look for me. The same way I know I'll never turn my back on her.

"Guess you might say it's almost like a family reunion," Dennis says, "seeing how I even met Mai's sister today."

I blink hard. "You saw Katy?"

"We ran into her earlier at a restaurant," Mai says. "Dennis and I met there for coffee, and Katy happened to be there. I introduced them."

"Did she say anything? About Chuck's, I mean," I quickly add, though it's not the question I truly want answered, the question I don't dare ask. Did Katy ask about me? She's about all I could think of today. Toward late afternoon, I was tempted to call, and I nearly did. Only the freak early start to our dinner rush stopped me from picking up the phone. But it's merely a matter of time before I crack. I'm aware things can't continue like this. Katy and I need to make up. We haven't seen or spoken to each other in nearly a week, and every day that passes, the truth weighs heavier in my heart. Part of this—most of it, if I'm being honest—is my fault. I was a jerk, and she called me out on it.

I love her. I miss her. I want Katy back.

"We didn't talk about the restaurant," Mai says. "She was there having coffee with Ellen."

"You mean, the felon?" I say, grunting at the news. Katy

isn't doing herself any favors. The last thing she needs is a so-called friend who sniffs around where she doesn't belong and steals things that don't belong to her. Hopefully Katy will wise up soon. "Mai told me how she caught her lifting money from the till," I tell Dennis. "That's all the proof I needed, and I fired her on the spot. Katy was probably mad about it, but she never should have hired her. Once a thief, always a thief."

Dennis's eyebrows rise. "She did time?"

"They locked her up in the county jail, but if you ask me, they should have slapped her with a lot more. I still don't get why the judge soft-pedaled her sentence. People like her deserve everything they get."

He nods. "Too many people think they can get away with stealing things that don't belong to them. Man, the stories we could tell." He glances at Mai. "Right, baby girl?"

She shrugs.

"Sounds like you've had your share of problems, Dennis," I say.

"Oh, yeah, I've been through it all," he confirms. "You think you know someone, then they go and knife you in the back, prove you wrong." He shakes his head. "It's all about trust, man. Not being able to trust people can destroy your faith in humanity."

"Exactly," I confirm, lifting my beer, chugging the golden foam. I set the empty bottle squarely on the table between us. "So, what type of business are you in, Dennis?"

"Sales."

"Retail?"

"Wholesale," he replies. "I trade in Island commodities."

"Global trading." I nod. "Don't know much about

that. But I do know something when it comes to running a restaurant."

"I'll bet you've got plenty of stories," he guesses.

"You got that right. It's amazing, the kind of crap people think they can get away with in a restaurant. They complain about the food being cold, the service too slow, the prices too high. I say, let them go right ahead and complain. If it's wrong, I'll fix it. But that doesn't mean someone has the right to rob me blind. And if a customer tries to walk off without paying, I'll prosecute, every time. Employees think they can get away with lifting a case of shrimp from the freezer, or stealing from my cash register? They better think again. Keep your hand out of my till, that's what I tell 'em. And they better listen, or they won't be working for me long."

"Sound advice, man." He nods at Mai. "Your dad's a pretty cool guy. I think you can learn a lot from him."

"I'm happy she's here, and I'm happy to teach her." After all, this is a family business, and she's part of the family. She deserves a seat at the table.

Mai leans over, grazes my cheek with a soft kiss. "Thank you, Otosan. You're a very kind and wonderful man."

I beam at the unexpected show of affection. Unlike Katy, Mai's usually quiet and reserved, but she's slowly coming around.

She glances at her watch, then points to it, eyeing Dennis. "It's getting late. We should talk after I finish work and the restaurant closes."

"Naw, that's okay. You take the rest of the night off." She's helped me out the past several nights with some of the simpler tasks involved in closing, but I don't want to impose with her friend in town.

"You're sure, Otosan?"

"Sure as the sun's going to come up tomorrow. Now, go on, get outta here. You don't want to spend the night cooped up in this place. It's a beautiful evening. You and Dennis take a walk on the beach, catch the sunset."

Dennis grins, clamps a firm hand on my shoulder. "You read my mind, man. Baby girl and I have lots of catching up to do." Standing, he lifts his hat and places it squarely atop his head, adjusting the wide leather brim so it covers his eyes. "Thanks again for the drink."

"Stop in tomorrow. I'll buy you lunch."

"Looking forward to it." He salutes me with a quick touch of a finger to his hat.

"Best deep-fried whitefish sandwich in town," I say. "Then again, Mai's pretty proud of the yakitori. She's added it to the menu, and people really like it."

"Mmm, yakitori." He smacks his lips. "One of my favorites. Taste of the Islands."

"Enough with the theatrics," Mai warns with a quick roll of her eyes before turning to me. "Otosan, you're positive you don't need me to stay? I can if you want."

"I'm all set," I promise. "Go on, skedaddle. No need to babysit the old man. I'll be fine."

CHAPTER TWENTY-ONE

~ I Can't Eat Another Bite ~

I NEED TO GO BACK. FORGET that Pop's been careless and insensitive. I'm solely responsible for having landed myself in this mess of misery and self-pity which I've been wallowing in for nearly a week. And *until* I take action—*unless* I take action—nothing will change. Pop's being his usual bull-headed self, and it's painfully obvious he isn't going to hoist the white flag any time soon. But things simply can't be allowed to continue the way they are. First and foremost, I can no longer stomach anymore fighting between us. Plus, I'm worried Pop's in way over his head. If I didn't know it before, I knew it for certain after running into Mai and her friend Dennis while Ellen and I were having coffee. Pop has no idea what Mai's like; no idea what he's up against. I can't stand by and allow him to unknowingly destroy everything he's worked so hard to build up during his life. Dealing with Mai by her lonesome is one thing, but now she's brought in reinforcements from the Islands?

Enough is enough.

So, I'm back.

"Let's leave well enough alone," Pop suggests my first

afternoon back working at Chuck's. It's Saturday of Labor Day Weekend, with all hands-on deck. "You're back, and that's all that matters to me. No need for us to talk about all that junk that happened."

It isn't junk, and he darn well knows it. And maybe he thinks there's no need for us to talk, but he's wrong. Pop and I *do* need to talk... and sooner or later, we will. But for now, I'm content just to be back near him, back on the job. I hadn't thought I'd miss it so much, or miss being around Pop. And right now, despite the fragile truce between us and the shaky ground surrounding our definitions of what being family means, I'm back on the job.

Until I forced myself out the door on my self-imposed sabbatical, I'd never truly understood how much Chuck's has come to be a part of my life. There's a comforting rhythm in the way things flow when you're working in a restaurant. It can be fun chitchatting with the locals who drop by on a regular basis. I like greeting and seating the steady flow of resorters streaming through our doors. I don't even mind picking up a table or two when we're super busy. Compliments, complaints, problem-solving. They're all part of what goes into running a restaurant.

The bell above the door tinkles and two customers straggle in. I glance at Pop, who's currently distracted by the television screen high above the neat rows of gleaming liquor bottles behind the bar. The score is tied and Detroit's about to come up to bat. I grab two menus and nudge him with an elbow. "Go on downstairs and watch the game. I'll take care of things up here."

"You sure? I can stay if you want." He glances around, scans the booths and tables.

We don't need him playing host right now. The restaurant's nearly empty.

"Go have fun." I lightly swat his arm with the menus. "I'll call if we need help."

He nods absentmindedly, rubs his chest with one hand. "Remember that guy who's buying my car, the one who never showed up like he promised? Well, he rescheduled, and now he's supposed to be here in about an hour. Let me know when he shows up."

"Will do," I promise.

"And keep your eye on the grill," he advises. "Pete said it was giving him problems before lunch. We need it up and running for the dinner crowd."

"Yeah, yeah, I've got it covered. Now go on, before somebody hits a grand slam home run and you're not there to see it."

"With the team Detroit's got this year? Ha! That'll be the day." He starts for the back, then hesitates, turns back to face me.

"Something wrong?"

"No." He lingers another moment. Then: "I missed you, Katy-Did. I'm glad you're back."

The soft lilt in his voice tugs at my heart. Maybe I've been too quick to judge. Maybe, when all is said and done, I'll find out Pop felt the same, too. "Ditto."

The table of two turns out to be the chatty type, pestering me with friendly questions about menu recommendations and tourist sites in James Bay. It's a good five minutes before I'm free again. I relieve Nettie from the floor, watching as she heads for the kitchen to grab a fifteen-minute break. I scan the room and take mental inventory of our staff. Pete's

216

behind the grill, with a prep cook nearby slicing tomatoes. Near the dishwasher, a busboy manhandles an empty tub. Out on the floor, the waitress Pop hired during my absence saunters between the tables. I try not to sigh. It'll be a few weeks before she's moving at full speed. Meanwhile, there's no sign of Mai, though I saw her in the restaurant when I came in earlier. Supposedly she's working four tables, according to the schedule someone drafted during my absence. If she feels comfortable handling those, then I'm going to assign her another two tables for tonight's dinner rush. The last thing I need is Mai with free time on her hands. She's already stirred up enough trouble.

I hear her before I finally spot her behind the bar, next to Jake, gaily chatting with him as he fixes a round of drinks. Strike number one. I head in her direction.

"No waitresses behind the bar," I remind her.

"Sorry," Mai says, shooting me a look that's pure evil. She slides away from the counter and resurfaces at my side.

"Catch you later, babe," Jake tells her, bestowing one of his brilliant smiles as he finishes pouring drinks.

She turns her back, so we won't be overheard. "You don't need to be so nasty."

"I'm not trying to be nasty," I reply. "It's one of the rules we have around here. A rule we've always had. No waitresses behind the bar. Or maybe you just forgot."

She *knows* it. I know she does.

"Whatever."

I bite my tongue, and attempt to keep my temper in check. I'm sick to death of the hypocritical persona she brings to the table. Mai's all sweetness and light whenever Pop's around, but remove him from the scene, and the woman displays a soul black as hell and owned by the devil.

"By the way, I'm giving you an extra two tables tonight," I say. "I know you were only scheduled for four, but I think you can handle the load. Unless you have a problem with that," I add.

"As a matter of fact, I do," she answers promptly.

"Excuse me?"

"I already worked lunch, and I'm not working the dinner shift."

I blink, the unexpected insurgency catching me by surprise. "You what?"

"You know exactly what I'm talking about," she retorts. "I'm done working for the day." She tugs at her apron strings, releasing the knot.

"But you're listed on the schedule." I don't have it handy, but I know I saw her name on it.

"You're not listening. Because if you *were*, you'd know that I just now told you I have no intention of working tonight. And even if I did—which I don't—it wouldn't be as a waitress. I'm supposed to be the hostess, remember? You're back. You can handle those tables yourself."

Who does she think she is, telling me which job assignments she's going to cover, and how I should do my job? Mai might think she can pull rank over the rest of our restaurant crew, but she can't do it to me. I'm the general manager. I'm the one who gets to decide who does what.

"Look," I say, struggling to keep my voice under control, "I don't know what your problem is, and frankly, I don't care. But this is Labor Day weekend. We need every available person on staff. That includes you. You're the one who decided to work here when Pop asked. You could have said no, but you didn't."

Mai shoves her apron into my hands. "I said I'm done working today."

I'm not about to allow her to suck me into playing semantics, or whatever other little game she's chosen to amuse herself with today. "Let's see what Pop says about it."

Her face morphs into a satisfied smirk.

"*Otosan*," she says, enunciating the three syllables slowly and distinctly, as if I'm a first-grader in need of extra guidance, "knows all about it. If you'd bothered to ask him, you'd know that."

"No way."

"Bye-bye, I'm leaving." She wiggles her fingers at me in a dismissive wave.

"You can't." Having Mai around is torture on any given day, but if she leaves, we'll be facing a potential disaster. "You can't just walk off the floor," I say, in one last-ditch effort to keep us fully staffed.

"No? Watch me," Mai advises. And then, to my utter disbelief, she does exactly that.

***

Somehow—the operative word here being *somehow*—we make it through the dinner rush. When the last customers finally straggle out the door, I rush to lock up behind them. We still have another two days to go before this weekend is over. "Good job, everybody," I say, trying to boost team spirit.

"I'm going home," Nettie says. "I need to get these shoes off my feet before they swell up worse than they already are."

"Thanks again for your help tonight, Nettie," I say. "And thanks for taking over part of Jenny's section. We would never have been able to manage without you."

Nettie rolls her eyes at the mention of our new waitress who, during the height of our dinner rush, managed to shatter a steaming tray of freshly washed glasses by filling them with icy pop, spilled a plate of barbecued ribs in a customer's lap—not once, but twice—and, despite the fact our POS is available to accurately assist, continued tallying up incorrect bills throughout the night. Jenny's sorely lacking in common sense, physical co-ordination, and rudimentary math skills. Why Pop hired her is beyond me.

"Hopefully Her Royal Ditziness shows up tomorrow with her brains intact," Nettie tosses over her shoulder as she heads for the door.

"'Night, Nettie," Pop calls.

I sink down in an empty chair beside him. "Well, tonight will go down as one for the books."

"Yep," he says, rubbing his forehead.

He sounds and looks more tired than usual. "You okay?"

"Lots of stuff going on." He shrugs off my concerns.

"Lots of caffeine going on," I remark, eyeing his coffee cup. "I thought your doctor told you to limit yourself to one cup per day."

He snorts. "Yeah, well, he says lots of stupid things. I'm starting to think the guy's a quack. Like I'm gonna drink that decaf crap."

Vintage Pop. God, I missed him. *"Coffee, black—"*

"And nothing fancy in it," he says, rounding out the chorus. "Am I right, or am I right?"

"I guess that depends on who you're talking to. I'm not sure your cardiologist would agree."

"Ha! What he doesn't know won't hurt him."

We sit for a few moments, each alone with our thoughts. Even though we're not talking, it doesn't matter. For the first time in weeks, there's no edge between us, only a comfortable silence that feels nice. Like, being home.

"Guess Jenny isn't exactly working out," he finally says.

"Guess not," I agree.

"Though I suppose we should keep her on through the weekend," he muses. "Probably a good idea."

"Probably," I echo, trying not to calculate the tally of broken dishes and upended dinners that are sure to accumulate before both the holiday and Jenny's brief stint working at Chuck's are over.

"What's the matter with people anyway?" he suddenly asks. "Why is it so hard to find competent help?"

"I don't know, Pop. I wish I did." It's a common complaint with local retailers, including the restaurants, clothing shops, grocery store, and our local pharmacy.

"It wasn't like this when I started the restaurant. Back then, I had plenty of good help."

I nod silently, thinking of Pete and Nettie. They're both seasoned employees and the only remaining members of Pop's original crew.

"We'll have to hire a few more people before the color season starts. Those tour buses are going to start showing up in town before we know it."

"I'll run an ad in *The Journal* next week," I promise. "I'm thinking another line cook, a dishwasher, maybe four waitresses?"

He nods, and swigs a last gulp of cold coffee. "Sounds good."

"Speaking of staff," I venture, "I probably need to tell you about something that happened earlier." Better I'm the one who brings up the issue of Mai's refusal to work, rather than have her running to him, complaining about me.

"What's going on?"

"It's about Mai."

Pop eyes me cautiously. "What about her?"

I pause, suddenly wondering if I'm doing the right thing by choosing to talk to him about this. Things have been going great between us all night. The last thing I want to do is wreck what we're building on.

"Come on, what's this about?" he presses.

It's too late for a reboot. I choose my words with caution. "I suppose you noticed she wasn't working tonight?"

He folds his arms across his chest and looks at me.

"She said she cleared it with you," I add.

"That's right," he replies. "Her friend Dennis is still in town and she wanted the night off." His eyes narrow. "You've got a problem with that?"

"No, not exactly." I bite my lip, trying to figure out the best way to proceed.

"Good," he says curtly. "She's been working hard around here. She deserved a break."

"She's a great asset to Chuck's." I hurry to agree. "And she does a great job. Customers love her."

It pains me to say it, but it's the truth. In fact, the only person who doesn't seem to love Mai is me.

"So, what's the problem?"

I should have left well enough alone. And now there's

no way out. And with the scowl on Pop's face deepening, I decide it's best to get this conversation over with, and quick.

"Mai told me she doesn't want to be a waitress anymore." The words rush out of me. "She only wants to be a hostess."

"That's it?"

What does he mean, *that's it*? Isn't that enough?

"I was hoping you could talk to her," I stumble on. "I tried to make her understand what we're up against when we run shorthanded. I told her everyone needs to step up and pitch in."

"Which she has," he says coolly. "What exactly is your point?"

"I guess it's that she wouldn't listen to—"

"No, you're the one who needs to listen," he says, crooking his finger at me. "I'm only going to say this once, so listen up good. Mai didn't go applying for the job, remember? I asked her, and she agreed. But she didn't have to. She did it out of the goodness of her heart. If I was you, I'd think about that long and hard. Seems like you should be thanking her, instead of complaining about when and what she chooses to do."

"But—"

He slams his palm against the table. "I said that's the end of it. I don't want to hear anymore! This isn't Mai's problem, and it isn't mine, either." Standing, he gives his chair a hard shove. "You're the manager around here, remember? If you have a staffing problem, then you need to figure it out. But don't go blaming Mai." He glares at me. "Now, is there something else you need to talk about, or are we done here?"

My face burns as hot and raw as if I'd been slapped. Though neither of my parents subscribed to the notion of corporal punishment, I'm sure this is exactly what it would feel like: degrading, humiliating. Why is Pop being so sharp with me? Are his meds off?

"I guess not."

"Good. I'm going to bed."

He stomps off, leaving me to sit alone with my thoughts. It's hard to wrap my brain around what just happened, especially since things had been going so well. But now, thanks to Mai, tonight's turned out to be yet one more in a string of major fiascos. I should have kept my mouth shut. Why did I think he'd be open to listening to me share my misgivings about her? If anything, it's pushed him right over the edge. Pop's furious, and I don't see him relenting any time soon. As far as he's concerned, Mai can do no wrong, and he'll defend her with every breath. Meanwhile, I've been relegated to younger-sister-status. And if I'm not careful, I'll soon be known as the bitchy one who constantly gripes and complains when things don't go her way.

Is it true? Am I being a bitch, ready to pounce on the slightest thing that advances my own interests? Do I relish the idea of someday being able to label her as a fraud and fake? Maybe I'm not being fair. Maybe if Mai and I had grown up together, it'd be a different story. If she'd been around when I was a kid, if she'd always been a part of my life, maybe I wouldn't resent her presence so much. She'd be part of the scenery, and I'd think of her as my big sister. I would have grown up happy.

I briefly chew on that thought, then bring myself up short. Am I crazy? There's no way I'd be happy having her around—in the restaurant *or* my life.

No way in hell.

Bouncing to my feet, I head for Jake's till. My adrenalin's

flowing, and I'm determined to put the energy to good use. I grab the credit card receipts, and tonight's batch report which Jake ran before he clocked out, and begin reconciling the accounts.

One hour later, I'm still at it.

"You've got to be kidding me," I mutter to myself, staring at the tape. No matter how hard I try, I can't get the cash to balance against the receipts. The drawer is off by an odd amount equaling roughly close to fifty dollars.

"*Any more shortages, overages, I want to hear about them,*" Pop's said more than once.

The last thing I want to do is head upstairs and give him the bad news. As he'd so succinctly pointed out to me not that long ago, I'm the general manager of Chuck's. It's my responsibility to deal with things like the shortage tonight.

But it's also my responsibility to report shortages to Pop.

Damned if I do, and damned if I don't.

Not to mention, the one glaring fact that keeps spinning in my brain. Pop won't like hearing it, but numbers don't lie. The truth is, we're facing a shortage tonight… despite the fact Ellen's no longer on staff.

Someone else stole the money.

Someone else has been stealing money all along.

And when it comes to the question of *who*, I have no doubt as to who precisely that someone might be.

I grab the cash, receipts, tape, and stuff them in the money bag, then cram it in the cash drawer, slamming it shut. Then I head upstairs to Pop's apartment. The more I think about Ellen, how Mai accused her of lifting cash from the till, and how she lost her job, the madder I get. And Pop's going to be plenty mad, too. He won't like hearing one of his daughters declare the other one to be a thief. But he's going to hear it, the whole sordid story. Because I'm not leaving until we finally have it out.

It's after eleven. Using my key, I let myself into Pop's apartment. All the lights are blazing, and from the living room's big screen TV, the familiar voice of the local sports announcer drones on about Detroit's doomed attempt to make the post-season playoffs. Pop's chair is empty. An empty pink plastic bottle stands on the nearby table, cap unscrewed, remnants of its thick chalky contents coating the inside. Pop's always been prone to a touchy stomach, and at one point in his life, lived on antacids. But as far as I know, he hasn't touched them in weeks.

Not since his latest heart attack.

"Pop?"

His bedroom door is half-open, and I give a tentative knock, then peek inside. The bed is empty, the sheets and blanket undisturbed, crisp and tucked in the military fashion he learned as a U.S. Marine. I cross the bedroom to the bathroom door, which stands ajar.

"Pop? Are you okay?"

When no answer comes, I peer around the corner.

And then I see him.

"Pop!"

I rush through the door. Pop lays crumpled on the cool tile floor. His eyes are closed. I sink to my knees, huddle over him, gagging at the horrible sweet stench of vomit dribbling from his mouth, congealing in a pool of nastiness around his head. He's been throwing up vomit and blood.

He isn't breathing.

CHAPTER TWENTY-TWO

~ Is There Anything Such as a Two Course Meal? ~
~ Part 1 ~

HOSPITALS ARE ALL ABOUT PAIN. Pain for patients, pain for their loved ones. For me, the pain is twofold. Part is waiting for news—any kind of news—about Pop. The other part is putting up with Mai, who's just rushed through the emergency room doors. Her cheeks are flushed, her eyes are panicky, and her voice screeches high as she demands details.

"Is it his heart? What are the doctors saying?"

"It's his gallbladder," I say, relaying news I learned moments before Mai showed up. I lean against the cinderblock wall, clutching tight to Pop's dog tags, which one of the nurses removed from around his neck when he was admitted. Right now, with my world in full tilt, I'm not surrendering the tags to anyone; it's like hanging onto a little piece of Pop.

"Are they sure it's not his heart?" she demands. "Tell me the truth, or else."

"Or else what?" I blow out a deep breath, struggling to keep my irritation at a manageable level as I realize Mai's as upset as me. "Look, at this point, I'm not sure about anything.

All I know is what they told me. They've already done two EKGs, and both showed his heart is fine. Supposedly, his heart enzymes look okay."

"Why do they think it's his gallbladder?"

"His blood work indicated an infection. They did an ultrasound, and it showed his gall bladder is seriously inflamed."

"What are they going to do about that? Will he be all right?" she presses. "Does it mean surgery? What else did they say? I want to know."

"And I'll tell you, if you shut up and give me a chance." Instantly I regret the harsh words. If Mai talked to me like that, I'd be furious. *Keep it together, Katy*. There's no need to be mean to her, I remind myself. Yes, we're both stressed. Being called to the ER in the middle of the night is a quick way to send anyone's stress levels soaring. Add that to the already strained relationship between us, and things are tenuous at best.

But at least she showed up. Mai cares enough about Pop that she came running over here when I called.

And at least I made the call. It would have been so much simpler on me without having her around; I could have spared myself the grief. In fact, those first five minutes alone in the ER, I debated the pros and cons of doing exactly that. Getting through this would have been so much easier without her around, especially since my thoughts keep circling back to the argument Pop and I had last night about Mai… how he defended her, then stomped out of the restaurant and headed upstairs. Hours later, I found him on his bathroom floor. My fault. All my fault.

No matter what I thought of her, no matter what's happened

between us; no matter if I'm correct and she does turn out to be a thief, I had to let Mai know what was happening. There'll be time enough later for accusations and recriminations, and rebuffing the excuses and alibis she'll probably invent. But not tonight. Tonight's about doing the right thing. I'd already messed up lots of my life, but I couldn't risk messing this up. If anything happened to Pop, I'd never be able to live with myself, knowing that I hadn't made the effort, but instead, allowed my selfishness to win.

Because no matter what I personally think of Mai, I know how much Pop loves her. He's accepted her as his daughter, and he loves her. He'd want her to know.

In the end, I had no choice.

And thank God for small favors. At least Mai didn't arrive with Dennis in tow. I only met the guy once, but that was enough. I don't like him, and I don't want him around. Not with Pop sick. Not even with Pop healthy.

"I'm sorry," I say. "I didn't mean to snap at you."

She silently pouts, her dark eyes fixated on me.

"They've put him on an antibiotic for the infection, and he's scheduled for surgery at six a.m. The doctor said that removing the gallbladder should be a simple procedure. If all goes well, Pop might actually be able to come home sometime later tomorrow."

"Tomorrow." Her face, already a map of worry lines, adds a few more roads. "Tomorrow sounds very soon."

I nod. For once, we're in complete agreement. "I think so, too."

"When can we see him?"

"I don't know. They didn't say." I glance up and down the corridor. If only there were someone we could ask. But no doctors or nurses are in sight, only a few aides gowned in differing hues of faded blue wandering in and out of glassed-in cubicles.

"I hate hospitals," Mai murmurs. "Nothing good happens in the hospital."

I nod. My experience with hospitals hasn't been the greatest.

"The last time I had a call in the middle of the night, my grandfather was dying. I rushed to see him, but I was too late. He was already gone."

"Mai, I'm sorry," I say softly.

She lifts her head and gazes at me a long moment. "Are you?"

I draw in a fast breath. Why is she challenging me? Then I suddenly recognize that she's probably hurting, too. I take in another breath. It will be up to me to decide which way things evolve.

"Yes, I am," I reply. "I know how much it can hurt, losing someone you love. And especially if it's sudden. It was like that with my mother. She died in a car accident. And just like happened with you and your grandfather, I never got the chance to tell her goodbye."

Mai keeps her silence, while I'm lost in my memory of that horrible day, the car crash which took my mother's life while I was confined to bed with an infection and a lingering fever. There was no time for my mother and me to make up. No time for me to tell her I was sorry.

But Pop isn't going to die. I'll see him again, and we'll have the conversation we need to have. And, unlike what happened with my mom, I'll have a chance to make this better. Pop and I are going to have a second chance.

They allow us to see him for a moment before he's wheeled down the corridor for one last series of tests. His eyes brighten as he catches sight of Mai, and his first smile is for her. And if I hadn't known it earlier, then I know it now: I did the right thing by calling Mai.

Then Pop reaches for me, clasps my hand, throws me a weak smile. I lean over the hospital stretcher, brush a kiss against his cheek. The fresh stubble of his gray-and-white whiskers scratches my skin in the all-too-familiar prickly tickle that made me squeal in delight when I was a kid.

"I love you, Katy-Did," he whispers, and squeezes my fingers.

"I love you too, Pop."

Then he's gone, scurried away by hospital staff. Mai chooses to stand and pace the floor, while I settle into a chair. I pull out my phone, check emails, scroll through my texts.

"There's nothing I hate more than waiting around," she says after a few moments. One toe of a stylish pump rat-a-tats against the tiled floor.

"I know exactly what you mean."

"How much longer is this supposed to take?"

"I don't know." I say, thinking of the time I've already spent here. Last night was insane, with the apartment door wide open, the medics and their steel gurney, and Pop strapped in tight. Strobe lights flashing a crazy red and white zig-zag that puddled against the dark street as the ambulance pulled away, me watching from the doorway. And suddenly, I find myself wondering: did I close the door? We left in such a hurry. And what about the lights? I flip to my phone, link to the live feed provided by the security cameras mounted around the restaurant. Pop's apartment isn't wired, but twelve different cameras provide live links to Chuck's.

I scroll through the footage, cringing as I catch sight of all the restaurant lights still ablaze. The front door is closed, but I'm guessing that if I didn't take time to snap off the lights, then I didn't take time to lock the door.

Leaping to my feet, I grab my purse. "I have to leave. I won't be long."

Mai shoots me a questioning look. "Where are you going?"

I hate leaving Pop, but I don't have much choice. "Back to the restaurant. I don't think I locked up. I can't leave it like that until morning."

"You stay," she says. "I'll go."

"No, thanks, that's all right. I can't let you do that."

"Yes, you can," she insists. "Obviously, someone needs to take care of things, and it should be me."

"Why?" But Mai's our thief. She can't be trusted... or can she?

"I should think that's obvious. I'm not the one Otosan needs to be here when he gets back. You are." Opening her clutch, she hunts for her keys. "Now quit wasting time and tell me what you want me to do."

My hesitation melts. While I hate the thought of her prowling around the restaurant, what's the point in arguing? She's lived with Pop for weeks now, and she's worked at Chuck's nearly as long. And while Mai can access the computer, she doesn't know any of the codes or passwords used by Pop and me. She'll be in and out; lock up, turn out the lights. It shouldn't take long.

And I can stay with Pop.

Gratefully, I hurriedly tick off a list of to-do things for

her. "Be sure and double-check the front door when you lock it. Sometimes it sticks. And don't forget to go upstairs. We left in a rush, and I'm pretty sure the apartment door is open."

"I will," she promises, keys in hand.

She doesn't have to do this. I don't have to let her.

"Thank you," I say, allowing the words to slip from my tongue before any filters can kick in and I revert to my earlier selfishness. Mai's doing me a favor, and I'm thankful she's helping me out. She's helping Pop out. "I appreciate it. And as soon as they bring Pop back and they let me see him, I promise I'll tell him why you left."

"Be sure and let him know I'm coming back," she reminds me.

"I will."

With a quick nod, she turns and disappears out the door.

It's another hour before Pop's finally settled in his hospital room for what's left of this long night. I chat with him briefly, make sure he's comfortable. His IV-cocktail of morphine and antibiotics have kicked in, and it's clear he's feeling no pain. He also can't remember anything from five minutes before, or why he's in the hospital. "Your gallbladder," I remind him, adding that the doctors have added him to their morning's surgery schedule. "Yes, Mai was here," I assure him. "Yes, she's coming back."

Then he sleeps, and I sit back, waiting.

Ten minutes later, I'm still waiting. Where is Mai? She should have been back by now. The hospital is only six blocks from downtown. I step outside Pop's room and make the call, listening in growing frustration as Mai's phone continues to loop to voicemail. After the third attempt to reach her, I give up and leave a message, then send her a quick text.

Maybe she'll respond to that. I can't imagine anything bad has happened to her. After all, this is James Bay.

After another five minutes, when she still hasn't responded to my text or voicemail, I weigh my options. The corridor outside Pop's room is empty, the quiet broken only by the intermittent eruption of a loud snore coming from the next room. I glance at Pop's door, knowing he'll be headed off to surgery in an hour or so. I should be in there with him, holding his hand. Still, I hate the thought of giving up without having any answers to my questions.

Then again, maybe I haven't been paying attention. Maybe, instead of asking, I should have been looking.

I pull up the live feed provided by the surveillance cameras positioned around Chuck's. Part of me relaxes as I take in the footage. It's obvious Mai has been there. The last time I viewed the feed, the dining floor and kitchen lights were blazing, but everything is dark now, with the tables and chairs shrouded in shadows. The kitchen is a gloomy gray maze of stainless steel counters, cooking grills, and dishwasher.

But where's Mai? Did she swing by the restaurant first, and then head upstairs to Pop's apartment? I scroll further, checking camera angles. Dining room, kitchen, front door.

No Mai.

Finally, I pull up the basement feed, and that's when I spot it. The unsteady beam of a flashlight coils its way around the floor, snaking across the pale linoleum, up the office door. Mai stands directly in front of the door, one hand clutching the flashlight, the other positioned boldly on the knob. I hold my breath, taking in the sight of her. Mai has no business being down there. I never told her to check on Pop's office. Besides, there's nothing there to concern her. His desk is littered with paperwork, and the safe is locked up tight, the same as Pop's office. Securely locked.

Or so I thought.

I watch in disbelief as Mai cracks open the office door, and slips inside.

CHAPTER TWENTY-THREE

~ Is There Anything Such as a Two Course Meal? ~
~ Part 2 ~

"WHAT THE HELL DO YOU think you're doing?" I burst through the basement office door, my words shooting through the air like a live round of ammunition.

Mai, crouched in front of the office safe, rights herself and turns to face me.

"Katy." Her voice is sharp, but her dark eyes are filled with alarm. "What are you doing here?"

"What am *I* doing? More like, what are *you* doing?" I made the drive from the hospital in record time, hands gripping the wheel in the ten-two position, heart pounding, anger mounting with every corner I took. By the time I busted through the door, my fury was bordering on rage. "Because the way I see it, you're the one who's breaking into our safe. How much money do you plan to steal?"

"It's not what you think."

"Really? You could have fooled me." I glare at her. "I think you'd better start explaining, and tell me exactly why you're down here. And I'd also like to know how you got in. This office is locked."

"I didn't break in." Her fists clench in a defiant pose. "Otosan gave me a key."

"Is that so?" I ask, attempting to keep a cool head. The news that Pop himself gave her carte blanche to his personal and business affairs makes me feel like losing it completely. But I can't afford to give in to my anger until I find out why she's in Pop's office and monkeying with our safe. Surely Pop wouldn't—he couldn't—have been so stupid as to hand her access to our cash. Only two people in the world have the safe's combination: Pop and me.

Or is it three? I glance at the safe. The door is still shut.

"What about the safe?" I challenge. "Did he give you the combination to that, too?"

"A moot point, baby sister," a low voice drawls from behind me. "When it comes to opening safes, Mai here is an expert."

Whirling around, I come face to face with Dennis, lounging against the door frame. The red hibiscus flowers of his Hawaiian shirt are the exact same color of the instant rage exploding in my head as I watch him casually salute me with two fingers to the brim of his stupid cowboy hat.

"You didn't know?" he says, relishing my astonishment and disgust. "Ah, let me tell you, Mai's a girl of many talents. You wouldn't believe all the things she knows how to do. Crack safes, fence jewelry, steal from her friends. Yeah, your big sister Mai is full of surprises."

"Leave her alone, Dennis," she says in a fierce hiss.

"Oh, I don't think so." Reaching out, he snaps on the light.

I catch the glint of burnished metal peeking out beneath his gaudy shirt at the top of his jeans. With a little shudder, I realize that Dennis has a gun.

"So, little sister decides to join us. Cool." He folds his arms across his chest. "Now this party can get started."

I dial my anger down to the lowest setting possible. The last thing I want is to do is find out first-hand if his gun is loaded.

"Why are you doing this?" Turning, I confront Mai in a shaking voice. Beads of sweat pop on the back of my neck, and I feel the damp moisture spreading under my arms. "After all Pop's done for you… how could you steal from him?"

"The old man?" Dennis steps up. "Yeah, Mai said he's in the hospital again. Tough breaks. Sorry to hear that. But hey, it's the law of natural order, or something, isn't it? You get old, and your body goes to hell, right? And talk about perfect timing. No need for us to do anything to get him out of the way. His gallbladder did it for us. Maybe I should send him a thank you note." He pauses, barks a short laugh. "Naw, I guess not. But give the old man my regards."

"Leave her alone, Dennis," Mai repeats. "She's not a part of this."

"That so?" he scoffs. "I'm thinking maybe she should be."

"That wasn't part of our deal," she insists. "I said I'd get the money for you, and I will. But not if you involve her."

His eyes narrow. "What's up with you, girl? You trying to tell me you got all caught up in this family stuff, and suddenly decided to grow a conscience? You need to be taking care of business, baby girl, not taking care of baby sister."

"This has nothing to do with her, and you know that as well as I do."

"You think I give a flying fuck?" Dennis shouts, his face

darkening in an angry red visage. In one fluid movement, he pulls out the gun and points it at Mai.

"Now maybe you'll think I'm serious," he says. "And I am, baby girl. Dead serious."

"You don't want to do something stupid," she says in a voice much braver than anything I'd be able to manage. "Put the gun away, Dennis."

"Shut up and open the safe." He urges her along with a quick thrust of the gun. "No more fun and games."

"Why are you doing this?" I ask him, even though I know I could end up very sorry for daring to open my mouth. Not to mention, I could also end up dead. "What do you want?"

"I'm only here to get what's mine. Isn't that right, Mai?"

"I told you, Dennis: leave her out of this."

I glance uneasily between the two of them. While Mai isn't backing down, she doesn't look or sound nearly as fearless as she did just a few minutes ago.

"You don't want baby sister to know?" He laughs. "Aw, come on, there's nothing wrong with having a little fun. Maybe Pops can't handle hearing the truth about his oldest daughter, about how she likes to steal people's money. But this one—" He leers at me, allowing his gaze to linger, slowly crawling the length of my body. "She looks plenty old enough to hear the truth. Oh, yeah," he croons, "plenty old enough. Baby sister is all grown up. She's a big girl now."

I force myself to stand there without flinching as he boldly stares me down. I've never been so scared in my life, but I refuse to give him the satisfaction of knowing his words have gotten to me.

"You know," he finally says, with a sideways glance at

Mai, "I'm thinking maybe we should let baby sister here take over."

"No," Mai says.

"Aw, why not?" He shifts his gaze back in my direction and winks at me. "I bet you could open this safe with your eyes closed, am I right?"

"Stop it, Dennis." Mai's fists curl into two tight balls as she stands her ground, small and fiercely defiant. "I told you I don't want her involved."

But I *am* involved, no matter what she thinks or says. I've been involved since that day she walked into our restaurant. And in some weird way which I barely understand, I'll grudgingly admit a sudden admiration and awe for Mai. Dennis has at least six inches and fifty pounds on her, not to mention a gun pointed at her chest. But she's not letting any of that stop her. Mai continues to resist, and she looks ready to wage an all-out battle with him.

Simply to protect me.

"Get out of the way." I shove her aside and plunk myself squarely in front of the safe.

"Katy, trust me, you don't want to do this," she cautions.

"Well, guess what?" I ask, feeling strangely calm and detached. "I don't think I have much choice… that is, unless your plan includes us being shot. And while I don't know about you, I'd prefer not to end up dead."

Dennis is openly laughing. "You never told me baby sister had a kick-ass sense of humor."

I'd like to kick his ass, all right; instead, I keep my mouth shut and begin working on the combination, fuming as I think about the nice piece of change Dennis will get out of this deal. Normally the safe holds five hundred dollars and some rolled coins, but with this being a holiday weekend, Pop upped the ante to one thousand dollars. And though today's deposit is still upstairs in the till, there's bound to be some start up cash for tomorrow's run. Then again, who cares? Dennis's snub-nosed gun planted between my shoulder blades proves a great incentive. I prefer to stay alive, thank you very much, and I intend to give him every bit of change we find in the safe. Maybe there's a few thousand dollars, at most; but Pop has plenty of insurance on the restaurant. Money can be replaced, but there's no replacing people, as he always says. So, Dennis gets whatever cash is available, and Mai and I get to live. Sounds like a fair trade to me.

With Dennis peering over my shoulder, I punch in the code, suck in a deep breath, and yank open the safe.

"Oooh, nice!" he croons, his breath hot and heavy against my ear. "Jackpot!"

I can hardly believe what I'm seeing. The safe is crammed with cash; stacks and stacks of neatly wrapped bundles. One hundred-dollar bills, bundled together like Monopoly money. Where in holy hell did Pop get all this money?

"Get the fuck out of my way." Dennis brusquely shoves me aside.

I sit back on my heels, wordlessly watching as he gleefully drags out one, two, five, ten bundles of cash. From the look of things, I'm guessing there's easily more than ten thousand dollars.

"And you told me I was wasting my time," he says, aiming his remark at Mai as he grabs an empty leather duffel bag near the door. Quickly he begins shoving the money inside. Finally, when the safe is empty, he zips the bag shut, bounces to his feet, and faces us.

"Both of you, over there." With the gun, he gestures toward the innermost corner of the room. "Move it. Now. Down on your knees."

"Don't be stupid," Mai warns. "You don't want to do this."

"Goddammit. Quit telling me what to do." The snarl rips through his words and across his face. "You've been yapping all night, and I'm sick of hearing it."

Mai clamps her mouth shut, and I hold my breath, not daring to move. Things were bad enough when I had his gun lodged sharp in my back, and I was trying to open the safe. But this is worse. Much worse, I realize, especially as I glimpse the panic beginning to flicker in Mai's eyes.

"You heard me. Move." Dennis waves the gun, prodding the two of us into the corner.

We huddle together on the floor, her head close to mine. Mai's breath comes in ragged little puffs, and I suddenly smell her fear, a thick cloying stink seeping through her skin. Knowing she's afraid scares me more than anything else happening. Mai's been brave through it all, but she's suddenly lost her nerve.

And Dennis knows it. Taking aim, he lands a swift hard kick against her leg with the toe of his leather boot. "Bitch. When I think of what you did—"

"Don't you touch her," I growl, my words and fury marching out of my throat before my better sense shuts me up. "Don't you dare hurt her."

He flinches, rearing back with a surprised look.

"Mai's right," I say, launching a second volley of attack before either can react. "You'd be stupid to try anything, especially if you killed us."

"Think so?" He smirks.

242

"I know so," I shoot back. "You'd never get away with it. The police would be on you so fast."

"In this hick town?" he scoffs.

There are moments in your life when you realize you won't take anymore. And for me, this is one of those moments. Pop's scheduled to be wheeled into surgery any minute, and he'll be all alone if anything happens to Mai or me. I can't let that happen. Pop always taught me to fight back against bullies. And if I've ever come up against a bully, tonight is the night. Dennis is the worst kind of bully, and I've had enough of his nastiness.

"James Bay might be a little town, but we're not hicks." Rising from my knees, I rear up to my full height of five foot ten. Dennis aims the gun at me, but I don't budge. When it comes right down to it, bullies usually are nothing but bluster and bragging; I'm about 99% sure he won't shoot. And though having a loaded gun pointed at your head is a great incentive to do what you're told, I refuse to be intimidated or browbeaten by this man any longer.

"I don't know who you are, or what you came here for," I say, "and frankly, I don't care. You've got your money, and that's what you wanted, right? So, take it and go. Get out of our restaurant and leave us alone."

Dennis blinks, then abruptly throws back his head and laughs. It's a deep throaty laugh that suddenly puts the fear of God in me. For sure, I've gone certifiable, taking a chance on talking back to him the way I did. I must be crazy. The guy is angry, and—more important—he has a gun. For all I know, he's going to pull the trigger. Who knows what he's capable of?

"Man, oh man, talk about an attitude. Who knew?" He

chuckles to himself. He wipes a few leftover tears from his eyes as his laughter slowly subsides. "You should be proud of your baby sister," he says to Mai, "sticking up for you like that."

But Mai isn't responding. She kneels with her head bowed, swaying back and forth, moaning nonsense.

"Typical," he says, grimly shaking his head. "That grandmother of hers did a real number on her."

"Are you going to shoot us?" I ask.

He glances back at me, barks a short laugh. "You want me to?"

"You heard what I said before," I say, swiftly shaking my head. "Just take the money and go."

Then, to my disbelief, Dennis lowers the gun. He stashes it inside his waistband, grabs the duffel bag with one hand, then turns to me with his other palm open.

"Sorry, baby sister, but I need your cell phone. I've already got baby girl's. Now I want yours."

Wordlessly I fish it out of my pocket, and turn it over to him.

Grinning, he tosses it inside the duffel bag atop the cash. Then nodding, he dips his head, touching two fingers to his hat. "Ladies, it's been a pleasure."

Dennis slips out the door fast and silent, the same way he entered. I watch him fade away, not daring to move, my every heartbeat pounding in rhythm with his heavy tread as he takes the steps and disappears upstairs.

I glance in Mai's direction. How long do we wait? Is he still in the restaurant? I thought things were bad while he held us at gunpoint, but now he's disappeared, it's even worse. It's only when you realize you've survived that the fear hits.

Maybe it's because you know how fast it happened, and you understand how quickly it could happen again. And what if he comes back? I stood up to Dennis once, but I'm not sure I have it in me to stand up to him again. I continue holding my breath, straining for any kind of noise from above that will let me know if he's still in the restaurant, or if he's left. Part of me thinks we should call the police, while another part struggles to grasp the incredible miracle that Mai and I are still alive, that he didn't shoot us, and we managed to escape with our lives. Long seconds pass, the silence broken only by the sound of Mai keening in the corner. I try not to let her distress unhinge me. One of us needs to stay calm. One of us needs to do something. Finally, I manage a tentative step, then another, and another. Eventually I find myself planted at the bottom of the staircase.

I gaze up the steps, listening, waiting, hoping for a sign, any sign, that Mai and I are safe.

Finally, from above, I hear the bell tinkle, and the distinct click of the restaurant's front door.

Dennis and the money are gone.

CHAPTER TWENTY-FOUR

~ How Do You Like Your Sushi? ~

I ALWAYS KNEW DENNIS WOULD COME looking for me. I just never thought he would find me.

"He's gone." Katy crouches close beside me. "We're safe now."

Safe? As usual, she is such a fool. There's no such thing as safe. I made two mistakes, and now I'm doomed to a life of forever glancing over my shoulder; wondering if someone's following me, fearing I won't even recognize the person who'll someday bring me down. Safe? I robbed myself for any chance of that happening the night I stole those diamonds from Dennis's *busu*, then ran away with his money. Safe? Even though he found me, it doesn't mean this is over. This will never be over.

I'll never be safe again.

"Mai, are you all right?" Katy touches my shoulder.

I resist the urge to flinch, to recoil from her touch. Instead, I rock back on my heels, forcing myself to bow slightly from the waist, exactly the way Obaa taught me. For Obaa, it was always about respect, and I know exactly what Katy wants. She wants me to respect her. She expects me to play the role of the penitent; to show my remorse, throw myself at her feet, and beg for mercy. Well, good luck with that one, bitch. She'll wait forever before I'll concede. She's seen me shamed, and now, finally, she's seeking revenge. She wants to see me humble myself, see me grovel in the dirt before her like some lowly dog, whimpering and whining. But that will be her downfall; in the end, I will triumph. Until then, I can play my role. One thing life has taught me is that showing deference to your elders makes things easier.

Although, in this instance, the role of the elder, of the oldest daughter, is rightfully mine.

"I'm sorry," I say, keeping my eyes averted so there's no need to behold the fool. "I didn't mean to bring this on you."

"He's gone now. We can call the police."

I lift my head, peer out from beneath fringed lashes to eye her. "What are you going to tell them?"

Katy gapes at me, and suddenly I want nothing more than to slap her. Doesn't she know how rude it is to stare? This fool would never last a day in Obaa's house. Then again, she was raised by Otosan. How can I fault him? He was all alone; he did his best. And despite that, she's so ungrateful. What I would have given to have had even the tiniest taste of the love he's shown her.

Wretched ingrate.

"Who the hell was that guy?" she asks, bouncing to her feet.

"Dennis Kailani." I rise with difficulty. It feels as if I've been kneeling in this cold, dark corner for what seems like forever. I lift my hands, smooth my hair and dress, try to shrug away the unwelcome senses that have followed me my whole life. The feelings of being dirty, unkempt. "He's no one."

"No one? For God sakes, Mai, he had a gun."

I bow my head. She will force the confession from me. "I owed him money."

"*Owed*? The way I heard it, it sounded more like you *took* his money." Katy's voice drops into that low whiny mode she always adopts when things aren't going her way. "I think I deserve an explanation, seeing as how we both could have been killed."

"We were never in danger. Dennis wouldn't have shot us. He isn't like that."

Her eyebrows lift. "It would have been nice if you'd shared that little fact with me earlier than this."

"I'm sorry you were afraid," I murmur, dipping my head low, silently railing against the imbecile. What else does she expect me to say? That it would have been nice if Dennis *had* shot her? That my life would then be so much easier? That finally, I would be the one to have the turn I never had, and that I deserve?

Katy has absolutely no idea how lucky she is.

"So, that's why Dennis showed up? You owed him money, and he came looking for you."

I nod.

"All the way from Hawaii." She peers at me. "That's a long way for somebody to travel. You must have owed him a lot of money."

Nearly one hundred thousand dollars, half of which is already gone, I silently reflect, mourning the loss. I never expected to run through the money so fast. I didn't give much thought as to how long it might last when I lifted the cash from his apartment that night; I just took it. It was a mistake. That entire night was filled with mistakes. I hadn't been thinking when I fled Obaa's house. Ojii was dead, his funeral over, the house still filled with relatives, mourning the only man who'd ever loved me. I had to get away. And as usual, no one noticed. No one missed me when I slipped out the door. Always the forgotten relative, the one who didn't count, except in Ojii's eyes. But he was dead, and there was no longer any reason for me to stay. I was happy to finally leave Kaneohe behind and head across the mountains for downtown Honolulu and that swear-to-God-baby-doll-I'll-find-us-something-better-soon shithole apartment Dennis and I shared. It was already dark when I finally reached the apartment and let myself in.

The living room was empty, but he'd been having quite the party while leaving me to deal alone with Ojii's death, Obaa, and the funeral. An empty bottle lay upended at one end of the couch and the room stank of whiskey. The coffee table was littered with stacks of cash and drug paraphernalia. Dennis wasn't only selling; he was using again. *Kono yarou.* Bastard. I'd told him to stay away from that shit. His job was to sell it, not use it. But he'd developed a taste for the sweet stuff. And other stuff that wasn't so sweet. I'd told him plenty of times that I wouldn't put up with other women. But, as usual, Dennis hadn't listened. That's what using did to him. He didn't listen. And what did he expect that I'd do when I found him passed out in our bedroom, naked on the bed, that *busu* with the big tits sprawled out beside him? He's lucky I didn't grab his gun and shoot them both dead right then and there.

Kono yarou. I'm better off without him.

Returning to the living room, I opened my purse and stuffed the bundles of cash inside. No drugs. I never touched drugs. Take the money and get out, I urged myself, before Dennis woke up. I slipped out the door with a grim smile, relishing what would happen when the two of them eventually came to, and discovered what had happened. It wouldn't be easy going for that *busu* of his, finding herself alone with Dennis when he realized the money was gone. And it wasn't even his money. Dennis was only the middle man. There'd be hell to pay when the men Dennis worked for came looking for their money.

My money, up until tonight… at least, all that was left of it. I gave Dennis most of what I had left; and now he also has the money from Otosan's safe. All that money, gone. I silently grieve, remembering how casually he'd tossed the bundles of cash into his duffel bag.

Kono yarou.

"How much money do you think Pop had in the safe?" Katy says.

"Twenty-seven thousand dollars," I say, thinking of how I could have put the money to good use.

"No way."

I shrug. If the fool wishes not to believe me, that's her choice.

She studies me. "Where would Pop get that kind of cash?"

"From a man who came into the restaurant earlier today." Katy hadn't been on duty yet, but I was there, stationed near the restaurant's front door as hostess when the man strode in asking for Otosan. The two of them disappeared downstairs for a while, then out back into the alley. Twenty-seven thousand dollars later, it was a done deal. "Otosan took the money, and the man took the car."

"Pop's car," Katy says. "The man finally showed up, and Pop sold his car."

I nod.

"For cash?"

I nod again. How many times do I need to explain this? Does the fool not understand English?

"And now Dennis has the cash." She trains her gaze on me. "Not only is Pop minus his car, but he's minus his money, too."

I lift one shoulder. Is it my fault things happened the way they did? If the man had come in earlier this week, as originally planned, Otosan would have already deposited the money in the bank.

"You intended to give Dennis the money," Katy accuses. "You were trying to open the safe when I found you down here. You were going to steal Pop's money and give it to Dennis."

Does the fool think I had any choice? Dennis didn't believe me when I pleaded with him that I didn't know the combination. He insisted I try. And, of course, if I'd thought things were that desperate, naturally I would have opened the safe. I've had the code since the second week I was here, when I accidently stumbled across a scribbled version of it while searching through the desk drawers one day. Not that I ever planned on stealing money from Otosan. Still, one never knows when a situation might suddenly arise. Having the code to the safe, and knowing that my secret was safe from everyone, was an opportunity I didn't dare pass up. I learned long ago it's best to keep all my options open.

"After all Pop's done for you," Katy says, staring at me with accusal in her eyes. "How could you steal from him?"

I'm not proud of what I did, but Otosan will understand. He told me I'm part of the family, didn't he? He said that everything that was his, was mine. And it wasn't as if I'd really been stealing. Eventually I would have found a way to replace the money. But at the time, I was more concerned with making sure Dennis didn't hurt me.

Better to keep my life, than keep the money.

"Pop trusted you, Mai. He's always trusted you. From that very first day, he gave you the benefit of the doubt." Her hands and voice tremble. "He accepted your word. He accepted you as his daughter."

For once, the fool and I are in total agreement. Otosan's always believed in me, and for that alone, I will love him forever. He took me in when I had no other place to go. He accepted me for who I was, and he never asked anything in return.

While it's true that I attempted to take his money from the safe, I did so only out of desperation. I never would have done it if I'd had another choice. Stealing money from Otosan will always be one of my deepest regrets.

But there's no use in trying to explain any of this to Katy. She wouldn't understand. She'll never understand. She fits into her family. She always has, and she always will. With Otosan to protect her, she never had to worry about cousins who pointed and stared, who doubled over in laughter, calling her names, shaming her in front of schoolmates when they caught her wearing leftovers from their own closets. Katy never knew how it felt to lie silent and wide-eyed in the darkness, listening as Obaa whined and complained to Ojii about their difficult and ungrateful granddaughter, lamenting the fact that they should be forced to raise her as their own. Katy would never understand how it felt to be treated as a second-class citizen; bad enough to be abused by your classmates, your teachers, your so-called friends... but also by your family. By your very own Obaa. *No wonder your mother doesn't come around*, Obaa would hiss in my ear as she cornered me in the kitchen, giving me hard, little shakes as she pinched my arm, her nails biting into my flesh. *Who would want to be around a girl such as you? No one, that is who*, she would answer to my growing silence. *Hafu*, she would whisper darkly in my ear. *Hafu,* she would mock me to my face, her nose inches from my own.

Yes, it is true. I am *hafu*; born of a Japanese mother, with a father who had come from—and returned to—a land far away. A land inhabited by people like him. People with a different culture than Obaa and Ojii. Different from all my cousins, from my mother... and from me. I'm all alone, and I'm like no one else in my family. I don't fit in. I've never fit in. And despite what Otosan told me, I don't belong here. I don't fit in James Bay.

"Do you think your tears are going to stop me from turning you in?" Katy's face flushes a dark ugly red. "You can get that thought right out of your head."

Tears? I touch my face with one hand, stunned by the unexpected wetness on both cheeks. I draw my hand away, impressed that I could be so good an actress. I was so deeply involved in playing a role, miming a well of sorrow and regret, that the actual physical reaction catches me by surprise.

I lift my head and meet her gaze. "I don't expect you to feel sorry for me."

"Good. Because I don't. As far as I'm concerned, I think you deserve everything you get."

"I know you wish I'd never come here," I say. "You've made that clear from the day we met. And now, finally, you'll have your wish."

"What are you talking about?"

"You're the one who will determine my fate."

"Quit the theatrics." Katy rolls her eyes. "We're alone, remember? And while I'll admit I haven't been exactly pleasant, what about you? You're no saint... and you're certainly not the big sister of my dreams."

Listening to her scolding me, I nearly laugh out loud. Katy's right. There's no love lost between us. And while I've been nasty and done some terrible things to her, the animosity goes both ways. She's been just as horrible to me. So, for her to blame me is pointless. She could have done more—so much more—to make me feel welcome... but she didn't. Katy was just as bad as any of my Japanese cousins. She was jealous and resentful of my presence in her life, and she couldn't find it in her heart to accept me.

And there's the tragedy of our family: Katy and I are sisters, but we're not friends. We'll never be friends. Otosan desires it, but it's not meant to be. We're sisters in blood, but we'll never be sisters at heart.

And while Katy will always have a home here, it's not meant for me.

"I have no regrets," I say.

"None?" she demands. Her eyes glitter as brilliantly as the diamonds I stole. "Not even about Dennis getting away with Pop's money?"

I shrug, not about to admit the truth to her. Let her think

what she likes. I can keep up the charade if I have to. "I did what I had to do."

"You realize there's no way out of this, correct? Everything that happened tonight—you and Dennis breaking into Pop's office, you trying to open the safe—it's all right there on tape." She nods toward the security camera mounted high in one corner of the room, its lens focused on the safe, and on us. Even as we speak, it continues capturing the logistics of our conversation on film.

"And now you're going to call the police," I say.

"Any reason why I shouldn't?" she shoots back.

"Go ahead," I say, already knowing exactly what she plans to do. Part of me isn't surprised. Katy's never liked me. She resents me deeply, and getting rid of me has always been her goal. And now it's payback time. She'll drag me down, drag all of us down, if that's what it takes. Some things are more important than money. That's how much she hates me.

And the feeling is mutual. I hate Katy as much as she hates me. As for that smug, superior smile on her face? It reminds me of my cousins, how little we have in common, and the miserable way they treated me while we were growing up. Forced to endure their merciless taunting, their cruel words, their many unkindnesses, I learned to hold my tongue. I'd think of my Ojii, of how much I loved him. I'd think of Ojii, how he sat with me and told me stories, reminding me that I was smart, I was beautiful, and that no matter what any of them said, I was better than them all. He protected me from my cousins and my Obaa. Obaa taught me how to suffer in silence, while Ojii taught me how to rise above them all.

I have learned my lesson well. I am Ojii's granddaughter.

I am proud, and I am strong. And if Katy thinks she can defeat me, she should think again.

Busu. Let the bitch try and drag me down.

"You have nothing to say for yourself?" Katy demands.

I raise my chin higher and glare at her.

CHAPTER TWENTY-FIVE

~ Can I Get This to Go? ~

NEVER HAVE I EVER WANTED to throw someone under the bus as much as I want to take Mai down. All my suspicions have finally been confirmed. She's lied, she's cheated. She's a thief.

And I'm willing to bet tonight wasn't the first time she stole money from us.

"It was you," I say in disgust, remembering how unjustly Ellen was treated. But now, finally, the real culprit has been exposed. "You've been stealing money from the till. Pop blamed Ellen and fired her, but it was you."

"You think so?" Mai brushes off my accusation with a short laugh and slight wave of her hand. "You're stupider than I thought."

She can insult me all she wants, but I know she's guilty, and I intend to make her admit it, if only for Ellen's sake.

"You might as well admit it," I say. "I know you're guilty."

"Sorry to disappoint you, but it wasn't me."

I glare at her. Why doesn't she simply confess?

"Think again, sister. It's true that your friend didn't deserve to be accused... but neither do I."

"Why should I believe you?" I challenge.

"Think what you like." She smiles with a confidence I don't expect. "But remember this: I wasn't the one constantly complaining about my tips."

Her cool composure catches me off guard. "What are you talking about?"

"It wasn't me, constantly making all those overrings," she reminds me. "And I wasn't the one with my hand in the till every night when Jake took his break."

I stand in stunned silence, flabbergasted by Mai's accusation. No way Nettie is our thief. She's been with Pop from the start, and she'd never steal from him. I've known Nettie since I was a kid. I looked up to her. I trusted her.

Yet Nettie is the one with the constant overrings. And Nettie's always been loud and vocal in her complaints about Pop's policy of waitresses having to share their tips with the busboys, dishwashers, and cooks. Plus, she has access to the till. She even has a key to the front and back doors, for the days she comes in early to prep.

Nettie.

There's no denying it. It was Nettie all along. My stomach yawns in a sickening lurch as I think of Nettie, how she commiserated with me the day Ellen was fired, but then how easily she betrayed us—betrayed Pop.

"You don't look so good," Mai says.

"Shut up." I close my eyes, close her out, thinking about Pop. He'll be devastated when he hears about Nettie.

Worse, how will he feel when I tell him about Mai?

Who knows how far she would have taken things, if she hadn't been caught? She's been using Pop, preying on his guilt. She's a master manipulator who knows how to twist people and events to suit her own selfish plans. And poor Pop was such an easy target. Given the circumstances, what father wouldn't want to protect his daughter? To give her what she never had, and let her know she was loved.

But Mai grew up without him. Now she's a woman. A woman who's done wrong. A woman who deserves exactly what she has coming.

Doesn't she?

All these days and weeks, I've waited for her to trip up. Tonight, it finally happened. Now I have the proof I need so that people will finally see Mai for the liar and cheat she is; the sneaky, vindictive woman I suspected all along. The surveillance footage will back me up. It'll expose Mai for who she is. I'll be free of her forever.

There's only one problem: Pop. Bad enough I'll have to tell him about Nettie. Learning of Mai's betrayal will be the ultimate blow. He's invested so much of his emotions in believing her story. It'll break my heart when he learns the truth.

How can I do it? It will destroy him.

I can't.

I won't.

"I can't believe I'm doing this," I say, my voice sounding distant and tinny to my ears, like I'm stuck in a tunnel. But I need to keep my feet on the road, and keep on keeping on. Because the way I see it, that's the only way out of this mess. "I'm going to let you go."

"What?" Mai looks at me like I've suddenly grown a Pinocchio-nose.

"You heard me. Go on, leave. You're free to go."

"You aren't going to call the police?"

259

"No." I slowly start to shake my head, then faster and firmer as my resolve hardens. "No, I'm not."

Her face morphs into stunned disbelief. "Why not?"

It's a stupid move on my part. Probably the stupidest thing I've done yet, especially now I finally have the chance to take Mai down. No one will question my version of events. I could use the tapes to make sure she pays for her crimes. I can get rid of Mai. I can put her away for years.

And I can break Pop's heart.

"No," I repeat. "I'm not going to call the police."

"But Dennis took the money. How are you—"

"That's none of your concern," I cut her off. "I'll see that it's replaced." I have plenty of money in savings. I can use that. Pop doesn't need to know about the theft. He will never know. "But don't think for one minute that I'm doing this for you," I warn. "Because I'm not. I'm doing it for Pop."

Yet even so, another part of me, a tiny part deep inside, wonders if that's true. Am I doing it for Pop, or am I doing it for myself, as well? Part of me would love to take revenge, while another part only wants all of this to be over and done. And there's still another part, a part which totally surprises me, lingering below the surface. A yearning, a strange kind of sadness, a longing that things might have been different. Given another time and place, would Mai and I found a way to live in peace? To be friends?

But we aren't. And I will never know.

"Here's the deal," I say. "Leave right now, and I promise I won't tell anyone what happened tonight. Go upstairs and grab your stuff."

"But it's already nearly morning," she says. "Where am I supposed to go?"

260

"I'm sure you'll figure something out. After all, you were smart enough to get out of Hawaii without being caught, right?"

Mai studies me for a long moment. Neither of us moves. I wait for her to challenge me, to mention Pop, to do something. She won't give up without a fight. She draws in a deep breath, and I steel myself for what's coming, for the words she's about to hurl at me. Then without warning, she lifts one shoulder in a sudden shrug. That's when I know that I did the right thing in following my instincts. Mai could care less about Pop, or how I handle the fallout from this mess. The only thing she cares about is herself.

"Go." My voice shakes, but the rest of me doesn't flinch. "Just go."

"*Busu*," she hisses. "You are such a bitch."

I stand there wordlessly as she pushes past me and pounds up the stairs. Closing my eyes, heart thrumming in my ears, I listen to the sounds from above as she slams one door, then another. Mai doesn't intend to go quietly. She's like a Cat 5 hurricane that blew in from Hawaii, wreaking havoc and destruction to everything and everyone in her path. Hopefully I managed to stop her in time from doing too much damage.

And hopefully, when I eventually head upstairs, I'll find her gone for good.

CHAPTER TWENTY-SIX

~ Tip Included ~

I ADMIRE THE BRIGHT FLORAL BOUQUET Don places on the hospital bedside table. "You're so sweet. Pop will love them." I nod toward the bathroom door. "He should be out soon."

"The flowers aren't for him," he says. "They're for his daughter."

I give an uneasy laugh as he sinks down beside me in an empty chair. The two of us haven't spoken since I found out Don was brokering the sale of Eva's property to Pop. "You brought the flowers for me?"

"I thought you could use a pick-me-up, especially after being here alone all night."

Briefly I consider telling him the truth: that I wasn't here all night, and that I wasn't alone. Part of me wants to spill everything, to share with Don exactly what happened, but my instincts tell me to keep my mouth shut. I know Don. Once he gets over his initial knee-jerk reaction to hearing about the robbery, he'll insist I go to the police. But notifying the police will trigger a staggering follow-through. I tick off the crimes in my head: safe-cracking, theft, guns. Warrants will be issued for both Dennis and Mai, and they'll probably be caught before either manages to secure a seat on an outbound flight for Hawaii. The police will haul them—separately or together—back to James Bay. Criminal charges will be filed, and I'll have to testify. And Pop would learn the truth. The good, the bad, the ugly. The truth about Mai.

I can't allow that to happen. I gave Mai a free pass last night when I let her get away scot free, but I'm only human. I'm not sure I have it in me to take the high road again, to resist the temptation to sink into an all-out dirty slugfest of *she said-she said* while the two of us break Pop's heart.

No. I'm doing the right thing by keeping my mouth shut.

"It sounds worse than it was." I offer Don a smile. "Pop came through the surgery fine. They decided to keep him an extra day because of his heart issues, but they're thinking he should be able to go home tomorrow."

He grabs my hand, gives my fingers a little squeeze. "If you need anything, I'm right here."

Why is he being so easy on me? How can he ignore how badly I treated him these past few weeks? If the situation were reversed, and I'd been on the receiving end of things, I wouldn't have put up with it. I would have walked away, and never looked back. But here he is, and with flowers, too. Despite my ignoring all his emails, phone calls, and texts, Don still showed up.

At least one of us hasn't given up on *us*.

I throw him a grateful smile. "Thanks, Don. It's good to know I'm not alone."

"You're not. I'm not going anywhere."

"I know that."

"Do you?"

"Of course, I do. Why wouldn't I?"

"Honestly, Katy, I'm not sure." He gives me a frank look. "Sometimes I wonder."

"What are you talking about?"

"You're great at managing things. You manage your life, you manage the restaurant, you manage the lives of the people around you. You even manage to get your dad to zip along to your beat. But people aren't machines. People make mistakes, Katy. And when they don't live up to your expectations, you shut them out."

I blink, pondering Don's words, and with a sinking heart, realize I can't deny any of it. Everything he's said is spot on. When I found out about how he was helping the sale for Eva and Pop, I didn't even give him the chance to tell me his side of things. I shut down and blocked everything out. I shut Pop out. I shut Don out. I shut myself out.

Lifting my hands, I grind the heels of my palms against scratchy eyes and push back the beginning of tears. I don't want to cry. I refuse to cry.

"I'm sorry," I murmur. "I didn't mean to hurt you. I didn't mean it."

Reaching out, he gently massages the back of my neck. "It's okay. Remember, plenty of people love you. Including me," he adds.

It's an offer of further commitment, and one which has me fingering away more tears before he can notice.

"All of us are here to help. Okay?"

"Okay." I offer him a weak smile and a shaky nod. Who knows? Maybe someday Don and I will end up together. Our history is contentious, with a multitude of sins on both our parts. But in the grand scheme of things, the good always outweighs the bad. And at this point, I'm thinking it always will. Meanwhile, I'm nothing but a weepy mess. It wouldn't be fair to Don or to me, trying to decide our future right here and right now. If things are meant to work out, they will.

"Katy? You still out there?" Pop hollers through the bathroom door, followed by a loud clunk. "Dammit!" he yells.

"Right here, Pop." I rise to my feet.

Don stands. "Maybe I'll wait outside."

I plant a quick kiss on his lips. "Don't go far."

"I'm not going anywhere," he promises.

"What do you need, Pop?" I start for the bathroom. "Do you want me to call the nurse? Do you need help?"

"What I *need*," he mutters, opening the door and hobbling out, "is to get rid of this damn hospital gown… and this stupid IV." He shuffles across the room, holding hands with his IV pole like the two of them are dating. "Damn nurses don't know what they're talking about. *This won't hurt a bit*," he mimics in a high, wobbly voice. "It hurt like hell!"

"You'll feel better tomorrow," I promise, stifling a smile as the cantankerous man I know and love begins to resurface. If Pop's feeling good enough to be complaining, then things will soon be back to normal.

His face is a menacing thundercloud as he makes a cautious first landfall on the edge of his bed, then winces. Shifting a bit, he glances expectantly at me. "Mai back yet?"

I hesitate. I'd love nothing more than to share all the dirty little secrets I've discovered about Mai. But what would be the point?

"I'm not sure. I haven't seen her for a while," I reply. The lights in Pop's second-floor apartment were still ablaze when I left the restaurant early this morning, but instead of checking things out, I headed for the hospital. Things were no longer in my hands. Mai already knew my terms of surrender, and exactly what I intended to do if she didn't leave immediately.

"Maybe she's at the apartment," I say. Hopefully by now she's far away from James Bay, waiting at a downstate airport, flight about to board, ticket in hand. A one-way ticket to Honolulu.

Aloha, big sister.

"I suppose we'll find out sooner or later," Pop says. "She's probably busy with that Dennis character. Or maybe she's working." His gaze travels to the hospital clock high on one wall. "It's lunchtime. Wonder if the restaurant's busy?" He pauses, glances at me. "Maybe you should go on down there, see if they need help."

"No." I already know they don't.

"It's a holiday weekend," he reminds me. "Lots of people will be in town."

"Pop, please! Would you stop already? The restaurant will be fine. Besides, do I look worried? No. And neither should you."

What I don't bothering telling him is the reason behind why there's no need to worry: Chuck's Tavern & Grill is closed today. I think about the temporary sign I taped to our front door, notifying customers we're closed due to a family emergency. It's the first time in the history of our restaurant that such a sign has ever been posted, and guaranteed Pop would have a fit if he knew what I'd done. But people do what they need to do. For today, I intend to concentrate on Pop.

"We're still running short-staffed," he says. "What if Mai—"

"Everything will be fine," I say.

And it will be, I reassure myself, trying not to focus on the fact that Mai's the one who's drawn his concern. Hopefully she's gone, and out of our lives for good. Will she return someday? But I can't let myself think about that. It's different for Pop. She's his daughter. Of course, he cares about her; he always will. He wouldn't be the man who raised me, the man I've always known to be decent and honest and kind, if he didn't care for Mai. Meanwhile, whiny-Katy, the bratty, self-centered only child who's always insisted on doing things her way and demanding that others follow, still has a few lessons left to learn. Beginning with letting go. *Que sera, sera.* I have no business allowing my fears and resentments to march me down paths clearly not meant for me to walk.

I lift the tight-woven hospital blanket, making it easier for him to slide into bed. I tuck the covers neatly around him, brush my lips against his forehead. "Anything else you need?"

Pop glances up at me, and for a brief instant, there's the oddest look on his face. I catch my breath, wait for him to say something that I'm sure will break my heart.

Then suddenly he tugs at my hand, and squeezes like he'll never let go.

"Thank you, Katy-Did. I think I'm all set."

I smile and let go. I let go of all the hurts and frustrations, of my anger and the fear.

"Me, too, Pop," I say. "Me too."

CHAPTER TWENTY-SEVEN

~ Every Good Meal Ends in Dessert ~

KATY CONSULTS HER NOTEBOOK, RUNS the tip of her pen down the margin, checks off another mark against an agenda item. It's her job to keep us on track during the weekly meetings the two of us recently started having every Tuesday morning.

"Here's something you'll be happy to know," she says. "We finally have a new waitress coming in next week."

"Why not have her start today?" I fold my hands over my stomach, eye her across the desk. While summer's over and the bulk of the tourists are gone, we're still running the restaurant short-staffed. "They're having that fall festival this weekend over in Billings, remember? Lots of people will be in the area. We could use the help now."

"Sorry," she says with a quick shrug. "When I hired her, I asked about having her start this week, but she wasn't available."

"There's your problem. You don't ask 'em, you tell 'em," I advise. Why is everything so complicated nowadays? When I started this business, people wanted to work. You gave them a job; they showed up. Simple as that. "She give you a reason why not?"

"She'll be out of town with her boyfriend, and she won't be back until Monday."

"Good Lord. How old is she, anyway?"

"Eighteen."

I run my hand across my buzz cut, against the rough stubble sprouting on my chin despite my morning shave. "She got any experience?"

Katy hesitates, and I have my answer.

"I'll train her myself," she promises. "It won't be a problem, Pop. She's young, but she wants to learn."

"Sounds like she wants to do the learning strictly on her terms. Listen, kiddo, you can't let them do that. You start kowtowing to 'em, and they'll—"

She raises one palm. "How about you cut me a break? I'm trying my best here."

It's the ultimate reminder, and it works. I sit back and shut my mouth. Not an easy task, but it's something I'm consciously trying to do more frequently these days. Katy doesn't need me criticizing her, or bringing her down. If she's serious about taking over the restaurant, then I've got to learn to let her take the lead. As for me, I need to learn to follow. She's done a fine job of stepping up and taking charge since I made her managing partner a few weeks ago.

Katy's the boss now. She's got authority over everything and everyone, including me. Lots of things are changing, and it's a different world. Some of the changes I like; some, I don't. I've been resistant to change, and I've spent lots of time wishing for a do-over. Given the chance, I'd do plenty of things different.

Nettie, for one.

I won't lie about how it feels, finding out Nettie was

our thief. And even after everything she did, I still miss her. While I was laid up, Katy discovered it was Nettie who'd been lifting money from the till. Learning the truth ripped me wide open almost as bad as those damn gallstones. I gave the woman a job when no one else would, and that's how she chose to repay me? I make it a point to try and be honest and fair with the people who work for me, and I trust they'll treat me the same. And I trusted Nettie. It hurts like hell, knowing she was the one stealing from us. Guess I'm a lousy judge of peoples' characters.

Case in point: Mai.

I shift in my chair, trying to settle myself, squint and point at Katy's notebook. "What's next? Or have we covered everything?"

"Just a couple more things," she says. "The dishwasher started acted up again last night. We should probably think about replacing it."

"Makes sense to me."

"Good. I'll contact our supplier and get him working on a quote." She ticks off another check. "That leaves us with the last item on today's agenda. Menus for winter."

I suck in a long breath. It's the same every year, and I figured we'd get around to having this conversation sooner or later. The heavy summer foot traffic prevents us from keeping up with demand for all those specialty items we offer in the off season. Come winter, knowing we've got the locals to see us through, we add things back to the menu.

"Our regulars are already asking when we plan on bringing back our Friday night all-you-can-eat fish fries."

"I don't know if that's such a good idea," I say. "Don't

forget: when we got rid of the all-you-can-eat part, we upped our profit margin substantially."

"Yes, but at the expense of our loyal customers," she counters. "Honestly, Pop, I think we need to bring the idea of all-you-can-eat back... and the sooner, the better. It won't kill us to swallow the cost."

Katy's got a good point. The locals cried foul after we dumped our popular fish fries. I don't want to give them an excuse to head out to Loon Lake. Rumor has it Sid Meyer's new seafood place is floundering. And while I feel for the guy, as a local business owner, I don't want to keep him in business at the sake of losing our own customers and declining sales.

"Yeah, let's do it," I say on second thought. Why the hell not? When it comes down to it, what's one or two extra pieces of fish?

"Great. I'll adjust the pricing." Katy dips her head, scribbles a few notes in the margin. "Okay, so that's it for the off-season menus. When do you want to start using them? The printer needs at least two weeks after we place the order."

No sense in me being the one making all the decisions. Katy's managing partner now. What she says goes. And if I don't like it, guess I'll have to learn to live with it.

"Whatever you think."

"Okay, we should probably get them finished this week."

"Great. Winter's right around the corner."

She jots another note, then abruptly stops, blinks, and regards me with a hoot owl stare.

"What's the matter?" I prompt.

"Winter."

"Okay," I say hesitantly. Katy doesn't like snow much, but I'm not sure what that's got to do with anything.

"It just started me thinking about the menu inserts we're still using," she says with an explanatory smile. "If you want to keep them, that's fine. But since we're talking money, I wonder if having the specialty dishes available is worth it... especially now."

Especially now that Mai is gone.

"What do you recommend?" I ask.

"We should keep them," she says without hesitation.

"Even the sukiyaki?"

"For now. I'll work with Pete and see if he can spice up the dish."

It's not the answer I expected. Katy opposed adding the items from the get-go. Not to mention, she's never been a fan of Mai.

I nod. "Sounds good."

"Great." She adds an additional note to her list. "And how about the pineapple ice cream? I think we should take it off the menu right now. We'll simply use up what's left, and then, no more orders."

"No problem. Can't say I'm surprised, though."

"What do you mean?" Her voice contains a catch.

"Just that I expected you to dump it faster than this. We all know how much you hate ice cream."

"Did I ever say that?" She pauses. "I guess I like ice cream as much as anybody else."

I stare at her with frosty amusement. "You could have fooled me."

She glances down at her checklist, her face flushing a deeper shade than the rosy pink found in a half gallon of Neapolitan.

"Did I say something wrong?"

"No, of course not." She lifts one shoulder, forces a faint smile. "I'm fine. Just thinking about Mom."

"Well, that's a good thing, right?" It's moments like this, I think about Katherine, too. And it's times like this when I miss her the most. It was Katherine, not me, who was good at dealing with emotions. She always knew exactly the right thing to say. "She liked ice cream."

"Yes, she did." A wistful look covers her face. "I miss her."

"Yep. I know what you mean." I gaze around the office, taking in its cinderblock walls. I'll bet, if Katherine had been around to see this place, it would look different. For one thing, the walls wouldn't be so stark. And it's a guarantee she would have spruced up the décor of Chuck's, too.

We sit there in silence, each of us with our own thoughts. And in thinking about Katherine, and in how much I miss her, my thoughts shift to Mai. She disappeared the same way she arrived in James Bay: without giving notice, and she's been gone for weeks now.

So much loss in my life. So many regrets.

But I can't afford to let *what-if* and *if-only* bog me down.

I blow out a long sigh, shift in my chair. "Well, we can't change what happened in the past. Life goes on, right?"

"It was my fault," Katy says.

"What?"

"There's something you don't know, Pop. Something I need to tell you. It's about how she died."

Blinking, I take in the solemn look on my daughter's face. Rarely, if ever, do we discuss Katherine's death.

"We know how she died," I remind her. "Her car was broadsided by a drunk driver."

"No." Katy shakes her head, hair swinging about her face, partially shielding her eyes. "It was all my fault. Because I'm nothing but a selfish brat."

"You're talking crazy." I stare at her across the desk. "You want to blame somebody for your mother's death? Blame that drunk who plowed into her car."

"No." Katy insistently shakes her head. "I'm the one to blame. Mom would still be with us if it weren't for me. If she hadn't... if I hadn't..." She falters a moment, then with a deep breath, steadies herself and lifts her gaze to meet mine. "It's time I told you the truth."

She's not making sense. No way could Katy had anything to do with her mother's death. She was sick in bed when Katherine died. Katherine was on her way home from work when that drunk behind the wheel killed her.

Yet watching the color drain from Katy's cheeks, milking her face in a chalky white, has me suddenly spooked.

"All right, I'm listening," I say, though I'm already certain I don't want to hear what she has to say.

"What happened to Mom was my fault." She bites her bottom lip. "After she got home that afternoon—"

"Katy, sweetheart, you got it all wrong. She never made it all the way home, remember? The accident happened right after she left school."

She shakes her head hard, ponytail whipping from side to side. "You're wrong!"

"No, I'm not. You were home, sick in bed. You don't know what happened."

"But I do," she insists. "I remember everything—*every*

detail—about that afternoon." She stands abruptly, the clipboard sliding from her hands, hitting the floor with a sharp clang. Her fists knot in tight balls as she faces me. "Listen to me, Pop. I'm not wrong about this. Let me finish. Please."

It's an urgent, eloquent plea, which has my heart galloping inside my chest like it's been hijacked by the Headless Horseman and he's about to take me for a wild ride down memory lane. I lift one hand and pat my shirt pocket, searching for the comforting shape of the tiny bottle. Maybe I should pop a pill, slip one under my tongue. A preventative dose to protect my heart.

I give her a nod. "I'm listening."

"It was on account of me that Mom came home early that day," she says slowly. "She came home as soon as classes ended, instead of staying late at school like she normally did. I heard her car pull into the driveway, and I knew she was home."

I think about our old house downstate, a rambling wooden two-story with drafty corners, leaky faucets, and creaky floorboards which Katherine turned into a home. But the *home* disappeared from our house the afternoon when Katherine died.

"She came upstairs and into my room. She took my temperature, saw I was still running a fever, and made me take more medicine. Then she got me a glass of ginger ale, which she said would help my throat. But I wouldn't drink it." Katy's eyes grow cloudy. "I told her I wanted ice cream. I'd eaten it all up the night before and Mom had promised to stop on her way home from school to buy more. But she forgot. When she told me, I yanked the blanket over my head, and screamed at her. I said horrible things, Pop." Her face is drawn. "I told her she was a horrible mother. I said that if she'd really loved me, if she'd truly loved me, she never would have forgotten to pick up my ice cream."

Katy pauses for a heartbeat.

"And then, she left."

I stand there, locked face-to-face with Katy, my metal desk and her dreadful story the only things between us. "What do you mean, she *left*?"

"She left because of what I said. Because I was being a brat. A greedy little brat." Her voice hitches. "I knew if I whined enough, she'd do what I wanted. And that's exactly what happened. Mom left me at home, and headed to the grocery store when the drunk hit her car. But she never would have left the house, she never would have been behind the wheel if it hadn't been for me complaining about some stupid ice cream."

The truth slams into me fast and powerful. What we had together, what our family had together, and everything we could have had: all of it gone in a heartbeat. I stare downward, take in some truths as cold and hard as the cement floor beneath my feet. The hurt and remorse of losing Katherine are as strong today as they were all those years ago.

But there's something else, too: the pain and regret of knowing what Katy's been living with—the tremendous guilt she's heaped on herself—all these years.

I want to reach out, wrap her in my arms, but something tells me not to touch her. She looks as if she might break.

"This? This is the truth?"

She silently nods.

"And you've been keeping this bottled up inside you... for all these years?"

Again, she nods, her face growing more miserable by the moment.

"But why didn't you say anything? Why didn't you tell me?" I ask gently.

"Why?" She licks her lips, her gaze darting around the room, as if on a frantic search for something she fears is already lost. "Why? Because I knew how much you loved her. And I knew that once you learned the truth, you'd blame me. I couldn't do it, Pop. I couldn't tell you. I'd already lost Mom. I couldn't bear the thought of losing you, too."

"Are you crazy? How the hell could you think that?" Without a second thought, I reach out and grab her, pull her close in my arms. "Do you know how much it hurts my heart to hear you saying these things? You're not to blame, not for any of it, do you hear me? My God, Katy, you were only a kid. Your mom loved you, and I love you. And I will always love you."

I press her close, wishing with all my might that she was ten years old again, with enough faith in my Daddy-Superhero-Powers that a few words and a big hug from me would magically make all the bad things vanish.

"I'm so sorry. I'm so, so sorry." With her head buried in my chest, her voice is slightly muffled. I feel, more than hear, her breath, which is coming in huge gulps. "All these years, I tried so hard, but I knew it could never be enough. I'd never be able to fix what I did."

"Katy, look at me."

She doesn't respond, and I grasp her shoulders, give her a slight shake.

"Look at me," I demand.

When she finally lifts her head, her eyes are shimmering with tears.

"I'm so sorry, Pop. I wish I could have fixed it. I know how much you loved her."

"We both loved her, remember?" I smooth the hair away from her face, brush away a few of the tears spilling down her cheeks. "There's nothing to fix, no reason for you to feel guilty. We got through it, didn't we?"

"But you deserved—"

"Shhh." I press a finger against her lips. "Let's let it be, okay? You're here, and that's all I want. That's enough for me. It will always be enough."

She stays silent, searching my face. And suddenly, I wonder if she's doubted it all along. The first time I noticed that same sort of look creeping into her eyes—doubt and apprehension, mingled with a touch of anger and a dose of fear—was the day Mai walked into our lives.

But Mai is gone now. I don't know when, or how, or why she left, but in the end, I suppose the whys and wherefores don't matter. Maybe she decided she needed some space. Or maybe Dennis convinced her to head back to Hawaii. Maybe someday we'll find out what happened. I hope so. Meanwhile, I can't live my life looking backward. Mai left our lives the same way she entered, drifting in and out the same way the wind catches a wave, then casts it wide, crashing it on the shore. Eventually the wave dissolves, and the water slips away, disappearing back into the sea from where it came.

And it would be a sin to squander the rest of my life wishing and hoping for something that wasn't meant to be. Not at the expense of squandering what I have right here at this very moment: this beautiful young woman, my Katy-Did, directly before me.

"I'm sorry we've been fighting, Pop. I've hated it, hated every minute of it."

"Me, too, kiddo," I say, mourning all those wasted weeks sitting behind us. Weeks the two of us can never get back. "Me, too."

She takes a deep breath. "I guess there's one more thing you should hear, as long as we're finally getting out the truth. It... it's about the restaurant."

"What about it?" There's not much left to discuss. I already told Katy that I've scrapped my plans to move forward purchasing Eva's store. Lucky for me, there were two more buyers waiting in the wings, and it wasn't hard getting out of the deal. And Katy is our managing partner now; from now on, she's the one who'll be running the show. If we expand, it'll be because Katy wants it to happen. "I trust your decisions."

"There's no easy way for me to say this."

"Just spit it out," I suggest.

She takes a long breath and squares her shoulders, the exact same way she used to when she was a kid and about to take that one final leap which would plunge her into the deep end of the pool. "I don't think I should be managing partner."

I blink. "Why not?"

"It's not that I don't appreciate it, Pop." The words rush out of her mouth in a slap-dash fashion, as if now she's started talking, she can't get things out quick enough. "I know stepping aside wasn't an easy decision for you. That restaurant is your world, and the last thing I want to do is mess up—"

"Whoa, stop right there." I gave her the job because I thought she wanted the authority. I thought she wanted to be in charge. These past few months, with things so awkward and strained between us, I thought that's what she was fighting for. More responsibility in the way things are run. More autonomy to make her own decisions. More power to do things on her own.

"If you don't want the job, it's okay," I say. "I understand. Believe me, nothing you say will ever change the way I feel about you. I love you, Katy-Did, no matter what. That's always going to be my bottom line."

"You've put so much faith in me," she says. "I don't want you thinking I'm not grateful. Because I am, Pop. I've very grateful. But lately I feel so messed up. And…"

"Go on," I urge.

It takes her a minute before she can compose herself enough to continue. "I'm not even sure I want to be involved in the restaurant anymore."

I let the news digest in my gut. She doesn't want to be involved? If she didn't want the job, why didn't she say so when I offered her the position of managing partner several weeks ago?

"I didn't realize you were so unhappy."

"Not unhappy. More like, confused." She lays a hand on my arm. "Bottom line, Pop? I need some time to think about things. And for right now, I think it's best if I'm not involved in the restaurant, at least not on a full-time basis."

"Are you telling me you don't want to work at Chuck's?"

She doesn't speak, but merely stares at me. There's no need for her to say anything. I can read the truth in her eyes.

"Good Lord," I mutter. "How long have you felt like this?"

"Quite a while," she finally admits.

"Why didn't you say something sooner?" I try not to raise my voice, but damn, this news comes winging in out of left field.

"I didn't want to disappoint you," she says in a small voice.

"Aw, sweetheart." I grab her again and hold her tight, try to ward off another occurrence of more unexpected tears. Anything is better than making Katy cry. "Don't you know by now you can never disappoint me? Never. Though I do wish you'd told me about all this, how you felt, long ago. If I'd known, I sure would have done things different. Remember how Sid Meyer tried to buy me out a few years ago? The only reason I turned him down was because I thought you wanted to take over the business."

Easy come, easy go. What's a bit of profit when it comes at the expense of the people you love?

"Pop, do you swear you're not making this up? I mean, the part about you not being mad at me?" She pulls back slightly. "Tell me the truth."

"No, I'm not mad. The only thing I want is whatever makes you happy." I study her face, try to analyze what's zipping around in that head of hers. Eventually I give up. This kid of mine has always been excellent at keeping her thoughts to herself.

"So, you're done working at Chuck's. Any idea what you might want to do now?"

A thoughtful half-smile begins to play around the corners

of her mouth. "I've been thinking about going back to school."

"College," I muse.

"I might start with a few classes, and see how things suit me."

Katy's finally going to college. Katherine would be ecstatic if she were still alive. Once upon a time, the news would have thrilled me, too. But now, I'm not so sure. I don't think she realizes how hard it's going to be to take herself out of the business world to sit in a classroom again. She'll be dealing with homework, late night study sessions, and final exams. She'll be competing with kids ten years younger than her—kids who, given different circumstances—Katy would be hiring to fill out our staff at Chuck's. Not to mention, she'll have to move. We don't have any four-year universities anywhere near James Bay. I feel the doubts beginning to suddenly creep in. Has she thought all this through?

"Pop? What's up? You've got that look on your face."

"What look?" I ask innocently.

"The one that says you're thinking in overdrive, and trying to figure out a way to make me happy."

"That's all a parent wants for their child."

"But I'm not a child anymore, Pop. And I think trying some things on my own, and going back to school, will make me happy. But there's only one way to find out, and that's for me to try. What I need from you is to let me try."

"I'm worried about you."

"Want to know a secret? I'm worried about me, too. But I'll be fine. And I think we both know it."

I draw in a deep breath, hold it for a second or two. Katy's right. She'll get through this. She's never been a quitter.

"Any idea what you want to study?"

"Well, definitely not math, I'll tell you that right now!"

Her attempt at humor puts the smile back on my face.

"I was thinking maybe psychology or counseling, or something like that," she says. There's a lift in her voice, an enthusiasm I haven't heard in a long time. "I've always been interested in people."

"Plenty of interesting people eat at Chuck's every day," I say. "You could stick around and analyze them."

A wide grin settles on her face. "Nice try, Pop, but I don't think so."

"A dad has to do what a dad has to do." I take a moment, trying to wrap my brain around the idea of my daughter in a white lab coat or professional dress. The Katy I know is usually out working the restaurant floor, t-shirt and khaki shorts, apron pocket jingling with tips. How am I going to manage without her? For the past few years, she's shaped her life to work around my definition of success.

My definition, I realize with a heavy heart. But what about what Katy wants?

Maybe it's time I step aside and give her the freedom to define her own life.

"You'll make a great psychiatrist," I say. "I can be your first patient."

"Don't book your appointment yet," she warns with a short laugh. "Being a psychiatrist means I'll need to go to medical school first, and I never was good at science or math. Private counseling might be an option. I like the idea of being involved with people, and helping them work through their problems." She turns toward me, a bright happy look lighting her face.

One word from me is all it would take. One word, and I know she'd give up everything. But how can I hold her back? It would be a selfish move on my part. Katy has so much to offer. I can't stand in her way. She deserves whatever life has in store for her, and she'll be an asset to whatever field or career path she chooses to pursue. And she brings plenty to the table, including a sharp mind and great business skills.

I should know. I trained her.

"So?" she prompts. "What do you think?"

"What do I think?" I take a deep breath, then blow it out in one long exaggerated sigh, the way I used to tease when she was a little girl. It's the one sure way I know guaranteed to keep a smile on Katy's face. "Here's what I think: whatever you decide to do, it will be great."

She catches me in a fierce hug. "Thanks, Pop."

"I'll miss you." I hold on tight. I'm a lucky guy, and I know it. "I love you, Katy-Did."

"I love you, too," she says, then draws back. Her gaze roams slowly across my face, as if she's committing my features to memory for some future time when she's no longer with me. And as I watch her study me, a small pain begins in my heart. It's nothing that will be soothed or relieved by one or two or even three of the tiny pills stashed inside my pocket. And there'll probably be more pain headed my way in the days and weeks ahead. Maybe someday, if I'm lucky, it'll eventually subside, be nothing more than a dull ache. It's a pain cursed with irony and satisfaction; the pain every parent feels on the day they watch their child make their own decisions and walk their own path, even though each step takes them further and further away.

Katy pulls back slightly, taps a finger against the top button of my shirt. "Where are your dog tags?"

You can't wear what you don't have. The last time I saw them was while I was in the hospital, right before they wheeled me into surgery. When I came home to my apartment two days later, Mai was gone, and so were my dog tags. I haven't got a clue why she decided to take them. But I refuse to sweat the small stuff. Mai needed them more than me. And it's as simple as that: if she needed them, she's welcome to them.

"Are we done talking?" I plant a kiss on Katy's forehead. "Frankly, kiddo, I'm exhausted."

Tired, but happy. And satisfied. It feels as if whatever was wrong between us has been resolved, and things are back to the way they should be. Katy no longer looks like she's about to jump out of her skin, and I feel the same. For the first time in weeks, the edginess is gone.

A bell tinkles upstairs, and Katy and I exchange glances.

"That must be Jake," she explains. "He's agreed to start coming in early to open."

I peer at her over the rim of my glasses. "Since when does the guy have his own key?"

"Since yesterday," she says, adding, "I thought it was time."

"You really think that's a good idea? He and Nettie could have—" I pull myself up short, remind myself that Katy made the decision while she was still managing partner of Chuck's. She has confidence in Jake, and I need to respect her judgment.

"Good call," I concede.

"Jake's a smart guy," she reassures me as I trail her out

of the office and we head for the stairs. "And he's not a thief, Pop. I know you got burned by Nettie, but that doesn't mean everyone else is out to get you. And he's not Ellen, either. Jake doesn't have a family or kids. He's ready for some responsibility. He can handle things."

"If you say so," I say. Being bossed around by my own daughter feels weird. I can see that this getting-used-to-Katy-being-more-assertive-in-establishing-her-boundaries concept will take some time. And since when did she get so smart about people?

On second thought, maybe Katy will make a good therapist after all. A damned good one.

"What's our special of the house for tonight?" I ask as we start up the stairs.

"Pete has a new recipe he's been wanting to try."

"Beef?" I ask hopefully. I wouldn't mind a new meat dish. My taste buds could use some jazzing up.

"I think it's something involving chicken."

"We've already got too much chicken on the menu," I grumble. "Tell him he needs to start using more beef."

Katy throws an amused look over her shoulder. "I'm not managing partner anymore, remember? You tell him."

"And don't forget the new dishwasher," I say, ignoring her light taunt. "You need to contact the supplier and check on prices."

"No, you're going to contact him," she counters as she reaches the top step, me trailing close behind. "I'll be busy researching colleges and classes."

"What the hell? I haven't got time for all this crap," I mutter.

"You can do it, Pop." She leans in close and plants a kiss on my cheek. "I have faith in you."

"Yeah, well... whatever." I swipe at my face, wondering if I've got lipstick smeared across my cheek.

And this is how life happens. In the moments slipped in between some hysterical kid who's crying because he accidently locked himself in the handicapped bathroom; with customers grousing and complaining when their orders get mixed up, or the food is cold; when the freezer decides to quit, and you're suddenly faced with a sweet, gooey flood as twenty-two gallons of ice cream begins to melt on a ninety-degree day; when there's a steady line of hungry people stretching out the front door on a busy Saturday night, and the cook yells you've just run out of barbecued ribs.

Life can be messy. Maybe it's late getting to your table, and maybe it turns out to be a bit overcooked. But you take what you have, and hopefully you've got lots of napkins around to sop up the mess. You keep going on, and you do your best. And in the end, when your order is served, somehow everything seems to work out. But here's the funny thing: you'll never know unless you give it a try.

And who knows? It might just taste delicious.

ALSO BY KATHLEEN IRENE PATERKA

The James Bay Novels
Fatty Patty (2012)
Home Fires (Book #2) (2012)
Lotto Lucy (Book #3) (2012)
For I Have Sinned (Book #4) (2013)
Deep Fried Reservations (Book #5) (2017)

Women's Fiction
Royal Secrets (2013)
The Other Wife (2015)

Nonfiction
For the Love of a Castle (2012)

**Turn the page for a bonus read
from *Fatty Patty*!**

FATTY PATTY

A James Bay Novel

KATHLEEN IRENE PATERKA

CHAPTER ONE

BRAND NEW SCHOOL YEAR. *B*RAND *new body. Brand new me.*

That's what I love about starting a new diet. The world seems bright and shiny, and I'm filled with happy hope. Anything is possible.

Like swimming twenty laps in James Bay's community pool. Losing thirty pounds before Christmas. Finally winning that contest.

Patty Perreault, Teacher of the Year.

I've got the smarts, I just don't have the body. And I never will—especially if I don't let go of the smooth tiled railing and start swimming soon. So long, contest. Hello, loser. Not to mention, that new mantra of mine will need some revising.

Brand new school year. Same old body. Same old me.

"Brrr." Priscilla dips one foot in the water, then quickly pulls it out. "Sorry, Patty, I just can't do it. You know I love you dearly, but the water is so cold, and—"

"Don't worry about it." I sidle alongside her, hugging the pool edge. God bless Priscilla. My fraternal twin would probably jump in the deep end if she thought it would help, but I'm not going to force her to endure this torture, too. Tiny and frail since the day we were born, she could stand to put on a few pounds. Plus, Priscilla's a worse swimmer than me. If she jumps in, the pimply-faced teenage lifeguard will probably end up having to rescue us both.

"But I feel so bad, just sitting here like this. After all, I promised to keep you company and give you moral support, remember?" Goose bumps pop up on her thin arms as she reaches for her towel, then she suddenly brightens. "I've got an idea. How about you swim and I count off your laps? That way you won't have to keep track in your head."

"Sounds good." I yank at the too-tight bathing suit creeping up my rear end. If I plan to keep up this swimming-laps routine, I might have to break down and buy a new one. This ugly pink suit has seen too many summers and too many cookies. I'm pretty sure the James Bay School Board of Education would not approve of one of their teachers being arrested for indecent exposure.

Plus, I doubt a criminal record would be helpful in winning that contest. I'm a good teacher; my evaluations plus the fact my fellow teachers keep nominating me prove it. So why haven't I won yet? I'm a quick learner, but this one has had me stymied. Four years worth of stymied. But not anymore, because I've finally figured it out: if I change the way I look, I know I'll win the contest.

And I am *determined* to win that contest.

"Okay, I'm ready." Priscilla's blue eyes shimmer like the pool water. "Whenever you are."

I grip the edge tighter, suddenly finding it hard to let go. There's twelve feet of water swirling below me. What if I sink? Is that lifeguard properly trained? I taught him in fifth grade, and he never was very good in school. How did he do

294

in Phys Ed? Is he any good at saving people's lives? I don't want it to be my life that puts him to the test.

"Patty? What's wrong?"

"Nothing. I'm thinking."

"Well, quit thinking and start swimming. How do you expect to finish if you never start?"

Easy for her to say, perched warm and dry, draped in a thick terry towel at the edge of the pool. I love my sister to death, but when it comes to dieting, exercise and food, she doesn't get it and she never will. They say twins have a psychic connection, and Priscilla and I have always been a team. We had our own secret language when we were small, and to this day still have this weird, uncanny ability to sense each other's thoughts. But when it comes to the way we look, we might as well be strangers, because the only thing that ties us together identically is our height. We are both short enough that we always ended up together in the front row during school musicals when we were little kids. But we're all grown up now and Priscilla, a thin delicate beauty, wears *short* well. On me, these extra thirty pounds make it look like I'm wearing an inner tube.

"Patty?"

"Okay, okay, I heard you. I'll do it." There's no use arguing with her. She's got my best interest at heart... plus a fiercely determined if-Patty-doesn't-start-swimming-soon-I'm-going-to-jump-in-that-water-myself look in her eyes. I finally let go of the slippery rail, sink below the surface, and start paddling toward the shallow end.

"One!" The faint shout of my twin's voice echoes through the water.

Great, just what I need. Priscilla keeping score, just like

she measures and tracks our food, courtesy of that little diet scale she recently bought for our kitchen counter. Whatever possessed me to tell her I'd started another diet?

Because I know she loves me. Priscilla's always been my champion and she only wants to help. And at this point, I'll take all the help I can get. I don't think I've got it in me to sit through another year of being nominated, endure another round of interviews, only to eventually lose out as Bay County Teacher of The Year. With the grand prize only one thousand dollars, it's not even like I'm in it for the money—though I've got to admit I wouldn't mind having my hands on that kind of cash. But after four years as a semifinalist-ultimate-loser, it's now a matter of personal pride—especially after last year's fiasco when I lost out to the ditzy third grade teacher everyone thought was so cute. So while it's not officially a popularity contest, who you know and what you look like is definitely part of the deal.

And if that's the case, I'll do whatever it takes. Schmooze whoever I can through the nomination process. Starve myself eating carrot sticks. Exercise by swimming laps.

And listen to whatever Priscilla tells me. She's not a teacher and doesn't need to lose weight. But when it comes to the looks department, there's no contest. Priscilla wins.

"I'm so proud of you," she says as I finally make it back into the deep end. "How many laps are you planning to swim today?"

"Twenty." I swipe the water stinging my eyes, gulp deep breaths, and hang on for dear life. Twenty laps? Dear God, what was I thinking? I'll drown before the day is done.

"You can do it, Patty." Her voice is as warm and bubbly as the nearby hot tub. "That's only eighteen more."

Only? I block out an overwhelming urge to yank my twin into the pool. No doubt some of her perkiness will dissolve in twelve feet of water. "I don't think I can do it."

"Oh, yes, you can. If anyone can, Patty, it's you." There's not an ounce of fat on Priscilla's body or smugness in her voice. "Why, look at that man over there. I'll bet he could do eighteen laps in no time. Just look at him go."

I follow her nod across the room. The pool is empty, save for us and the lifeguard, plus the guy two lanes over. He's big and bulky, with strong even strokes despite how heavy he is. He cuts through the water like a fish, taking the lane in easy rhythm, then—flip! With a furious splash, he slips under the water, turns, and races back down the length of the pool.

Damn. Why can't I swim like that?

Priscilla cocks her head, eyes him for a moment. "He's wearing goggles. Maybe you should buy yourself a pair."

"I don't need goggles."

"But—"

"No goggles," I say firmly. "They're just one more thing I can't afford. Besides, they won't help me swim any faster."

Still, I can't help wondering. Could goggles help? I slip another peek at the swimmer. The guy is fast. Really fast, despite his size. A flash of neon whips through the water as he nears the end of the lane.

"They can't cost that much. Look, he's headed our way. Let's ask him." Priscilla lifts an arm.

"No, don't!" I make a grab to stop her, but, as usual, I'm too late.

"Hello!" She waves him down as he comes up for air.

"Are you nuts? Stop that," I hiss. "What do you think you're doing?"

Priscilla blinks. "Trying to help. I thought you wanted advice."

"Well, I don't. And even if I did, I certainly wouldn't ask some guy wearing..." I squint, sneak a better look as he grabs the pool edge. Gaudy neon plastic covers his eyes. "From some guy wearing purple goggles."

"What's wrong with purple? I think they're cute."

"Maybe on a five-year-old," I mutter.

He steadies himself with a beefy hand. "Something wrong, ladies?" His voice hangs cool in the humid air and the look he shoots me isn't much warmer.

Oh, God, did he hear what I said?

"We were admiring your goggles." Priscilla flashes him a smile that lights up the pool. "Patty's not much of a swimmer and I was telling her maybe she should get herself a pair. What do you think? Would goggles help?"

"I suppose that would depend on the color." He yanks the goggles from his face and splashes them through the water. "Then again, your friend looks a little older than five."

Me and my big mouth. When will I learn to keep it shut? I cling to the edge when suddenly my hand slips and I sink like a stone, ending up with a mouth full of water.

A burly hand grabs me. "Whoa."

I sputter and cling tight, gasping and coughing as he thumps my back a few times. His arms around me feel like a big safety net.

"You okay?"

"I'm fine," I choke, though my self-esteem is plenty soggy.

Priscilla kneels at pool side. "Patty, for God's sake, what are you doing?"

I have no clue. I finally quit coughing, but it's hard to catch my breath. Brawny shoulders keep me upright, and his arms hold me close. His face is round and ruddy, and he's older than me, maybe mid-thirties. Neatly trimmed moustache. Nice eyes, especially without all that purple plastic hiding them. Soft brown eyes. Eyes that smile.

Not that he's smiling. And I don't blame him. I'd be mad at me, too.

One corner of his mouth turns up. "A five-year-old, hmm?"

"Sorry," I say quietly. "Sometimes I talk way too much."

"No problem." His smile widens. "Goggles might not be a bad idea. They add lots of chemicals to this water. My eyes get irritated if I swim without them."

I nod toward his lane. "We were watching. You're good." Especially for someone so big. It's hard to tell since we're both in deep water, but I'd bet a week's paycheck he could stand to lose at least fifty or maybe even seventy pounds.

"Swimming's a great workout." He swishes his goggles through the water, snaps them in place, covering up those soft brown eyes. "Sorry, ladies, I don't want to lose my stride."

He ducks under the lane dividers, then heads down the length of the pool, picking up his former rhythm in merely a few strokes.

"You should move into the next lane," Priscilla urges. "The two of you could race."

"Get real," I mutter, watching him. "I'll never be able to swim like that." He's already reached the far end of the lane while here I am still languishing at poolside like a beached whale. This whole losing-weight-by-swimming isn't going to be as easy as I thought. I felt so righteous yesterday, plunking

299

down money to buy a pass at our little town's community pool. Money I can't afford. Money swirling down the drain if I don't get moving.

Brand new school year. Brand new body. Brand new me.

"Come on, Patty, I know you can do it."

Good thing Priscilla has faith in me because suddenly I'm not so sure. Is there something wrong with me? I'm lousy when it comes to money and math. Maybe the other teachers have it all wrong, nominating me year after year. Maybe the final panel of judges knows something I don't. Maybe I don't deserve that award.

Do I really look that bad?

"Patty, you've got to stay focused. You're so good at everything you do. Just keep your mind on that, and I know you can do this. You can't quit now."

Priscilla's right. If I quit now, I'll be nursing another heartache at this year's award ceremony.

Maybe, if I concentrate on the three P's—Professional, Polished, Perfect—and never let my eyes slip from the prize, maybe, *just maybe*, I'll come out the winner.

"Okay, start counting." With one last yank at the bottom of my suit, I slip back under the water.

***

Four laps later, my body refuses to go another inch, and I call it quits for the day. Every muscle—muscles I didn't realize I had—ache as I wade up the gentle incline of the handicap ramp. Thank God school doesn't start for another two weeks. That gives me fourteen days to get myself in gear.

Priscilla halts at the door to the shower area. "I don't think I need to bother. I never even got in the pool."

I reek of chlorine. "Meet you outside. Promise I won't be long."

"That's what you always say. I'll wait in the car." Priscilla starts for the women's locker room and I head for the shower. Our small northern Michigan summer resort community of James Bay is renowned for its beautiful beaches, but personally I've always thought Lake Michigan way too chilly for my tastes. And while the upper stratosphere of elite residents are wealthy enough to indulge their up-north style with vacation homes, private pools, and facilities at the James Bay Yacht Club, locals like me are lucky to have this community pool. I fling my towel on a hook, flick on the water, and soap up, welcoming the feel of the hot stinging needles hitting my body. Despite my time in the pool, I still feel grubby. I spent the afternoon at school on my knees, unpacking textbooks. Last I heard, they still haven't hired a replacement for the other fifth-grade teacher and I've been doing all the prep work by myself. Hopefully the school board will get their act together and hire someone soon. I might be gunning for the grand prize, but there's no way even Teacher of the Year can be expected to handle a class of fifty kids all by herself.

The shower room is big and wide. Cool blue tiles line the walls and there's room enough for ten women. But whoever designed the place forgot the shower curtains. I lather bubbles on my arms and legs, and swish them across my bathing suit. I'm alone now, but that doesn't mean some skinny little thing who wears a size four won't waltz in here at any moment. I'm not taking a chance and showering in the nude. Bad enough being forced to share a dressing room with women like that. Showering naked in front of them with no curtain to hide behind would be the ultimate in humiliation.

It's hard enough facing myself in the mirror every day.

If only Priscilla and I were identical twins. Either God has quite the sense of humor or our guardian angels took a vacation the day we were born. Priscilla weighed in at barely two pounds and was whisked off to the neonatal unit to be coddled by nurses who cooed over the precious baby with raven black hair and delicate features. Meanwhile, I came squalling into the world, tipping the scales at a healthy seven pounds with a hearty set of lungs and orangey-red curls. The hospital sprung me after four days while Priscilla didn't come home for another two months. Except for the time I spent away at college, we've been together all these years.

Thirty years, to be exact. You'd think the two of us would be settled down by now, happily married, with families of our own. We're settled down, all right... just me and Priscilla, rambling around together in the big old pink Victorian Mama left us—a shabby house with rotting windows, ancient plumbing and a habit of draining our joint checking account. If life's supposed to be a journey, I'd much rather be zooming down a freshly paved highway than bumping through potholes like we've been doing the past couple years. Maybe I need to buy us a GPS. If I could convince Priscilla to sell the house, that GPS could steer us straight down the road to a brand new condo.

Then again, who am I kidding? Priscilla refuses to consider selling... and she's not exactly the condo type.

Take care of your sister, Patty. She'll never be healthy and strong like you. Mama's voice dances in my head.

Poor Priscilla. Allergic to everything, she's always been

a homebody. She swears she's content working from home at her job transcribing medical reports, but I'm not buying. Being cooped up like she is with only the occasional trip to the mall or weekly visit to the grocery store would drive me nuts. Plus, with her looks, Priscilla could have her pick of any man. But how's he supposed to find her if she stays home all the time?

And if he doesn't find her, I'll be doomed to living out my life in that pink monstrosity of a house we call home. I'll never convince her to sell.

I wiggle out of my wet bathing suit and into my favorite t-shirt. It's loose and comfortable, unlike the snug blue shorts pinching around my waist. Another summer gone, another few pounds found. Whatever possessed Priscilla to bake all those cookies? She knows better than to listen when I beg.

I jam my gear in an old school bag and head out into the empty lobby. The unmanned counter has a display of swimming goggles under glass. I crouch closer for a better look. Maybe Priscilla is right. If I plan on getting serious about this exercise routine, I should plan on getting serious about the equipment, too. Besides, how much can goggles cost? Five dollars? Ten?

"Decide to buy a pair?"

I glance up and see goggle-guy himself strolling up to the counter, gym bag in hand.

"I'm debating." My knees creak and I try not to wince as I struggle to stand. People my age shouldn't be this out of shape. "Payday isn't until next week."

He's taller than I expected but the extra inches around his middle are no surprise. Doesn't he realize he'd be seriously attractive if he lost some weight? Crisp white shirt and tailored pants. Brown hair, still wet from the pool, tending to curls. Dark brown moustache framing his mouth. And those warm brown eyes. A woman could get lost in those eyes.

He drops his locker key in a plastic tub on the counter. "If you're worried about money, you could probably pick up a cheap pair at the sporting goods store downtown."

"I'll think about it."

"Just thought I'd mention it." His gaze sweeps slowly across my body, then finally returns to meet my eyes. "I don't remember seeing you around here before."

Good God, did he just give me the once-over? I feel the hot flush shoot up my face as I struggle not to tug at my waistband. Whatever possessed me to go out in public wearing these shorts?

"I just started swimming laps," I stammer. "Today's my first day."

"Sam Curtis." He sticks out a hand. "And you're Patty, right?"

"Patty Perreault." The firm, smooth touch of his hand is a surprise. Do men use hand lotion? I sneak a peek at his left hand. No wedding ring. "How did you know my name?"

"Your friend." He glances around the lobby. "Did she already leave?"

I'm not surprised he noticed. Priscilla's looks attract men the same way hot fudge sundaes make dieters drool. Why should Sam Curtis be any different? Overweight or not, he's still a man.

"Priscilla is my sister and she's waiting in the car." I tug my hand out of his. "I have to go."

Sam grins. "Worried she'll get mad and drive away without you?"

The thought of Priscilla leaving in a huff makes me laugh out loud. "I don't think so. Besides, it's my car, and I've got the keys." I jingle them with a smile.

He leans one elbow against the counter. "So... you're going to start swimming laps. Coming back tomorrow?"

Tomorrow? Ouch. Climbing out of bed is going to be torture. Every part of my body already aches, down to and including my toes. "I don't know," I hedge. "Maybe."

"I'm usually here every afternoon at five. Early mornings tend to be pretty crowded. I like having a lane to myself."

"Are you in training?" I eye him carefully. Sam doesn't look like an Olympian, but you never know.

"Me? I'm no health nut." He gives an easy laugh. "I just like to swim. How about you?"

"I'm not sure."

"About what? The training part or the swimming part?"

"Both, I guess," I surrender with a grin. "Mind if I ask you a question?"

"Shoot." He shifts his weight against the counter.

"How many laps did you swim today?"

"Fifty."

My heart skips a few beats. I barely managed six; I can't imagine doing fifty.

"I've got a dinner meeting tonight, so I cut my workout short. Normally I average about one mile."

"You swim a mile every day?" I think about the informational sign posted near the pool's edge and quickly do the math. "That's eighty laps."

"Don't let it scare you. It sounds harder than it is."

"If you say so." I hear the doubt creep in my voice.

Eighty laps is a lot of swimming back and forth. Maybe I should save myself the grief and give up right now.

He studies me for a moment, like he's weighing whether I'm serious or not. "I'll let you in on a little secret. Don't think about the bigger picture. Try taking it one lap at a time."

One lap at a time? Who does he think he's kidding?

Sam grabs his gym bag. "I've got to get going or I'll be late. Maybe I'll see you tomorrow. And by the way, in case you do decide to buy a pair…" He nods at the goggles in the display case as he starts for the door. "The pink ones get my vote. They match your bathing suit."

I stand there with my mouth open, watching as he strides out the door. Someone—a man!—noticed this ugly pink suit? No doubt about it. I'm definitely shopping for a new one tomorrow. Damn the cost.

A pretty blond teenager strolls out of the office. "Need some help?"

"No thanks, I'm just looking."

She shrugs, and turns back toward the office. I take in her clinging t-shirt and tight shorts. With that kind of body, she probably swims one hundred laps a day. I could never look like that.

And I never will, if I don't try.

"Wait. I've changed my mind." I point through the glass. "I need some goggles."

"Which color?" Her hand hovers over the array.

"The blue ones, please." I count out the money and hand it over. Forget that crazy idea of Sam's. Whoever heard of color-coordinating goggles with a bathing suit? At least the blue ones match my eyes. And as for that ugly old pink suit? Headed straight into the trash, as soon as I get home.

Two minutes later I bounce out the door with swimming gear in one hand and a small plastic bag containing a twenty-dollar pair of goggles in the other.

Priscilla eyes me as I open the door. "I was beginning to wonder if you fell in the pool."

"Sorry. I didn't mean to take so long." I throw my gear in the backseat, snap my seatbelt, and start the car. Fading sunlight in my rearview mirror glints against a steel-blue Jeep as it backs out of a narrow parking space. Talk about inspiration. A big sturdy car for a big sturdy guy. I return Sam's wave as he drives past us.

Priscilla stares. "Was that the man with the goggles?"

"His name is Sam." I shoot her a fast smile as we head down the driveway. "Sam Curtis. I bumped into him in the lobby and we started talking about goggles. And guess what? I bought myself a pair."

This time Priscilla is the one who smiles. "And they're purple, right?"

"You'll have to wait and see."

"I thought you said they were too expensive," she teases.

"A girl's got a right to change her mind."

"I don't think it was the girl who changed her mind. Sounds like the man did it for her." She settles back in her seat with a curious smile. "I like him, Patty. He seems nice."

I swing into traffic, my mind spinning along with the wheels of my tires. Sam Curtis *is* nice. What more could you ask for? He's attractive, easy to talk to. He's even the right age. The more I think about it, Sam might just be perfect.

Perfect for Priscilla.

Well, maybe *perfect* isn't the right word. He'd be perfect if only he wasn't...

The F-word eludes me. How can I call him that? I know how much it hurts when I notice people noticing my own extra pounds. I refuse to use the F-word about myself and I won't use it about him.

If only Sam wasn't so... hefty.

"Are you coming back tomorrow?" Priscilla asks.

"You bet I am."

"Good for you, Patty. I'm proud of you."

I'm proud of me, too. I can do this. Sam can spout off all he wants about swimming being fun, but this is serious business as far as I'm concerned. The contest nominations open up in November and I'm determined to lose this extra weight. Two pounds a week? I can do that. Maybe even three. Four, if I'm lucky. And who knows? I might even give Sam's crazy theory about *one lap at a time* a try. A good teacher is open to different methods and uses what works. Plus, I'm nowhere near as overweight as Sam. He might be able to swim laps around me today, but give me a few months and I'll blow him out of the water. I've got a goal: thirty pounds, eighty laps, and a grand prize waiting at the end of the lane.

Patty Perreault. Teacher of the Year.

Brand new school year. Brand new body. Brand new me.

CHAPTER TWO

J AMES BAY IS AN UP-NORTH dream. Sprawled along the shore of Lake Michigan, the bay curves inward to provide yachts, sailboats and swimmers a natural shelter from the storms. Its pristine beaches are perfect for swimming and summertime picnics. The town itself boasts a year-round population of three thousand, which easily swells to nearly twenty thousand on any given day during the ten weeks of summer. With the auto factories shut down for their annual two-week retooling for new car lines, downstaters flood our little town, anxious to escape the heat of the city. They fill our hotels, shop the upscale stores the locals can't afford and dine at restaurants offering gourmet cuisine. Gourmet cuisine? Not at our house. Especially not tonight.

Tuna salad? *Yechh.*

Priscilla's dinner concoction—tuna, celery and dill pickle chunks on a bed of lettuce with tomatoes circling the plate—is meant as a dieter's delight. But tuna is tuna, no matter how you dress it up. I'd much rather be eating something tasty, like a grilled Reuben sandwich stacked high with corned beef, smothered in melting cheese, dripping with sauce...

"I know tuna isn't one of your favorites." Priscilla's voice wafts across the kitchen table. "But I made it with a yogurt dressing, so there's hardly any fat. And the best part is, it's only three hundred and fifty calories per serving."

"Really." I stare at the tuna and then at my sister. Poor Priscilla. She's much too excited about this fishy subject. I definitely need to figure out a way to get her out of the house more often.

"And you don't have to worry about the calories, either, because I weighed both our portions. Aren't you glad I bought that little diet scale?"

Her face glows and suddenly I'm ashamed. If memory serves correctly, Priscilla doesn't care much for tuna, either, but she's not complaining. Not to mention she doesn't need to measure her food—or lose weight, either. She's so thin, she could use a few Reuben sandwiches.

I poke my fork through the cold salad, force down another bite, and wash it down with a swig of ice tea. "It's good."

She beams. "I'm glad you like it. It was on sale, so I bought a whole case. I read somewhere that tuna is a great source of protein. Plus, we're saving money on our food budget. It's a win-win, all around."

"Wonderful," I mutter. Win-win? I think about the contest and choke down more tuna.

"I'll go online tomorrow and find some tasty tuna recipes."

For a minute I think about telling her not to bother, for she'll only be looking for something that doesn't exist. And I'm in big trouble if Priscilla plans on adding tuna as a regular staple to our dinner menu. Even diet Jell-O tastes better than this.

"How did things go at school today? Have they hired another fifth-grade teacher yet?"

"If they did, nobody bothered to tell me." I drain my ice

tea in a long gulp. "Maybe I'll hear something at the staff meeting tomorrow."

"They'll find someone soon."

"They'd better. I can't have fifty kids crammed in my classroom."

"Patty, you are such a worry wart. Every one of those kids would be lucky to have you as a teacher."

"I won't feel lucky until the James Bay School Board has someone's signature on a contract." I push away my plate.

Priscilla stares. "You hardly ate anything."

"I'm not hungry." I hate lying to her, but it's safer than admitting the truth. She's trying so hard and I don't want to crush her spirits. Although I'd love to crush that case of tuna stored in the pantry.

But I am not going to sabotage myself this time. Today is the second day of my new diet and exercise plan. *Brand new school year. Brand new body. Brand new me.* And brand new goggles, too. I tried them out today after school, as well as Sam's theory. *One lap at a time.* Who would have thought it would actually work? I managed ten laps before I finally gave up and quit.

I prop my elbows on the worn kitchen table, watching as Priscilla stacks the plates and silverware and squirts pink dish soap into the sink. Doing dishes is a tiresome chore and one I'm sick of. "I wonder how much a dishwasher costs?"

"More than we can afford."

"They can't be that expensive." I wrap my toes around the thin rungs of the chair that's been my seat since childhood. The wood is smooth under my feet, worn from years of constant use and Priscilla's dust rag. But the chair legs wobble if I push too hard and the back rung is loose. I need to get some super glue. Or maybe a new chair.

Better yet, a new life.

The chair squeaks in protest as I shove it aside and join her at the sink.

"What's wrong, Patty?" Her hands swish efficiently through the hot, soapy water as she washes the glasses, then moves on to the plates. "You don't seem yourself tonight."

"I'm okay." I grab a dish towel and start drying. No use moping about it, and Priscilla doesn't deserve to get stuck doing all the work herself. "Just a little moody, I guess."

But moody isn't the word for it. I'm sick of doing dishes by hand, of living paycheck to paycheck, of scrimping to get by. If things don't improve in the next few months, I might even have to suck it up and take on a second job during summer vacation.

I grab another glass, swipe it dry. "Sometimes it doesn't seem fair. Why us? I mean, other people can afford dishwashers. They don't have to live this way."

Her hands stop midstream in soap suds. "What's wrong with the way we live?"

"For God's sake, Priscilla, do you have to ask? Open your eyes and take a look." I snap my dishtowel at the high-ceilinged kitchen. The cupboards, so old they're back in vogue, could probably get by with a new coat of paint... but the rest of the room, with worn linoleum floors and old countertops with permanent stains, is in desperate need of a make-over.

Just like the rest of the house.

Just like me.

"This place is falling apart," I mutter.

"That's not true," she shoots back. "Don't forget the new roof we put on last year."

"Don't remind me. I feel sick whenever I think about how much it cost." I never should have touched the home equity loan line of credit we took out after Mama got sick. Priscilla and the bank talked me into it, assuring me it would take care of Mama's mounting medical bills... and eventually, the funeral expenses, too. Then, after that nearly-a-tornado-storm blew though last summer, Priscilla convinced me to use it again. I didn't want to, but with the roof full of leaks and minus lots of shingles, I didn't see where we had a choice. Now we're deep in debt. The monthly sum we owe the bank is higher than a mortgage payment.

"It still needs a new furnace, plus some paint, inside and out—"

"So, we'll buy some paint." Priscilla goes back to washing dishes, and for a moment the muffled clink of submerged knives and forks is the only sound between us. "Paint's not that expensive. Although we might have a problem trying to match the color."

God help us, if that's what she's thinking. There is no way in hell I'm letting Priscilla re-paint the house in that hideous shade of Barbie-doll pink Mama picked out years ago. When it comes to house paint, pretty-in-pink does not apply.

"I'm not just talking about the paint." I grab some silverware, give it a hasty swipe. "We need new windows, too. That tiny one in my bathroom is almost rotted away. It needs to be replaced, just like every other window in this house."

"Then we'll buy new windows. We can go to Home Depot on Saturday."

But I don't want to go to Home Depot. I don't want to buy new windows. I don't want to paint the house.

I want something else. Something more. Something I can't put a name to, something no one else can give me... except myself.

Well, plus the people that vote for me.

I don't care what it takes. I have got to win that contest.

"Patty, pay attention to what you're doing, or don't do it at all." Priscilla plucks the silverware I shoved into the drawer back out and sticks them in the rack. "They're not even dry."

"Who cares?" I drop my rag and turn to face her. "Look, let's be realistic. The house needs an update, and that means money... money we don't have. We can't let things fall apart like this. It's not fair to the house and it's not fair to us."

Her eyes are wide and round. "But we've got the bank loan. You know we'll pay it back in time. Why not use the money when we need it? Let's just write a check."

"No," I say firmly. Priscilla's never been good when it comes to money matters, and I'll admit I'm not much better, but there's no way she's talking me into touching that home equity line again. I swallow hard, chewing on my thoughts. Is now the time to bring up the subject of a condo with top-of-the-line appliances? If only I could bring Priscilla to buy into my way of thinking, it would be an easy trade-off. With the right buyer, we could get a pretty penny for this old Victorian if—and that's a big *if*—I can convince her to sell. Up until now, she's stubbornly refused to consider the idea.

Well, I can be just as stubborn. Although I need to be careful how I do it. Priscilla isn't always strong enough to handle things. Hopefully this time she's ready to listen. I take a deep breath. "I think we should consider listing the house."

"I cannot believe you're bringing that up again." She throws me a wounded stare. "We grew up in this house, Patty. It's home. And it's all we've got left of Mama. Do you want to give her up, too?"

She leans over the sink, pulls the stopper. Water gurgles as it sucks down the drain. Too bad it can't suck away my guilt. Both of us loved Mama, and both of us grieved when she died two years ago, but Priscilla took it hardest. Maybe because she was the one who nursed Mama through her cancer. Long black hair swirls around her face, hiding her eyes. Is she crying? Priscilla often retreats to her bed, but she never cries in front of me. I don't think I can stand it if she starts to cry.

"I love this house, Patty." She turns to face me, eyes shimmering. "And I don't want to move."

Oh, God, she *is* going to cry, and it's all my fault.

"I'm sorry." She grips the counter. "You don't deserve this. It's all my fault."

I blink. "What?"

"It's my fault we don't have the money." Her voice is barely above a whisper. "I haven't worked much in the past month or so and I know I'm not doing my share. But I promise you, all that is going to change. There's no need for me to sit around, being lazy."

"Don't be silly," I scoff. "You are not lazy. You already do too much as it is. Besides, you just got over being sick, remember?"

"I'm not sick now."

"Let's keep it that way. I don't want you having a relapse."

Her chin tilts high. "I'm fine, Patty. When you are going to quit babying me?"

As soon as someone else steps up to take my place.

"Dr. Brown called from the clinic a few weeks ago and offered me more work, but I told him no. I let him think it was because I was still sick, but the truth is... well, the truth is, I didn't want to work." She bites her bottom lip. "You're going to think I'm horrible when I tell you this."

I try hard not to roll my eyes. Priscilla, always thinking up some new drama. "You are not horrible."

"I am," she insists. "And I'm ashamed. Only a horrible person would be so jealous."

I feel the frown pinch my face. "Jealous of what? Of who?"

"You."

I stare bug-eyed at my twin, certain Priscilla has lost her mind. She's got things twisted around. She's the ravishing beauty: sweet, delicate, patient, and kind. While as for me...

"You have every summer off." Her eyes glisten blue and enormous. "You do so much for us and I know I shouldn't complain. You work hard, Patty, and you carry most of the load. That's not fair." She halts, her voice growing thinner by the minute. "Teaching isn't easy and you deserve a break. But you get Christmas vacation, plus a week at Easter... and then all summer, too. And having you home these past couple months, I started thinking it might be nice if I could take a little vacation myself every once in awhile, too."

Now I'm the one who feels horrible. Here I am, griping about what a horrible fiasco it would be to pick up a summer job, while Priscilla works all year round. Her job is a perfect fit for someone in poor health and she's comfortable in the cozy sterile niche she's created for herself. Medical summaries needing transcription are delivered daily by a runner from the clinic and a computer keeps her networked to the medical world, producing a small, steady income. But it isn't enough. It will never be enough. And while we're not on the edge of financial ruin, sometimes it feels like we're tottering dangerously close. It's a scary, lonely feeling.

"Starting tomorrow, things are going to change." Her eyes glow with a fierce determination. "I'll call Dr. Brown and ask him to send me more files. From now on, I'm going to work harder and smarter. I'll bring in more money and you won't need to worry so much. I can do it, Patty. I swear I can do it."

She grabs me in a fierce hug. Her shoulders feel painfully thin. "Things will all work out. We've lived in this house all our lives and I know you love it as much as I do. We can do this, Patty. We can save it."

My heart sinks. Priscilla would faint if she knew how I really felt. I've never dared admit the truth.

"I've got faith in you," she says. "You'll think of something so we don't have to sell."

Good thing she's got faith in me, because I'm totally without a clue. Mama left things in a tidy legal knot, putting the title to the house in both our names. Without Priscilla's signature, there will be no sale.

"You've always been the smart one, Patty. You'll figure out what we should do."

Smart one? I've got my doubts. But my twin is right about one thing. It's going to be up to me to figure out a way through this financial mess.

Problem is, I don't want to find a way through it.

I want out.

***

Ten years of humdrum staff meetings have taught me there's no need to hurry. I make it through the library door with minutes to spare. The room is crowded with familiar faces and loud chatter. I wave at a few teachers and head for the snack table where I pour myself a cup of lukewarm coffee and turn my back on the tray of assorted cookies. Those coconut macaroons can whisper sweet nothings all they want, but I'm done listening. Day Six of my brand new life. Cookies not included.

I scan the rows of chairs for Ruth Proctor, one of our school's fourth grade teachers, my former mentor, and now good friend. Ruth always saves me a seat. I finally spy her in the second row and start toward her—only to halt halfway up the aisle as I spot the man slouched comfortably next to Ruth... in what should be my chair.

Wavy hair, sparkling brown eyes. I peer at the stranger who's usurped my space. He looks flirty, fast and dangerous—the type of man Mama constantly warned Priscilla and me about. The kind of man you can't take your eyes off. The kind of man women dream about. The kind of man who would never spare me a second look except at the spare tire sitting around my waist. What's he doing in our stuffy school library, chatting with Ruth? He looks like he belongs on a billboard, or a beach somewhere, playing volleyball with bikini-clad girls.

I head toward the back of the library in search of an empty seat. Maybe he's a guest speaker at today's meeting. Strange, Ruth didn't mention anything about him earlier this morning when we were chatting. She knows everything that goes on at James Bay Elementary. Ruth's been here twenty years and she's an excellent teacher. Her Teacher of the Year Award she won years ago proves that. She's also one of the select few who serve as mentors to new teachers hired each year...

My heart skips a beat. New teacher? Fifth grade?

Could it be? What if...

No. The gods of the Human Resource Department would never be so generous. I squeeze in between a kindergarten aide and the sour-faced library assistant I normally try to avoid. Who am I kidding? I must be suffering from a drop in blood sugar. The notion that Blond Adonis could be my new colleague is crazy thinking. Maybe I should have grabbed a couple cookies after all.

Five minutes later, Chuck Stevens' introduction reaffirms my faith in the heavenly powers.

"People, I'd like to introduce Nick Lamont. Nick's been hired to teach fifth grade at James Bay Elementary this year. Nick, glad to have you on board. Stand up so everybody can see you. People, let's give Nick a big James Bay welcome."

Blond Adonis has a name. My hands sting from furious clapping as Nick Lamont slowly comes to his feet with a modest grin and a quick wave for the room.

"How could you hold out on me like that?" I hiss in Ruth's ear an hour later when a break is finally called. I slip into the seat vacated by Nick moments earlier and give Ruth's arm a little shake. "You knew about him all this time, didn't you? And you never said a word."

"I'm sorry, Patty, but I had to wait until it was official. Nick only signed the contract this morning."

Brand new school year. Brand new body. Brand new CUTE male teacher in the classroom next to me!

"Quick, tell me everything you know." I shoot a glance at the door. Ruth needs to talk fast. Breaks never last long, and soon he'll be back to reclaim his seat. "Where's he from? How old is he? When did they decide to hire him?" I suck in a quick breath, feel the heat rush through my cheeks at the one question burning through my brain. I'd never dare ask anyone else, but this is Ruth. "Is he married?" I whisper.

She laughs and shakes her head. "No, Patty, no wife. I don't know much about him, but that much I do know. His application and résumé came in at the last minute. His credentials are perfect. They snapped him right up."

"I can see why." With eye candy like Nick Lamont behind the teacher's desk, any subject—even math—would be a pleasure studying. "I bet he's an excellent teacher."

Ruth clears her throat. "I'm sure he'll do fine."

I hear the catch in her voice. "What's that supposed to mean?"

She hesitates, one eye on the door. "He doesn't exactly have much experience."

I swing my head and catch a glimpse of him as he heads back into the room. Nick doesn't look like he's fresh out of college, but more around my own age. He must have at least eight to ten years experience in a classroom.

"How much is not much?" I ask, watching as he heads for the cookies. "Come on, Ruth, you owe me the truth."

She sighs. "He just finished his student teaching."

"They hired a first-year teacher?" I stare as Nick samples the coconut macaroons. How could the school board do this to me? I've been praying all summer that we'd luck out and snag someone with years of experience, brimming with energy, plus the knowledge and skills to put into team-teaching fifth grade with me. All those prayers and what do I get? A first-year teacher. I've never been so disgusted with our school board in my life.

And I don't care how gorgeous Nick Lamont is. I hope he chokes on those cookies.

"According to Mr. Stevens, Nick comes highly qualified," Ruth adds. "He has his certification plus a little something extra. Something they were looking for. Nick's a coach. He's been hired to coach the high school's varsity basketball team."

I slump back in the folding chair. No wonder the school board caved. James Bay is a sports-crazy town and Chuck Stevens' fanaticism with sports is legendary. Plus, he and the district's athletic director are chums. Who cares if Nick has no teaching experience? Obviously Mr. Stevens, the athletic department, and the school board are all on the same page and made their decision based on what matters most—the fact our basketball team hasn't won a district title in years.

"You worry too much, Patty." Ruth pats my hand. "Once Nick gets accustomed to being in a classroom and nailing down a routine, he'll be fine. And so will you. I had a nice little chat with him this morning after he signed the contract and I told him all about you."

Ruth's crazy if she thinks I'm letting her off so easy. "Exactly what did you say?"

"That you were an excellent teacher and could be a big help to him. Remember your first day teaching? How nervous you were and how I found you crying in the bathroom before the first bell rang? I'll bet Nick feels just the same."

Somehow I doubt I'll ever find Nick Lamont crying in the men's room—especially since I'm not about to go looking.

Plus, Ruth needs glasses. Nick doesn't look nervous. More like damn sure of himself.

I give him the evil eye as he strolls to where we sit.

"Patty Perreault?" His face lights with interest and he grabs my hand as Ruth introduces us. "Just the person I've been wanting to meet."

I don't want to like him. I don't want to be impressed. But I'm fighting a losing battle. Half a room away, Nick was gorgeous. Up close and personal, he's perfect. Perfect hair, perfect smile. The warm press of his hand on mine sends a surge of adrenaline—pure feminine pleasure—shooting down my spine, straight into my toes. I wiggle them in my new pair of too-tight shoes and curse myself. Betrayed by my own body.

Is the word *scrumptious* on fifth-grade vocabulary tests?

"Nice to meet you. I'm sure we'll talk later." Standing, I suck in my stomach and start to brush past Nick.

"Where are you going?"

I nod toward the back of the room and my empty chair. The dour-faced library assistant blows her nose.

"Wait a minute." Nick grabs my arm. "Not so fast."

"But..."

His hand tightens on my elbow. "The fifth-grade team should sit together. Take my seat. I'll grab another chair."

Even if I wanted to argue, it's already too late. He places his hands on my shoulders and suddenly I find myself sitting again. I fight down a surge of desire at the touch of skin on skin, of male-female contact. Biology normally isn't a subject taught in fifth grade. Maybe our curriculum could use some revising. A few seconds later, Nick is back with another chair that he wedges in between us. "Now isn't that better?" His eyes sparkle.

"Fine," I whisper.

"Just so you know, I plan on sticking close," he confides in a low voice. "Ruth told me you'd teach me everything I need to know."

"She did?" I suck in a deep breath as his knee grazes mine and I try not to stare. God, when did it get so hot in here? Someone should turn on the air conditioner.

"I want things to work out between us."

"Of course." I breathe softly, catching a delicious whiff of the cologne he's wearing. It smells expensive, exotic, exciting. I close my eyes, thinking about being marooned with someone like Nick on a tropical island. You wouldn't care if you were ever rescued.

"This whole team-teaching thing? Just tell me what to do and you've got it. You're in charge," he whispers.

I suck in a gulp of air. Nick's breath is sugary-sweet, like coconut macaroons.

"You okay with that?"

I blink. Is he nuts? How could it not be okay?

"Yes. Absolutely. Whatever you want," I manage to sputter.

"Great. The two of us need to stick together. And now I've met you, I can see that won't be hard." He settles back in his chair with an easy smile. "I think the two of us are going to be great friends."

Chuck Stevens drones on from the podium. Something about lunch tickets and the new reading series. It's hard to hear over the pounding of my heart.

I chance a peek and catch Nick staring.

At me.

And then he winks.

At me.

God bless the James Bay School Board for hiring Nick Lamont. Maybe he doesn't have any teaching experience, but he looks like he can handle anything thrown his way... even by a group of rowdy ten-year-olds.

And who knows? Maybe if I'm lucky, Mr. Lamont will teach me a thing or two.

CHAPTER THREE

MY HAND GRAZES THE POOL'S rough surface as I reach the end of the lane. *Finally*. I tug off my swim cap and goggles, grab my towel, and head for the hot tub. A good long soak is just what I need to soothe my weary muscles and wash away the day's frustrations. Crummy doesn't even begin to describe it. I should have stayed in bed.

Thunder rumbling in the distance as I hit the alarm should have been my first clue. Breaking the zipper on my favorite pair of shorts was the second. Strike one, hoping to impress Nick. Rain pelted against the window as I finally settled on comfortable jeans, loose black t-shirt, and strappy sandals. Priscilla and I have started giving each other manicures and pedicures. At least my toes will look good if Nick finally showed up at school today.

Breakfast didn't improve my attitude. Dry toast is dry toast no matter how you slice it. Four ounces of juice chugged over the sink and out the door I went, my gloomy mood following me right down the driveway as I backed into the street. My car brakes have been acting up again. One more thing to add to the growing list of things that need fixing. By the time I finally made it to school, my depression was official—especially when I discovered the classroom next to mine still dark and empty. Exactly the way it's been all week.

Where is Nick? He's yet to put in an appearance. Doesn't he realize school starts in a few days? Cartons of textbooks, which I've opened for him, sit pushed against the wall near his door. The classroom is stark, walls bare, student desks still clumped together in a corner where they were pushed aside for summer cleaning. If Nick doesn't show up and get himself organized, he'll find himself a prisoner in his classroom before the first bell rings.

I drop my towel at the edge of the hot tub, hit the button starting the jets, and ease myself into the frothy water. Outside, the raindrops pound a steady rhythm against the windows. Days like this are meant to be spent cuddled up with a good book, not swimming laps. And so much for Sam Curtis and his stupid theory. Swimming laps isn't getting any easier. My patience is wearing thin and my appetite is growing. Ten days in and I've only lost three pounds. This dieting thing isn't going to be as easy as I thought. There's nothing more depressing than knowing you can't trust yourself when it comes to food... especially cookies.

I'd give anything for one of those pecan chocolate chip cookies Priscilla's got hidden behind the vegetables in the cupboard. Does she actually think a few cans of green beans can stop me? My food radar was finely tuned years ago and lately it's been operating on maximum power. Even now, I can hear those cookies calling my name. I swallow hard, close my eyes, imagine the sweet crunchy flavor melting against my tongue. Maybe when I get home, I should give myself a little reward. I've been so good up until now and everyone deserves a treat now and then. Besides, how many calories can there be in one little cookie?

Ha! I'll bet Priscilla knows.

Eighty calories in a slice of bread. Ninety calories in one ounce of meat. Priscilla's little diet scale reigns supreme. Who would have guessed that naked chicken breast I devoured at dinner last night contained a whopping three hundred calories? No skin, no bones, and no taste, either. Barbeque sauce would have helped, but as Priscilla so *thoughtfully* pointed out, just one dollop adds an extra fifty calories. My twin is worse than Old Mother Hubbard. She's swept the kitchen bare of anything remotely edible or delicious. No more moist chewy cookies, no more salty chips. No more pop or ice cream. All my favorites, banished by Priscilla to dieters' never-never-land.

Except for that bag of cookies stashed behind the green beans.

"Well, look who's here."

My eyes fly open and I peer up at Sam Curtis, poised on the hot tub steps. He snaps his towel in greeting.

"Want some company?"

"Be my guest." I don't even hesitate. Not only do I like the guy, but there's this little matter named Priscilla. Sam doesn't know it yet, but he could very well be the answer to my prayers. If I play things right, Priscilla's little diet scale will be sitting on his kitchen counter one day.

I scoot toward the middle of the bench. The hot tub is big, but so is he.

Sam eases into the bubbling water and makes himself comfortable directly across from me. "I've been wondering about you."

I eye him warily. "Good or bad?"

He grins. "That depends. I haven't seen you around here since the day we met. I thought maybe you gave up and quit."

Do I admit the truth? I *have* been thinking about quitting. Achy muscles and itchy dry skin are the only things I've gained from all this swimming back and forth. But if anyone has a right to complain, it's Sam. He submits himself to daily torture here at the pool.

"I haven't been coming as often as I should," I finally say. "I probably shouldn't have bought that pass. It's going to expire soon and I'll have wasted the money."

"Don't be so hard on yourself. Showing up is half the battle. Besides, you're here now, right?"

I feel the beginning of a smile tug at a corner of my mouth. "That's true."

He settles deeper in the swirling water. "Rough day?"

"Rough week. School starts soon and I'm still not ready."

"You're in school?" His voice carries a hint of interest. "What are you studying?"

I laugh out loud. How old does he think I am? "I'm a teacher, not a student. Fifth grade. I've spent all week prepping my classroom and I'm still not done. Twenty-five fifth graders will show up next week raring to go. Just thinking about it makes me tired. I don't know; maybe I'm getting old."

Good God, now I sound as bad as Ruth. I offer him a quick smile through the steaming bubbles. "Sorry, don't get me wrong. Normally I love my job."

"Today was just one of those days?" he suggests.

I nod. "The rain messed up my plans." More like, a certain fifth-grade teacher who continues to be a no-show.

"Plus my car has been giving me problems," I add.

So is my memory. I think it's playing tricks on me. There's no way Nick can be as fine as I remember.

"Everybody's entitled to do a little complaining now and then," Sam says. "Besides, I've got broad shoulders."

No kidding. His shoulders and arms are solid, like flesh-colored rocks. I slip further into the foaming water and try not to stare.

"Stress can get to you, if you let it. That's one reason I hit the pool every day. Swimming relaxes me. Once I'm finished, I reward myself with a ten-minute soak in the hot tub."

The irony isn't lost on me. Sam rewards himself by soaking in the hot tub, while I dream about cookies…

"What's wrong with your car?"

I blink. "Excuse me?"

"Your car. Didn't you say it was giving you problems?"

Why does he care about my car? Is he an auto mechanic? Seeing a person stripped down to their swim trunks doesn't exactly provide you with clues as to what they do for a living.

"I think it's the brakes." I know how to fill the windshield wiper fluid but I missed the chapter in Driver's Ed that dealt with brakes, transmissions, and all that greasy stuff lurking under the hood. "They're making this funny grinding noise."

"That doesn't sound good. You should get them checked out."

"How much would that cost?"

"No idea." He shrugs. "My friend Rod owns a repair shop. I could give him a call if you like. He'd give you a good deal."

"Thanks, I'll think about it." I sink back into the foaming

bubbles. So much for Sam being an auto mechanic. And maybe that's a good thing. I'm not sure how much money they make. Priscilla needs someone financially secure who'll be able to take care of her. But there's good money in construction. And with those big beefy arms, Sam looks like he could spend all day swinging a hammer.

"By the way, I like your new bathing suit."

"You do?" I peer down at the one-piece suit I purchased last week, which now officially qualifies as the most expensive piece of clothing I own. I nearly fainted when I saw the price tag, but buying it was a no-brainer. It's a perfect fit: tight across the tummy, ample coverage in the rear.

"The blue matches your eyes."

"Thanks," I stammer. Sam might not be a heavyweight in the looks department but he's no lightweight when it comes to flattery. Suddenly the hot tub seems like it's shrunk. This isn't the way the conversation should be going. What am I supposed to say? Do I talk about Priscilla? I'm not used to chatting with men, except at parent-teacher conferences. Men speak a language all their own, with talk of sports, hardware stores, and how to land that really big fish.

My thoughts drift to a certain basketball coach with sparkling brown eyes and tousled blond hair. Would Nick be interested in teaching me his language?

"So, you're a teacher. Can't say I'm surprised. You seem like the perfect type to work with kids."

I check his left hand one more time. He's not wearing a wedding ring, but given the way things have worked today, that doesn't mean anything. Sam could have kids of his own—plus one or two ex-wives lurking in the background. And I don't care how nice he seems. If I'm going to play matchmaker and set him up with Priscilla, he needs to be single. The last thing she needs is someone with baggage.

"Do you have children?" I ask politely.

"Me, kids?" He looks startled, then breaks out in a grin. "Not unless you count my niece and two nephews. I spoil them rotten every chance I get." His smile broadens. "And just for the record, I've never been married."

Good God, did he notice me checking out his ring finger? Talk about embarrassing. Still, it seems odd that a nice guy like him isn't settled down by now. Maybe he's gay. But just as quickly as I come up with the thought, I toss it away. I'm not picking up any of those vibes. So, if Sam's not gay and he's never been married, what is there about him that scares women off?

Maybe the same thing about me that scares away men.

"Actually, when I started college, I planned on going into education," he says. "I'm good at math and I think I would have made a good math teacher. But being on my feet all day didn't sound particularly appealing, so eventually I switched majors and settled for a sit-down job. Can't say I regretted the decision, either." He chuckles. "I've grown pretty attached to my leather chair."

Sam doesn't look like someone who wears a suit and tie to work. I sneak a peek at his hands—beefy and broad. They're perfect for swinging a hammer or laying brick; yet the fingernails are neatly trimmed, with no sign of grease or dirt staining the edges.

"Guess you could say that leather chair of mine is one big reason I work out at the pool. My doctor was pretty blunt when I went in for my annual physical. He told me if I didn't lose some weight and start exercising, I'd be headed

331

for a heart attack. I showed up here the next day and bought myself an annual pass."

Suddenly he points at me. "Hey, there's an idea. You should buy yourself an annual pass. It's only three hundred dollars."

Only three hundred dollars? He tosses off the figure like it's chump change. I can think of plenty of ways to spend three hundred dollars. Property taxes, insurance, the home equity loan. "Thanks. I'll think about it."

"It's the best deal they've got. Plus, with an annual pass, you don't have to worry about an expiration date."

"Hmmm." I close my eyes and try to shut him out. Hopefully he'll take the hint. And that part about him being a heart attack waiting to happen? Best thing I can do is write him off right now as potential husband material. Priscilla needs someone to take care of her, not the other way around. If they ended up together and then he got sick, I'd be stuck taking care of them both.

"If I were you, I'd buy that pass soon. They jack up the rates before the end of the year."

I've heard enough. If Sam Curtis thinks he has such a good handle on what and how I should spend my money, let him buy me the damn pass. Obviously he doesn't know much about money—or women, either, for that matter.

"Do me a favor?"

He eyes me with an easy smile. "Sure."

"Just stop with all the talk about that pass... because frankly, I don't want to hear it."

His eyebrows pinch together in a frown. "But—"

"Look, I should think it would be obvious. Do I have to spell it out? I'm broke, okay?" I feel the stony pride settle on my face. "I don't have thirty dollars, much less three hundred."

His face turns as bright red as his swim trunks, and I myself am mortified. How could I have embarrassed him like that? Good Lord, what if he has a heart attack right here? He was only trying to help. Maybe I should do us both a favor and drown myself right now. Quick and easy. Death by hot tub.

"I didn't mean to offend you. Sorry." He grabs the metal railing and stands. "Guess my sister is right. She's always telling me I need to learn to keep my mouth shut."

"Wait, please don't go." It's a miracle he hasn't already bolted, seeing I was screeching at him like a banshee just a few seconds ago. "I'm the one who owes you an apology. My money problems aren't your fault."

He shakes his head, starts up the steps. "People don't like talking about money. I know that. I had no business giving you advice."

Sam sounds as sincere as one of my fifth graders when they know they've messed up. "How about we agree we both were wrong and leave it at that?" I suggest. "Just... please. Don't go away mad." I hate it when people are mad at me. "Please? Sit back down."

He eyes me warily.

"Please?" I'm not proud. I know how to beg.

The hiss of bubbling water jets is the only sound between us for a few seconds as he stands there eyeing me. Finally he eases himself back onto the bench.

"Look, Patty, don't take this wrong—but if you've got financial problems, I think I might be able to help. I wasn't kidding when I told you I'm pretty good with money. Plus, you said you taught school, right? Teachers make a decent salary."

I blow out a long sigh. Men! Don't they ever listen? "Thanks, but I don't think so…"

His eyebrows rise as I sputter into silence. I don't want to talk about this. It's bad enough trying to hash things out with Priscilla. I don't need the grief. I came here to calm down, not get myself revved up. "It's a difficult situation," I add. "You wouldn't understand."

"Try me," he suggests.

I shake my head. "You can't help. No one can."

But Priscilla could, if she tried. If only I could get her to sign a realtor's agreement, we could list the house, find a buyer, and hopefully end up with a nice profit once the sale goes through. Enough profit for a brand new condo.

"It's our house. I hate the place. It's old and needs lots of work."

"Why not sell it and move?"

"It's not that simple." The smile on my face feels snug as my bathing suit. "It's a huge old place with stained glass windows, gingerbread trim, and a furnace that should have been replaced years ago. The heating bills last winter were ridiculous. It needs new windows, plus a new paint job inside and out, and I just don't have the time or energy." Or the heart for it, either. Not anymore. "I'd give anything to sell."

"Sounds familiar. Is it one of those Victorians over on Mulberry?"

I nod.

"Nice area."

"Nice enough when you drive by," I grudgingly admit, "but you wouldn't want to live there."

"What's holding you back? Sounds like it's a great house, even if it does need work."

"Maybe you'd like to buy it?" I ask hopefully.

"Me?" He gives a big belly laugh and water sloshes round us. "No thanks. I'm happy in my condo."

Sam lives in a condo? Lucky him. Obviously he doesn't have a twin brother fighting him about where to live. I try and hold back the flood of resentment threatening to suck me down.

"There are always plenty of people with money looking to find a deal."

He's got to be a realtor. He's good with money, he knows the neighborhood, as well as the ins and outs of the real estate market.

"If you're serious about selling, you shouldn't have a problem."

I've got a problem, all right. One delicate beauty with a mind of her own and a stubborn streak that might as well be forged of steel. "It's Priscilla," I confess. "We've lived in the house since we were born. She refuses to even consider selling."

"Priscilla." His brows furrow. "That's your sister?"

I nod. "You met her once, remember? She was here with me that first day at the pool. We're twins."

"Twins?" Surprise spreads across his face. "I wouldn't have guessed. She's..."

I push down the flash of annoyance. For once in my life, it would be nice if people didn't act so shocked when they learned the truth. It gets irritating after awhile. Thirty years worth of irritating.

"Obviously, we're not identical." Better to admit it

myself, than wait for him to point it out. "Priscilla is thin and gorgeous and I'm... well, I'm stuck with these stupid red curls."

"What's wrong with your hair?" he asks with an indulgent smile. "I like it. It suits your personality."

I grimace. With all the humidity in the air, my curls at this point probably resemble a frizzy wet mop.

"They make you look a little wild," he adds. "Saucy and sweet. I think it's cute." He settles back in the foaming bubbles. "So, you've got me intrigued with this talk about your sister and the house. Let's hear the rest of the story."

"It's much too complicated." We've been sitting in this hot tub far too long. If Sam thinks I'm cute, the heat has definitely warped his thinking.

"Sounds like you could use some help. Professional help."

"And I suppose you're a realtor, right?" Everybody has an angle.

"No, I'm talking about an accountant."

"Thanks, but I don't think so. Accountants cost money... way more money than I have to spend."

He chuckles. "If you're so bad at math, what makes you such an expert at what you can or can't afford?"

I roll my eyes. "I can't even afford to fix my car. How do you expect me to pay an accountant?"

"There are always ways to work things out."

"And I suppose you're going to recommend someone, right? Like the guy who does your taxes?"

"Actually, I do them myself," he volunteers.

"Some advice guru you turn out to be. You tell me to hire someone but you don't even follow your own advice. Why should I listen to you?"

"You might say I have a professional interest in the matter."

I right myself on the slippery bench. Sam's got an office job with a leather chair. He knows people don't like talking about money. Suddenly things are beginning to make sense. "You're an accountant," I accuse.

"Guilty as charged." A slow grin spreads across his face. "I'm a CPA and CFP."

"Okay, I get the CPA part, but what's a CFP?"

"Certified Financial Planner. Someone who can help put your financial affairs in order and plan for the future. I'd be glad to take a look at your portfolio and offer some suggestions."

My portfolio? I nearly laugh out loud. I doubt my checking account qualifies for such a fancy term. It rarely carries a balance of more than a few hundred dollars, except on payday. "Thanks, but I don't think so."

"I'm serious, Patty," he urges. "I'd be glad to help. You should think about it."

"I should think about a lot of things." While Sam seems like a nice guy, I know his services won't come cheap. And I can't afford to waste one penny. Besides, what do I really know about him except that he likes to swim and he thinks I'm cute?

That last fact alone has me questioning his judgment.

"Maybe you could give me your business card."

He hesitates.

"You do have one, don't you?" I press. What kind of businessman doesn't have a card handy to offer potential clients?

"Not on me," he finally admits. His brown eyes twinkle.

"Business cards aren't something I normally carry when I'm wearing swimming trunks."

"I guess they would get pretty soggy." I slump deeper in the swirling foam. Death by hot tub is sounding better by the minute.

"I started my own firm about five years ago. I've got four people working for me now. We're small and I intend to keep it that way."

It sounds legit. He seems nice. How can I go wrong? Still, it's a lot of money. But what if hiring him ends up saving me money? It might all work out, just like he's said.

"If—and this is a big if—I did decide to go with your firm, who would I work with? One of your associates?"

"I would handle your account personally. Being the boss has its advantages. I get first pick of clients." He eyes me with a confident smile. "I've always had a thing for redheads."

Good God, he's flirting with me! What am I supposed to do now? Flirt back? Other women would know what to do, but not me. This is not what I bargained for.

"Look, Sam, you're sweet to offer, but I think I'll pass. I don't have the money."

Or the courage. I close my eyes so I won't have to look at him. I'm not sure what's going on, but he scares me in a way I don't understand. But why should I be scared? Sam is just a guy. Still, there's something about him...

"We could barter for it. I help you out and you give me lessons."

I open an eye and squint at him. "What kind of lessons?"

One corner of his mouth lifts. "I suppose swimming lessons are out, since we both know you're clueless about that."

"Don't be so sure. Give me a few months and I might surprise you."

"You're on." He matches my grin with a steady one of his own. "Meanwhile, how about dinner?"

"Did you just ask me out?" I blurt.

"No, you're asking me out," he counters. "I do your financial work-up and you buy me dinner. Sound fair?"

How can I refuse? "I guess you've got yourself a client," I stammer.

His eyes light up. "I'll get you one of my business cards before we leave. Give me a call and we'll set up an appointment."

Much as I hate to admit it, just talking with him makes me feel better. Being with Sam is like sinking into an overstuffed couch with plump cushy pillows. He's like a neighbor who's lived next door all his life but doesn't know the details. Someone who can help. Someone guaranteed not to poke fun when he learns all the financial horrors I've hidden from everyone, including myself.

Maybe, with Sam's help, there's hope after all.

Never lose faith, Mama always said. Sooner or later, an answer will be provided.

But who would have thought I'd find it sitting in a hot tub?

ABOUT THE AUTHOR

KATHLEEN IRENE PATERKA IS THE author of numerous women's fiction novels, including **The Other Wife**, **Royal Secrets**, and the acclaimed series 'The James Bay Novels': **Fatty Patty**, **Home Fires**, **Lotto Lucy**, **For I Have Sinned**, and **Deep Fried Reservations**. Kathleen is also co-author of the non-fiction book **For The Love of a Castle**. She and her husband Steve live in the beautiful north country of Michigan's Lower Peninsula.